Join the army of fans who LOVE Scott Mariani's Ben Hope series . . .

'Deadly conspiracies, bone-crunching action and a tormented hero with a heart . . . Scott Mariani packs a real punch'
Andy McDermott, bestselling author of *The Revelation Code*

'Slick, serpentine, sharp, and very very entertaining. If you've got a pulse, you'll love Scott Mariani; if you haven't, then maybe you crossed Ben Hope'
Simon Toyne, bestselling author of the *Sanctus* series

'Scott Mariani's latest page-turning rollercoaster of a thriller takes the sort of conspiracy theory that made Dan Brown's *The Da Vinci Code* an international hit, and gives it an injection of steroids . . . [Mariani] is a master of edge-of-the-seat suspense. A genuinely gripping thriller that holds the attention of its readers from the first page to the last'
Shots Magazine

'You know you are rooting for the guy when he does something so cool you do a mental fist punch in the air and have to bite the inside of your mouth not to shout out "YES!" in case you get arrested on the train. Awesome thrilling stuff'
My Favourite Books

'If you like Dan Brown you will like all of Scott Mariani's work – but you will like it better. This guy knows exactly how to bait his hook, cast his line and reel you in, nice and slow. The heart-stopping pace and clever, cunning, joyfully serpentine tale will have you frantic to reach the end, but reluctant to finish such a blindingly good read'
The Bookbag

'[*The Cassandra Sanction*] is a wonderful action-loaded thriller with a witty and lovely lead in Ben Hope . . . I am well and truly hooked!'

Northern Crime Reviews

'Mariani is tipped for the top'

The Bookseller

'Authentic settings, non-stop action, backstabbing villains and rough justice – this book delivers. It's a romp of a read, each page like a tasty treat. Enjoy!'

Steve Berry, *New York Times* bestselling author

'I love the adrenalin rush that you get when reading a Ben Hope story . . . *The Martyr's Curse* is an action-packed read, relentless in its pace. Scott Mariani goes from strength to strength!'

Book Addict Shaun

'Scott Mariani seems to be like a fine red wine that gets better with maturity!'

Bestselling Crime Thrillers.com

'Mariani's novels have consistently delivered on fast-paced action and *The Armada Legacy* is no different. Short chapters and never-ending twists mean that you can't put the book down, and the high stakes of the plot make it as brilliant to read as all the previous novels in the series'

Female First

'Scott Mariani is an awesome writer'

Chris Kuzneski, bestselling author of *The Hunters*

THE BABYLON IDOL

Scott Mariani is the author of the worldwide-acclaimed action-adventure thriller series featuring ex-SAS hero Ben Hope, which has sold millions of copies in Scott's native UK alone and is also translated into over 20 languages. His books have been described as 'James Bond meets Jason Bourne, with a historical twist'. The first Ben Hope book, *The Alchemist's Secret*, spent six straight weeks at #1 on Amazon's Kindle chart, and all the others have been *Sunday Times* bestsellers.

Scott was born in Scotland, studied in Oxford and now lives and writes in a remote setting in rural west Wales. When not writing, he can be found bouncing about the country lanes in an ancient Land Rover, wild camping in the Brecon Beacons or engrossed in his hobbies of astronomy, photography and target shooting (no dead animals involved!).

You can find out more about Scott and his work, and sign up to his exclusive newsletter, on his official website:

www.scottmariani.com

By the same author:

Ben Hope series
The Alchemist's Secret
The Mozart Conspiracy
The Doomsday Prophecy
The Heretic's Treasure
The Shadow Project
The Lost Relic
The Sacred Sword
The Armada Legacy
The Nemesis Program
The Forgotten Holocaust
The Martyr's Curse
The Cassandra Sanction
Star of Africa
The Devil's Kingdom

To find out more visit **www.scottmariani.com**

SCOTT MARIANI

The Babylon Idol

avon

HarperCollins
PUBLISHERS
Since 1817

AVON
A division of HarperCollins*Publishers*
1 London Bridge Street,
London SE1 9GF
www.harpercollins.co.uk
A Paperback Original 2017
1

Copyright © Scott Mariani 2017

Scott Mariani asserts the moral right to
be identified as the author of this work

A catalogue record for this book is
available from the British Library

ISBN 978-0-00-748622-9

Set in Minion by Palimpsest Book Production Ltd, Falkirk, Stirlingshire

Printed and bound in Great Britain by
Clays Ltd, St Ives plc

MIX
Paper from
responsible sources
FSC™ C007454

FSC™ is a non-profit international organisation established to promote
the responsible management of the world's forests. Products carrying the
FSC label are independently certified to assure consumers that they come
from forests that are managed to meet the social, economic and
ecological needs of present and future generations,
and other controlled sources.

Find out more about HarperCollins and the environment at
www.harpercollins.co.uk/green

'O King, we will not serve your gods, nor worship the image of gold you have set up.'

The Book of Daniel 3:15–18

PROLOGUE

For all of his sixty-three years Gennaro Tucci had lived in the same small cottage on the edge of the same rural village in Umbria. He had been a carpenter much of his working career, but now spent most of his time pottering about his house and garden, keeping himself to himself with little need for much in the way of a social life, apart from a cat. He was a simple, gentle, kindly man with few needs and no regrets in life, whom it took little to make happy. Every Friday morning, Gennaro would amble up the road to the tiny village church, which was usually empty, sit in the same pew within its craggy whitewashed walls and bow his head and offer a few simple prayers. Then he would amble home again, feed his cat and while away the rest of the morning until lunchtime.

One particular Friday morning, in the summer of what would turn out to be Gennaro's final year, he arrived in the church to find that it wasn't empty – though he took little notice of the well-dressed stranger sitting in one of the pews across the aisle, a man of the same approximate age as he was, with grey hair turning white, and a broad, deeply lined face with penetrating eyes, who had looked at Gennaro fixedly as he came in.

Gennaro never asked himself who the stranger was,

1

whether a newcomer to the village or someone just passing through. He smiled, nodded politely and got on with his habitual prayers, oblivious of the way the stranger kept staring at him. He remained in his pew the same length of time he always did, then left the church and began walking home under the warm sunshine, sniffing flowers and feeling happy at the beauty of the day.

Had Gennaro Tucci's mind not been fully taken up with such pleasant thoughts, he might have noticed that the mysterious stranger had left the church at the same time, and was following him at a distance, staring at his back with an expression Gennaro might have found unsettling.

And, once he'd reached his little cottage on the edge of the village, had Gennaro happened to look out of the window he'd have noticed the stranger standing there by the front gate, watching as though unable to tear his gaze away.

But Gennaro saw nothing, and after a few minutes the stranger disappeared. The next day came and went, as peacefully as ever; then the next.

The following evening, they came.

Gennaro was upstairs, getting ready for bed, when the lights shone through his windows and he heard the thump of someone crashing through his front door. Frightened, he padded down the stairs, calling, '*Chi è là?*'

When he saw the three intruders, masked and armed, Gennaro almost died of fright. At first he'd thought the men had come to rob him, but that was unthinkable – he had nothing to steal, which was why he'd never locked his door in all these years. But they hadn't come for valuables. It was him they wanted.

Gennaro struggled and cried out as they grabbed him. One of the men jabbed a hypodermic syringe into his arm, and after that things began to go hazy for the sixty-three-year-old. They dragged his half-unconscious body outside and bundled him into a black van, shut him up in the back and sped off into the night.

Many hours later, some four hundred kilometres north of the home Gennaro would never see again, the van finally stopped and his captors dragged him out. By then the drugs had begun to wear off. Gennaro blinked in the strong sunlight and gaped at his new surroundings, too terrified to ask what was happening to him and why he'd been kidnapped. He was in the grounds of some magnificent house by a lake. Poor Gennaro had never left rural Umbria, and had no recognition of where he'd been brought. But he did faintly recognise the man who stood before him as the three thugs shoved and dragged him inside the big house, then threw him down on his knees on the hard marble floor. The man smiled down at him with an expression that was almost benevolent. Gennaro blinked up at him and struggled to remember where he'd seen him before.

The stranger from the church.

Now that Gennaro saw him more closely, he was even more confused. It was like looking into a mirror. They could have been identical twins.

'What is your name?' the man asked.

'G-Gennaro T-Tucci,' Gennaro managed to quaver.

'Gennaro,' the man said with a broad smile, 'you are a gift from God.'

Chapter 1

So many times in the past, Ben Hope had vowed and declared that his crazy days of running from one adventure to another were over, and that he was going to stay put at home for the foreseeable future. And every time he'd said it, before long some new crisis had come barrelling into his life and whisked him off again – the latest in a sorry, never-ending series of broken promises, to himself, and to others, which had sometimes made him wonder if he was cursed by fate.

This time, though, he was determined to be true to his word. This was it. Mayhem, violence, war, intrigue, chasing around the world – he was done with the lot of it, once and for all.

It wasn't so much that, as his longtime friend and business partner Jeff Dekker sometimes joked, 'We're getting too old for this shit.' In his early forties, Ben had plenty of life left in him and could still outrun, out-train and, if necessary, outfight guys half his age. But he would have been lying if he'd said that the recent African escapade hadn't taken a lot out of him, physically and emotionally.

The same went for Jeff, who'd been right there at Ben's side in what had to be the deadliest, most complex and disturbing rescue mission either man had ever experienced, either during their time in British Special Forces and in the years since. Likewise for Tuesday Fletcher, the young ex-trooper who had not long since joined their small staff at the Le Val Tactical Training Centre in rural Normandy but already proved himself ten times over to be a stalwart asset to the team and forged bonds of comradeship with Ben and Jeff that could never be broken.

Less than a fortnight had passed since they'd all returned to Le Val, to find a mountain of mail waiting for them. The business was growing by the month, attracting so many bookings from military, law enforcement and private close-protection agencies worldwide looking to refine and extend their tactical skillset that it was hard to keep up with demand. Now that the operation had received a substantial cash injection in the wake of the Africa mission, they were set to grow still further.

But all of that had been set aside for a week, as an official Le Val holiday was declared.

Ben had spent that time recuperating. For most people, 'recuperating' might have meant lying in bed, or sitting around idle, licking their wounds and feeling sorry for themselves. For Ben it meant getting back into the punishing exercise routines he'd followed for most of his life. Working back up to a thousand push-ups a day, lifting weights, honing his marksmanship skills on Le Val's pistol and rifle ranges, scaling cliffs and sea-kayaking off the Normandy coast, and going for long runs through the wintry countryside with Storm, his favourite of the pack of German Shepherds that patrolled the compound. The harder Ben trained, the more he emptied his mind and the further he left the horrors of Africa behind him.

Jeff Dekker was no slouch either, but he'd used his recuperation period differently. His romance with Chantal Mercier, who taught at the *École Primaire* in the nearby village of Saint-Acaire, had grown more serious over the last months, and he'd spent his time off with her. In all the years Ben had known Jeff, throughout the never-ending sequence of on-off, part-time, short-term girlfriends whose names were too many to remember, he'd never seen him so committed to a relationship. He was happy for his friend, and Jeff seemed happy too. Even Jeff's French had improved.

Meanwhile, Tuesday Fletcher had taken advantage of the week's holiday to fly home to London to see his parents, Rosco and Shekeia, second-generation immigrants from Jamaica. Tuesday was still recovering from a gunshot wound to the arm, sustained during their flight from the Congo. Ben had no doubt that he'd come up with some white lie to conceal from his parents just how close he'd come to being killed. If anyone could make light of a bullet in the arm, it was the ever-cheerful Tuesday.

The second week since their return, the three of them had started easing themselves back into business-as-usual mode and begun working their way through the backlog of emails, letters, accounts, orders, bookings and the process of hiring new staff to cope with the expanding Le Val operation, and a hundred other matters that had accumulated during their absence.

That was where Ben found himself at this moment, sitting alone in the prefabricated office building across the yard from the old stone farmhouse. It was an early December morning, and the icy rain that had been drumming on the office roof since dawn was threatening to turn snowy. The fan heater was blasting waves of warm air that engulfed Ben as he sat at the desk sipping from a steaming mug of black coffee. Storm and two more of the guard dogs, Mauser and Luger, appeared to have given themselves the morning off and were curled contentedly at his feet, like a huge hairy black-and-tan rug spread over the floor. Ben didn't have the heart to kick them out into the cold.

From where he sat, through the window he could see the parked minibus that had brought the current crop of trainees to Le Val: eight agents from the French SDAT anti-terror unit anxious to up their game in expectation of more of the troubles that had been rocking Paris in recent times. Tuesday was currently out with them on the six-hundred-yard range, the group probably all freezing their balls off as he took them through their sniper paces. Trembling hands and numb fingers were no great boon to long-range accuracy. Poor sods. Ben was scheduled to teach a two-hour session that afternoon in the plywood-and-car-tyre walled construction they called the 'killing house', covering elements of advanced live-fire CQB, or close-quarter-battle, training that they were unlikely to learn anywhere else. At least they'd be indoors out of the wet. Two more members of the Le Val team who'd be happy to huddle indoors with mugs of coffee were Serge and Adrien, the two ex-French Army guys who manned the new gatehouse – the latest addition to the complex – and controlled people coming in and out.

As for Jeff Dekker, Ben wasn't quite sure where he was at that moment. He'd said something about checking the perimeter fence for wind damage; the region had been buffeted by one winter gale after another that week. With the kind of arsenal that Le Val kept locked up in its special armoury vault, and the sort of work that went on within the various sections of the compound, government bureau-cracy insisted on the property being ultra-secure. Not that Ben had lately noticed any gangs of jihadist terrorists roaming the Normandy countryside in search of military hardware. But rules were rules.

Ben reached for his Gauloises and Zippo lighter, flicked

a cigarette from the familiar blue pack, clanged open the lighter and lit up in a cloud of smoke. It suddenly felt even better to be home. Puffing happily away, he reached across the desk for the stack of mail he'd been sifting through. So far it had all been bills, bills, and more bills.

But this letter looked different.

Chapter 2

The letter certainly was unusual. More than the Italian postmark, Ben was surprised to see the ink-stamped legend ISTITUTO PENITENZIARO BOLLATI on the envelope. He'd heard of the Bollati medium-security prison in Milan, but never been there, could think of no connections the place could have to him, and wouldn't have expected to receive a letter from anyone there.

Yet there was no denying his name and address neatly handwritten on the front of the envelope. Above them, the date on the postmark showed that the letter had left Milan while Ben was struggling to survive somewhere in the middle of the Congo jungle.

'Hm,' he said.

At his feet, Storm cocked an ear and glanced up as though to see what the fuss was about, then lost interest and went back to sleep.

Ben took another slurp of scalding coffee and another drag on the Gauloise, then put down his mug, rested the cigarette in the ashtray and picked up the old M4 bayonet that served as a letter-opener in the Le Val office. He carefully slit one end of the envelope, reached inside and was about to draw out the single folded sheet of paper when his phone suddenly came to life and started buzzing on the desk like an upturned bee.

'Got a problem in Sector Nine.' Jeff's voice was barely audible over the crackle of the wind distorting his phone's mic. Sector Nine was what they called part of the east perimeter fence. 'That sodding apple tree Marie-Claire wouldn't ever let me cut down? Well, we won't need to now. Sorry to drag you out here, mate, but I need your help.'

Ben could imagine what had happened. He'd read the letter later. He grabbed his leather jacket from the back of his chair and slipped it on.

'You want to come?' he said to Storm, who instantly sprang to his feet as though it were feeding time. Life was simple if you were a dog.

Outside in the biting wind, the sleet was turning snowier by the minute. Ben pulled up the collar of his jacket and crossed the yard, past the minibus and over to the ancient Land Rover. It was a tool box on wheels, filled with all kinds of junk including a greasy old chainsaw. Storm hopped in the back and found a space for himself while Ben got behind the wheel, and they set off across the yard and down the rutted track that ran between the buildings parallel with the rifle range and led across the fields towards Sector Nine. He heard the muffled boom of a rifle coming from the range, the ear-splitting report and supersonic crack of the bullet in flight muted by the high earth walls that ran parallel from the firing points to the butts at the far end and prevented any 'flyers' from escaping the range boundaries. Not that such elementary mistakes could happen under Tuesday's expert supervision; he could splatter grapes all day long at five hundred yards with his modified Remington 700, and he was one of the best instructors Ben had ever seen.

The old tree had been a bone of contention for years. Marie-Claire, the local woman they'd employed from day one as an occasional cook, swore the particular apples it produced were essential to her mouth-wateringly delicious traditional Normandy apple tart recipe. As popular as her tart was with the parties of hard-worked and hungry trainees at Le Val, Jeff had always griped that the tree was too close to the fence and had argued that they could get perfectly decent apples at the grocer's in Saint-Acaire or the Carrefour in Valognes. It had been an endless and hard-fought debate, with neither side giving an inch, while the tree kept growing taller and spreading outwards year on year. Now it looked as if the winter wind had settled the argument for them.

The track wound and snaked through the grounds. To Ben's right, he passed the patch of oak woodland, now bare and gaunt, that in summer completely screened the ruins of the tiny thirteenth-century chapel where he sometimes retreated to sit, and think, and enjoy the silence. To his left, beyond hills and fields and forest, he could see the distant steeple of the church at Saint-Acaire pointing up at the grey sky.

He loved this place, in any season. He couldn't imagine why he'd ever wanted to leave it.

But then, he'd done a lot of things in his life that he couldn't understand why, looking back.

As Ben approached Sector Nine, he saw Jeff's Ford Ranger over the grassy rise up ahead. Then Jeff himself, arms folded and frowning unhappily at the branches that had become enmeshed in the wire. The whole tree had uprooted and toppled over, flattening a thirty-foot section of fence with it. Those ever-lurking jihadis had only to come leaping through the gap, and they'd be just a step away from total European domination.

'What did I always say?' Jeff said, pointing at the fallen

tree as Ben stepped down from the Land Rover. 'What did I always warn that old bat would happen one day? And did she ever listen to a word? Did she buggery.'

'No use crying about it now,' Ben said. He grabbed the chainsaw from the back of the Landy. The dog clambered into the front seat, fogging up the windscreen with his hot breath as he watched the two humans set about dismantling the tree.

Ben started with the smaller branches, trimming them off while Jeff dragged them away and tossed them in a heap to one side. Once the gnarly old trunk was as bare as a telegraph pole, it was time to start chopping it up into sections before the real work of rebuilding the broken fence could begin. By then, the sleet had delivered on its threat to turn snowy. Ben and Jeff took a break, and sat in the Land Rover watching the snow dust the landscape. Ben lit another Gauloise, smoking it slowly, savouring the tranquillity of the moment.

'I love her, you know,' Jeff said, out of the blue after a lengthy pause.

'The old bat?'

'Chantal. I'm in love with her, mate.'

Ben had never heard his friend say anything like that before. From his lips, it was like Mahatma Gandhi saying how much he loved a good juicy beefsteak.

Jeff shook his head, as though he could hardly believe it himself. 'I mean, I know what it sounds like, and I never thought this would happen to me. But I think she's the one. Christ, I really fucking think so.' He glanced at Ben. There was a look in his eyes something like helplessness.

'Chantal's great,' Ben said, even though he'd only met her briefly a couple of times.

'Yeah, she is.' Jeff swallowed, like a man about to make

a confession. 'Listen. I . . . uh, I asked her to marry me. She said yes. Wanted you to be the first to know.'

Ben masked his complete astonishment and said, 'I'm sure you'll be very happy together.' The subject of marriage wasn't one that was ever discussed between them, given Ben's patchy history in that department. He was more unqualified than most people to extol the joys of married life, but it was all he could think of to say right now.

'Thanks, mate.' Jeff smiled, then pointed through the windscreen, obviously keen to change the subject. 'Look at this frigging snow.' It was thickening by the minute, blown about in sheets by the increasing wind.

'No point waiting for it to stop,' Ben said. 'Let's get on.'

The chainsaw buzzed and snorted and kicked in Ben's hands as he sliced the tree into sections, bending over the prone trunk, with Jeff standing at his shoulder waiting to grab each piece as it came loose and toss it into the pile. Ten minutes later, the top half of the tree was next year's firewood logs ready to be loaded on a trailer and split and stacked in the barn.

Two minutes after that, it happened.

There was a strong gust of wind, followed immediately by a strange whizzing crack that was only faintly audible over the noise of the saw. At almost the same instant, Ben heard Jeff's strangled cry of shock and pain. He looked quickly around, just in time to see the blood fly. As if in slow motion, like a scarlet ribbon fluttering from Jeff's body, twisting in the air. Jeff doubling up. Falling against him. Collapsing into the trampled grass. Mud and snow and sawdust and more blood. Lots of it, spilling everywhere. Ben yelling Jeff's name. Getting no response. The sudden fear twisting his guts like a pair of icy gripping hands.

In those first confused instants, Ben thought that the

chain had broken and gone spinning off the bar of the saw, hitting Jeff in some kind of freakish accident. In a panic he hit the engine kill switch. The saw instantly stopped, and Ben realised the chain was still intact.

He threw the saw down and fell on his knees by Jeff's slumped body. Jeff wasn't moving. The snow was turning red in a spreading stain under him. Ben yelled his friend's name. Tried to shake him, to roll him over, to understand what was happening. Blood slicked his hands and bubbled up between his fingers. So much blood.

Now Ben was thinking that the spinning chainsaw might have dislodged an old nail or fencing staple buried deep in the tree trunk from long ago, and sent it flying through the air like a deadly piece of shrapnel.

'Jeff!'

Jeff's eyes were closed. His face was white, except where it was spattered red. His jacket and shirt were black and oily with blood. Ben ripped at the material.

And then he saw the gaping bullet wound in Jeff's chest.

Chapter 3

You didn't need to be a forensic pathologist to recognise the devastating effect that a high-velocity rifle bullet could have on the human body. And Ben was no stranger to gunshot wounds.

This one was bad. It was very bad.

A gust of wind slapped a fresh flurry of snowflakes over them, and suddenly it was blizzarding. Ben crouched in the mud and the blood and the snow, bending over his friend's inert body, blinking away the flakes that swirled into his eyes. His hands shook so violently that he could barely control them enough to check Jeff's pulse. Inside the Land Rover, Storm was howling and barking and scrabbling at the window to get out.

There was no pulse. The shock of the impact had stopped Jeff's heart. He wasn't breathing. Red froth was bubbling at his lips.

Ben closed his mind to the panic that rushed up inside him, and dived into action with artificial respiration to try to force Jeff's lungs to start working. His own face was soon slick with blood. He could taste the coppery saltiness of it on his lips. He spat and kept trying.

After ten breaths there was still no response. No breath. No pulse.

16

Using the edge of his hand Ben gave a sharp rap to the lower part of Jeff's breastbone in the desperate hope that the cardiac compression would jar his heart back into life. That was, if the bullet hadn't carved it into butcher meat.

No pulse.

Jeff was dead.

But Ben couldn't allow that to happen. He yelled, 'No!' And hit him again, terrified of doing further damage to the wound but not knowing what other choice he had. Blood sprayed from the impact. Jeff's flesh felt cold and lifeless to the touch.

One more time, Ben resorted to the mouth-to-mouth to try to force oxygen into Jeff's inert lungs.

And this time, Ben's own heart soared as he suddenly felt a pulse, as ragged and delicate as a damaged butterfly's wingbeats. 'You're not dead yet, Dekker!' Ben yelled, wanting to shake him, slap him. Jeff's body convulsed and a spout of blood burst out of him with a rattling gasp. He was alive, though Ben knew he could slip back down at any moment and not come back up again.

There had been no more shots. In his near-panic, Ben struggled to think straight. He remembered that Tuesday was out with the trainees on the long rifle range. Could a bullet have gone astray somehow? Impossible. Not on Tuesday's watch. And in any case, the shot that had hit Jeff had very clearly come from the opposite direction.

Beyond the fence. *Outside* the boundaries of Le Val. Logic dictated that the shooter had hidden himself among the wooded hills somewhere between here and Saint-Acaire. He could have been half a mile away. Waiting, watching through his scope, biding his time for the perfect moment to pull the trigger.

But who was he? And why had he done this?

The landscape was rapidly turning white, visibility suddenly diminished to not much better than a hundred yards. There was no sign of anyone. Nothing moved or made a sound, except for the whistle of the gusting wind and the swirl and patter of the falling snow. Ben didn't want to leave Jeff, but it haunted him that the faceless shooter was still out there, somewhere, perhaps hundreds of yards distant, or maybe moving in closer to finish what he'd started. Ben ran to the Land Rover, wrenched open the tailgate and grabbed the old shotgun that kicked about in the back among the shovels and other tools. A rustic twelve-bore against a long-range rifle was no match, but it was better than being unarmed. He rummaged inside the vehicle for the green plastic first-aid box and shoved it under his arm.

'Storm, go find Tuesday!' Ben told the German Shepherd. 'Fetch!' The dog was trained to know the names of everyone at Le Val, and to locate and alert them on command. Storm cocked his head, understood what Ben was asking him to do, bounded out of the Land Rover and streaked away through the snow like a heat-seeking missile.

As he ran back to Jeff, Ben tore out his phone and dialled 15, the emergency SAMU number for urgent medical assistance. He forced himself to speak clearly and slowly as he explained what had happened. 'Please hurry.'

The nearest hospitals were in Valognes and Cherbourg, both miles away. Jeff was going to need everything Ben could do to keep him alive until someone got here. He was still losing blood much too fast. The bullet had passed right through his body, making an exit hole between his shoulder blades that Ben could have poked three fingers inside. More blood was leaking from that hole than the entry wound, but he'd have to stem the bleeding from both before Jeff lost a fatal amount.

Ben pulled open a bandage pack from the first-aid kit and tore it in half. Struggling to get Jeff's dead weight rolled over a little he wedged one knee under his friend's back with a wad of bandage pressed tightly between it and the exit wound, and used both hands to maintain pressure on the entry wound with the other wad. He squeezed with all his might to staunch the deadly haemorrhages. It could take ten or fifteen minutes of steady pressure to stem the flow – by which time it could all be over. Blood quickly soaked through the bandages until they were saturated.

It wasn't long before Storm came pounding back through the snow. Tuesday was sprinting after him, still clutching the scoped rifle they'd been using for their training session. The dog was barking frantically and running circles around Tuesday to guide him on. In their wake came the eight SDAT guys. Tuesday's jaw dropped in horror at the sight of Ben crouching over Jeff's bloody form in the snow.

'He's been shot,' Ben said tersely. 'Don't ask me more, because I don't know. Just help me. I've called for the ambulance but I need more bandages from the kit. Quickly. And keep your head down. The shot came from that way, eleven o'clock. The shooter could still be around.'

Tuesday nodded dumbly, dropped the rifle and set about tearing open more bandage packs. He knew better than to ask questions. Once a soldier, always a soldier; like Ben he was no stranger to dealing with gravely injured comrades in the field. The SDAT guys were good at what they did, and they were experts in looking tough and intimidating in the black balaclavas and tactical armour they wore on the job, but they had about as much real-life battlefield experience as any other cops, and in those first shocked instants they could do little but watch grimly as Ben discarded the blood-soaked pressure pads and replaced them with the fresh ones Tuesday quickly handed him.

The SDAT team leader was a tough, gruff Frenchman called Roman Vidal. He took out a phone and urgently, efficiently called in police reinforcements, then picked up the rifle and the shotgun and began delegating orders to his men, marshalling them as though they were dealing with a terrorist attack.

Which maybe they were. Ben had no idea what was happening, and right now it was the last thing on his mind. Jeff's pulse was vacillating wildly, sometimes barely there at all. The blood kept coming, though now the flow seemed to be easing a little.

With Tuesday's help Ben laid Jeff out flat on the ground with his legs elevated to make it easier for his weak heartbeat to pump blood to the head. Ben had taken off his bloody jacket and laid it over Jeff to keep him warm. That was all they could do, except hope they could get their friend out of here as soon as possible.

The SDAT guys fanned out along the perimeter, keeping low and scanning the terrain beyond the fence for any sign of the shooter. The falling snow wasn't helping. It was becoming hard to tell where the horizon ended and the sky began. Tuesday stayed close by Ben and Jeff, biting his lip in agonised worry and holding in the thousand questions that were bursting to come out.

'Hang in there, Jeff,' Ben kept saying in his ear. 'Help's on its way. You're going to be all right. You're going to be fine.'

He didn't even know if Jeff could hear him.

Finally, after what seemed like hours, Ben caught the sound of an approaching helicopter. He looked up and saw the aircraft thudding towards them out of the grey clouds.

Ben would never know the pilot's name, but he would forever bless the guy's heroism for having flown out in such bad weather. The white SAMU air ambulance landed just inside the perimeter, whipping up powdery snow from the ground by the blast of its rotors. Two paramedics jumped out and hurried over.

It took a monumental effort for Ben to stand back and let them take charge of the situation. Within minutes, Jeff was being stretchered aboard the chopper. Ben kept his hand from shaking as he scribbled out a few details on a form: Jeff's name, address, blood type and next of kin, which Ben wrote down as Lynne Dekker. Jeff's father had walked out when he was eight. His mother Lynne had emigrated from the UK to Australia's Northern Territory a few years back, where she and her new man, an outbacker called Kip Malloy, ran a crocodile farm supplying leather to the cowboy boot industry. Ben couldn't remember the name of the place.

As he handed the form back to the paramedics, blood smeared all over the paper from his fingers, he asked if there was room for one more on board the chopper and was told, without hesitation, no chance.

Ben said, 'At least tell me where you're taking him.' The paramedic replied that Jeff would be flown direct to the Centre Hospitalier Louis Pasteur, the big hospital in Cherbourg, being the nearest facility equipped to deal with major trauma. Ben thanked him and let him go. He stood back, and he and Tuesday watched in silence as the hatch slammed shut and the chopper took off.

Both thinking the same terrible thought.

That they might never see Jeff Dekker alive again.

Chapter 4

The distance from Le Val to Cherbourg was almost exactly thirty-five kilometres by road. Ben couldn't get there as fast as a chopper, but he was damned well going to try.

'I'm coming too,' Tuesday declared as Ben clambered into Jeff's truck. It was faster than the Land Rover, not that Ben intended to make the drive in either.

Ben shook his head. 'Someone's got to hold the fort, Tues. In a few minutes this place will be crawling with police. In the meantime, kennel the dogs, lock the weapons up in the armoury and get ready for a lot of questions. If they want me, they know where to find me.'

Tuesday just nodded. He looked as ashen and pallid as it was possible for a healthy twenty-four-year-old Jamaican guy to look. Ben briefly laid a hand on his shoulder. He wanted to give him some kind of reassuring smile, but he couldn't. He slammed the truck door, fired up the engine and took off over the bumpy ground, wipers slapping, lights burning twin beams through the drifting snow. Tuesday, Vidal and the others shrank in the rear-view mirror until the white veil swallowed them up.

Ben hammered the truck back towards the house. Less than a minute later he was skidding to a halt in the yard, piling out without shutting the door and sprinting past the big stone farmhouse towards the lean-to garage where he stored his personal car.

The old BMW Alpina turbo was neglected and dirty, but its 4.4-litre V8 motor could get Ben where he wanted to be just about as fast as anything else on the road, especially when he was the one behind the wheel. He punched it out of the yard and down the rutted track to the security gates that shut Le Val off from the big, bad world. He left those open, too, for the contingent of gendarmerie vehicles that would soon be descending on them in force. Then he was off, heading north, shifting as aggressively as the untreated and slippery rural roads would let him.

His mind was empty, numb. There was no point in trying to make sense of what had happened. That would come later. And when he figured out who had done this . . .

He gripped the steering wheel. He couldn't afford to let his grief and rage take him over. That would come later, too.

Traffic grew steadily thicker as he left the countryside behind him and joined the N13 heading towards the city. The sudden snowfall had caught a lot of people unprepared, and the road was heavily congested with sluggish bumper-to-bumper lines of vehicles. Twice he veered off onto the verge to roar by the dawdling drivers blocking his way, and forced past them with his horn blaring to warn them of his approach. People gawked at him from their car windows. He didn't care.

A few minutes later, he left the *nationale* and carved his way into Cherbourg-Octeville. The hospital was located in the north of the city, not far from the port. He screeched through slippery, twisty streets, attracting more stares from drivers and pedestrians, burning through red lights and ignoring one-way systems and not giving a damn about police, until he spotted the sign with a red cross and the words 'HÔPITAL PASTEUR URGENCES'. Moments later he swerved into the hospital car park, skidded into a space, burst out of the BMW and ran for the entrance without bothering to lock the car.

It wasn't until Ben shoved through the doors into the hospital emergency-room reception area that he realised that his hands, face and clothes were still covered in blood and he looked like someone who'd just been dragged out of a train wreck. That probably accounted for some of the looks he'd been getting on the way here. The same expressions were on the faces of the hospital staff as they came rushing to meet him, intent on grabbing him and shoving him onto a gurney before he collapsed on the floor.

'It's not me. I'm not hurt,' he explained to the nurses, putting out his bloodstained hands to ward them off him. 'Jeff Dekker. He was brought here by helicopter. Less than an hour ago. Where is he? Is he—?'

Not dead, was all the information he could glean from any of the tight-lipped nursing personnel. A large matron kept insisting that if he would please settle down and wait, Docteur Lacombe the head surgeon would update him as soon as possible. Ben got the impression that Lacombe was deep in the middle of working on Jeff at that very moment. Which explained why the nurses were being noncommittal about the condition of the patient. Which in turn implied that things were very much in the balance and could go either way.

Ben did what they said and went to a small waiting area with banks of plastic seats and a vending machine. He sat by a window that overlooked the hospital car park and gazed out without seeing anything.

The wait was agonising. He took a few sips of eighteen-year-old single malt scotch from his old steel flask, then stared at it for a moment, thinking back to the time when it had turned a bullet that had been heading for his heart. Perhaps it could have done the same for Jeff. The thought made him want to swallow the whole contents of the flask, but he fought the urge and put it away.

He paced and sat down. Paced and sat down. The snow had stopped falling outside. The sky was leaden, threatening a downpour of rain that would thaw the streets of Cherbourg to a brown slush. Restless and badly in need of something other than alcohol to settle his nerves, he wanted to duck outside for a cigarette but worried that he might miss speaking to this Lacombe guy. After another half-hour he dialled the Le Val office number, and Tuesday snapped up the call before the first ring was over.

'Well?' Tuesday sounded breathless with worry.

'Nobody wants to tell me anything much,' Ben said. 'I think they're operating on him as we speak.'

'Then there's a chance,' Tuesday gasped. 'Thank Christ. When the phone rang I thought—'

Ben preferred not to dwell on what might all too well turn out to be false hopes. 'What's happening there?' he interrupted.

Tuesday let out a frustrated grunt and replied all in a flurry, 'Jesus, what *isn't* happening here? Now would be a good time to rob a bank, because it seems to me every cop in Normandy's turned up to get a piece of the action. Not long after you left, four NH-nineties landed in the field, full of guys in black. Then about thirty more vehicles rolled up. They've got the whole place surrounded and they're combing through every square inch like it was the biggest terrorist incident in French history. It's mayhem. I've repeated the whole story so many times I'm beginning to feel like a bloody parrot.'

'Let them do what they have to do,' Ben said. 'Maybe they'll find something.'

He very much doubted they would. More likely, the guys in black body armour would strut about feeling pumped up and hungry for Muslim extremists to gun down, then they'd eventually get bored and go home to their shoot-'em-up video games.

He asked, 'Is Vidal still there?'

'Overseeing his troops like he's General Patton. There's something else, Ben.' Tuesday paused, sounding uncomfortable. 'I'm really sorry. I had no choice.'

'What?'

'They demanded access to the armoury, and I had to let them in. They took the lot. Stripped it totally bare.'

'What do you mean, took the lot?'

'Every last scrap, down to the empty spare magazines. They even took the slings and bipods for the rifles. Said it was a precaution in accordance with the new anti-terror legislation. So if I tried to stand in their way, that pretty much made me a terrorist myself. They loaded everything into an armoured van and gave me a slip of paper that says it's being kept in secure storage at a government facility until further notice. Which basically means we're out of business for the foreseeable future. I'm sorry, Ben. If you want to fire me now, I'd understand.'

'No, Tuesday. You did the right thing and I wouldn't blame you for a minute, and neither will Jeff. Listen, do me a favour. Middle drawer of Jeff's desk there in the office. There's a tatty address book. Look under M and give me his mother's number in Australia.'

'Got it,' Tuesday said after a moment, and Ben scribbled

26

the number down on the back of his Gauloises packet. Then he remembered the other call he was going to have to make, a prospect that felt like a cold knife going into his belly. 'Now look under C.'

'Chantal,' Tuesday said with a groan. 'God, I'd forgotten all about her. The poor woman. Hold on. Yeah, there's a mobile number.' He read it out. 'You want me to—?'

'I'll do it,' Ben said grimly. 'Thanks, Tuesday. I'll keep you posted when I know anything.' He ended the call. Then took a deep breath and made the first of the two other calls he was dreading. As the dial tone was pulsing in his ear he tried desperately to formulate what he had to say. A woman's voice answered at the fourth ring, ten thousand miles away.

'May I speak to Mrs Lynne Dekker?'

'Speaking. Who is this?'

'Mrs Dekker, you don't know me. My name's Ben Hope. I work with Jeff.'

It was one of the worst calls he'd ever had to make. But the next one, to Chantal Mercier, was even harder. First the same stunned silence, then the same cry of anguish, the same gulping sobs. Then, to make Ben even more miserable, followed the rage, the recriminations, the bitter accusations. Chantal was certain that it was as a result of all the awful and dangerous things they did at Le Val that Jeff was hurt. Ben tried to placate her, but could think of little to say.

When it was over, he put the phone away and went back to the slightly lesser ordeal of waiting. He wasn't counting the minutes. He was counting the seconds.

About nine thousand more of them had ticked by in his head, and the hands on the wall clock in the waiting room had left midday far behind, by the time a door swung open and a figure in a blue doctor's overall appeared, spotted him and started walking briskly over. Ben stood up on jelly legs, his heart rate suddenly doubled. He stopped breathing.

Here it comes, he thought.

Chapter 5

Dr Lacombe was a she, with a mop of streaky blond hair that would probably have reached down past her waist if it hadn't been scraped back from her face and heaped and plaited into an elaborate French braid. She was probably around thirty-five but looked older, with shadows under her eyes as if she'd been up all night and was ready to drop from stress and exhaustion. Ben could picture how she must have looked just a minute earlier, in a surgical mask and apron and latex gloves, with even more of Jeff's blood spattered on her than he had.

'Sandrine Lacombe, head surgeon,' she said, offering a hand, and Ben could tell from her tone that the news couldn't be entirely bad. Relief flooded through him like warm honey pouring through his veins. He started breathing again.

The doctor's grip was firm and dry. She had a clipped, efficient manner that Ben liked instantly as she started briefing him quickly on the situation.

It wasn't as bad as it could have been, but it could have been a lot better. Jeff had lost a tremendous amount of blood, necessitating an emergency transfusion the moment he'd been brought in. Meanwhile the path of the bullet, narrowly missing his heart, had caused massive tissue damage and internal bleeding in the chest cavity and collapsed a lung. They'd almost lost him twice during the three-hour operation. Now moved to the intensive care unit, he seemed to have stabilised. Holding on, but still deep in the woods.

'We've done all we can,' Dr Lacombe sighed. 'I managed to sew up and reinflate the ruptured lung. As for the rest of the damage, now only time will tell if he's going to pull through.'

'Thank you,' was all Ben could reply.

Dr Lacombe puffed her cheeks and gave a little shrug as if to say, don't thank me too soon. 'The next twelve hours will be difficult,' she warned. 'There's a high risk of complications. Frankly, given the extent of the trauma I would give him little more than a sixty per cent chance of surviving this. He wouldn't have made it even this far, if someone hadn't prevented him from bleeding to death at the scene.' Her weary but sharp blue eyes flicked up and down, taking in Ben's bloodied appearance. 'I take it that someone was you, Monsieur—?'

'Hope. Ben Hope.'

A flicker of surprise in her eyes, that she wasn't speaking to a Frenchman. Ben spoke the language without any trace of accent. She went on, 'It was also you who provided the patient's blood group. Thank you for that. If we hadn't known in time, there's little chance he would still be with us now. It appears you have some medical training?'

'British Special Forces, a long time ago. They teach you a few basics to keep your people going when they've been shot, burned or blown up.'

She nodded pensively. 'I thought you looked *militaire*. Anyway, you've helped to save his life for the moment, and with any luck he may live to thank you for it. We'll do everything we can from here. But please don't get your hopes up.'

'I appreciate your directness, Doctor. That's exactly what I need.'

'May I ask what is your relation to the patient?'

'Friend and business partner.'

'This business, it's in Basse-Normandie?'

'We've been based here for a number of years.' Ben left out what she didn't need to know: that he'd spent a good portion of that time flitting from place to place and getting himself into trouble all over the world, and could speak a variety of languages as well as French. Jeff was Mr Stay-at-Home by comparison.

'I see. What about his family – has Monsieur Dekker any relatives?'

'A mother who emigrated to Australia. And a fiancée a little closer, in Saint-Acaire. They've already both been notified. His mother's got a long way to travel to the nearest big airport, but I'd imagine she'll be on her way soon.'

'It'll be a while before I'll allow him to have any visitors.' Dr Lacombe paused. 'What about you? You have a contact number?'

'I'm not going anywhere. Any changes in his condition, I'll be right here.'

'Just in case,' she said, handing him a card, 'this is my personal cell number, if you need to talk. I don't give this out to everyone, you understand?'

'I appreciate your help, Doctor.'

She paused again, fixed him with those sharp eyes, as blue as topaz, and said, 'You know I have to report this, don't you? A gunshot wound of this kind—'

'I understand,' Ben said, 'but the police already know all about it. Some of them were already there just after it happened. I'm afraid more of them will be landing on your hospital pretty soon, looking for me.'

She shook her head. 'What did happen?'

'He was shot.'

'I can see that. I mean, what *happened*?'

'We were cutting up a fallen tree. Talking about this and that. He'd just told me that he was getting married. It was a happy time. We had no idea that someone was watching us. Someone hidden, quite a distance away, with a rifle. Then they fired. One shot, one hit. You know the rest.'

'I don't understand.'

'Neither do I,' Ben said. 'Not yet.'

'Does your friend have, I don't know, enemies?'

'Looks that way,' Ben said. 'One with a rifle, and who knows how to use it. Sniper-style, probably set up on a bipod and fitted with a scope. Judging by the ballistics, the gun's something around a thirty-calibre, like a .270 or a .308. Maybe fitted with a silencer too, which could explain why I heard nothing over the noise of the chainsaw. Those are the only clues I have so far, for what they're worth.'

'I don't know anything about guns, except what they can do to people,' Dr Lacombe said with a faraway look and a slight shiver, as if she was visualising a whole back-catalogue of horrors she'd personally witnessed in the course of her surgical career. 'And I don't like them.'

'I don't much like them either,' Ben said. 'Except when they're used for good.'

'How can a tool of violence and death be used for good?'

'When it's deployed against the person who spilled first blood,' Ben said.

'You're talking about justice. That's a job for the police.'

'When they can find the guy. *If* they can find him.'

'Are you saying you intend to find him?'

'I'm saying I intend to make this right.'

She looked at him. 'This is not a war, Monsieur Hope.'

'Tell that to your patient,' Ben said.

'When he recovers,' she said. '*If* he recovers.'

'He's tough as an old boot,' Ben said. 'He's been hurt before and pulled through.'

'As badly as this? Then I hope for your friend's sake that he's as fortunate this time.'

Ben felt suddenly weary and dizzy, as if all his energy had drained out through his feet. He glanced around him for something to lean on. 'No,' he admitted quietly. 'Not as badly as this.'

'You don't look good,' Sandrine Lacombe said, frowning at him. 'I think we should take a look at you.'

'I'm not hurt. None of this is my blood. I already told them that.'

'I know a delayed shock reaction when I see one.'

'I'm fine.'

'No, you're not. Trust me, I'm a doctor.'

33

Chapter 6

Despite his protests, Sandrine Lacombe dispatched a squad of nurses to attend to Ben while the doctor herself hurried back to the ICU to check on Jeff and see to the rest of her rounds. Ben was taken into an examination room where he did his best to fend off the nurses' attentions, but gave in when he caught a glimpse of himself in a mirror and didn't recognise the wild man looking back at him: the figure of an escaped desperado who had taken refuge in a slaughter-house. 'You can't go around the hospital looking like that,' said the head nurse. 'You'll frighten the patients.'

Once they'd exchanged his bloody rags for a hospital gown and confirmed what he already knew, that none of the blood was his, they started insisting on treating him for shock. Ben drew the line at sedatives. He needed to keep his wits about him. But a hot shower seemed like a good idea, and he gladly followed the head nurse down the corridor to get himself cleaned up.

He stood under the splashing hot water for fifteen long minutes, trying to wash away the tension that locked up his neck and shoulder muscles. Looking down at his feet, he saw the cloudy rust-coloured swirl of Jeff's blood running off him and circling the drain. He still felt strangely numb. It all seemed somehow surreal, as if he were watching himself from the outside; as if these events were just an awful dream from which he half expected to awake at any second. One instant Jeff had been there at his side, his usual self, cheerful and focused and content with the future; the next there was an empty, desolate space where Jeff used to be. Good old solid Jeff, who was always there when you needed him, whose spirits were so hard to dampen, who had saved Ben's skin on more than a couple of occasions. Someone like that couldn't just disappear from your life and not be there any more.

No, it didn't seem real. But reality would bite soon enough, all right, if Sandrine Lacombe returned to break the news that the patient had slipped away despite all their efforts. Ben had lost enough people close to him to know exactly how he would feel then.

One step at a time, he decided. There was no other way to deal with this.

After his shower Ben towelled himself and put on the clothes that the nurse had left folded on a chair for him. His own, except for his leather jacket, were probably already in the hospital incinerator. What they'd brought him would have fitted a man two inches shorter and forty pounds heavier, but at least he wouldn't have to meet the cops dressed like an in-patient.

Just as he'd expected, there were six plain-clothes officers waiting for him in the corridor when he emerged from the bathroom. During his years as a kidnap rescue specialist and since, Ben had dealt with a lot of police officers in a lot of countries. A few notable exceptions apart, he'd never been able to form much of an affinity with them. But in this situation, he promised himself, he would try to keep it civil.

It proved to be a hard promise to keep. Even as he walked towards them along the corridor and saw them all turn to stare at him, Ben's eye had picked out the most officious-looking one and decided he must be in charge. He was right. Inspector Sébastien Tarrare couldn't have been more puffed-up if he'd been personally appointed by the president as commander-in-chief of French national security.

They waved him into the same small waiting area whose walls Ben had already spent three hours studying. The shortest and fattest of the cops, with a bristly neck and protruding teeth, helped himself to a Coke from the vending machine. Ben gave him a hard look. Tarrare invited Ben to sit. Ben preferred to stand. They'd barely exchanged ten words yet, and already it wasn't going too well. All six cops looked on edge, shooting him cagey looks as though he was some kind of terror suspect himself. It was a good thing his name was Ben Hope and not Bin Hossain, he thought, or Tarrare and his little posse would have cordoned off a security zone several blocks around the hospital and called in tanks and artillery support by now.

Inspector Tarrare briefly introduced his five colleagues, whose names Ben dismissed from his memory the instant he heard them, and then went on to offer a few insincere-sounding condolences for what had happened.

'He's not dead yet,' Ben said.

'But I am given to understand he is mortally wounded,' Tarrare replied, arching an eyebrow.

Ben definitely didn't like him now.

'In any case we are obliged to treat this as a matter of the utmost priority. Especially under the circumstances, considering the nature of the target.'

Now it was Ben's turn to arch an eyebrow. 'The target?'

'A terrorist's dream. Your place of business has more military hardware all stockpiled in a single place than any French Army base.'

Ben said, 'If that's true, then the government had better step up its defence spending. We have a small armoury, kept highly secure and subject to regular inspections, every item in it registered and licensed down to the last round of ammunition, with a stack of official paperwork to prove it. Which I know you already know, Inspector, so let's cut the bullshit. Besides, as far as anyone can prove at this point the target was a man, not a place of business. My friend was shot. I didn't see a terrorist raiding party storming the compound to blow open the armoury for its contents. Nor did any of the witnesses to the immediate aftermath of the shooting, including several officers of your very own SDAT.' So put that in your pipe and smoke it, he wanted to add, but didn't.

'All the same,' Tarrare said without missing a beat, 'this is an extremely serious situation.'

'No argument there,' Ben told him. 'You have an attempted murder to solve and a guy running loose with a rifle. Maybe that should be your priority.'

'And maybe you should read the papers,' said the porcine cop with the can of Coke, tipping it towards Ben as he spoke. 'France is under attack from radical extremists. Any day now, another major incident is expected to happen anywhere in the country. But you don't seem to think this incident is connected with the current national state of emergency?'

'By radical extremists, I take it you mean Islamic ones?'

Tarrare pulled a face and grunted, 'Who else?'

'Just making that clear,' Ben said. 'I mean, for all we know it could have been anyone from the National Liberation Front of Corsica, to the Basque separatists, to the Unité Radicale bunch who tried to shoot your president a few years back. Or maybe those Action Directe guys or the Red Army Brigade are back in business and looking to procure some weaponry for a new wave of terror attacks that will

37

shake things up like nothing Europe has ever seen before. Basically, it could be anyone at all. I'd say you boys have your work cut out for you, for sure.'

Nobody replied. The cops all glared at him.

Ben pointed up at the big clock on the waiting-room wall, which read 2.15 p.m. 'But you must be hungry, missing lunch over this stuff. Why don't you do what you do best, head down to the nearest bistro for a nice meal and a bottle of wine and spend an hour or two working out how to become the heroes who saved the republic? Then maybe you'd like to call Commander Roman Vidal and ask him if they've found a single scrap of evidence down there at Le Val linking the shooting with the activities of any known or suspected terror group of any kind.'

The cop with the can pulled a nasty sneer. 'If it wasn't terrorists, then what? Maybe a hunter let off a stray shot? Thought your friend was a wild boar?'

Ben stared at him coldly and wondered how fast the guy's smirk would disappear with that Coke can rammed down his throat. 'Wild boar hunters shoot in groups, with spotters and beaters. They don't snipe at their quarry from extreme ranges, with no safety backstop except someone's wire fence. They don't use silencers and they don't generally confuse a human with a large hairy pig. Though,' he added, giving the cop a deliberate up-and-down look, 'in some cases I can see how that misunderstanding might arise.'

The cop's eyes narrowed and he flushed scarlet. 'Then who did this? Enlighten us, as you're obviously so knowledgeable.'

'That's a very good question,' Ben said. 'I don't know who did this, any more than you do. But then, I'm not the police, am I? I'm just a visitor to this hospital, waiting to find out if my friend in there is going to live or die, and having to waste my time answering pointless questions while you guys should be out there searching for the answers. So how about you leave me alone now?'

When the disgruntled cops eventually did leave, Ben called Tuesday again to update him on Jeff's condition. Moments after he'd put his phone away, Ben heard footsteps and turned to see Dr Lacombe approaching. The look on her face made his heart jerk to a stop for a moment. Even before she opened her mouth to speak, he knew she'd come to deliver bad news.

'There's been a complication,' she said gravely.

'What kind of complication?'

She sighed. 'I'm very sorry. I was afraid something like this would happen.'

'Talk to me. Tell me he's alive.'

'He's alive. But—' She went into a rapid stream of medical terminology like post-traumatic pulmonary thromboembolism and right ventricular failure and circulatory failure and mechanical ventilation, until Ben stopped her.

'I don't understand. What happened?'

'He had a blood clot in the lung. It caused a severe stroke and he's no longer able to breathe on his own. We gave him a massive dose of barbiturates to induce deep unconsciousness, so the machine could breathe for him. I have no idea how long we might have to keep him under. Worst case, perhaps indefinitely.'

Ben could only repeat her words dully, as if he'd become stupid. His brain couldn't compute what she was telling him. 'Are you saying—?'

'I'm afraid so, yes. He's in a coma.'

Chapter 7

'There's nothing you can do here,' she told him. 'You might as well go home and rest. You look like you need it.'

'Maybe I'm not the only one,' Ben said. Sandrine Lacombe looked every bit as wrecked as he felt.

She shrugged. 'I'll stay with him as long as I can. I might go home myself for a couple of hours' sleep, but I'll have my colleague Dr Sauveterre call me if there's any change in his condition. I live nearby, so, any developments, I can come straight over.'

Ben was touched by her determination to do whatever she could for Jeff. 'I'll go,' he agreed. 'There are some matters I need to attend to back at the house. But before I do, can I see him?'

Dr Lacombe frowned and seemed about to say no, then relented. 'Just for a minute, okay?'

She was about to lead the way when a movement outside caught Ben's eye and he looked out of the window to see a black Peugeot taxicab come speeding into the hospital car park. It pulled up close to the entrance and a pretty brunette in a tweedy winter coat clambered out, her face red and streaked with tears.

Sandrine Lacombe noticed Ben's expression. 'The fiancée?'

He nodded. Chantal Mercier had arrived.

Moments later there was commotion in the reception area. Ben grimly went to meet her, but didn't have a lot of talking to do as the doctor took charge of the emotional scene and broke the news of the latest negative developments with a level of calm, sympathetic but firm professional control that a lot of top-rank military commanders would have envied.

Chantal sniffed, wiping her eyes. 'Where is he?' Her voice was hoarse from crying.

'You can see him,' Sandrine Lacombe said gently with a glance at Ben. 'But only for two minutes.'

Chantal barely looked at Ben as the doctor led them down a series of corridors to the ICU. Jeff had been moved into a room behind a glass partition. His bed was surrounded by so much equipment that he was barely visible. A coloured monitor on a stand showed his heartbeat, slow and steady. More screens and racks of beeping electronics were flashing up streams of data that were meaningless to Ben. A drip bag dangled above his friend. Lying there completely still in the middle of it all, Jeff looked shrunken and frail under the sheet, as if all the vital force had been sucked out of him. The respirator tube was attached to a mask over his mouth and nose. Dozens of smaller pipes and hoses hung off him like snakes. His eyes were shut. He was barely recognisable.

Chantal let out a stifled cry when she saw him, raced to the bedside and clasped Jeff's hand in both of hers, her face contorted and streaming with tears all over again. 'Oh my God, oh my God,' she kept murmuring. 'He feels so cold.'

'That's normal,' Sandrine Lacombe said, but Ben could see the sharp worry lines etched into her face.

Chantal pulled herself as close to Jeff as all the tubes and wires would let her. '*Mon pauvre amour, est-ce que tu m'entends? Réponds-moi.*'

'He can't hear you,' Sandrine Lacombe said softly. 'He's far away.'

Chantal looked up, eyes swimming and full of terror. 'How long will he be like this?'

'I can't say.'

'What does that mean? Are you trying to tell me he could be like this for *ever*?'

'I can't say,' the doctor repeated, tight-lipped.

'If he wakes up, will he be . . . like before?'

'I'm sorry. I can't say that either.'

An angry flush of colour came back into Chantal's cheeks. 'You're supposed to be a doctor. How can you not know these things? I want a second opinion. I *insist* on—'

Ben couldn't stand it any longer. He stepped around the foot of the bed, gently took Chantal's arm and said, 'Dr Lacombe is doing all she can. Let me drive you home. We can come back when it's okay to visit.'

But Chantal jerked her arm away and shook her head furiously. 'I want to stay with him.'

'That's not an option,' Sandrine Lacombe said, gentle but firm. Chantal opened her mouth to protest, but all that came out was sobbing.

It was a long and sombre drive back. The cold rain was lashing down, and all that remained of the earlier snow was the dirty roadside slush. Chantal sat with her head bowed and her face in her hands all the way, not speaking. Ben didn't know what to say to her. He was having a hard time dealing with his own emotions, and in the end he fell into silence too.

The short winter day was darkening by the time they reached Saint-Acaire. When the Alpina pulled up outside her little terraced house on the edge of the village, Chantal got out and ran to her door and disappeared inside without a word. The door slammed.

Ben sat for a moment, lit a Gauloise and then drove on.

When, a few minutes later, he turned off the road onto the innocuous farm track that led to Le Val's entrance, he found its floodlit security gates partially blocked by a TV crew van and alive with a throng of reporters armed with cameras and microphones and clamouring for details about the shooting. A cop car was in attendance nearby but the gendarmes seemed content just to smoke and watch from a distance as Serge and Adrien, from inside the locked gates, were kept busy holding the noisy crowd at bay, repeating 'No comment, no comment' to a thousand insistent questions fired at them like bullets.

Ben slipped the BMW through the chaos, as thankful for the tinted glass shielding him from flashing cameras as he was for the tall fence and barbed wire keeping the zombie horde from invading the private sanctuary inside.

Once he'd made it through the gates and down the track to the heart of the compound, Le Val had never seemed to him so empty and desolate. The fleet of police vehicles had all gone. Jeff's Ford Ranger was still where Ben had left it. Parked behind the pickup was the old Land Rover, and behind that was a little Renault Clio hatchback he didn't recognise, but he was too tired and upset to think about it.

Tuesday must have seen the approaching lights of the BMW. He stood silhouetted in the glow from the open farmhouse door as Ben stepped out of the car and walked up the steps. Tuesday's face was drawn and grim, and became even more so when Ben gave him the latest update on Jeff. They spoke for a few moments in the kitchen, where a bottle of scotch and a half-empty glass rested on the table. It wasn't like Tuesday to drink, but he'd made some inroads into the bottle already. Ben fetched down another glass from the cupboard, filled it to the brim and knocked half of it down in a long, stinging swallow that made his eyes water.

'We're all over the TV news,' Tuesday said. 'It's a bloody circus. I've given up watching.'

'What do they know?'

'Just that some British guy got shot. None of the details have been released yet. But watch this space. This is going to be terrible for the business.'

'To hell with the business,' Ben said. He slumped at the kitchen table with his drink. It was only now that the full reality of the situation was beginning to kick in. It would be a long night. And a long day to follow. The first of many long days.

Tuesday was shifting about uncomfortably as though he wanted to say something but didn't know how to put it. Ben looked at him. 'What aren't you telling me?'

Tuesday pointed in the direction of the living room. 'You, um, you have a, erm, visitor.'

Ben's heart fell, remembering the strange car outside. Tuesday's nervousness and the way he suddenly made himself scarce a moment later, told him all he needed to know. Left alone in the kitchen, Ben refilled his glass. He walked slowly from the room. Paused outside the living-room door. It was ajar and he could see a dim light on inside.

He pushed the door silently open and stepped through it.

She was standing with her back to the doorway. Her rich auburn hair was shorter than it had been last time he'd seen her. The sight of her brought a whole new flood of emotions that Ben didn't know if he could handle, not at this moment.

'Hello, Brooke,' he said.

Chapter 8

She turned. Apart from her hairstyle, she hadn't changed. She was as achingly beautiful as ever. More, even, but maybe that was just because he hadn't seen her in such a very long time. But there was no smile. Not that he'd expected one from her, even on a better day than today. Her green eyes, vivid even in the dim light of the single side lamp, were moist with tears.

'I came as soon as I heard,' she said.

Brooke was officially still on the books as a member of the Le Val team, although she hadn't worked there lately. Tuesday must have called her earlier that day. *Thanks for letting me know*, Ben thought.

'What happened?' she said. 'Who did this?'

He shook his head. 'I wish I knew what to tell you.' A long mournful silence filled the room. He took a step towards her. 'It's good to see you again,' he said, because he didn't know what else to say. In any case, it was a lie. Seeing her again, especially now, like this, was indescribably painful.

'Whatever,' she murmured.

'How are you?' It sounded so lame.

She shrugged. 'There isn't much to say, Ben. I'm working. Living in London again. Life goes on. I'm with someone else now.'

Ben said, 'I hope you're happy.'

'Don't try so hard to sound like you mean it.' Her voice rose a tone, cracking out at him like a whiplash. Then she paused, softened a little, let out a sigh. 'I'm sorry. I shouldn't have said that. Yes, I'm happy. I think I am. That is, I was, until today, until I heard about Jeff. This is so awful.'

He hesitated, knowing that the question bursting to come out was the wrong thing to say, especially at this moment. But then he thought, Fuck it, and let it out anyway. 'Please don't tell me you're back with that prick Rupert Shannon again.'

She stiffened. 'Give me some credit, will you?'

'That's something, at least. Then who is he?' Ben asked, knowing very well how badly he was crossing the line. But he'd committed himself now and there was no turning back.

Brooke folded her arms across her chest and gave him a piercing look. 'What I do and who I see is my business. You took yourself out of my life when you walked away. Your choice, Ben. Live with it.'

He had been living with it, not always successfully. 'Yeah,' he muttered. 'I'm sorry I asked. It was wrong.'

'Is Jeff going to be okay?'

'They had to induce a coma.'

Brooke's face fell. She'd known Jeff for years, going back to when she'd first come to lecture classes at Le Val as a visiting expert on hostage psychology. Dr Brooke Marcel, one of the leaders in her clinical field. One of the great lost loves of Ben's life. Letting her go the way he had was his biggest regret – it hurt him every day, like an old war wound that could never quite heal.

'I booked a room at the Manoir in Valognes,' she said. 'I'll drive up to the hospital in the morning, but then I have to rush back to London for work.'

'Thanks for stopping by.'

'I don't know why . . . I just thought . . .' Her voice trailed off, and then she shook her head. 'God, what a mess. Who could have done this to him? I can't understand. I mean, Jeff never hurt anybody.'

Ben thought about that. You couldn't be the high-level military operator Jeff Dekker had once been without hurting anyone, or at least being involved in a good deal of it. Special Forces made enemies around the world and there was no shortage of folks who would go to all kinds of lengths to get back at them if they could. But the shroud of secrecy around the Special Boat Service, Jeff's old unit, was no different from the impenetrable cloak that protected the identities of operatives within Ben's own former 22 SAS regiment. Practically nobody on the outside knew who these men were. Targeted revenge attacks against individuals in response for things they had done in the name of their country were pretty much unheard of. Unless someone within their own unit had somehow been turned or manipulated by a third party with an axe to grind, or gone bad themselves. Ben had already worked through a mental list of possible candidates, and crossed their names off one by one until none remained.

'Whoever it was,' he said, 'they've just made the biggest mistake of their life.'

She looked at him, understanding from the look in his eyes what he was thinking. Brooke knew him well enough, from long experience, to know exactly how he was liable to respond in this situation.

'Leave it to the police, Ben. Hasn't there been enough trouble already?'

'It seems to me that the shooter isn't having any trouble at all,' Ben said. 'He got in, did his work, and got out. Job done, nice and easy. Now he's out there somewhere enjoying life with a clear conscience. I can't let that happen.'

'So you're taking it upon yourself to sort things out. As usual.' Brooke said it with an exaggerated tone of resignation.

'You haven't met Inspector Tarrare and his goon squad. They couldn't catch the flu in the middle of an epidemic. Don't try to twist this around, Brooke. If that was me lying in that hospital bed, breathing through a machine, Jeff would do the same thing and you know it.'

'Jeff needs you here.'

'As in, don't go running off and getting yourself killed?' he said. He almost added, 'Why should you care anyway?' But he bit his lip. He'd already said too much.

She gave a sour laugh. 'What am I saying? As if anyone had a chance in hell of stopping you, once your mind's made up. Running off when people need you around is what you do best, after all.'

That hit below the belt. Ben could have replied, 'You were the one who broke off the engagement, not me.' But this was no time for a drawn-out argument. He clenched his teeth and said nothing.

'I didn't come here to fight,' Brooke said sadly after a beat. 'I'll go now, before one of us says something we'll both regret.'

There was no physical contact between them as she was leaving. He wanted to reach out to her, even if he didn't deserve the comfort of her touch. He stood in the door and watched the tail-lights of the Renault Clio disappear up the track towards the gates, where she'd have to run the gauntlet of zombie reporters clamouring for their story. Then she was gone, and the rainy night closed in behind her.

Ben could have done with some company, but Tuesday had disappeared. He returned to the kitchen and swallowed down some more whisky. Still the best cure ever devised for delayed shock, and other things.

He wandered back outside into the rain. Out of the darkness came a familiar shape, and a wet nose nudged Ben's hand in greeting. Storm trotted by his side as he crossed the yard, looking up at him curiously. The dog seemed subdued, as if he understood something.

Ben walked over to the dark, silent office building opposite the house. Inside, he flipped on the light. Looked at Jeff's empty desk. Sat down at his own, and stared into space. It was cold inside the office building, but Ben was too numb to feel the chill. Just like he was too sick to feel hungry, even though his stomach was empty apart from ten-year-old Laphroaig. Maybe he needed to drink some more, because the image of Jeff lying there in the hospital kept coming back to him. He tried to flush it out of his mind's eye by picturing the unknown shooter. The blank face behind the rifle. Ben wondered what he was doing right this moment, what he was thinking.

'I'll find you,' he said out loud. 'Don't ever think I won't.'

But he wasn't going to find him tonight. Wherever the shooter had gone, he had a head start that Ben knew he couldn't hope to make up by going off half-cocked, jumping in his car and tearing off on a revenge mission with not a single clue or lead.

Tomorrow would be another day.

Until then, Ben could only bide his time, lay aside his restless thoughts and try to relax.

As he sat there at the desk, he looked down and saw the unopened letter from the Bollati penitentiary in Milan, lying there exactly where he'd left it that morning when he'd gone to help Jeff with the fallen tree. He'd forgotten all about it until now.

He gazed at it for a moment. He had nothing better to do, and maybe it would help take his mind off things. He picked up the envelope, slipped out the letter. Unfolded it. And began to read.

Chapter 9

The letter was handwritten on three thin sheets of headed Bollati prison paper. The first thing that caught Ben's eye was that it was in Italian, a language he spoke less fluently than French but in which he nonetheless could hold his own pretty well. The second thing he noticed was the handwriting itself, a fine flowing italicised script that very few people could produce any more, and which clearly showed its author as being someone of a certain age and education.

At the top of the first page the November date, a few days earlier than the postmark on the envelope, told him that it had been written while he, Jeff and Tuesday were fighting for their lives in Africa. No indication of the writer's identity, so Ben flicked over to the last page and ran his eye down to the bottom. His eyes narrowed in surprise when he saw the signature.

The letter's author was one Fabrizio Severini.

A name Ben recognised immediately. It flooded his mind with memories from years back, returning him to a chapter in his life when he'd still been working freelance as what people in that little-known trade called a 'K&R crisis consultant'. The K and R stood for kidnap and ransom, which had been Ben's particular area of expertise in those days. When vulnerable, innocent people – many of them children – were taken by ruthless criminals looking to extort money from their loved ones, and when the conventional avenues for getting them back had been tried and failed, it had been Ben's job to employ his own specialised means to hunt the kidnappers and bring the victims home as unscathed as possible. The kidnappers had rarely come out of it unscathed themselves. It had been a dangerous business for them once Ben was involved.

Dangerous for Ben, too. And the strange mission that had indirectly brought him into contact with Fabrizio Severini had been one of the most hazardous of them all. What had started as the race to save the life of a child had led Ben through some unexpected twists and turns before placing him in conflict with one of the most tenacious, ruthless enemies he'd ever encountered, a man named Massimiliano Usberti.

Usberti was a rogue senior Italian archbishop who controlled a secret and powerful Christian fundamentalist cult called *Gladius Domini*: Sword of God. Its brainwashed members, branded with a tattoo to show their allegiance, were prepared to kidnap, torture or assassinate anyone who stood in Usberti's way. One of Usberti's trusted inner circle had been a psychopathic killer called Franco Bozza. Another had been his close aide and personal secretary, Fabrizio Severini. Ben had worked alongside the only law enforcement officer he'd ever trusted, the intensely cerebral, sharp-witted and fiercely driven Parisian cop Luc Simon to bring down Gladius Domini. In the process, Ben had been shot, almost stabbed, come within a whisker of being crushed by a speeding train, and been very nearly incinerated in a burning mansion. All more or less run-of-the-mill stuff for him. He'd also found love, not lastingly, in the form of the American scientist Roberta Ryder.

During the final shakedown that brought the cult to its knees, Massimiliano Usberti had been arrested while many of his cronies, Severini included, had fled for the hills. But Severini had proved much less wily than his leader: INTERPOL had scooped him up just a few weeks later, while over the next few months – pretty much as Ben had expected might happen – Usberti had used his influence in high places, his power and his wealth, to oil his way out of trouble. In the end Usberti had walked away from the affair a free man – albeit disgraced, broken and barred from ever again regaining his old position in the church.

When the news had broken that the charges against Usberti had been controversially dropped, Ben had already been moving on with his life and becoming involved in the hunt for a missing girl abducted by an international child sex trafficking ring.

For a while afterwards he'd toyed with the idea of going after Usberti to deliver some natural justice where the courts had failed. But he'd reluctantly given up on the plan. If anything untoward had happened to the former archbishop, Luc Simon – by then promoted from the Paris police to a desk at the INTERPOL HQ in Lyon – would have known about it, instantly put two and two together and jumped on Ben with all the force of his new position. Ben had thought about it less and less over time, and eventually let the whole thing fade from his mind. It wasn't a perfect world. The bad guys sometimes walked: you just had to deal with it.

If there was any consolation, it was that not all of Gladius Domini's surviving members had got off so lightly. Quite how Usberti had managed to get Severini to take the fall for him, Ben would never know and had long ago stopped caring. But the prison notepaper in his hands was certainly proof, if nothing else, that Severini's plunge had been a spectacular and enduring one. Ben wondered how many more years the man had left to serve.

That wasn't all Ben was wondering as he returned to the start of the letter and began reading, translating from Italian as he went. Why on earth was Fabrizio Severini, a man he'd never even seen in the flesh, writing to him after all this time? He was about to find out.

Dear Signor Hope,

It is with a heavy conscience and only after a great deal of soul-searching that I write to you, as well as with the heartfelt wish that you will both forgive this unsolicited and most unorthodox personal communication and treat its content as an expression of my utmost sincerity.

Considering we have never met in person and never shall, you are doubtless wondering why I have chosen to send you this letter. I fully understand that you may not wish to read it and will instead feel impelled to tear it up; but for reasons that will become clear below, I beg you to read on and hear what I must tell you.

In the years since its downfall, I have always remembered you as the man primarily responsible for bringing to an end the insidious organisation in which I once so strongly believed, and whose name I cannot now bring myself to mention. Nor do I find it easy to express the deep shame I continue to endure each and every day, as I sit here in my cell with little to do except think back to those dark times, to the many and terrible sins committed, to which I was so blind, and to the man I once idolised and trusted as though he were my own father. I believed myself at the time to be collaborating with a true visionary, a man of God. Instead, as I later came to realise, I was in fact working in league with the Devil. I allowed myself to become an unwitting instrument of this maniac whose pure evil is matched only by the cunning that has, to this day, enabled him to evade justice.

I was a fool, and I have been rightly punished for my mistakes. I deserved all that befell me: to have lost my cherished family, my home, my position within the Church, and my freedom. It is not to gain sympathy that I tell you of the complete psychological breakdown and the torment of mental illness I suffered for so long following my arrest and incarceration. The experience broke me and, in effect, I went mad. I spent an extended period of time in a facility for the criminally insane, and only after prolonged treatment were my rational faculties slowly restored, permitting my transfer here to the Istituto Penitenziario Bollati – where in the last two years I have received far more humane and compassionate treatment than I could ever hope to merit.

Though the horrors of my insanity are now largely behind me, the burden of guilt I suffer can never be lifted from my shoulders. Every day I have prayed for God's forgiveness for my part in the unspeakable crimes Massimiliano Usberti perpetrated in the name of the Catholic faith. I was once a man of God, blessed each day by His love and guidance; but that source of Divine wisdom was lost to me as the Lord turned His back and spoke to me no more, however much I begged Him to reveal Himself to me as He once did. His long silence has in many ways been the hardest punishment for me to bear.

Finally, after all these years of torment, God in His mercy has spoken to me once again. But now that He has taken me back into the favour of His Divine goodness, it pains me deeply to say that He has only confirmed to me what I have always dreaded to be the case.

And this brings me, my dear Signor Hope, to my reason for penning this letter to you – a reason so terrible that the very thought makes me shake with fear as I write. For I am now more utterly certain than ever, in my heart of hearts, that we have not seen the end of this evil maniac Massimiliano Usberti. A man like him does not simply fade into the background. If he has managed to remain in the shadows for so long, it is only because he is hatching some dreadful new plan that eclipses even his monstrous exploits of the past. Moreover, I am convinced that he will return to seek vengeance against those he perceives as having wronged him – those who prevented him from carrying out his pernicious goals and may attempt to do so again when he inevitably rises once more from the darkness.

Signor Hope, I beg you to be vigilant and pray that you will take heed, for I am one of the few people alive who understands the power and depth of the merciless hate that motivates Usberti. I am weak and vulnerable, trapped as I am behind these bars. If his villainous influence can reach me inside prison by the hand of some assassin, so be it; I deserve little better. But you are strong, and free. You must do all you can to guard yourself from him. Not only yourself, but every one of those virtuous, wholly innocent individuals who played a part in his downfall. With all my heart and for their sakes as well *as your own, I beseech you not to take this warning lightly.*

May God in His infinite glory watch over you and protect you.

Your humble servant,

*Fabrizio Severini
Prisoner 56139*

Chapter 10

The letter left Ben stunned. He clutched the thin sheets tightly in his hands and read them again, twice, word by word, in case he'd somehow misunderstood or mistranslated.

He hadn't. The message couldn't have been clearer. Fabrizio Severini, repentant sinner, acting on a mystical revelation from God, was warning him that his old enemy Massimiliano Usberti was coming back for revenge.

And with those three pages of elegant handwriting, it was as though the planet had suddenly flipped its magnetic polarity, turning everything upside down.

For the thousandth time since that morning, Ben revisualised the awful memory of the shooting. The details were exactly the same, yet everything was completely different. In his mind's eye he pictured the two of them standing by the fallen tree: Ben cutting, Jeff close by waiting to grab the next section of log and toss it on the pile. Then, like an extreme slow-motion replay: the bullet closing in from nowhere. The blood spray. Jeff falling. The entire nightmare sequence happening a fraction of a second *after* the gust of wind that had buffeted them with a fresh snow flurry. A gust of wind that could very easily have diverted the trajectory of the bullet just those few critical inches and caused it to hit . . .

The wrong target.

It seemed so obvious to him now that Ben was furious with himself for not having thought of it before. As a trained sniper himself, it had been drilled into him long ago that even a 10mph gust of sidewind, coming in right-to-left from three o'clock or left-to-right from nine o'clock, could blow a medium to long-range rifle shot far enough off course in either direction to spell the difference between a hit and a miss. Even the most experienced rifleman could be caught out by a sudden change in windspeed and direction. At a range of three hundred yards, the deviation could be a full seven inches left or right depending on which way the gust blew. At five hundred yards the shot could veer off by up to twenty inches or more; and at a thousand yards it could be off by over fifty inches, missing the bullseye by a whole four feet. And that was the data for a ten-mile-an-hour gust. A stronger wind could affect the shot even worse.

The realisation made Ben's mind reel. Because if Severini's warning could be believed in any way, it meant that the bullet hadn't been meant for Jeff at all.

It had been meant for him.

He was clutching the letter so tightly in his hands that the paper ripped. He let the torn pieces fall to the desk as his mind raced and filled with questions. Had the sniper known he'd hit the wrong man? Was it possible that the gust of wind, whipping in a fresh snow flurry between him and his distant target, could have obscured the view through his scope just long enough to mislead him? He pressed the trigger; he saw a man go down; he packed up his kit and hurried from the scene, running back to his hidden vehicle, getting on the phone to report back to base that his mission was accomplished.

Whereupon, the assassin might have gone after the next target on his list.

Ben looked down at the torn letter. *You must do all you can to guard yourself from him. Not only yourself, but every one of those virtuous, wholly innocent individuals who played a part in his downfall.*

The next question that flashed into Ben's mind was: what other names were on the hit list?

He could think of four apart from his own. Four people whom Usberti would have blamed and never forgiven for their involvement in the affair. The first and most obvious was INTERPOL Commissioner Luc Simon, Ben's main ally in bringing down Gladius Domini.

The next was Roberta Ryder, who had become entangled in the intrigue through no fault of her own and become Usberti's target for assassination and kidnap, narrowly escaping with her life.

Then there was Father Pascal Cambriel, the elderly French priest who had sheltered Ben and Roberta at his humble village home after Ben had been shot, and ended up playing a key role.

And lastly there was Anna Manzini, the scholar and expert on the history of the Cathars, who had helped Ben unravel the bizarre background behind Usberti's obsession with alchemy and after whom Usberti had sent his murderer Franco Bozza, to butcher her in her villa near Montségur in southern France. Like Roberta, Anna Manzini had had a close call and only just survived.

Usberti's henchman Franco Bozza was out of the picture now. Ben had seen him get shot in the throat and die right in front of him. But the world was full of eager professional killers hungry for work, at the right price. And Massimiliano Usberti was a rich man, from an aristocratic family with enough property and investments to shield him from even the most catastrophic financial loss. If Severini was right, the fallen archbishop had his own twisted reasons for wanting to get even with all four people on the list, and the means to carry it out.

If Severini was right. If, if, if.

Everything depended on whether Ben could trust this crazy letter from a recovering mental patient living under massive psychological stress, who based his claim on a direct communication from heaven above. Either the guy was a nut, and Ben could throw the letter away, or he was for real, and Ben needed to act on it. There was very little middle ground between those two options, and no room for mistakes. He had to know more before he could let himself jump to conclusions. He swivelled his chair around to face the computer terminal on the desk. The sleeping screen flashed into life and he started urgently hitting keys.

The name Fabrizio Severini threw up a smattering of search engine results that were mainly old news archives related to the fall of Gladius Domini and the subsequent police investigation, the arrests, the court cases, the sentencing, the scandal that had rocked the church and drawn all kinds of censure from the Vatican. Ben didn't see anything he hadn't seen before.

But then he found something new.

The item was a cursory, low-key article from the Italian current affairs website *La Repubblica*, too insignificant to have been picked up by other news agencies. It took Ben only a second to read it: an announcement of the recent suicide of the disgraced former senior Church official Fabrizio Severini, found hanged in his cell at the Istituto Penitenziaro Bollati in Milano. Checking the reported date of his death, Ben saw that it had happened just three days after the postmark on the envelope. The letter might not even have reached Le Val by the time Severini's body was discovered.

Ben didn't know what to make of it. Had someone got to Severini, as he'd seemed to resign himself to the fact that they might? Or had the demons in his own mind got to him in the end? Again, it was impossible to tell.

Undecided, Ben ran another internet search, this time keying in the name Massimiliano Usberti. The computer did its thing, spat out its findings, and Ben found himself being taken back to *La Repubblica* and a report dated from just over six months earlier.

'I'll be damned,' he muttered to himself.

The former archbishop Massimiliano Usberti, previously stripped of his title by the Vatican following allegations that he was the leader of a radical fundamentalist cult linked to suspected murders and racketeering, has died in a bizarre boating accident near his home on Lake Como. Usberti, who since his dismissal from the Church had filed for bankruptcy and been treated for depression and alcoholism, is believed to have fallen from the deck of a motor yacht and been caught up in the propellers, resulting in such extensive cranial and facial injuries that the coroner's identification needed to be carried out using dental records . . .

The piece ended with a line or two about the private funeral ceremony that had taken place at Usberti's family estate, where he had been laid to rest in the ancestral chapel.

If Ben felt any satisfaction from the news of Usberti's death, it was swamped by his utter confusion about what was going on here. Sitting back in his chair he lit another cigarette and closed his eyes as he tried to puzzle it out logically. Le Val hadn't existed when Ben and Usberti's paths had crossed; so, for Severini to have traced him there and known where to address his letter, he must have been allowed some limited internet access by the relatively relaxed system at Bollati, and been able to Google Ben's name just as Ben had done with Severini's. The bookish, educated ex-clergyman was just the kind of inmate who would spend a lot of time in the prison library, enjoying the privilege of keeping up with what happened out there in the world.

Was it believable, then, that he wouldn't have learned of his hated former employer's death? Could such an important piece of news have gone unnoticed? Or had he been aware of the facts, but preferred to listen instead to the imaginary voices in his head telling him otherwise? Ben could well imagine that to be the case. If his suspicion was right, and if Severini was really nothing more than a poor raving lunatic racked with guilt and suffering from hallucinations and delusions, the letter was worthless junk and Ben was left with nothing.

It was rare for Ben to be lost for ideas, and even rarer for him to feel the need for another man's counsel in a moment of crisis. But with his best friend in a coma and his mind jangling with confusion and fatigue, he badly needed to reach out to someone he could trust. He took out his battered old leather wallet, thumbed through the collection of business cards inside, and found the one that bore the blue-and-gold emblem of INTERPOL. He reached for the phone and dialled the direct line number on the card.

The evening was wearing on, but calling at this late hour didn't matter. Luc Simon wasn't the kind of guy to clock off when the factory whistle blew. He ate most of his meals at his desk, and probably slept there most nights: his wife would no doubt have confirmed that, before she'd got sick of being married to a ghost and left him for someone who could pay her a little more attention.

Luc's phone answered on the second ring. '*Bureau du Commissaire Simon.*'

Ben said, 'It's me.' He was about to say more, when he realised that the voice on the line was quite different from the smooth Gallic tone of Luc Simon's. This man sounded older, coarser. And even more worn out with exhaustion than Ben felt.

'Who's calling?' the voice asked.

Ben gave his name. 'I was looking for the commissioner. This is his direct number, isn't it?'

'Yes, it is,' the voice said, wearily, maybe slightly suspiciously.

'Is he there? It's okay. My name's Ben Hope – he knows me. Check me on his database if you want.'

A silence. Then, 'He's not here. He's gone.'

'Gone?' For Luc to have gone home before midnight would have been a record. For him to have left his job would have been unthinkable. 'Gone where?'

The second silence on the line was heavier than the first, and it brought a chill that went down Ben's spine and told him something was wrong.

'If you know Commissioner Luc Simon,' the voice said, laden with sadness, 'then I regret to inform you that he is dead.'

Chapter 11

Ben couldn't reply for several seconds. He wouldn't have called Luc Simon a close friend, but they'd known each other a long time and collaborated on more than one occasion. The news hit him deep and low in the stomach. Finally he was able to say, 'When this did happen?'

'The commissaire didn't come into work today, and didn't respond to phone calls. As you know, he lived alone. We thought perhaps he had been taken ill. When agents visited his home this afternoon, they found him in his bathroom. He was stabbed to death in the shower, either this morning or last night, we don't yet know for sure. Nobody knows anything,' he added. 'It's chaos here. We're putting together a press release, but so far—'

'You have no idea who did it,' Ben finished for him.

'That is all I can tell you,' the voice said. 'I'm sorry.'

Ben muttered a word or two of thanks, then put the phone down. He was wishing he'd brought the bottle from the house, to help chase away the visions of a slashed shower curtain and blood-spattered tiles that were crowding into his mind. But there was no time to dwell over his shock and sorrow. Because Severini's warning letter had just come back into sharp focus. Ben no longer cared if the guy was crazy or not. This was happening.

'Roberta,' he said out loud. His arm shot across the desk to snatch up the phone again.

When Ben had first met her, she'd been a struggling independent research scientist living in Paris. In the wake of the Gladius Domini affair she'd relocated to Ottawa and Dr Roberta Ryder had become Dr Roberta Kaminski, to protect her identity, and had slipped out of Ben's life until she'd needed his help once again. The last time he'd seen her had been an emotional farewell in Indonesia, and even though he still had her mobile number he'd always avoided calling it. He knew why that was. The chemistry between them had been one of the factors behind his relationship breakdown with Brooke.

Ontario was six hours behind, making it afternoon there. 'Come on,' he muttered as the dial tone burred in his ear. Then his heart jumped as he heard her voice. 'Roberta?'

'Who is this?' She sounded as if she was walking somewhere briskly. Always in a hurry, that Roberta Ryder.

'It's me.'

'*Ben?* What—?'

'Where are you?'

'Carleton. Where else?' Carleton University in Ottawa was where she taught now. 'Freezing my ass off in the snow outside the main science block, about to head across campus to the cafeteria for a badly needed coffee before my next class begins in exactly twenty-four minutes' time. If you really needed to know, which frankly is a mystery to me. But then, you always were one of life's great mysteries, weren't you?'

'Are you okay?'

'You sound weird, Ben. And why do I get the feeling this isn't purely a social call?'

'Just tell me. Are you okay?'

'I was doing great, until a moment ago,' she replied acerbically, and he could just see her, halted in the snow, one hand on her hip, one eyebrow raised, in that questioning way of hers. 'Living the dream. Single, free and contented, and I gave up long ago waiting for you to call me. Yet now here you are. What's the matter?'

'I don't have time to explain,' he said. 'Listen to me. You need to get out of town, right this minute.'

'Wow. Not a word from you for months and years, now this. You really know how to lay the charm on a lady, Hope. In the desert of life, you are my mirage.'

'I'm serious. Something's happening. Don't ask me what, because I don't know. Just get away from there immediately.'

'Are you nuts? Just like that? Get out of town, no explanations, no nothing? I have classes. I have a *job*, Ben.'

'Never mind all that. You might not be safe and I need you to do as I say.'

'Why – am – I – not – safe?'

'Someone tried to get me. They got Luc Simon.'

'The Paris cop? What do you mean, *got?*'

'He wasn't a Paris cop any more. And I mean, they killed him. They could be coming after you next.'

Her tone changed to one of shock. 'What the hell's happening? Are you okay?'

'It's not me I'm worried about. It's you.'

'I can look after myself,' she said defiantly. 'Remember?'

'So can Jeff Dekker. But he's lying in the hospital with a bullet hole in his chest, meant for me. These people aren't messing about. How much money have you got on you?'

'About seventy bucks. You are officially freaking me out right now. Is Jeff going to be all right? Who's doing this?'

'No more questions, Roberta,' Ben interrupted. 'Please, just do as I say. Don't go back to your apartment. Grab all the cash you can from the campus ATM and jump on a bus. Keep changing buses, taxis, whatever you have to do to cover your trail. You see anyone following you, anything out of the ordinary, go straight to the police.'

'*Following me?*'

'Keep your eyes open. Head north into the mountains, where nobody can find you. Book into a hotel, cash, using a different name, and don't do anything until I call you again. Promise me you'll do that.'

'Ben, I—'

'I mean it, Roberta. I know how it sounds. But you have to promise me. I can't have anything happen to you.'

'Does this mean you love me after all?'

'No jokes. Do it.'

'Who said I was joking?'

'I'll be in touch.'

'I've heard that one before. I can't wait.'

'Will you do it?'

'YES! All right! I must be even crazier than I thought, but I'll do it. This is going to cost you big-time, Ben Hope. Of all the goddamn lunatic things I ever did for y—'

He cut her off by ending the call. He could only pray she'd take him seriously. What was it with red-headed women? Without a doubt, she was the most stubborn, head-strong person he'd ever known. That was, besides himself.

The next name on Ben's list was Father Pascal Cambriel. Ben had checked in on him now and then since the Gladius Domini business, mostly to ask after his health. Now in his mid-seventies, the old priest still lived in the same humble cottage in the little village of Saint-Jean in the south of France. A little slower, more dependent on his walking stick, but still active and enjoying his simple rural existence – feeding his chickens, tending to his little vineyard, kindling his fire and reading the Bible by candlelight every night as he puffed on his old briar pipe and indulged in more of his homemade wine than perhaps was good for him. Life didn't change a great deal for Pascal Cambriel, including his tendency to not always answer the phone, a piece of modern technology the old man could take or leave. If he even possessed such a thing as a mobile, it wouldn't survive the first battery discharge.

Ben dialled Pascal's landline number. He wasn't surprised when it rang and rang, but it didn't allay his worry much either. Le Val to Saint-Jean was an eight-hour drive that Ben was prepared to make if he got no response that night.

In the meantime, he had one more name to check on the list.

Ben had lost contact long ago with the dusky, black-haired history professor Anna Manzini. The last time he'd seen her had been in the private hospital room, filled with the scent of scores of red and white roses, where she'd been recuperating after the violent assault by Franco Bozza that had nearly killed her. Ben had gone there to say goodbye and tell her how sorry he was that she'd become involved. Even bruised up from the attack, with a dressing on her right cheek where Bozza had slashed her with his knife, she'd managed to look beautiful.

That day, Anna had told him she'd had enough of France and was going back to live in Italy to take up her old university professorship. Her last whispered words to him, as he'd sat on her bedside and she kissed him tenderly on the cheek, had been: 'If you ever find yourself in Florence, you must give me a call.'

Ben hadn't found himself in Florence since then, and he didn't have a number for her in any case. Returning to the computer, he Googled the *Pagine Bianche*, the white pages online phone directory for Italy. When the website came up he entered MANZINI and FIRENZE into a search box and punched TROVA. The computer came up with '*30 Risultati trovati*', lots of Manzinis but not the one he was looking for. Unlisted. Damn.

Next he brought up the Florence University website and clicked open the faculty page to check through the list of academic staff. Unlikely that the university would divulge the phone details of faculty members, but there might be an email contact.

He found neither, because Anna Manzini was no longer listed there. Instead, he found her on a separate page for former faculty members, which gave no details at all except her name, department and the dates of her service. She'd left Florence University nearly two years ago.

It looked as though he'd lost her trail, until a new idea came to him. Anna had always been more than just an academic; she was a successful writer too, which was what had brought her to live in France in the first place, where she'd been researching a new project on the Cathars. 'Who knows?' she'd said to Ben during that last meeting. 'Perhaps one day I'll finish my book.' When he widened his online search on her, Ben discovered her author website and found that she'd not only finished it, but that it had been a best-seller – the first of several successful works of historical non-fiction she'd churned out in the last few years. Her latest biography of the mystic, visionary, and polymath, Hildegard of Bingen, had sold quarter of a million copies.

Anna's picture beamed at him from the screen. She'd been forty-two when he'd known her, but looked thirty-eight. She seemed not to have aged a day since. Either thanks to the wonders of plastic surgery, or else maybe the miracle of Photoshop, there wasn't a trace of a scar from Usberti's attempt to kill her. But selling a truckload of books wasn't going to protect her from this renewed threat. Ben had to warn her, and fast.

Her author website gave no email address or social media handle, just a generic form. Frustrated, he filled it in, giving his mobile number and a brief note saying it was vital that she contacted him immediately. All he could do then was hope she'd respond.

He'd been sitting in the office far too long. The last thing he did before leaving was to try Pascal's number again – to no avail.

'Damn,' he muttered. Then there was nothing else for it.

'Let's go,' he said to Storm. The dog followed him as he sprinted back to the house. He ran upstairs to Tuesday's room and banged on the door. Tuesday answered. The sound of Levi Roots' reggae music was coming from his stereo in the background, but it didn't seem to be cheering Tuesday up. He looked even glummer than before.

'You can come out now. Brooke's gone,' Ben said.

'I only wanted to give you guys some space.'

'So we could rip each other's guts out in private. Thanks. Listen, Tues. Remember I said about you having to hold the fort here? Well, you're going to have to hold it a little longer. There's been a development and I have to go.'

'Go where?' Tuesday said, blinking.

'I'll call you from the road,' Ben replied. 'Any news about Jeff, any news about anything at all, keep me updated.'

Tuesday said he would. Without another word, Ben hurried to his own quarters on the top floor of the rambling old house. It was a small, simple space, which he kept uncluttered with a minimum of belongings, as neat as a military dorm. He rummaged through his cupboard, then grabbed his battered green canvas bag. The old army haversack was

71

permanent home to various items that tended to come in handy when Ben was on his travels, such as his mini-Maglite torch with LED upgrade for when he found himself in dark spots, and a roll of super-strong duct tape that was useful for anything from trussing up captives to making improvised field dressings. Ben stuffed in a couple of changes of underwear, two pairs of Helikon winter socks, the same ones the Norwegian Army used, a spare pair of black Levi's and a heavy denim shirt identical to the one he was already wearing. From a box on the dresser he took a thick roll of cash without counting it, wrapped it up with his passport inside a double skin of two plastic Ziploc bags and tucked the package in on top of his spare clothes. Then he jammed in two packs of Gauloises, his whisky flask, and a can of fluid for his lighter.

Finally, there was the other item he kept hidden under the loose floorboard at the foot of the single bed: one piece of hardware that the anti-terror cops couldn't confiscate, because no official knew it even existed. The nine-millimetre Taurus automatic had belonged to a Romanian drug dealer called Dracul, before Ben had commandeered the handgun as a trophy of war. He snicked a full magazine of Federal +P hollowpoints into its butt, cocked it and locked it and tucked it into the bag where he could get to it quickly. Because in situations like this, it was a lot better to have it and not need it, than to need it and not have it.

Three minutes later, Ben was jumping into the Alpina, flinging his bag onto the passenger seat, firing up the engine with a throaty blast and gunning the car out of Le Val's yard.

Eight hours to Father Pascal's village of Saint-Jean. He aimed to make it there in seven.

Chapter 12

Ben drove hard and fast through the night. Rain and sleet battered his windscreen, turned to snow for a while around Orléans, and then petered out again as he hammered southwards. He chain-smoked his way through the rest of his current pack of Gauloises, then broke into a fresh one. The strong, unfiltered cigarettes did little to settle his tension; the frenetic modern jazz station blasting from the Alpina's sound system didn't help much either.

Approaching Bourges, running low on fuel and energy, he pulled off the motorway into an *aire de service*. The night was chilly and damp. After he'd finished filling the tank, out of habit he parked the car in a corner of the rest area car park where it was shaded under the trees from the lights. He took his pistol from his bag and slipped it into his belt, behind the right hip where it was hidden by his jacket. Then he locked up the car and walked to the nearby all-night café and shop to get something to eat. He felt hollow and weary, yet jumpy and agitated. More conscious than usual of the hard steel lump of the gun nestling against the small of his back, he walked wide of any corners or doorways where an attacker could suddenly leap out. None did, but the edginess remained.

He walked into the café. It was warm inside. Tall windows

offered a view of the brightly illuminated fuel station on one side, the darker car park on the other. Piped muzak was playing quietly in the background. There were a few late-night travellers taking a rest, some couples but mostly solitary men, sitting at plastic tables and desultorily sipping coffee while fiddling with phones or tablets. Nobody took any notice of Ben as he went in, but he eyed each one, sizing them up as though they could be a potential threat.

Maybe he was being paranoid, he thought. Or maybe he wasn't. If the shooter had figured out by now that he'd got the wrong target, he could have hung around Le Val and picked up the trail of the Alpina. Ben was pretty sure nobody had followed him, but you could never be one hundred per cent certain of spotting a skilled tail. Especially when they worked in a team, relaying one another, keeping in contact by phone or radio, maintaining a constantly-shifting net of surveillance around their target. Ben had worked in enough of those teams himself to know exactly how they operated. If somehow Usberti was behind this – despite apparently being dead – then there was no telling how many paid guns he could have brought on board.

Ben bought a pack of sandwiches and a carry-out paper cup of steaming black coffee, paid cash and made his way back to the BMW. Nobody followed him. He locked himself inside the car, took the gun from his belt and laid it on the centre console close by his right hand. He tore open the sandwich pack: Gruyère cheese and pâté de campagne. His body craved food but he had no appetite. As he ate mechanically and slurped the hot coffee, he checked the latest news reports on his smartphone.

One small consolation was that the media were still in the dark about the details of the shooting incident at the obscure training facility in rural Normandy. *The as-yet unidentified victim is believed to be a British national residing in France, with unconfirmed reports suggesting an ex-military connection. The British Ministry of Defence were unavailable for comment. Details of the victim's condition have not yet been released and the exact circumstances of the incident remain uncertain . . . SDAT anti-terror officers have said they are involved in the investigation but have not revealed whether the shooting may have been carried out by a member or members of an extremist Islamic group.* And on, and on.

The other news item he wanted to check was much more forthcoming on detail, but no more conclusive. INTERPOL's fury in the wake of Luc Simon's murder was splashed all over the media, along with gruesome images of the shower unit, post-body-removal, that looked as if a butcher had hung up a live pig in there by its hind legs and slit its throat.

It was no way to go for a good guy like Luc Simon.

INTERPOL were lining up suspects on the working theory that the killing was an act of revenge, carried out either by someone Luc had put away or on their behalf. No charges had yet been brought. Inevitably, the media were whipping up their own storm of speculation that the murder of a high-ranking law enforcement officer was yet another terrorist atrocity. Ben wouldn't have been surprised if, in the next day or two, the cops pinned it on some claimed Muslim fanatic they found on an intelligence watch-list, complete with the 'discovery' of maps and photos of Luc Simon and his home in the suspect's apartment, along with the requisite anti-West hate literature and bomb-making materials under his bed. And maybe they'd be right. But Ben didn't think so.

Next he tried Roberta's number, but her phone was switched off. Then he tried Pascal's landline number once more for luck, and gnashed his teeth in frustration until the dial tone went dead. So much for the communication age.

But at least someone was answering their phone. The third number he tried, he got a reply after three rings.

'Dr Lacombe? It's Ben Hope.'

'This is why I don't generally give out my personal number,' complained the sleepy voice on the other end of the line. 'Do you know what time it is?'

'How is he? Any change?'

'There hadn't been, when I came home to get some sleep. They haven't called. So, no, none.'

'I'm sorry if I woke you, Doctor.'

'It's okay. And you can call me Sandrine.'

'Are you alone, Sandrine?'

'What kind of question is that?' she said sharply. 'Yes, I do happen to live alone, for your information. Did you call to ask me on a date or something?'

'Not exactly,' Ben said. 'The reason I asked is because I need a favour.'

'What kind of favour?'

'The sensitive kind that needs to be strictly between you and me. One that concerns Section Forty-Five of the French Code of Medical Ethics.'

'I see. Regarding patient confidentiality?'

'Specifically, the matter of releasing a victim's identity to the media. Or not releasing it, more to the point.'

'And you have some reason for having it kept quiet, I suppose.'

'I have reason to think the shooter got the wrong guy, but doesn't know it yet. I'd like that knowledge to be kept from him for as long as possible. Now you understand what I meant by sensitive.'

A rustling sound as she sat up in bed, fully awake now and unlikely to get any more sleep that night. 'What are you telling me here? If he was the wrong guy, then who was the intended target?'

'Let's just say if they'd succeeded, it would have been a little hard for me to call you.'

'Someone tried to kill *you*? But who?'

'A dead man,' Ben said. 'Or so people believe. If he isn't one already, he soon will be.'

'Do the police know this?'

'They're fixated on their own ideas of what this is about. If I told them I thought I was the target, I'd spend the next week sitting in an interrogation room being hammered with all the questions they can't ask Jeff.'

'Where you'd at least be safe.'

'But other people wouldn't be. And I can't have that. So no, I have no intention of telling the cops what I know.'

'This is just plain crazy. Things like this don't happen in my world.'

'Things are a little different in mine,' Ben said.

'I can't be drawn into this intrigue,' she said. 'Have you seen the news? The story's getting bigger by the hour. I'm a doctor, not a spy. There are rules, you know?'

'I understand. Forget I mentioned it.' He was about to end the call when she said, 'Hold on, don't go.'

'I'm still here.'

There was a pause on the line, followed by a sigh of resignation; then she said, 'To reply to your question, the answer is no, I haven't signed off on that disclosure, and can't, without the consent of the victim or their next of kin, which I haven't got at this point. If this was an instance of, say, rape or child abuse, where there's a clear case for withholding the victim's identity, that's one thing. But where a violent crime has been committed involving firearms, especially in this day and age—'

'The media are hungry for all they can get and the police can release the details themselves, I know. They haven't yet, but it could all change by morning. I was hoping you could exert some professional influence.'

'When you said you wanted a favour, you weren't kidding.' She heaved another sigh. 'All right. I can try to delay things from my end, but probably not for more than a day, maybe two. And I know someone who knows someone in the police media liaison department. It's possible that I can pull a few strings there, too, assuming I can come up with a plausible-sounding reason to persuade them. It won't be easy.'

'Whatever you can do, it's appreciated.'

'I can't promise anything,' she warned him. 'I don't even know why I'm agreeing to this.'

'I'll bring you a big bunch of flowers.'

'Your friend needs them more than I do.'

'He's not really that into them.'

'You take care,' she said. 'Don't do anything stupid.'

'Why change the habit of a lifetime? I'll be in touch.'

Chapter 13

Ben sped on southwards through the night. As he drove, he made one last call.

The kind of help Ben needed to ask for next could only be had from certain highly specialised quarters. And sixty-odd-year-old former sergeant Boonzie McCulloch, once Ben's military instructor, later his friend and mentor, long since retired to an idyllic rural life in Campo Basso but still with a few fingers in a few pies, was just the man to go to.

Along with the rest of the world, Boonzie had seen the news about the shooting at Le Val and had been just about to call when Ben beat him to it. The Scotsman's shocked silence quickly turned to molten anger as Ben described Jeff's condition. 'If I'm right, whoever did this is after me. And the moment it leaks that they got the wrong guy, they'll be back.'

'Aw, fuck this for a game of soldiers,' Boonzie's gravelly voice rumbled over the line. 'I'm on ma way. Tonight, reet noo. I'm gettin' in the car and I'm comin'.' It was like letting a rabid pit bull off the leash. Ben could almost hear the phone cracking in Boonzie's iron fist.

'That's not what I want,' Ben said firmly, reining him in. 'I've already dragged you into too much trouble in the past.

I'll deal with this my way, alone. But I could use some backup.'

'Say the fuckin' word, laddie,' Boonzie rasped, wanting blood.

'I need six guys. I was thinking maybe McGuire, Fry and Blackwood, if they're available, plus three more. How fast can you get a team together for me?'

'For you? They'll be trippin' over themselves tae help, son. And woe betide these murderin' basturts when we get oor haunds on them. Leave it wi' me. I'll get back tae ye asap.'

By the time Ben had reached Limoges in west-central France, it was all arranged. Within a few hours three good ex-regiment men would be rolling up at Le Val, two of them flown in from London and the third from Germany where he'd just finished a VIP close protection stint. They'd be heavily armed, and they wouldn't need to use the main gate. Their mission: to back up Tuesday and the others in case the bad guys tried to strike again. Meanwhile, another trio urgently summoned in from various parts of Europe would speedily converge on Cherbourg, where they'd station themselves in and around Louis Pasteur Hospital to spot, intercept and detain anyone suspicious who might come snooping in the event of an information leak.

Sandrine Lacombe would flip if she knew her place of work was under guard by professional hard men with guns. But the good doctor would never know. Unless something happened – in which case all hell might just break loose.

With his insurance policy in place as best he could arrange it, Ben stormed on through the night. The Alpina ate up the distance as he carved southwards on the A20 motorway. Driving, driving, driving. A cold stream of wind whistling from the cracked-open window. The heater blasting, the radio blaring. Fists clenched on the steering wheel, eyes wedged open against his growing fatigue and burning with anger as he thought about Jeff lying there in that hospital bed and about Luc Simon in the morgue. When his thoughts turned to Father Pascal, to Anna Manzini and Roberta Ryder, frustration and impatience scoured him like acid and he willed the car to go even faster.

From Limousin he passed into the Midi-Pyrénées. A while later the signs for Toulouse flashed by. He left the motorway and veered south-east into Roussillon, then due south from Carcassonne, deep into the rugged landscape along ever narrower and twistier roads, slippery with ice, that led him up dizzying mountain passes where the ruins of medieval castles stood silhouetted on craggy snow-capped peaks against the winter sky; then plunged steeply down into green pine valleys, through small towns and villages and hamlets too small to feature on the map. Couiza, Quillan, Montségur. He passed within a couple of kilometres of the villa that had been Anna Manzini's base for her research on ancient Languedoc history and the mysteries of the Cathars. The same villa where Franco Bozza had almost managed to kill her.

Being back here again for the first time since that summer brought back memories he'd thought he'd left far behind him: he and Roberta Ryder dodging bullets and chasing clues all over the Languedoc; the deadly running pursuit on which Usberti's hired killers had led them; playing tag with Luc Simon and an army of police; finding Anna battered and unconscious after Bozza's attack; the final bloody standoff with Bozza in an underground cavern buried deep in the heart of a mountain. And Ben remembered the kindness that Father Pascal had shown him when he'd turned up on the priest's doorstep, badly hurt. The old man had been more of a father to him than his real one ever had. The memory sent a painful stab of guilt deep inside Ben as he replayed those images inside his head.

He should have done more to stay in contact. But keeping in touch with people who had been important in his life had never been one of his greatest talents.

If you ever find yourself in Florence, you must give me a call.

In the desert of life, you are my mirage.

Running off when people need you around is what you do best, after all.

Their voices echoed in his mind. He'd let them all down. For that, he was truly sorry.

Soon, his speeding headlights lit up a road sign for the village of Saint-Jean. Dawn was still a couple of hours away. He'd made good time.

The village was still more or less as Ben remembered it – a few new houses might have sprouted up at its edges, and more of the ancient red-tiled roofs were incongruously decorated with recent add-ons like solar panels and satellite dishes. He passed the drystone wall that had been painted with blood from his gunshot wound, then winding deeper into the village he passed the little church in which he'd prayed alone in the dead of night; then he saw the graveyard, and beyond it the slope of scrubland leading up the hillside where Pascal tended to his vines; and then he saw the priest's cottage. The same old pale-blue Renault 14 was parked in the narrow, winding street outside. Ben's spirits brightened seeing it, knowing it meant Pascal was at home.

He pulled the Alpina up at the kerbside and got out. Looked up at Pascal's windows, dark and shuttered like every other window in Saint-Jean. The cold stillness seemed to hang over the place like a shroud, and he shivered. He didn't want to wake Pascal, and thought about sitting a while longer in the car, but changed his mind, walked up to the door and knocked softly.

There was no response after a couple of minutes, so Ben made his way around the back, through the neat yard, past the henhouse. A goat bleated from somewhere in the darkness. The back porch was open. He creaked the door ajar and stepped into the narrow hallway. He smelled the rich cherry and vanilla tang of aromatic pipe tobacco that had soaked into every crevice of the old stone walls. An antique case clock ticked steadily, sonorously from within. He called out softly, 'Father Pascal?'

'*Arrêtez!*' The voice behind him made him tense and whirl around. Yellow torchlight shone in his face and glinted off something that Ben instantly recognised as a wartime French service revolver. One that was pointed right at him.

Ben froze and put up his hands. Normally, when faced with a firearm aimed in his face, he would have done either one of two things: move in faster than a striking cobra and take control of the weapon, breaking the fingers of the person holding it. Or, if that wasn't tactically favourable, he would have drawn out his own gun and fired first. And so far in his life, Ben had always been quicker.

But he wasn't about to do either of those things when the person with the gun was a little old woman as frail as a sparrow, so frightened that the weapon was fluttering in her skinny hand. 'Who's there?' she quavered.

'Don't shoot,' he said in French. 'It's all right. I'm a friend of Father Pascal. My name's Ben.'

The woman hesitated, then reached tentatively out and clicked on the wall light. She was in her seventies, with thinning grey hair, wearing a dressing gown topped by a shawl draped around her shoulders. Her eyes were reddened as though she'd been crying.

'I couldn't sleep,' she said. 'I saw the car lights. I thought perhaps *they* had come back.'

'You thought who had come back?'

'Those men. The men who—' Her voice trailed off. She sniffed.

'You don't have to point the gun at me,' Ben said, eyeing the antique revolver and her finger on the trigger. It might be a relic, but if it had been good enough to kill Germans in two world wars, he didn't want to be on its business end. 'I promise I won't hurt you. Where's Pascal? What men are you talking about? Is everything all right?' But it obviously wasn't. He sensed something was terribly wrong.

The gun drooped in her thin hand, pointing at the floor. The old woman's eyes filled with tears. And now Ben knew for sure, and he felt his own shoulders sag.

'When?' he asked.

'Two days ago.'

'What happened?'

'There was an attack. At the church. The police think it was two intruders. Nobody knows. Nobody saw anything.' She sniffed again, and shook her head. 'Pascal . . . I knew him all my life. And now he is gone.'

Ben's throat was so tight that he could barely speak. 'What did they do to him?'

'They beat him. They killed him, *les salauds*. The funeral is this morning.'

Ben was numb as he walked back to the car. He watched the old woman disappear inside her house, her head bowed. He sat and smoked, letting his mind become empty.

Dawn came; the sky lightened in gradual shades. A fog hung over the mountains in the background. The old woman reappeared, dressed in boots and a coat. If she was still carrying the gun out of fear that the attackers might return, it was hidden in a pocket. She let Pascal's hens out and fed them, moving stiffly in the morning cold. Seeing Ben sitting there in his car, she came over with a sad smile and asked if he'd like to come inside for coffee. He said no, thanks, and apologised for having scared her earlier. He told her the men wouldn't be back, and that she shouldn't be afraid.

There was nothing more to say. Nothing more to do here. He'd be on his way, after the funeral.

At ten o'clock in the morning, Father Pascal Cambriel was laid to rest in the graveyard of the church of Saint-Jean where he'd spent so many years caring for his community. Many had turned out to pay their final respects to the much-loved priest they'd known all their lives. Ben stood at the back of the crowd and watched with a clenched jaw as the coffin went into the ground. There were tears and sobs. A younger priest drafted in from a neighbouring town said a few solemn words. Ben spoke to nobody.

He was the last to leave the cemetery. As he knelt alone by the fresh grave, he made his promise. Then, slowly, calmly, he walked back to the car and drove away, never to return to Saint-Jean.

Gentle, kind Pascal wouldn't have approved of the vow Ben had taken at his graveside. But Pascal hadn't lived in Ben's world and had only the smallest understanding of what motivated evil men and the cruelty they were capable of. Those were things Ben understood very well indeed. And whoever was doing this, whoever was hurting his friends, he was going to track them down, and find them, and destroy every single one of them.

They wanted blood. They were going to get it.

Chapter 14

'Gennaro, you are a gift from God.'

When Massimiliano Usberti had uttered those words six months earlier, he'd meant them literally. For a man of such profound religious faith as his, there had been no other way to describe an event so serendipitous. It was the act of Divine providence he had been praying for. Now that it had come, with it came the long-cherished opportunity to start putting his plans into action.

He'd been waiting a long time.

Life was quiet when you were a disgraced former archbishop. Too quiet. For years, Massimiliano Usberti had seen almost nobody, spoken only to the small band of faithful disciples who hadn't abandoned him since his fall from grace. And what a spectacular fall it had been. The pain and humiliation of his rapid, sudden descent remained with him every waking moment. His private retreat, the villa set into its own four acres on the shores of Lake Como, was his only comfort, though for all its opulence it was a far cry from the magnificent Renaissance palace outside Rome that had been his main residence at the peak of his career as a senior archbishop.

Back in those halcyon days, it had seemed as if nothing could stop him. He'd been on track to become a cardinal.

One day, perhaps even Pope. Anything, everything, he dared to dream felt within his grasp. *Gladius Domini*, the Sword of God, his brainchild, his life's work, had secretly attracted powerful investors from every fundamentalist Christian enclave across the world and mighty friends in China and the USA. Its goal: to re-Christianise the globe and destroy once and for all the rising Islamic threat that was spreading everywhere like a cancer; to bring about a new golden age of holy crusade against the heathen menace in the East. Its mission statement was *Necos eos omnes. Deus suos agnoscet.* Or, in layman's terms, 'Kill 'em all and let God sort them out'.

When the crash had come, thanks to the combined efforts of Usberti's enemies, the blooming flower that had been Gladius Domini had been trampled into the dirt. All but a handful of his powerful friends in high places had deserted him in the wake of the disaster. The investors had dropped him like a hissing stick of dynamite and run a mile. His dreams had crumbled into ashes as he escaped imprisonment by the skin of his teeth, letting minions like the hapless Severini take the fall in his place.

And so, with his power hugely diminished, his ambitions crushed and his once-substantial wealth slowly eroding, Massimiliano Usberti had become a virtual recluse. No longer the proud, physically imposing, leonine man he once had been, he grew scraggy and wrinkled and started paying less attention to his personal appearance. He lost interest in food and gained a little too much interest in strong spirits. His beloved motor yacht, in which he'd once merrily sailed the sparkling blue waters of Lake Como, no longer held any joy for him. He would sometimes be confined to his bed for days on end by fits of black depression from which not even his new assistant, a devoted young priest called Silvano

Bellini who had joined his shrivelled retinue a few months earlier, could rouse him.

When he did take Bellini's advice to get some fresh air and exercise, all he could do was pace restlessly about the lakeside estate, brooding and muttering to himself. Indoors, he became glued to the internet, obsessing over the state of the world. Was he the only one who could see how desperately, now more than ever, God's guiding hand was needed to avert the catastrophic decline of civilisation? The more he scoured the web for fuel to feed the fire burning inside him, the more evidence he saw of the entire globe's descent into ruin: heading faster and faster towards utter degradation as the situation that had seemed untenable even at the height of Gladius Domini's glory days now seemed to spiral ever further into complete chaos.

Usberti was convinced that the age of Sodom and Gomorrah was returning in modern times exactly as prophesied in Scripture, bringing with it a plague of abominations that were the sure signs of the approaching apocalypse. The holy institutions of family and marriage breaking down. Promiscuity and drugs, pestilence and mental illness everywhere, perpetrated and encouraged by a subculture of corrupt intellectual elitists who had turned their back on God's wisdom and taught others to follow their disgraceful example. Men marrying men now, heaven help us. What next, sheep and goats? As if that perversion were not gruesome enough, barely a day seemed to pass without Usberti wanting to throw up at the sight of yet another aberrant bearded transsexual being fêted by the online media. The Western world was in the throes of lunacy, celebrating bestial sin and surrendering to all manner of vile unnatural passions and self-obsessed neurosis, even as the invading enemy hordes came flooding through their open borders: a never-ending army of so-called refugees bringing with them a wave of crime, rape and violence perpetrated against the decent Christian people who had welcomed them into their lands. Roaring in like a rogue wave, the heathen invaders were set to colonise all of Europe and beyond, one nation after another. The weak, ineffectual puppet governments of those countries, paralysed by the spell of political correctness and terrified of committing what the propagandists defined as a 'hate crime', would simply stand back and do nothing, until the faithless and dissolute West ultimately fell to the invasion of Islam and Shariah law.

Needless to say, Usberti had seen the whole ugly mess coming a long time ago; nobody had wanted to listen to his warnings and now it was almost too late to stem the tide. It was left to a brave few to fight back, and Usberti yearned to take his place at the head of a righteous campaign to restore sanity and godliness to the world. But what could he do? His money was dwindling, his influence was dead and his name was a joke.

However badly his frustration over the state of human affairs consumed him, it was his bitter hatred of his personal enemies that ate deepest of all into his soul. He spent hours daily plotting all kinds of bitter revenge against those who had engineered his downfall. One in particular: Ben Hope.

Ben Hope.

Even the sound of the name made Usberti want to spit bile. For years, the only thing that sustained him was to dream about the terrible things he would do to the despicable swine who, more than anyone, had destroyed his future. Not just Hope, but all the others too: a list of names that Usberti recited endlessly in his mind and often wrote down by hand, scratching the letters so deep that his pen would wear right through the paper and mark the surface of his desk.

Those filthy pigs thought he was finished. They thought they had stopped him. How wrong, how oh-so-very wrong, they were. And how pitifully they would all squeal for his mercy when he was restored to his former power, one day.

One day.

But he knew that could never happen. Oh, he had the means to take his revenge, all right. He wasn't broke, not yet, and he still commanded the loyalty of followers who would do whatever he asked. Neither his personal assistant Silvano Bellini nor his administrator Pierangelo Volpicelli were coarse or brutal men, but Usberti had made sure he surrounded himself with others who were exactly that: men such as Ennio Scorceletti, known simply to his associates as 'the big man', along with Renato Zenatello, Federico Casini, Aldo Groppione, Luca Iacono, Maurizio Starace and half a dozen others who lived in barrack-style accommodation on the estate, were uncompromisingly vicious thugs from a variety of criminal backgrounds. The hulking Scorceletti was a staunch Catholic who had beaten his estranged wife to death with a hammer after she left him for another woman. Zenatello, a former carabiniere, had done time in prison for his role in the murder of four Afghan immigrants. Convicted rapist Groppione had performed similar tricks against a Nigerian asylum seeker and his wife, killing them in their car outside Fermo with a hunting rifle. Iacono was a computer hacker by trade, who had proved his fealty to God by setting fire to a mosque in his home town of Naples.

The list went on.

For all of these men, the primary appeal of their employer's brand of Christian fundamentalism was that they could vent as much hatred as they liked against homosexuals, Muslims, atheists, liberals and other filthy servants of Satan. They each loved nothing more than being sent on a vigilante mission of faith-inspired violence in the sure knowledge that they were consolidating their places in heaven. Some of them, like Scorceletti, had been recruited into the ranks of Gladius Domini back in the glory days, before the fall; if anything, Usberti's topple from grace had only intensified the fierceness of their loyalty to him. He had only to give the order, and he could unleash all manner of bone-breaking, razor-slashing nastiness on those he dreamed of punishing.

So many sleepless nights he'd spent working out his vengeful plans, he knew exactly what form the punishment would take. But as much as he yearned to give the order, he knew that the moment he took any such action against his list of enemies, his involvement would be so transparently obvious to even the most obtuse law enforcement official that he'd be instantly whisked away to prison for the rest of his life. And however much he detested the scum who had brought him down, he wasn't prepared to give up what little freedom and luxury remained to him.

Then how could he strike back at them? He couldn't think of a solution. It would take a gift from the Lord above to make it happen. Every day he got down on his knees and prayed for Divine help in making his plans possible. Had he not been a loyal servant of God all his life? Didn't he deserve just one break?

Usberti seldom ventured from the privacy of his sanctuary. That summer, however, he had taken a rare road trip to visit his last surviving relative, an uncle who lived in a luxury residential clinic for the elderly not far from Assisi in Umbria.

Usberti's reasons for travelling four hundred kilometres to see the old man, on whom he hadn't laid eyes in at least thirty years, were by no means sentimental: Fortunato Usberti was two months shy of his hundredth birthday, reportedly possessed barely an organ in functioning condition, had completely lost his marbles and was as rich as Croesus. His devoted nephew therefore felt obliged to rekindle the somewhat lapsed relationship between them, in the hope that the ailing Fortunato might consent to leaving him a little something when he shuffled off to a better place, which with any luck wouldn't be too long away. *This is what it's come to*, Usberti seethed on the journey south.

A double disappointment awaited him in Umbria. On arrival at the rest home he found his uncle disturbingly alive and plenty chipper enough to molest the nurses, while now so senile that he didn't even know he had a nephew, let alone one he recognised. Usberti didn't stay long. He got back in the Mercedes and instructed his driver to get him out of here. Soon afterwards, as they passed through a small village, Usberti spied a little church and felt the urge to go inside. Maybe the Lord would grant him some new miracle.

And that was exactly what the Lord did.

Usberti's heart nearly stopped beating when he saw Gennaro Tucci walk into the coolness of the empty church. Then, of course, he didn't know the man's name or anything about him – except that this complete stranger could have been cloned from Usberti's own flesh and blood. The resemblance was uncanny, quite stunning, although Usberti was the only one who seemed to spot it as the man barely glanced at him with a quick smile.

That was when the idea had come to him, in a flash. It was so simple, so blindingly obvious; and Usberti realised that God, in those mysterious ways of His, had provided

His loyal servant with the perfect means to take his long-sought revenge.

The decision that followed was an easy one to make. Gennaro Tucci lived alone, a poor man with a simple life and few friends. That much had been easy to find out, and it was all Usberti needed to know.

Two days later, his men Casini, Zenatello and Scorceletti seized their victim at his home and brought him back to the Lake Como estate. There Gennaro was kept locked in a disused wine cellar for a week, while Usberti quickly and secretly, through a defunct company name, allocated a substantial part of his remaining fortune to the purchase of a small island off the Sicilian coast. The moment the sale went through, it was time to move briskly to the next phase. They brought the hapless prisoner up from the cellar, forced cognac down his throat until he was half unconscious, dressed him up in some of Usberti's own clothes, then dragged him to the boathouse where the motor yacht was launched for the first time in years.

The rest was history. When the disfigured body was dragged from the water later that day, it was an open and shut case: death by misadventure. Nobody would lament the passing of the disgraced former archbishop, just as little was made of the disappearance of a retired, penniless carpenter from Umbria. Even if it had, nobody would ever connect the two.

And now Usberti, whisked off in the night to live in hiding on his island off the coast of Sicily, was ready to strike back at his enemies from a position of absolute safety, where nobody would suspect him, let alone come looking for him. Vengeance would be his, and it would be carried out from beyond the grave.

He couldn't wait.

But what Massimiliano Usberti couldn't possibly have known back then, six months ago, was that his revenge quest would lead him to a greater reward by far. A treasure he couldn't have imagined in his wildest dreams of wealth and power.

Usberti was soon to make the discovery of his life.

Chapter 15

As Ben drove away from Saint-Jean, he considered his priorities. The first of which was to understand who was doing this. Was someone else carrying out these attacks on Usberti's behalf, or was Usberti alive? If he was alive, where was he?

If the situation had been different, Ben could have picked up the phone and talked to Luc Simon. Now that the one cop he trusted in the world was gone, he might have been thinking about driving east, over the Italian Alps, to pay an unscheduled visit to Usberti's home estate. But that wasn't his only or even his main priority, because there still remained one name on the hit-list to be ticked off. Ben had to find Anna Manzini and make sure she was safe.

He checked his email – still no reply to the message he'd posted via her author website. Looking again at the site, he noticed the name and number of Anna's literary agent in Florence on the 'contacts' page. It was worth a try.

'*Agenzia letteraria* Carlo Scanzi,' said a gravelly voice.

Ben hadn't spoken Italian in a while. He politely introduced himself, explained that he was a friend of Signor Scanzi's client Anna Manzini, said he urgently needed to contact her and asked if he could have a number or address, preferably both.

The agent responded with a snort. 'Sure. If you're such

a close friend of my client's, why are you calling me? You people will do anything to get your little feet in the door, won't you?'

It wasn't a good start. Ben asked, 'What people?'

'You're the second one today. What's it this time, trawling for a free signed copy? A referral to a publisher? Help with some crappy project you think's gonna make you rich? Dream on. Wait, I know who you are. You're not Italian. You're that freaky Dutchman who tried to shove your manuscript on Signora Manzini at the Turin book fair and chased her into the ladies' bathroom. I'm onto you, pal. You breach that restraining order and I'll have the carabinieri down on you so fast it'll make your head spin.'

'I told you who I am,' Ben said coolly. 'And when I said this was important, I meant it. Anna knows me. Call her, tell her I'm trying to get in touch with her and that it's urgent. Give her this number.'

'Stick it.' Scanzi hung up.

In truth, Ben couldn't blame the guy for protecting his client. What troubled him the most was that he hadn't been the first one to call that day, trying to find out Anna's details. It appeared that he had competition, and perhaps from more than just an overzealous book fan.

Which meant two things: first, if he couldn't get in touch with Anna by phone or email, he was going to have to travel the 750 kilometres to Florence and reach her in person; and second, he was going to have to get there before someone else did.

The quickest flight he could find online from Montpellier Méditerranée to Peretola Florence was a one-stop with Alitalia that was going to take over eight hours all told, with a long connection in the middle, on top of which would be the extra time-wasting hassle of hiring a car at the other end. He reckoned he could drive there in a little over six hours, if he kept his foot down and avoided police entanglements.

But he couldn't do it without getting some rest first, or he risked falling asleep at the wheel. Kipping in the car in a cold December was inviting hypothermia, so he hammered up the coastal A9 motorway as far as Montpellier, located a little hotel called the Ibis in a pine forest off exit 32 and crashed fully dressed into bed, where he tossed and turned for a couple of hours. He awoke feeling as refreshed as he was ever going to, whether he slept two hours or twelve. After a fast shower and a change of clothes he checked his email once more: still no reply. Committed now, he jumped back into the Alpina munching on a brioche and raced eastwards, stopping only for fuel and coffee. The French and Italian Rivieras flashed by unnoticed. Marseille, Cannes, Monaco, Genoa. By eight that evening, he was arriving in a wintry-looking Florence.

Carlo Scanzi's office was on the top floor of a handsome old apartment building off Via dell'Agnolo, near to the historic centre's limited traffic area. Ben drove slowly past the building to check that the upper windows were in darkness, then parked two blocks away, grabbed his bag and walked back. The temperature had dropped below zero and a freezing mist cloyed the narrow streets, but the cold night air wasn't Ben's sole reason for having slipped on the pair of Blackhawk light assault gloves that he kept in the car.

Ben waited in a shadowy doorway across the street from the apartment building, watching the windows and the entrance until a young couple came out and hurried off, arm in arm, braving the chill. Before the door had swung shut, Ben was across the street and inside.

Nobody was about. He padded silently up the spiral stairs

to the darkness of the top floor. From his bag he fished out the mini-Maglite and turned it on. He shielded its bright, thin beam with his gloved hand as he hunted for the agency office's door and quickly found it, marked by a brass plaque. Ben reached back into his bag and took out the small pouch that contained his lock picks. If Scanzi didn't want to talk to him, then he'd have to access the agent's client files by other means.

But when Ben went to pick the lock, to his surprise he found the door was already open. He put away the picks and stepped quietly inside, pausing to listen and let his eyes adjust to the dark. He was in a short hallway with a door at its far end. He moved towards it in absolute silence, gently turned the door handle and slipped through.

Scanzi's office was in pitch blackness and utterly still. The torch beam swept back and forth like a laser, picking out glass-fronted bookcases, artwork and tasteful furniture until it landed on what Ben was looking for, the antique desk cluttered with papers, piled-up books and a shiny Dell laptop. On the wall behind Scanzi's desk chair hung a framed blow-up taken at some book event, where a small balding man in his sixties, wearing a rumpled suit and with skin the colour of tea stains, was shaking hands with a tall, immaculately dressed younger man baring perfect teeth at the camera. Ben was no authority on Italian authors past or present, but he figured the glamorous one was some famous writer and the small rumpled unhealthy-looking one must be Scanzi.

As he approached the desk, Ben's torch beam picked out something else that made him stop in his tracks.

He said, 'Hm.'

It seemed that Carlo Scanzi hadn't gone home after work that day. Because he was lying twisted on the rug in front of his desk. And he looked even less healthy than he did in his photo. In the photo, he hadn't had his throat cut and his chest and belly perforated by at least a dozen knife wounds that had turned his white shirt black with blood. Scanzi's glassy stare seemed to be aimed right at Ben. His face was contorted with terror and agony. He hadn't died pleasantly, but there didn't seem to have been much of a struggle. His murderer was evidently a much larger, more powerful man. Whoever he was, he was long gone. Ben didn't feel the need to draw his pistol.

Ben crouched by the corpse, cautious not to step in the blood that had saturated the rug and was still drying, telling him that Scanzi hadn't been dead for too long. That impression was confirmed by the rigor mortis that had frozen his face in a mask of horror but not yet fully spread to his limb muscles, which could take five or six hours. Scanzi had probably died sometime that afternoon. Stepping over the body and exploring further with his torch beam, Ben could see none of the pictures of wife, kids and grandkids that a man of Scanzi's age might have added to the clutter on his desktop. The agent wore no wedding ring, either: not a family man, then. Which could account for why nobody had come looking for him when he hadn't returned home that day. If nothing else, Ben could at least rest easy in the knowledge that he wouldn't be disturbed in the next few minutes while he searched for what he needed.

The Dell laptop had gone to sleep, and flashed into life when Ben touched the power button. What came up on-screen was the most recently opened file. It was an agency agreement, a kind of document Ben had never seen before but which he guessed must be a standard boilerplate contract between authors and literary agents. It was dated two years earlier. The bold print header read AGENZIA LETTERARIA

CARLO SCANZI. On the line below was the name and address of the client who had signed up to be represented by him.

Anna Manzini.

With a sick feeling, Ben realised he'd been right. Someone else had been following up the same line of inquiry as him. Someone who was now a critical step ahead of him and knew where to find her. Someone with a knife that had already been bloodied once that day.

Ben left the apartment and raced back down to the street. He wanted to sprint the two blocks back to his car, but kept to a brisk walk in case a report of a man running from a murder scene later attracted suspicion. Anna's address was scrawled on the notepad in his pocket. He punched her postal code into his sat nav. Moments later he was screeching through the streets of Florence, heading south.

The sat nav led him eight kilometres outside the city, into rolling countryside dusted with frost. Judging by the place she'd rented in the Languedoc when he'd known her, she had a taste for elegant and secluded homes; as he turned through the gates and found himself winding up a long, private tree-lined driveway, it was clear that her new residence was no exception.

As the villa came into view, Ben's already rapidly beating heart stepped up a notch. The blue lights of emergency vehicles swirled through the mist up ahead. The property was swarming with cops. Paramedics were carrying a body on a gurney from the house towards a waiting ambulance.

Once again, he'd got there too late.

Chapter 16

The villa was fronted by a grand paved circular courtyard with an ornate baroque-style fountain as its centrepiece, all illuminated in the hard glare of the swirling blue lights and the softer glow from the house's many windows, all of them lit up. Ben hurriedly parked the BMW away from the cluster of police cars, got out and ran towards the boil of activity, taking in the scene. There was only the single ambulance, accompanied by five blue Florence police Alfa Romeos and a Lamborghini fast pursuit car belonging to a pair of swaggering plain-clothes guys who had taken charge of the dozen or so uniformed cops present.

The paramedics had nearly reached the ambulance. Pushing his way closer, Ben saw that the body on the gurney was covered in a bloody sheet. His stomach twisted up at the sight. *Anna.*

But as he pressed onwards through the police cordon he saw that the sheet wasn't pulled up right over the victim's face the way they did with dead bodies – and that the face, wearing an expression of agonised pain, wasn't Anna Manzini's. It was a male, youngish, dark-haired, thirty or less. He didn't look fatally injured, but he'd been pretty badly cut up.

Ben felt a presence and turned to see one of the plain-clothes men approaching. He was thirty-something, dressed in an immaculate Burberry trench coat, and looked like he spent more time in the gym and at the hairdresser's than chasing bad guys. Eyeballing Ben suspiciously he took an ID badge from the right hip pocket of his coat and flashed it. 'Detective Tito Bellomo. Who're you?'

'I'm a friend of Anna Manzini, the owner,' Ben said. 'Where is she?'

'This is a police crime scene,' he said. 'You've no business here, so move on, please.'

'Is she here?' Ben insisted. 'Is she all right?'

'I said move on,' Bellomo said, giving Ben a scowl that he probably practised in the mirror every day. 'Or I'll arrest you for loitering.' He tucked his ID badge back in his coat pocket.

Ben held up his hands. 'No problem, officer. Hey—' He pointed at the sleek blue-and-white police Lamborghini that was gleaming in the villa's lights. 'Is that your car? Wow, that's really something, isn't it?'

Bellomo couldn't resist looking round to admire it himself for a moment, before he turned back to Ben with the scowl. 'Are you still here?'

'On my way, Detective. Sorry I troubled you.'

Ben made as if to head back to his car, but the moment he saw Bellomo walk off, he slipped into the shadows and watched the scene unfolding. From here he could see through the tall front doors of the villa and into the entrance hall, twice the size of Le Val's living room and gleaming with marble, a broad sweeping staircase in the background.

Observing the crowd of people in the hall, Ben couldn't see Anna among them and wondered where she could be. There were two young women dressed as though for a night out, bare-armed in flimsy dresses and shivering and hugging themselves in the cold from the wide-open door. Both were crying and being gamely consoled by the pair of men they were with, who looked about the same age as the victim being loaded aboard the ambulance and just as traumatised as their female companions. The four of them were being questioned by Bellomo's plain-clothes partner and a team of patrol officers.

If they were witnesses to whatever had happened here tonight Ben wanted to speak to them, but there was no way he could get close.

Then he noticed a third young guy, dressed similarly smart-casual as the first two and about the same age, who had wandered outside to sit on the low wall surrounding a little patio or barbecue area off to one side of the house, half-lit by the swirling blue lights. The cops either hadn't noticed him, or for some reason they were less interested in speaking to him than to his friends. He didn't seem particularly upset by the evening's drama, more concerned with the cigarette he was trying to ignite from a lighter that was sparking but wouldn't produce a flame.

Ben walked over, sat next to him on the wall and offered his Zippo. 'Try mine,' he said in Italian.

The young guy puffed ferociously on the lit cigarette, passed Ben back his Zippo and muttered, 'Thanks, man.' He was in his mid-twenties or thereabouts, with a scrappy beard and long black hair that kept flopping into his eyes. He paused for a moment to glance Ben up and down, then pointed at the villa. 'Look, I already told Detective Franciosa in there all I could. I was barely involved in this whole thing, you know?'

Ben nodded sagely, took out the ID card he'd just lifted from Bellomo's trench-coat pocket after distracting him and let the young guy have a quick glance at it, keeping his thumb over the mugshot photo. 'Detective Bellomo, Florence CID. Just a minute of your time, Signor—?'

'Morante, Luciano Morante. Where you from, Detective? If you don't mind my saying, your accent's kind of weird.'

'I worked abroad a long time,' Ben said, taking out his notepad and jotting down Luciano's name, just like a real detective would.

'That's what I'd like to do, you know, see the world. Hey, man, that police Lambo is the coolest car. What's it like, being in your job? You get to shoot a lot of people?'

Ben looked at him. 'You wouldn't believe me if I told you.'

Luciano's eyes twinkled. 'You got a gun? Can I see it?'

Ben hesitated. 'If I show it to you, will you answer my questions?' He was wondering if it would be quicker just to put the gun to this twerp's head and give him three seconds to spill what he knew, but maybe even Italian detectives didn't behave that way towards members of the public.

'Sure.'

Ben slipped out the Taurus, dropped the magazine, jacked the round from the chamber and let Luciano fondle the unloaded weapon. Satisfied, Luciano passed the pistol back to him, took another draw of his cigarette, blew out a gigantic cloud of smoke and motioned towards the house.

'Man, what a scene, huh? Never even met Gianni Garrone before. Poor bastard. I only came along for the ride; I'm a friend of Pietro there, you know?' He pointed. Pietro was one of the two men in the hallway, still talking to Franciosa and the uniforms.

Luciano went on, shaking his head, 'It's unreal, man. I'm new in town, first party I get invited to, next thing I know I'm walking in and there's the host, this Garrone dude, tied to a chair and some big psycho maniac carving him up with a knife in one hand and a fucking digital recorder in the other. One glance at us, and he takes off. The sicko probably gets his kicks playing back the screams of his victims. I saw that in a movie.'

It felt like history repeating itself. Another Manzini villa, another sadistic knife attack. As though Franco Bozza was back, and up to his old tricks. But that couldn't be. In his mind, Ben was seeing the bloodied, ripped shower curtain at Luc Simon's apartment in Lyon. Picturing the blade shearing through thin plastic and slicing into vulnerable, naked flesh. He asked, 'Did you get a good look at the attacker? Would you recognise his face?'

'No way, man. He was wearing a mask, like a ski mask?'

'You said he was a big guy.'

'No, not big. Huge. Definitely over two metres tall. All bulked up like he was a powerlifter or something, but fast on his feet. He disappeared into the woods on the other side of the house. A minute later we saw a car go speeding off. Might've been a van, probably dark-coloured or black, hard to say.'

It was a usefully detailed description. Ben jotted it down. 'Your friend, you said his name was Pietro—?'

'Rossi. We work at the International Film School together. I just started there a couple months ago.'

Ben's list was growing. He scribbled the name Pietro Rossi next to Luciano Morante, circled them together and wrote beside them, FLORENCE INT. FILM SCHOOL. 'So the victim, Gianni Garrone, he's a buddy of Pietro's too?'

'Yeah, though like I said, I never saw him until tonight. It's my first time coming here. Pietro's been to a few of Garrone's get-togethers. Said there were going to be girls. Well, I count two. For three guys, plus Garrone makes four. Some night this turned out to be. Can you believe I've been here two months and I still haven't got laid?'

Leaving aside Luciano's frustrated love life, Ben asked, 'Does Garrone live here?' Thinking that maybe Garrone was Anna's current younger male squeeze, who could have moved in with her. That didn't seem like Anna's style to Ben, but it occurred to him that perhaps he didn't know her as well as he thought he did. That still wouldn't explain where Anna was now.

Luciano shook his head. 'He lives here, but not like, it's his place. He works here. The owner's a woman. Hot stuff, too.' He grinned. 'Pietro said, first time he saw her, he thought she was Valentina Del Cuore. You know, the movie star? Absolute dead ringer.'

Ben grunted, pretending to have heard of her.

'This Manzini chick's a writer, apparently. Gianni's, like, her assistant. Helps with research and stuff, makes phone calls, runs errands. Lives over there, in the annexe next door, but she lets him have parties and stuff in the big house when she's away.'

'And that's where she is, away?'

Luciano blew more smoke. 'I guess she must be, yeah. She's not here, anyhow. If she was here, you guys would've found her when you searched the house, no?'

Ben's relief was outweighed by his frustration. 'Did Pietro happen to say if he knew where she'd gone?'

'Nah, man, not to me.'

'But if Gianni's her assistant, he must know where she is.'

'I guess so, yeah,' Luciano said noncommittally, puffing like a steam train. 'What's the deal with her? She in trouble or something?'

Ben put away his notepad, stood up and offered his hand. 'You've been a big help to the investigation, Signor Morante. I'll know where to find you if we need to talk again.'

'Detective Bellomo, right?'

Ben walked away. He wanted to confirm what he'd learned with Pietro and perhaps find out more, but Pietro was still deep in conversation with the cops. Meanwhile, the paramedics had finished loading the injured Gianni Garrone into the ambulance and were closing the doors. If Ben wanted to find out where they were taking him, now was his only chance. If he drew a blank, he could always pay a visit to the Florence International Film School later to catch up with Pietro Rossi.

Making his choice, Ben trotted to the Alpina and fired it up. He waited for the ambulance to go first, making its way down the villa's driveway with its headlamps burning beams through the mist.

He followed.

Chapter 17

The ambulance headed back towards Florence with its blue lights flashing. Ben had expected it to lead him to some modern hospital on the outskirts of the city, but instead it led him deep into the historic centre, to the Piazza di Santa Maria Nuova where it pulled up outside the portico of an ancient hospital building by the same name. Ben tucked the Alpina into a parking space off the square a short distance away, and watched from behind the wheel as the paramedics and a team of hospital staff unloaded Gianni and hustled him quickly inside out of the cold.

Ben waited an hour in the car, during which time he got back on the phone. Still no email response from Anna. Frustrated, he dialled Sandrine Lacombe's number. She sounded anxious. There had been no change in Jeff's condition and she had little to report, except that his mother had arrived from Australia and had to be sedated after the shock of seeing him. Sandrine seemed totally unaware of the armed guard Ben had posted on her hospital. But something in her tone made him suspect she wasn't telling him everything.

Next, he called Le Val for an update on things there. Tuesday told him that McGuire, Fry and Blackwood had arrived early that morning. Between them, they were watching the perimeter day and night and if anyone was lurking nearby, they'd know about it. 'Have you seen the news?' Tuesday added in a dark undertone.

When Ben checked the online media channels immediately after ending the call, he fast discovered what Sandrine Lacombe hadn't wanted to tell him. 'Shit,' he muttered.

It had to have happened sooner or later – and it had, while he was heading towards Italy. The BBC, Euronews. com and the other channels had all broken the story more or less identically:

'The victim of the recent suspected terrorist incident in Normandy has been named by French police as Jeff Dekker, a British ex-serviceman and director of the Le Val Tactical Training Centre near Valognes, a shooting gallery used by law enforcement and the military, as well as civilians. Mr Dekker is currently being treated for gunshot wounds at Louis Pasteur Hospital in Cherbourg, where he remains in a critical condition. Le Val co-director, Benjamin Hope, was unavailable for comment. France's Secretary General for National Defence, Henri Couillon, yesterday expressed grave concerns over the security risk posed by private firms such as Le Val, where large arsenals of deadly assault weapons are vulnerable to easy theft by extremist groups . . .'

Ordinarily, Ben would have been irritated by the 'Benjamin' part, as well as the article's misleading sensationalism and description of Le Val as a 'shooting gallery'. But right now, what concerned him was the fact that his enemies, whoever they were, knew that they'd got the wrong man. They wouldn't have to be geniuses to figure out that their intended target was still out there, and gunning for them.

In other words, his element of surprise had just vaporised.

Ben quelled his annoyance with a couple of cigarettes. As his thoughts calmed, he realised that the leak also meant that Jeff was no longer at risk in Cherbourg – not from sneak assassins, at any rate. He made a quick call to Boonzie to instruct him to pull the two guys off their post in Cherbourg and send them down to Le Val to fortify the defences there.

Once that was done, Ben looked at his watch and decided that Gianni Garrone's doctors had had plenty enough time to do whatever they needed to do to patch up their patient. He left the car and wandered inside the old hospital building, keeping an eye out for cops but, so far, spotting none. At the front desk, he flashed the police ID and asked to see the patient. He was ready to bolt at the first sign of trouble, but the real Detective Bellomo obviously hadn't yet sounded the alarm over his stolen badge, and the hospital staff were happily taken in by the impostor – weird accent or not. The nurses tried to insist that he should come back later as Signor Garrone was in no fit state to receive visitors yet. Ben sweet-talked them into letting him have ten minutes alone with the patient. This kind of work was so much easier when you could open doors with a wave of your badge. He wished he could be a cop more often.

The hospital wasn't much more modern inside than it was outside. A nurse led him to a curtained-off corner of a ward, where he found Garrone propped up in bed, heavily bandaged and even more heavily drugged.

Ben pulled up a chair. When the nurse had gone, he said, 'I'm Detective Bellomo. You had a lucky escape tonight, Gianni. I know you're hurting, so this won't take long. I need to know where Anna is. I don't have time to explain, but she's in serious danger.'

Garrone couldn't turn his head. His bloodshot eyes rolled sideways to peer at Ben in surprise at the mention of Anna. He was pumped full of so many painkillers that his lips barely moved as he croaked, '*Is . . . she . . . okay?*'

'I hope so, Gianni, and I mean to keep her that way. But I need your help.'

'*Left . . . three days ago . . . research trip . . .*' The patient winced as though every breath was causing him terrible pain, which Ben didn't doubt it was. '*Really big . . . Important,*' he added.

'I don't care what she's researching, Gianni. That's not what I need to know. Just tell me where she went.'

Garrone's eyes drifted shut, and for a moment Ben thought he'd passed out. He had to lean close to hear the murmured word, '*Olympia.*'

Ben didn't think he meant the capital of the state of Washington, USA. Or the exhibition centre in London. 'She's in Greece?'

Almost inaudibly, Gianni whispered, '*She went . . . to meet a man . . . Theo Kambasis.*'

'Kambasis,' Ben repeated, writing it down.

Gianni nodded. The drugs were rapidly carrying him under.

'Stay with me, Gianni. One more question. The man who attacked you. He was after her, wasn't he? He hurt you so you'd tell him where she'd gone. That's why he had the sound recorder.'

Another barely perceptible nod. Gianni's breathing had slowed down to the merest sigh.

'Did you tell him, Gianni? Do they know where Anna is?'

But by then, Gianni Garrone was far away in a chemical haze from which he might not emerge for hours. Ben had got all he was going to get, and it was time for him to leave.

He just had to hope he could find her before the killers did.

Chapter 18

As Ben was leaving the hospital, he was scanning a mental map of Europe and measuring distances. Olympia was a long way away, right down on Greece's Peloponnese peninsula. To travel there by road represented a monster journey back north past Bologna and Ferrara, then over the arch of the Gulf of Venice to Trieste near the Italian border. Once out of Italy would begin the long slog southwards through the snowy forests and mountains of Slovenia and Croatia, across Bosnia and Herzegovina, through Montenegro and Albania and much of Greece itself. Such a long drive was out of the question, time-wise. As was the prospect of hacking all the way down to Ancona or Bari on Italy's east coast to catch a ferry – if ferries even operated at this time of year.

No: it was clear he was going to have to leave the car here in Florence and jump on the first flight he could get. Assuming he could locate Anna Manzini in Olympia when he arrived. Assuming she was still there by the time he did. Assuming she was still alive when he found her.

A lot of assumptions, but it was all he had.

Ben's mind was working fast as he walked away from the hospital portico arches and headed across the square towards where he'd parked the Alpina. Piazza di Santa Maria Nuova was cordoned off by stumpy chained-together bollards, to stop cars blocking up the parking spaces for ambulances. He stepped over the drooping iron chain and walked a few paces up the narrow street towards the car, lighting another Gauloise.

He was so consumed with his thoughts that he at first failed to register the pair of blazing headlights approaching the wrong way up the street, from the opposite direction. Snapping back to the present moment he turned and saw the black van.

Going much too fast. Heading right for him.

By the time Ben realised that the driver's intention was to run him down, it was almost too late to get out of its path. He leaped back over the chain cordon, placing the two-foot-high concrete bollards between him and it.

The van didn't slow down. It rammed into the bollards with a crunch of crumpling metal. Its front rode up off the ground as it smashed the concrete into rubble and kept coming, like a tank, bearing down on him.

Ben ducked through the rapidly narrowing gap between the corner wall of the square and the oncoming vehicle. He made it to the first parked car, a yellow Fiat, dived for it, slid sideways across its bonnet and landed on his feet. Immediately he was running up the street towards the Alpina, knowing he had little chance of reaching it before the van caught him.

With just one headlight still intact and its bumper and grille twisted and mangled, the black van ploughed through the remains of the bollards and entered the mouth of the street, the roar of its engine echoing between the tall buildings either side. Its left-side wing caught the front of the yellow Fiat and rammed it violently into the car behind it, a red Alfa that bounced sideways out of its parking space and almost flattened Ben as he raced past.

Ben was still ten long strides from his BMW. The van smacked the wreckage of the cars aside and kept coming. The passenger window was rolling down. A black-gloved hand was reaching out, clutching what took only a split-second glance for Ben to identify as a SIG Sauer MPX machine pistol.

The weapon opened fire, filling the narrow canyon of the street with noise and releasing a stream of bullets that stitched a ragged line of holes in the sides of the parked cars in Ben's wake, punching through metal and glass.

He reached the Alpina's driver's door, but there was no time to get in. Ducking around the back of the car he fell into a crouch and whipped his Taurus from his belt. In advanced pistolcraft classes at Le Val, they taught the art of high-speed combat fire without using the sights. Things were happening too fast to take aim in any case as the van bore down on him, the machine gun snorting from its passenger window. He let off three fast snap-shots, saw his bullets splat into the van's crumpled bonnet and windscreen. The MPX opened up with another strafing volley, blowing out two of the Alpina's side windows, shredding the rear door and wing and forcing him to duck. The car shielded him from the gunfire. Solid German engineering. But if they'd been using a rifle-calibre assault weapon the bullets would have torn right through and found him on the other side. Some things in life, you had to be grateful for.

The van slewed to a skidding halt, blocking the street. Its doors burst open and two men jumped out. They were wearing ski masks and body armour. The one on the passenger side, dumping the spent mag from his machine pistol and slapping in a fresh load from a tactical pouch on his belt, was small and slightly built. The driver was a monster, muscular and tall, and the Franchi Spas combat shotgun he was wielding like a claymore was built to match.

Ben remembered the witness description of Gianni Garrone's attacker. *A huge guy, bulked up like he was a power-lifter, but fast on his feet.* Same guy – and maybe also the same bastard who had shot Jeff and murdered Father Pascal, Luc Simon and Carlo Scanzi. He and his accomplice must have been hanging around the villa, waiting for the ambulance to go by so they could tail it to the hospital in Ben's wake and lie in wait for their moment to finish the job and eliminate the witness.

And Ben had walked right into their path. They'd obviously watched him go inside the hospital, and decided to make their move when he reappeared. But Ben wasn't about to let himself be picked off so easily.

Firing past the van's open door the big man let off a roaring blast from his shotgun that ripped away part of the Alpina's rear wing and tail-light, inches from where Ben was crouching. Then another, blowing out most of the rear window pillar and spraying Ben with broken glass.

Pinned down, he used the moment to consider his tactical options. In an ideal world, the torturer needed to be taken alive. The big man had been the one sent into Anna's villa to gain the information; hence he was the most trusted and senior member of the hit team; hence he was more likely to know who they were working for. By contrast, the little guy on the passenger side was expendable.

So in the next instant, when Ben felt a pause in the gunfire and reared up from his cover to take another shot, it was the little guy he fired at. When the enemy is wearing armour, you abandon the traditional centre-of-mass approach and aim a little higher. Ben held the Taurus tightly in both hands and snapped off a double-tap, BANGBANG, that took him right in the head, a little off-centre but who would quibble. The little guy jerked backwards off his feet and went down on his back, the MPX clattering from his hand. Before he'd hit the ground Ben was swivelling the pistol a few degrees sideways to open fire on his muscular pal, hoping to wing him and take him out of the game without inflicting a lethal hit.

But the big guy was as fast on his feet as Luciano Morante had said. He ducked behind the open door of the van, clambering back inside with surprising agility for a man his size. Ben fired at the windscreen, turning it into a web of cracks. The van's engine roared. It lurched forward and took off, leaving the dead man lying in the road. As it sped past, Ben rattled off a string of shots and shattered the passenger window. But the van kept going, making its escape the wrong way up the narrow street.

Ben could have run to check the dead man, but he had two reasons for ignoring him. One, as a source of information he was past his best; two, Ben could hear the growing wail of police sirens through the ringing in his ears, a sound he didn't want to hear any more than the enemy did.

He scrambled out from behind his car. The Alpina looked as if the SAS had been using it as a shooting-range target. He could only hope it still went. He wrenched open the bullet-riddled door, dived behind the wheel, twisted the key in the ignition – and to his relief the engine burst throatily into life.

The van's impact against the row of parked cars had squeezed them up nose-to-tail like railway carriages. Ben slammed the gearbox into forward drive and rammed the car in front, then crunched it into reverse and rammed the one behind him, trying to widen the gap so he could batter his way out. The van was getting further away every second.

The Alpina surged out of its parking space, wheels spinning. Both headlamps were smashed, but that was what street lighting was for. He punched the gas, roared into the square and pulled a 180-degree handbrake turn to bring himself facing the right direction. In terms of the traffic system that was also the wrong direction, but all that mattered was catching up with the van.

There was no time for anything like fastening the seat belt. Ben accelerated hard and the narrow ancient street with its crumbling stone walls and barred windows and shuttered doorways and graffiti became a tunnel. Cold air whistled in through the shattered windows.

There was the van, racing wildly ahead. Amid a screeching of brakes and blaring of horns, a bus appeared, blocking the van's way. But a side street lay between them to the left, and the big guy threw the van down it, rocking hard on its suspension as he rounded the tight bend and almost flattened an old man and his dog who were crossing the road. The bus driver kept coming, then had to slam the brakes back on again with a shake of his fist as Ben forced him to a halt a second time.

The Alpina hammered down the side street. The van had lost precious seconds of lead. Ben was catching up, but the van driver had no intention of slowing down for anything, any more than he had respect for the one-way system.

Ben felt the fierce thrill of the chase as he sped after his enemy. He was the predator now, and he wasn't going to let the big man get away from him.

Chapter 19

On they went, reaching insane speeds as they zigzagged this way and that through the maze of narrow streets that was the heart of the old city, so tight in places that the van was scraping its sides to squeeze between the lines of parked cars on one side and the walls of shops and houses on the other. Oncoming traffic veered onto the kerb to avoid a collision, adding to the cacophony of angry horns. A lone motorcyclist braving the chill did a panic-brake to avoid being run down, lost control of his machine and went sliding off in a shower of sparks.

The van skidded right, left, right again. Ben grimly chased on after it, battering past the traffic that swerved aside to let them through. The police sirens were still there in the background but he couldn't see any cop cars in his mirror – yet.

Suddenly the street opened up and they were tearing through one of Florence's great landmarks, the Piazza del Duomo. The lit-up Gothic facade of Santa Maria del Fiore cathedral towered magnificently over them like a giant black-and-white cake. Its great dome and Giotto's bell tower stood shrouded in mist. On a less freezing cold night the square might have been crowded with pedestrians, and Ben was thankful it was almost deserted as the two vehicles went chasing across it at breakneck speed, sliding and fishtailing on the slippery paving stones.

The chase had to end soon, and it wasn't going to end well for either of them if the lunatic behind the wheel of the van kept this up much longer. The night was murky and with only one working headlamp between them, it was virtually certain that either the van or the car was going to end up piling into a wall or a lamp-post.

Just when Ben was steadily gaining on his target, he had to brake hard and almost lost control as a taxicab pulled out in front of him. Gritting his teeth he saw the van's taillights vanishing off ahead and jammed the accelerator down hard in pursuit. The cold air streaming into the car was whipping the breath from his lungs and making his eyes water, while his fists were going numb on the steering wheel.

They were carving southwards now, away from the cathedral district. The Alpina was closing the gap once more – but now Ben could see the inevitable flashing blue lights in his rear-view mirror. More lights were in the sky above, strong white search-lamps cutting through the mist as the Florence police helicopters joined the chase.

He couldn't give up. The van was just thirty yards ahead of him, racing up a narrow street called Via del Moro, veering left and right and scattering rubbish bins into the Alpina's path and sending Ben into a slalom that took up what width the street had to offer. The end of the street raced towards them and Ben glimpsed another square and a big junction up ahead, flanked with red lights. Traffic was streaming across their path, but the van roared across the junction without slowing down and Ben had no choice but to go right after it, bracing himself for a collision that never happened as cars streaked and swerved past and horns chorused all around him.

Ben realised they'd reached the point where the River Arno bisected the city. Ahead of him, the wildly careering van was heading for the Ponte alla Carraia, one of the most famous bridges in Florence. Behind, the lights of police cars behind were filling the street in an ocean of blue. The beat of helicopters was clearly audible over the wind and engine roar.

Ben chased the van onto the five-arched stone bridge. Either side of them, the waters of the Arno were a broad stretch of black between the city lights. He gunned the throttle and the rear of the van seemed to accelerate towards him. With a crunch of buckling metal the Alpina rammed it, the impact jarring Ben against the steering wheel. The van wobbled. The Alpina fell back, came on again, rammed the van a second time.

Halfway across the bridge, the van's crumpled rear doors suddenly burst open. And that was when Ben realised that the big guy wasn't alone inside it. Another man in body armour and a black ski mask crouched on the floor of the van, facing the open doors. In his gloved hands he was clutching a long, bulky shape that Ben didn't need headlights to recognise.

The rocket launcher filled the back of the truck with a blinding flash as it fired. At point-blank range the missile would tear a car in half and incinerate anything inside in a fireball hot enough to melt steel. And nobody could miss at this distance, not even from inside the back of a wildly swerving and rocking van.

Ben wrenched the BMW's steering wheel violently to the right. Felt himself thrown to the left as the car went into a skid. There was a bright orange-white explosion behind him. The missile had hit one of the chasing police cars, ripping it to pieces. Ben scarcely had time to register it as the Alpina, skidding out of control, crashed violently into the low side wall of the bridge. The impact flung him almost over the wheel. The car's nose dropped. The blackness of the river rushed up to meet him.

Then it hit.

The torrent of foaming water burst through the cracked windscreen and swallowed Ben up with an icy shock that felt as if it could stop his heart. He groped around inside the sinking car, bubbles erupting from his mouth. The Alpina was going down fast as the river flooded in through its broken windows. He could hardly see. One groping hand found the strap of his bag. The other found the door handle, but the door wouldn't open, so he turned himself round and kicked it hard with both feet to burst it open against the pressure of the water. The car was turning end over end as it sank. Ben grasped his bag and launched himself from the open door. His lungs were bursting. He would not drown. He would get out of this.

He kicked and struggled through the black water, only half-sure of which way was up. His head broke the surface and he gave a wheezing gasp. Sirens and thudding helicopters filled his ears. Treading water, he looked up. The bridge seemed a long way above him, and he could see nothing past the angle of its side wall. Just the fierce glow from the burning police vehicle and the flicker of blue lights lighting up the night sky above. The blazing wreckage must have blocked the whole bridge.

A chopper was circling over the river where they'd seen the BMW go down. Its searchlight was combing the water. Ben gulped air and dived back below the surface, swimming hard until his lungs couldn't take it any more and he resurfaced. He looked back at the hovering choppers. They hadn't spotted him, or they'd be turning the spotlamps his way.

Ben swam on until he reached the far bank, which was sloping and thick with reeds. The cold water seemed to have drained every last reserve of strength from his body, but somehow he managed to drag himself ashore, coughing and spluttering, breath rasping, his clothes streaming and his whole body shuddering with the crippling chill. He had to find shelter, dry himself off, seek warmth, or he could go into hypothermic shock.

He made it up the bank and hauled himself over a wall that separated the riverside from the street. Then he ran, or staggered, towards the quayside buildings that could hide him from the hovering choppers. Pausing against a wall, he looked around him. He could see another bridge further downriver, running parallel with the Ponte alla Carraia and dotted white and red with the lights of slow-moving traffic. Before the bridge, on his side of the river, a car park was set off the street behind a low wall. He broke into a run towards it and saw the camper van sitting in the shadows. He made his way towards it.

Ben had broken into a good number of considerably more secure vehicles in his time, and it didn't take much to force the lock. Nor did it take much to get the engine started without a key. Shaking so badly that he could hardly control the steering, he pulled out of the car-park entrance and drove for ten minutes until he was well away from the drama; then he found a quiet spot off the street and pulled up.

The camper had a small stove running off a butane bottle. Almost praying out loud that it would work, he turned on the gas and pressed the piezo-ignition lighter switch, and his prayer was answered by the whoosh of blue flame. He quickly pulled down all the blinds so that he couldn't be seen from outside, then returned to the stove and stripped off his wet clothes. The spare clothing in his bag wasn't any less soaked. Naked and shivering, he huddled as close to the heat as he could without burning himself and rubbed his hands, arms and thighs to get the circulation going again. They said that alcohol only made the body lose heat even more, but what did they know? A few swigs of whisky from his flask made him glow inside, even if it was an illusion.

When he felt warm enough to drag himself away from the stove he wrung out his clothes over the sink, then hung them up to dry over a cupboard door. Inside his bag he found his passport and the rolls of cash still perfectly dry within their plastic wrapping. He wasn't so sure about his phone, which he'd have to take apart to let the water trapped inside evaporate before using it again.

His gun was lost, now somewhere at the bottom of the Arno along with his car, but he'd have had to abandon both anyway, where he was headed next: to the airport, and from there to Olympia, Greece.

Chapter 20

By morning the news channels and the city of Florence were ablaze with last night's dramatic events, which the media had managed to circumbobulate into yet another terrorist atrocity with the Italian police emerging as the heroes of the hour. City authorities wept over the damage to the Ponte alla Carraia while tributes were paid to the fallen officers and hundreds more of their incensed and heavily armed comrades scoured Florence for the presumed Muslim extremists responsible, still at large, with photos of bearded, olive-skinned, villainous-looking likely suspects plastered online.

Cops were swarming all over the airport as Ben sat waiting to embark on the next leg of his journey, which was giving him headaches on top of a sleepless night in his stolen camper van. If the epicentre of ancient Greek culture was one of Europe's most frequented visitor destinations in the peak of the high season, during wintertime it seemed by contrast almost as though they were actively trying to keep people out. Kalamata Airport near Olympia was essentially closed up during the colder months, forcing Ben to opt for a flight to the more distant Athens with the plan to double back on himself by road, a drive of over 300 kilometres.

He twiddled his thumbs for hours, wolfed down some breakfast, gulped a pint of espresso, smoked and paced outside in the cold, checked his email, called Tuesday, called Sandrine Lacombe, learned nothing new.

The delays meant that he didn't land in Athens until midday, there to face the complications of getting hold of a car. He'd wrecked so many hire vehicles and been blacklisted by so many rental companies in his time that it was becoming a problem. The agent at Auto Europe proved so intransigent that Ben eventually walked out of his office in disgust, grabbed a taxi into the city and found a backstreet car dealer who sold him a ten-year-old Opel for under a thousand euros, no papers, no questions asked.

Finally, still seething at the loss of precious time, he was on his way. He took the motorway route via Patras that hugged the coastline, to avoid meeting snow and ice on the more direct roads further inland that cut through the forests and mountains of the Peloponnese mainland. The Opel was basic and rusty and battered, and the scrapheap was in its near future, but it didn't seem at imminent risk of blowing its engine, and after a few kilometres he felt relaxed about caning it mercilessly.

That freed his mind to agonise instead over how he was going to find Anna, if indeed she would still be in Olympia when he got there, or if the bad guys hadn't reached her first. While waiting for his flight to Athens Ben had searched online for Theo Kambasis, the man Anna had gone there to meet, but found nothing. How much information had Gianni's torturer pressed out of his victim? Ben couldn't afford to assume the enemy's intel wasn't a step ahead of his own, any more than he could afford to assume that the two thugs who'd tried to kill him last night hadn't escaped Florence sooner than he had. Even if the police had caught them, it was safe to bet that whoever was behind this could easily deploy more manpower wherever needed.

Whoever was behind this. The big question. Of all that was bad about the situation, what Ben liked least of all was still not knowing who the enemy actually was. Was Massimiliano Usberti dead, or alive? It was like chasing a ghost.

With no answers, all he could do was press on as fast as he could, pushing the Opel to its limits through landscapes that were stunning even in winter, but which he barely noticed as he focused completely on his objective. Four hours after leaving Athens, he was rolling into the sacred valley of the gods where, according to mythology, Zeus had inaugurated the very first Olympic Games in celebration of having defeated his Titan father, Kronos, in a wrestling match.

Ben didn't know it yet, but the ancient site was about to become the scene of a new, deadlier conflict.

The modern town of Olympia was small, making the job of finding one person out of only a thousand or so inhabitants somewhat easier. Its single main street was dotted with souvenir shops, bars and cafés, most of which seemed mainly to exist for the coachloads of tourists who descended upon the place en masse in summer, and were now either running on a single cylinder or closed up altogether. According to Ben's web search there were at least thirty-seven hotels and guesthouses in the immediate vicinity. He'd already narrowed the list to sixteen, eliminating the places that shut in winter and focusing, at least initially, on the more upmarket ones where an affluent woman of taste like Anna Manzini would be more likely to be found.

But sixteen hotels was still sixteen hotels, and he was going to have to do it the hard way, hoofing it to each in turn in the hope that he might get lucky. Moreover, and more troublingly, he was well aware of Anna's liking for expensive private rentals. There must be hundreds of villas available for rent locally in the dead season, and she could be in any of them.

The day was growing darker by the time he'd drawn a blank at the first four hotels he tried. Feeling suddenly weak with hunger, Ben grabbed a sandwich of spicy lamb in pita bread and a foaming Greek coffee in the bar of the fifth and sat down in a corner to eat it. The bar was almost empty, apart from a few locals and a pair of oversized Cockney tourists weighing down a table in the middle of the room, whose blaring conversation it was impossible to avoid listening in on. 'I *told* you it would be freezing here in bloody December, Alf,' the woman was scolding her husband in a voice to wake the dead. 'Nothing's bleeding open, is it? Some bloody holiday idea this was. Should have gone back to Lanzarote like I kept telling you.'

'Been there, done that,' Alf said glumly.

'Well we're not coming to this dump again. I'm bored to death, my feet are killing me after traipsing about that bleeding museum, and all *you* can bang on about is some bloody actress you *think* you saw.'

'I'm sure it was her,' Alf protested. 'I'd know her anywhere.'

'Bet you would, and all,' his wife sneered at him. 'You spend enough time drooling over her pictures. If you think a dolly bird like that would even look twice at a bald old git like you, you need to take a butcher's in the mirror.' She gave a derisory snort.

'Should have got her autograph,' Alf said with a wistful shake of his head. 'Wonder what she was doing there. Maybe she lives here. Just think, Deb. Valentina Del Cuore, in the flesh.'

'Flesh, flesh, that's all you bloody think about, innit? Honest to God, I don't know what's the matter with you.'

They both looked up, startled by the tousled-looking stranger who had suddenly appeared at their table.

'Did you say Valentina Del Cuore?' Ben asked.

Chapter 21

Alf's description of the dark-haired beauty fleetingly glimpsed that afternoon left Ben, posing as a reporter hunting for a snap of the movie star, in little doubt that the woman he'd spotted was in fact Anna Manzini.

The holidaymakers had been labouring their way through an unentertaining tour of the Archaeological Museum of Olympia when they'd seen her enter, briefly speak to one of the staff and then disappear through a door marked 'private'. Her famously lavish black locks were half-hidden under a hat and she was draped in a long winter coat with a big fur collar, but Alf swore it was her. Maybe she was scouting locations for a movie, he suggested, still dazzled by the sighting and virtually offering to carry Ben's camera equipment for him as he went off in search of her.

If the lead was a solid one, it meant Anna had turned up at the museum just an hour or so ago. With luck, Ben would still be able to find her there. Abandoning his half-eaten meal he rushed out to the car and checked Alf's vague directions against the map on the museum's website, which proclaimed: '*The permanent collection contains finds dating from prehistoric times to the Early Christian period. Among the many precious exhibits, the museum's famous sculpture collection, the bronze collection which is the richest of its kind in the world, and the large terracotta collection, are especially noteworthy.'*

The Archaeological Museum was situated just out of town, in a wintry valley north-west of the Kronion Hill. Ben left the Opel in a parking area and walked up to the museum via a columned walkway that led to a paved courtyard surrounded by trees. The main building was filled with the reverent hush of a cathedral. Ben found himself surrounded by gleaming statues of bronze and marble and stone and a dizzying array of artefacts from the dawn of antiquity. He could see why the place might have little to offer Alf and Deb in the way of entertainment value, lacking the interactive digital displays, virtual tours or emotion-driven social experiences required to shore up the limited attention span of the smartphone-toting modern breed of tourist. For an old-school appreciator of history and aesthetic beauty in the raw, though, it was a candy shop of eye-popping wonders.

But that still didn't explain why Anna Manzini should have travelled all this way from the culture-rich environment of Florence when she could have done all the research she needed in the comfort of her luxury villa, including talking to this Kambasis guy. The telephone was a wonderful invention. Whatever she'd come here for, she'd clearly had a very specific intention that could only be addressed by a visit in person.

There was no sign of Anna in any of the exhibit rooms. Ben quickly found the door marked 'private' and was considering going through it when he spotted a female staff member in an apron, dusting the glass front of a display cabinet containing a collection of ancient bronze helmets. Putting on a nervous expression and glancing at his watch, he went over to where she was working. He spoke English, on the assumption that every single employee of the entire

Greek tourist industry probably spoke it better than most Brits.

'Excuse me, but I'm looking for my wife. I was supposed to meet her here about an hour ago but I got held up. Black hair, wearing a hat and a long coat with a fur collar – you wouldn't have seen her, by any chance?'

His linguistic assumption was correct. The woman shook her head and said no, she'd only come in for a couple of hours to do some cleaning and hadn't been here long. Nobody answering that description had arrived in the last forty minutes or so, as far as she knew.

'She had an appointment with someone named Kambasis, Theo Kambasis?'

At which, the woman's face brightened with recognition. 'Oh, yes, Mr Kambasis is an assistant curator here. But I'm afraid you've missed him, too. He told me yesterday that an Italian history professor was coming to see him today, to discuss something about Phidias' workshop.'

'That's her.'

'I assumed it was a man.'

'She gets that a lot.'

The woman glanced at her plastic watch. 'If you're quick you might find them still over at the workshop.' She added with a smile, 'Mr Kambasis can't tear himself away from that place, once you get him talking.'

Ben visualised some kind of restoration workshop attached to the museum, with rows of benches and priceless relics sitting here and there in the process of being reconstructed. 'Which way do I go?' he asked.

'Oh, it's not part of the museum,' she explained. 'It's part of the ruins of the ancient site of Olympia. It's not far. You'll find it over on the west side of the sacred enclosure, directly opposite the Temple of Zeus. Here, let me give you one of the museum's leaflets. There's a little map on the back that shows you the layout of all the buildings.'

Ben thanked her for her help, and left. The ancient site was within easy walking distance and cars weren't allowed access, so he left the Opel outside the museum and set off at a trot, map in hand, hoping he wasn't going to miss Anna again. Dusk was creeping in. His breath misted in the cold air as he hurried on his way.

What had once been one of the most spectacular visions of ancient Greece was now an extended field of ruins, spread out among groves of trees with the rolling background panorama of hills and mountains still visible against the darkening sky. Using the map to orient him he made his way through the maze of tumbledown arches and buildings; there was little remaining of Olympia's former glory except partial walls and the occasional segment of stone column standing here and there.

The workshop of Phidias was his target. Whoever this Phidias was or had been, Ben had little idea and even less interest. The woman at the museum had said that it was near the Temple of Zeus, and the map seemed to concur, but he couldn't see anything resembling a temple – only a rectangular patch of what was basically a rubble field. He was reminded of some of the devastated ancient temples he'd seen in the Middle East during his military days, victims of tank battles and bombing raids, millennia of history wiped out at a stroke. Here, the slow ravages of three thousand years of natural decay and earthquakes had taken a more gradual toll.

He wondered whether those smoking battlefields, still echoing in his mind with the crackling of blazing vehicles and the screams of the dying, could ever become as serene and tranquil as the spot he was standing on now. There was something almost meditative about the ruins of Olympia, a stillness he hadn't experienced since the brief months he'd lived the life of a lay brother in a monastery in the French Alps, so secluded from the hectic buzz of the modern world that it was easy, and very tempting, to forget it even existed.

But there was no time for contemplation as he walked on, looking and listening for any sign of anyone around. Just as he was becoming certain the place was completely deserted and he'd got here too late, he heard voices in the distance and picked up his step. It looked as if he'd found the workshop of Phidias. As he drew closer, he could see that it was one of the only areas where the ruins were still fairly intact: a once-grandiose building with walls and columns miraculously unharmed by the wrecking ball of the ages.

Then he saw them: two figures slowly picking their way through the dusky shadows of the ruined building, some sixty yards from him. One was a man, stooped and walking with the gait of an elderly person. The other was a woman he instantly recognised. Slim and statuesque, in a long elegantly tailored winter coat that couldn't be anything other than Italian, her black hair spilling out from under a fur hat. Beautiful even from the back. He knew right away that it wasn't Valentina Del Cuore.

Anna Manzini. He'd found her, alive and safe.

The man she was with, whom Ben presumed must be Kambasis, was pointing this way and that as the pair meandered along what had once been a corridor or passageway, now just the low remains of one wall. Anna was listening to him, pausing every few steps to raise an SLR camera that dangled from her neck and snap a photo while enough light still remained. They were too engrossed in their conversation to have spotted Ben coming their way.

He was about to call Anna's name when he realised the three of them weren't going to be alone for long.

The lights of an approaching vehicle were cutting through the dusk, bouncing up and down as the suspension rocked over the bumpy ground. A white panel van had emerged from behind a stand of trees at the edge of the ancient site, where he guessed there must be a limited access road leading in for authorised users. At first he thought that it might be a maintenance crew come to carry out some kind of repair work on the place. But what kind of maintenance crew would start work at dusk? Something was wrong.

The van's headlights darkened, then its engine cut out. It didn't stop. It coasted on between the ruins, steering a lurching, bumping course over the uneven ground towards where Anna and Kambasis were strolling along in conversation. They didn't seem to have noticed it.

Something was definitely wrong.

The van braked silently to a halt. Its doors opened, soft and quiet. The dark figures of three men got out. Ben was much further away from them than they were from Anna and Kambasis, but even from this distance the way they moved had alarm bells shrilling in his mind. They walked from the van three abreast, confident yet stealthy, heading right towards Anna and Kambasis who were still too taken up by their intense conversation to have seen they weren't alone.

Ben kept going, moving faster, watching the three men. The dark jackets they were wearing let them blend into the shadows. The two either side were large men, over six foot. The one in the middle dwarfed them both.

The big guy. Gianni Garrone's attacker. The driver of the black van in Florence.

As Ben watched they broke their line and split up, the

outer two peeling off at an angle, so that they converged on their target in a pincer movement like a pair of stalking predators creeping up on their prey. The two flankers were each drawing out stubby black objects that, even at this distance in the growing darkness, were unmistakably hand-guns. The big guy in the middle unslung a heftier weapon from under his jacket.

Ben let his bag fall from his shoulder and broke into a sprint. It went against all his training and experience to give away his own presence and position to the three stalkers, but he had to warn Anna and her companion before some-thing terrible happened right here in front of him. He let out a yell.

'Anna! Look out!'

He saw her tense, then whip around in surprise and confusion to see who was calling her name.

But Ben's warning was too late. Suddenly, through the stillness of the falling dark, came the first snap of gunshots.

Chapter 22

If this had been the summer season, hordes of tourists would have been fleeing amid scenes of mayhem. Now in the dead of winter with nobody around to raise the alarm, the ruins of Olympia were the gunmen's own private shooting range and they could expend all the ordnance they wanted.

The gunfire punched ragged holes in the silence of Olympia. Anna Manzini and Theo Kambasis froze like two rabbits paralysed in the headlights of an oncoming car. To the sound of another shot, Kambasis staggered and clutched at Anna's arm. Still some forty yards away and running fast, Ben couldn't tell if the old curator was trying to protect her, or was clinging to her for support. Anna let out a cry. The two of them fell back over the low wall by which they'd been strolling, and disappeared from view.

Ben ran harder, his heart thumping with anxiety, partly because it was impossible to know whether Anna had ducked out of sight, or been shot, and partly because rushing unarmed, empty-handed and in plain view towards a trio of heavily armed attackers wasn't tactically the soundest option in anyone's book.

A beat later, he knew that his warning yell had had exactly the effect he feared. Pausing in their stride towards the wall behind which Anna and Kambasis had disappeared, the gunmen turned and gazed in Ben's direction, then raised their weapons and opened fire on him.

Ben had reached a crumbly archway that stood supported on a pair of columns. Whatever temple or shrine the arch had once been a doorway to, the rest of the building lay collapsed and strewn all over the ground, and it was behind those ruins that he dived under cover, pressing himself flat as scores of bullets cracked into the ancient stonework, stinging him with flying chips of masonry.

The big man motioned to his companions, as if to say, 'I'll take care of this guy, you deal with those two.' The others turned back towards the low wall where Anna and Kambasis had dropped out of sight, while the big man started ambling casually towards Ben. If he seemed almost nonchalant, that was because he knew that if Ben had come ready for a gunfight, he'd have already returned fire.

On his hands and knees in the dirt, Ben looked desperately around him for some kind of improvised weapon. Even a handy chunk of stone would be better than nothing, but the only rocks he could see were broken segments of ribbed cylindrical columns and large square blocks that must have weighed two hundred pounds apiece.

The big man came closer, holding his weapon at waist level. It was the same kind of SIG Sauer MPX machine pistol they'd used to try to kill Ben in Florence. Possibly the very same weapon. It was fitted with a red-dot optical sight and long curved magazine, with a spare protruding from his hip pocket. He had the fire selector set to three-shot bursts, which hammered the stonework in percussive snorts as he walked closer.

Ben could almost hear him laughing.

Tactical advantages were few and far between in this situation, but Ben had one thing going for him: if he kept low enough the big guy couldn't actually see him. Pinned under fire, he inched forwards like a crawling snake, until he'd managed to work his way out of the hot zone and could peer around the edge of a big stone block and see the big guy just feet away, blasting at the spot where he thought Ben was sheltering. He was grinning ear to ear, clearly a man who enjoyed his work. In the background, Ben saw the other two stepping closer to the low wall over which Anna and Kambasis had disappeared. They raised their pistols and let off two shots each, BLAMBLAM – BLAMBLAM, firing over the top of the wall at an angle towards the ground. It was exactly the angle they'd have been shooting at if they were executing two injured victims lying at the foot of the wall on the other side.

Ben went cold. Anna had just been murdered right in front of him and there'd been nothing he could do to save her. He'd been too late. It had been all for nothing.

The big man had reached the solitary stone arch and was peering over the piles of ruins strewn around it, the contented smirk on his face turned to a perplexed frown as he realised that his helpless target wasn't where he'd thought he was. He stood bulkily framed beneath the archway, searching left, searching right. His eyes darting in all directions except for the one he should have been looking in, which was directly above him.

Ben had clambered up the rocks unseen and was perched on top of the archway right over the big guy's head. The two other gunmen had only to turn round to spot him and open fire, but they seemed too busy admiring their handiwork over by the wall. Ben waited for the perfect moment, holding his breath, every muscle coiling like a spring. Then he pounced, like a leopard dropping from the foliage of a tree to surprise a gazelle grazing below.

Except this gazelle was more like a Cape buffalo. From a little distance away, the guy was huge. Close up, he was enormous. Ben's 165 pounds landed squarely across his broad shoulders with an arm hooked around his throat, and he hardly seemed to sag under the sudden impact. Ben locked the stranglehold tighter and rained blows on his face and head. A massive elbow lashed backwards and caught Ben in the ribs, ripping his grasp loose and sending him sprawling to the ground.

Towering over him with a look of rage, the big guy pointed the machine pistol in Ben's face. Before he could shoot, Ben lashed out with a prone kick and swept the man's legs out from under him. This time he did go down, and hard, all that bulk raising his centre of gravity to bring him slamming to earth like a sack of concrete.

Then Ben was up on his feet, stamping on the guy's throat and face as he tried to protect himself with his arms. Ben might as well have tried stamping on a tree trunk. Moving back, he snatched up the fallen gun, pointed it, squeezed the trigger – and nothing happened. In the failing light he'd missed what the big guy had missed moments earlier. The gun was empty, the bolt was locked to the rear, the breech open, good for hammering nails and not much else.

In the split second it took Ben to realise it, the big guy had scrambled back to his feet. A normal man would have been crippled by Ben's surprise assault, but if he was hurt he didn't show it. Now the two of them were circling one another beneath the archway. Ben was no dwarf at a shade under six foot, but he had to look up to make eye contact. The monster was at least a foot taller, and two feet wider. With a grin, he bent down and picked up a stone block that probably weighed more than Ben, as though it were made of polystyrene. He raised it to his shoulder and heaved it at Ben like a shot putter.

Ben ducked out of the way of the skull-crushing missile, tripping backwards as the block flew past him and struck the middle of one of the archway columns with a massive thud that left a crater and seemed to rock the whole arch on its shaky foundations. A shower of dust and loose chippings sprinkled from overhead. Ben hurled the empty machine pistol at his opponent. A hefty chunk of steel and aluminium hardware that bounced off his bunched pectorals as though Ben had pinged a pebble at his chest.

The big man bent down to pick up another rock. This time, he wouldn't miss. He raised it high above his head, preparing to hurl it down and crush his enemy like a worm.

But he never got the chance as a ton of crumbling ancient blockwork came crashing down on him and flattened him to the ground. The impact of the hurled rock had finally proved too much for the supporting archway column. After withstanding all the ravages that two and a half millennia could inflict on it, now it gave way and buckled in the middle like a broken knee. The arch collapsed with a roar, burying the man's head and torso under a pile of stone so that only his lower half protruded. His legs gave a couple of twitches, then stopped moving.

Covered in dust, Ben picked himself up and retrieved the empty machine pistol, then the spare magazine protruding from the hip pocket of his half-buried enemy. He quickly searched the rest of the guy's pockets for things like ID, but found nothing. Then he reloaded the gun, scrambled over the pile of stone that had been the archway and peered through the falling dusk.

And what he saw next made his heart skip a beat.

Chapter 23

The big man's companions had got what they'd come for, but Ben realised now that he'd been wrong about their intentions. Their mission wasn't to kill Anna Manzini, and she wasn't dead. The shots he'd heard had been for Kambasis, who most certainly was.

They had Anna and were dragging her in the direction of the van. It was just like Anna Manzini to go walking in winter wearing high-heeled shoes, and she was kicking out with them at her attackers for all she was worth. The victim was proving to be quite a handful, keeping both of them much too busy for them to think about where their large companion had gone. Too busy, also, for either of them to notice Ben walking towards them with their companion's machine pistol in his hand.

Thirty yards away, Ben steadied the weapon over a ruined wall and took aim, but the light was fading fast and he couldn't risk a shot at this range for fear of hitting her by mistake. Then, as he watched, Anna used another weapon on the one who was clutching her arm: her teeth. He let out a howl as she bit his hand, let go of her and staggered back a step.

One step was enough to make him a safe target. Ben centred the glowing red dot of the optical sight on the guy's chest, magnified twice in the reticule. Fired. Saw the dark shape crumple and fall.

Two down. One remaining. Not for long, either.

The third guy saw his comrade go down, and he did what all frightened amateurs do when holding a loaded weapon and coming under fire from unknown, unseen assailants. He grabbed Anna and pinned her against his chest like a human shield, then started blasting off shots in all directions, as though a whole regiment was hiding among the ruins. Next he must have spotted a movement in the semi-darkness as Ben advanced closer, because he aimed the pistol over Anna's shoulder and loosed off two more shots in Ben's direction. He wasn't much of a marksman even when he knew what to shoot at.

But now Ben had a problem, because he couldn't shoot back. If he was going to save her, he had to get in closer. And the closer he got, the easier a target he would become.

He hurdled a low wall, then another, and raced for the nearest cover between them and him: the workshop of Phidias. The pistol cracked three, four, five times and bullets spat off the stonework as Ben darted into the semi-intact building. Keeping his head low he stole a glance through a ragged hole in the wall that had once been a magnificent arched window, just in time to see Anna's kidnapper holster his pistol and unclip something else from his belt.

It wasn't a gun.

The small object sailed through the window, bounced and rolled to a halt near Ben's feet. The quarter of a second he stared at the khaki-painted metal canister before he reacted was all the time he needed to know what it was, or more importantly what it contained. Forty-three grams of TNT and dinitronaphthalene wrapped in a wire shell and aluminium casing that would burst outwards into lethal shrapnel, blowing a crater in the ground and destroying everything within a ten-metre radius, including himself if he didn't move very, very fast.

So he did.

The percussive blast ripped through the air behind him as he dived for a gap in the wall at the rear of the workshop. The explosion lit up the shadows with a bright flash, searing the back of his neck with its heat. The outer wall where the window had been blew outwards, stone blocks crashing down. Ben hit the ground with a painful scrape and instantly rolled back up to his feet, still clutching the gun. Running through the acrid smoke that engulfed the remains of the building he skirted the shattered wall and emerged from the other side. Anna's captor had redrawn his pistol and was pressing it to her head as he hustled her away. By now he must have realised he was on his own, and he was desperate. In one tiny twitch of his trigger finger, he'd blow her brains out even if he didn't intend to.

But not if Ben could get him first.

Ben stepped out of the smoke and said, 'Hey.'

The guy stopped and turned, whirling Anna around with him with the pistol pressed to her temple. The light was fading fast but Ben could see the expression of surprise on his enemy's face. As well as the look of utter amazement in Anna Manzini's dark eyes. Of all the people she might have expected to appear at this moment, Ben Hope must have been the last.

'Is that the best you've got?' Ben said to the guy, jerking a thumb back at the demolished workshop behind him. 'Your boss should have told you, I'm not that easy to get rid of.'

'I'll kill her,' the guy said in Italian.

'Then why haven't you already?' Ben said. 'Like you did the others?'

143

The guy said nothing. He was doing everything he could to shield himself behind his hostage, but she was five-nine in high heels and he was six-one in combat boots, which was making it hard for him to hide. At this range, his head was as big as a pumpkin through Ben's sights and the optical red dot was trained right on the middle of his brow.

'Put the gun down,' Ben told him. 'This isn't going to end well if you don't.'

Confusion flickered in the man's eyes. He ground the muzzle of the pistol against the side of Anna's head, and her face contorted in pain and fear. 'Ben—' she gasped, but the guy clamped his other hand over her mouth and stifled her words.

Ben took a step closer, the weapon unwavering in his grip, the red dot of his sight hovering over his target like a bright crimson drop of blood. He said, 'Let's deal. You do three things for me, in the exact order I tell you, and I'll do something for you. One, lose the weapon. Two, let her go. Three, tell me who sent you. If you do those things, I'll let you walk. Your choice.'

The guy shook his head. Sweat was pouring off his face, even in the chill of the falling winter night. 'If I drop the gun, you'll kill me.'

'Think about it,' Ben said. 'You don't have a lot of choices here. You know as well as I do that if you shoot her, your boss won't be too pleased with you. He must already be pretty pissed off that his paid killers shot the wrong guy when they tried for me, as I'm sure he knows by now. And if he's who I think he is, and if he's half as ruthless as he used to be, he just might decide to gralloch you like a deer if you screw this up as well.'

'He'll kill me if I go back empty-handed,' the guy said.

'You may be right,' Ben said. 'But that's your problem,

not mine. If you want to take my deal, it's a limited time offer. You have three seconds.'

The guy hesitated for two of them. Before the third ticked by, he tossed the gun and let Anna go. She ran to Ben, still staring at him in disbelief.

Her would-be kidnapper now stood alone and helpless.

'Good move,' Ben said to him. 'You just bought yourself some time. You're two-thirds of the way to me letting you walk. Now let's keep it going. Why don't you confirm what I already know, and tell me who sent you?'

'The old man,' the guy said, with a look of terror.

'I'm allergic to vague answers,' Ben said. 'When I hear them, I get this uncontrollable twitch in my right index finger. Let's try that one again, shall we?'

The guy gulped and glanced around him, as if dreading that his boss might hear him give his name away.

'Usberti,' he muttered in a low voice, almost boggle-eyed with fear. Usberti had always had that effect on people.

'Massimiliano Usberti? Just to be clear on this. We're talking about the archbishop.'

The guy nodded. Anna's eyes had filled with horror at the mention of the name. She was too stunned to speak.

'Funny thing is,' Ben said, 'I'd heard he got carved up in a bizarre boating accident. Imagine, the media getting something like that wrong. Have you actually seen him? In person? Spoken to him?'

The guy nodded again, more emphatically.

'Before or since he died?'

'He didn't die. That was all a setup.'

So now there was no more doubt over who was behind all this. Ben demanded, 'Why were you ordered to kidnap this woman? What does Usberti want with her?'

'I only do what I'm told. I promise you, I know nothing.'

'How about your name? Do you know that?'

'Federico Casini.'

'What about your friend there?' Ben asked, waving the gun towards the body of the man he'd shot. 'And the big fellow who's underneath all those rocks?'

Federico Casini gulped. 'Renato Zenatello. The big guy's name is Ennio Scorceletti.'

'All right, Federico. You're just a foot soldier, so I believe you when you say you don't know much. You fulfilled your side of the bargain and I'm letting you walk. Here's what's going to happen next. You're going to go back to your boss and take your chances that he doesn't skin you alive and have you turned inside out. And you're going to deliver a message for me.'

'Message?'

'That's exactly right. You're going to tell Usberti that Ben Hope is coming for him. Tell him there isn't a crack or a hole on this planet where he can hide and I won't find him. And that when I do, I'm going to feed him feet first through a mincer. Slowly, with a glass of chilled champagne in my hand and a string quartet playing a Strauss waltz in the background. Think you can remember that, Federico?'

Casini nodded.

'Then get moving.'

Casini couldn't suppress the grin that spread all over his face. He turned and started walking away through the ruins. Five yards. Ten. Faster and faster, jittery in his step and on the point of bolting.

Anna was clutching at Ben's arm, blinking with shock and confusion. Ben said quietly to her, 'You okay?' and she gave an uncertain nod.

Ben watched Casini hurry away. Observing his body language, and reading his thoughts. This guy knew perfectly well what awaited him if he delivered a message like that to Massimiliano Usberti. Casini was going to run a thousand miles in the opposite direction, go to ground on the far side of the world and never show his face to his employers again. Then new employers would pay him to do more dirty work. And more innocent people would die. Scumbags like Casini just couldn't help but be what they were.

Ben said quietly to Anna, 'Close your eyes.'

'Close my eyes?'

'I don't want you to see this.'

Casini had managed to get some twenty or so paces away when Ben called out, 'Hey, Federico.'

Casini froze and slowly turned back to stare at him.

Ben said, 'I changed my mind. I'll tell him myself.'

Casini's mouth dropped open. The MPX spoke once. Its single report was flat in the cold, damp air. Casini flinched, then dropped to his knees. He put his hands to the bullet wound in his midriff, gaped at the blood leaking through his fingers.

'You . . . you said . . . you'd let me walk,' he croaked.

'And I did let you walk,' Ben said. 'Twenty whole paces. Which I'm betting is more of a sporting chance than you and your cronies gave to my friends Pascal Cambriel and Luc Simon. Not to mention my friend Jeff, who sadly can't be here today. Because I know how much he'd have loved to put this second bullet in you. I'm just going to have to do it for him, and tell him all about it when I get home so we can have a good laugh.' Ben glanced at Anna. 'Anna, you didn't close your eyes.'

She shook her head vehemently, with a defiant set to her jaw. 'I want to see him get what's coming to him. They killed that poor innocent man.'

'Fair enough.' Ben raised the MPX, placed the optical red

dot on Federico Casini's forehead and squeezed the trigger. To the sound of the final gunshot that would be heard among the ruins of Olympia for a very long time, the kneeling figure keeled over backwards, twitched once and lay still.

Anna was trembling. Ben took her hand gently in his and said, 'Let's get away from here.'

Chapter 24

He kept a tight grip on her hand as they hurried away through the ruins of Olympia. For the moment, he ignored the questions she kept firing at him: 'What's happening? What did those men want with me? Why are you here? What are we going to do about Mr Kambasis?' He had plenty of questions of his own to ask her, but talking could wait.

As Ben had anticipated, Usberti's crew had left the keys in the white panel van's ignition for a fast getaway. Its doors were still open and the engine was still warm. It had Greek plates. Probably stolen, or paid for in cash under a false name, like his Opel.

The van had fared better in the firefight than its former occupants, but it hadn't survived Casini's random shooting spree completely unscathed. There was a bullet hole punched through the skin of the front passenger door and another in the flimsy steel of the wing panel, where part of the headlamp was blown away and dangling from its mount like a popped eyeball. Neat, round black holes on white bodywork were a little more conspicuous than Ben would have liked, but there wasn't much he could do about it, and he didn't plan on using the van for long.

Inspecting the back, he found that the cargo bay contained a dirty single mattress and had been hastily, not very neatly, lined with thick building-grade plywood to deaden the screams and thumps of an unwilling passenger. The classic kidnap setup Ben had seen a hundred times.

Up front, there was food and bottled water in a plastic bag, ready for a long drive to wherever they'd been planning on taking her. The interior cab light shone on a small zipper pouch that lay on the dashboard. Inside it, Ben found a hypodermic and a small glass vial. The syringe was loaded with a colourless liquid. Ben pressed the plunger until out a single drop trembled on the end of the needle. He waved it under his nose to get a whiff. No mistaking what it was. Once upon a time, kidnappers used chloroform. Nowadays they'd moved on to more sophisticated stuff.

Anna almost fainted when she saw the needle. '*Dio mio.* They were going to drug me?' Up close, even pale and in shock, she looked radiant. The picture on her website couldn't do justice. The photographer hadn't needed to use Photoshop to iron out the old scar on her cheek. It was already invisible.

'Only for as long as it took to deliver you to their boss,' Ben said, helping her into the cab. He shut her in, then ran around to the driver's side, stashed his bag behind the seat and got behind the wheel.

She said, 'Why would they do that? I don't understand.'

'Nor do I,' Ben replied. 'But I soon will.'

'We have to call the police.'

'They'll be here soon enough, if anyone heard all the noise back there,' he said, firing up the van's engine with a dieselly rasp. 'And they'll want to know all about the Italian lady history professor who travelled to their country to pay a visit to Theo Kambasis and was with him when he got shot to bits. You want to spend the next forty-eight hours in an interrogation room with a bunch of suspicious cops hungry for a murder conviction, not to mention all those angry culture officials who want to know why their best tourist attraction just got blown up?'

'I have nothing to hide. I'm innocent.'

'So was Kambasis. Didn't do him much good.'

Ben bumped the van up onto the road and drove fast through the darkening night, the heater blasting, sticking to the back roads, aiming to put as much distance between themselves and Olympia as possible in the short time they could afford to stay with this vehicle. He couldn't risk returning to the museum to retrieve his car.

'I rented a house,' Anna said. 'Not far from here.'

'Sorry,' Ben replied. 'You can't go back there. Too dangerous.'

'But my travel bag is there,' she protested. 'My laptop, my clothes, my things . . .' She shook her tiny handbag. 'All that's in here is my purse, my passport, some tickets and a hairbrush.'

'It can't be helped, Anna. I'm certain that the person who sent these men after you also would have found out where you were staying locally. That wouldn't be difficult. More of them could be watching the place.'

'How can you be so sure of that?'

'Because it's what I would have done.'

She sighed, then gave a resigned sort of shrug. 'It's only stuff, as they say. Losing my laptop is the worst thing, but its contents are encrypted and all backed up online, so I can retrieve everything easily. Where are we going?'

'Not the Ritz-Carlton. But somewhere safe, where these people can't get to you.'

'Is there really no other choice?'

'None,' he replied.

'Then it's not a dream. This is really happening to me.

I'm frightened, Ben. I don't understand. Why are you here?'

'Let's find a place to stop. Then we'll talk.'

She shook her head. 'I always knew I would see you again. Just not like this.'

'That's me all over,' he replied. 'Always full of surprises.'

Twenty kilometres further south-east, on a deserted, bleak and icy mountain road near the small town of Andritsaina, Ben finally decided to pull up. He turned off the lights and checked in the mirrors.

They were alone. Leaving the engine running to give them warmth, he turned to her and said, 'All right, let's talk. You want to know why I'm here? I tracked you from Florence because your name is on a list of targets, Anna. So is mine.'

'List?' she gasped. 'Why?'

'Because someone from our past, someone we thought we'd never hear from again, is back and he means to do us harm.'

'Usberti? The archbishop?'

'Former archbishop. Thanks to us.'

'I was barely involved.'

'He's not the most forgiving type of person.'

'But what does he want with us?'

'Revenge, pure and simple. We hurt him, now he wants to hurt us back. And he's doing a fine job of it so far. You remember Father Pascal, the old priest from Saint-Jean in the Languedoc who helped us?'

'I never met him. I spoke to him only on the phone, just one time.'

'You won't be speaking to him again. They beat him to death inside his own church.'

'My God.'

'How about Luc Simon, the Parisian police detective in charge of the Gladius Domini case? Promoted to a desk at the INTERPOL HQ in Lyon afterwards. I've been in contact with him now and then over the years. Not any more. He was stabbed to death in his home the same day they murdered Pascal. Not long after someone took a shot at me at my place in Normandy and put my best friend in a coma from which he might never wake up. It's an orchestrated hit, one after another, all over France and Italy. Yesterday they attacked your villa outside Florence, and pressed it out of your assistant Gianni that you'd travelled to Greece to meet Kambasis. I was just a step behind them.'

'Gianni! Is he—?'

'He's in hospital. And lucky to be alive. I'm afraid that your agent, Carlo, wasn't as fortunate. I found him in his office, with his throat cut.'

'I think I'm going to be sick.'

Ben reached into the plastic bag, opened one of the bottles of water left for them by the would-be kidnappers, twisted off the cap and passed it to her. She took a long gulp, passed it back to him with a nod of thanks and then leaned back in the passenger seat with her eyes closed for a moment as she fought her nausea.

'Feeling better?' he asked after a few moments.

'Not really. Not at all. Because what you say means that poor man Theo Kambasis died because of me. I barely knew him, but he seemed so nice. He didn't deserve to die.'

'Nice people don't last very long when Usberti's around.'

'If I hadn't come to meet him – if I hadn't told Gianni I was coming here – but Ben, how could I have *known*?'

'None of us could have known,' Ben told her. 'I wouldn't have had any idea what was happening if Usberti's former assistant, a man called Fabrizio Severini, hadn't written me a letter from jail to warn me that his old boss was back and on the warpath. And until tonight I still had no idea of what was really happening. Because I thought Usberti was planning to kill you, too. But I was wrong. There's something else going on here, Anna. Something about you breaks the pattern. He might have started out with the intention of taking you out just like the rest of us, but he changed that plan. Now he wants you alive. Not out of compassion, or softness, or because you're a woman. I know this man. He doesn't *do* compassion, and he enjoys the hurt that's inflicted on women almost as much as the sadists he hires to do it for him, like your dear departed pal Franco Bozza. If he's decided he wants you taken alive, it's because now he thinks you're worth more to him that way.'

Anna instinctively put her fingers to her cheek, where Franco Bozza's knife had cut her. Scars could heal, but some memories lingered forever. 'What could he want from me? Money?'

'I wondered about that,' Ben said. 'You're successful, you're wealthy. A lot wealthier than someone on an INTERPOL commissioner's salary, let alone a rural priest. But I don't think this is about money.'

'Then what? Who am I? I'm just a writer.'

'You're a little more than just a writer,' Ben said. 'You're a highly regarded scholar with a knack for digging up bits of history that nobody knew before you came along.'

'All the same, why would that make a difference?'

'You tell me,' Ben said. 'Gianni couldn't say much when I spoke to him, because he was all banged up and pumped full of drugs. But I think that when Usberti's goon, that big bruiser back there, turned up at the villa and put the squeeze on him, he told them a lot more. Which you can be certain reached Usberti's ears absolutely verbatim, because the guy was recording every word of it.'

'Poor Gianni. I have to call him, tell him how terrible I feel about what's happened.'

'Not advisable. He'd probably ask where you are, assuming he's well enough to talk at all. And that's not something we want our friends to know, in case they go back to chat with him again.'

She blanched. 'Please tell me you don't really think that. You're just being careful.'

'Being careful is what keeps me breathing air. Chances are they won't, because Usberti's goons already found out all they wanted. Whatever he let slip to them that was so important, it's the only thing that prevented you from becoming just another dead body in Usberti's revenge campaign. I wouldn't have been able to save you, Anna.'

'But you did. And it's not the first time.'

'I'd like it to be the last,' he said. 'That's why I need to understand what's going on here.'

'I have no idea.'

'I think you do,' Ben said. 'You just don't see the connection. It can only be about one thing. Your research.'

'My research?'

'Something big. Really important. That's what Gianni told me you were working on. You didn't just visit Kambasis to talk about Phidias' workshop, did you?'

'Just as well,' she muttered unhappily. 'There's not much left of it to talk about.'

'Then there's more to this.'

'Oh yes,' Anna replied. 'There's much more to it. Just that I can't understand why—' She broke off mid-sentence and her face fell as the realisation hit her. 'Or maybe I do understand.'

'Then tell me.'

'It's complicated,' she said. 'To help you understand what

I've been researching, I'd have to go right back to the beginning and fill in a lot of detail.'

'Then I suggest we find ourselves a place to hole up in for the night,' Ben said. 'Then, you can explain this entire thing to me.'

Chapter 25

The winding mountain road led them down towards Andritsaina, which was little more than a village nestling on the forested slope. Not wanting the van to be seen in case it drew the wrong kind of attention, Ben found a wooded layby a kilometre outside the town. It wasn't the perfect hiding place, but it would have to do. He wiped down the steering wheel, door handles and anything else they might have touched, and then they set off on foot, using Ben's torch to light their way on the dark road.

On a winter's night the village made Olympia seem like a bustling metropolis by comparison. An icy rain began to fall as they made their way through the narrow, almost deserted streets, looking for somewhere to shelter from the cold and get something to eat.

Anna shivered. The Italian designer coat she was wearing scored high on style but was next to worthless as a winter garment. Her legs must be cold, too. The hems of her light-weight trousers were wet and wrinkled and speckled with mud. 'Look at me,' she complained. 'I look like a vagrant. And I can't walk another step in these shoes.'

'I don't know why you do it,' he said, frowning down at her feet. 'I don't mean you personally. Women, in general. Most of them, at any rate, in my experience, which isn't vast.'

'Do what?'

'You're a historian. You ought to know that the history of feminine footwear runs right alongside the history of female oppression. Going all the way back to ancient China a thousand years ago, when they invented foot-binding. Like hobbling slaves by chopping off their toes to stop them from escaping, or rebelling. You might as well be wearing barbed-wire slippers.'

'So shoe design is a male conspiracy?'

'How many top shoe designers are women?'

'I don't know. Some, I would imagine.'

'Then they should know better. They're selling you all out.'

'Women feel the need to be attractive,' she said with a shrug. 'That's why we do it.'

'You'd look fine in a pair of combat boots.'

'You can't be serious.'

'Bin the rest of the designer junk while you're at it, in exchange for something more practical.'

She peered at him, smiling a little. 'Is that what you go for in women, the butch look?'

'Whatever works.'

'Perhaps there's a military surplus store in this town, where I can buy a whole new outfit.'

'Unlikely,' he said.

'More likely than finding any decent kind of accommodation,' she replied. 'This is the kind of place where the hotels open in April and close in October.'

If Ben had been on his own, he'd just as happily have roughed it in the woods with a makeshift bivouac, a fire made of cut branches and a wild rabbit roasting on a skewer for dinner. But Anna Manzini wasn't someone you could easily take camping. 'Let's try there,' he said, pointing as they rounded a corner and saw a bar that was open for business.

Inside, the place was half-empty but warm and welcoming: part hardcore drinking joint, part fast-food grill house, part family restaurant. The owner was a jovial bear of a man named Kris Christakos, who was proudly fluent in English. 'You are the first tourists I have seen for months,' he commented as he brought over a whisky for Ben, red wine for the lady, and took their food order.

Ben explained that they were on their way south towards Messini, but their car had broken down on the mountain road and they'd had to walk all the way here. Was there anywhere in the village they could get a room for the night? Kris beamed and pointed a finger straight up at the ceiling above him. 'We have a couple of rooms to let upstairs. It's not much, but it's better than the mountain. My brother Nick, he drives a taxi and is also a mechanic. In the morning he can take you back to your car and fix it for you.'

'Sounds good,' Ben said with a smile and no intention whatsoever of letting anyone connect them with a stolen kidnap van.

While they were waiting for their meal, he took out his phone. 'Who are you calling?' Anna asked.

'Someone you know,' he replied.

Roberta Ryder and Anna Manzini had met briefly, years earlier, at Anna's villa in the Languedoc during the Gladius Domini affair. It hadn't been a comfortable meeting, with Ben caught in the middle of two otherwise highly rational and intellectual women who, for reasons he never could fathom, were potentially ready to start clawing each other's eyes out over him.

When Roberta's distant voice came on the line, she didn't sound any happier. 'It's me,' he said. 'Are you okay?'

'Oh, I'm having a whale of a time out here in sunny Jerkville, Ontario. There's ten feet of snow outside the window of my shack and I can't sleep at night because of wolves howling. As long as I don't run out of firewood to feed my little stove, I'm just peachy. Any idea when I can go back to my life?'

'Stay tight. I'll call you again soon.'

'That was quick,' Anna commented with a raised eyebrow as he ended the call. Ben didn't reply. He instantly started punching in another number. When a different female voice answered after two rings, he launched straight in. No greeting, just an urgent 'How is he?'

'I'm with him now,' Sandrine Lacombe said. 'Still no change. He's stable, but that's the best I can say.'

Ben took a deep breath and let it out slowly.

Sandrine said, 'You know the police came here again, looking for you?'

'Good luck to them,' Ben said.

'Where are you?'

'You don't want to know,' he replied. 'I have to go, Sandrine. Call me if there's any news about Jeff.'

'You know I will. Take care, okay? Wherever you are.'

'It sounds as if there are a lot of women in your life, as ever,' Anna said with a wry smile as Ben put the phone away. Then, seeing his look, her expression became serious. 'That was about your friend?'

'He still hasn't woken up.'

'I'm so sorry.'

The food arrived a minute later, served by Kris's daughter Talia. Ben hadn't eaten more than a bite since arriving in Greece, and attacked his plate of *paidakia*, which was essentially just grilled chops with potatoes. Anna contented herself with a salad, most of which she just shunted around her plate, picking at just a couple of morsels until she finally gave up. 'I can't eat. I keep thinking about that poor man.'

'Kambasis?'

'Such an interesting person,' she went on, shaking her head, as though the violent sudden death of a less interesting individual could be construed to be a less tragic event. 'Archaeology was in his bl— was in his family. You know his father, Leonidas Kambasis, was the local Greek archaeologist who assisted with the German-led project to excavate the workshop of Phidias in the fifties?'

'It's amazing just how little I know,' said Ben, still waiting to find out a lot of things.

Anna went on, 'In fact, people tend to forget that it was actually the Nazis, not the Greek government, who enabled the first really extensive modern excavation of Olympia, starting in 1936, to mark the opening of Hitler's grand Berlin Olympic Games that year. The Nazi engineers in charge of the excavation project were Emil Kunze and Hans Schleif, who as well as being a classical archaeologist was also an SS Standartenführer. Hitler was passionate about the preservation of the site, regarding his Third Reich as a cultural and aesthetic successor to ancient Greece. The Olympia project became known as the *Führergrabung* or "Führer excavation". There was even a special *Kunstschutz* department within the Wehrmacht responsible for its protection, which issued orders to German soldiers not to urinate on the ruins as it damaged the marble.'

'Too much schnapps in their bloodstream,' Ben said. It was just like Anna to dwell over historical detail at a moment like this, and he had to hold back from pushing her onto more important matters.

'After the war, Emil Kunze returned to oversee the continuing excavations, as though nothing had happened. It was ironic that after three and a half years of Nazi occupation, the execution of a hundred and thirty thousand innocent Greek civilians and the decimation of the population, the Olympia site was completely unscathed.' Anna shook her head sadly. 'And even more ironic that it survived all those terrible times, only to be demolished seventy years later because of us.'

'We didn't demolish all of it,' Ben said. 'Only the bits that were still standing. In another few centuries, who'll know the difference?'

If Anna sensed the attempt at levity, she didn't show it. 'Anyway, you wanted to know why I went to see Kambasis. You were right, Ben. My reason for talking to him was very central to my new research project. Nobody in the world knows more about Phidias than he did, as he inherited his passion for the subject from his father. He was the best person to talk to, in order to find out if it was feasible.'

'If what was feasible?' Ben asked, pouring himself a glass of wine.

'Do you know anything at all about Phidias?'

'No, but I have a feeling you're about to enlighten me.' Ben wanted to add, 'And I wish you would.'

'He was a master sculptor who lived and worked in Olympia two and a half thousand years ago, during the fifth century BC. Phidias was renowned for many great works but his most famous creation was a giant gold and ivory statue of Zeus, which became known as one of the seven wonders of the ancient world. It stood twelve metres in height, a spectacular monument, quite magnificent.'

'It's not in the museum,' Ben said. 'The ceiling's not high enough.'

'It's not in any museum,' Anna replied. 'For a thousand years it remained housed in Olympia's Temple of Zeus,

162

which as you've seen is now completely ruined. Sometime in the fifth century AD, it disappeared from there. Stolen, dismantled, broken up into pieces, nobody knows. What we know of it in modern times comes only from ancient texts and images on old coins. Having inherited his father's fascination for all things related to Phidias and his works, Theo Kambasis made it his life's goal to rediscover the statue's remains, as he was convinced they were still somewhere in the vicinity of the Olympia site. He spent much of his time there, searching for clues, and wrote numerous papers and articles on the subject. That was how I came to learn about him, and why I wanted to talk to him in person.'

Ben was beginning to understand, or at least he was trying to. Chewing a mouthful of *paidakia*, he said, 'So that's what this big new research project is — you're looking for the statue of Zeus?'

Anna shook her head. 'No, that's not my interest.'

'Then what?'

'As I said, what I wanted to discover from Theo Kambasis was whether or not the technology truly existed in the fifth century BC to create an enormous golden statue of that kind. How feasible was it back then, with the facilities available, to create an object so huge out of precious metals?'

Anna shoved her unfinished plate out of the way and leaned eagerly across the table with her hair falling across her face, looking at Ben with a sparkle in her dark brown, almond-shaped eyes. 'You see, before I went any further with this, I needed to know whether the story could be true or not. Now, together with the evidence I've already collated, what Theo Kambasis told me has got me convinced.'

'Convinced about what?' Ben said, now thoroughly confused. 'What evidence? What story?'

'The story of the biggest, most legendary, most fabulous golden statue in all of history,' Anna replied, spreading her arms wide with a flourish. '*That's* what I've been working on for my new book, and I'm certain it exists.'

Chapter 26

'It all begins with the Bible,' Anna said. 'I don't suppose you would be especially familiar with the Bible, Ben?'

He was aware how little she really knew about him, or his past. When they'd first met, he'd been posing as a journalist. She'd soon come to realise he was a little more than that, but he'd never told her many specific details. He smiled. 'I've heard of it, though. Isn't it that book all about God and Jesus and stuff?'

She reddened. 'No need for sarcasm. I just meant—'

'It's okay. It has been a while since I did any of that kind of reading.'

'Then let me explain. We're concerned here with the ancient text that belongs to the *Ketuvim*, or writings, of the *Tanakh*, that is to say the Hebrew Bible. In versions of the Christian Old Testament it's grouped with the Major Prophets and is commonly known as the Book of Daniel. Traditionally it's attributed to Daniel himself, a noble Jew who was a captive exile in the ancient kingdom of Babylon, though most modern scholars now believe the author to be pseudonymous.'

'All right,' Ben said. 'Go on.'

'First, let me fill you in on the background. The kingdom of Babylonia, as you may or may not know, was a powerful and enduring historic empire that occupied part of ancient Mesopotamia, in what nowadays covers much of Iraq, Kuwait, Syria, and extends into Iran and Turkey. Babylon's origins date all the way back to the Bronze Age, and it was ruled over by a long succession of dynasties over the course of many centuries. Perhaps its most famous, or infamous, ruler was Nebuchadnezzar the Second, who took the throne in 605 BC. He was an aggressive and ruthless empire builder who reconstructed the ancient capital and sought to extend his kingdom's influence far and wide. At the height of Babylon's glory under his reign, the city was said to have covered an enormous area, bigger than modern-day London. Inside its giant walls, which according to the historian Herodotus were some sixty metres high with huge brass gates and watchtowers all around, were magnificent royal palaces and gardens, even a grand observatory where the Babylonian astrologers made their celestial observations.'

Ben drank more wine.

Anna went on, 'Nebuchadnezzar's foreign policy was just as ambitious. He crushed and swallowed up many smaller kingdoms, waged war against the Egyptians, and also attacked Israel where he succeeded in taking Jerusalem, sacked the Temple of Solomon and deported much of the city's population to Babylon. The Book of Daniel relates the story of three young Hebrew prisoners whom Nebuchadnezzar's soldiers had captured and brought back as slaves. Their names were Hananiah, Mishael and Azariah.'

'Better known as Shadrach, Meshach and Abednego,' Ben said.

Anna looked at him in surprise. 'Yes, those were the names given to them by their captors, to facilitate their integration into Babylonian culture. But how do you—?'

'I studied theology, in another life. That's why I said my Bible knowledge might be a little rusty. Once upon a time, I could have quoted you chapter and verse.'

He might as well have told her he was from the planet Zog. She stared at him in amazement. 'No.'

'Told you, I'm full of surprises,' he said. 'In fact there was a time when that was going to *be* my life. The church. Reverend Ben Hope, living in an ivied vicarage with a bored wife, two kids, an estate car and a yellow dog. Can't you see it?'

'I had no idea. I would never have taken you for a religious person.'

'Who said I was?'

'You don't believe?'

'Probably not, any more.'

'But you did, once. Nobody would seek a career in the church if they didn't believe in God.'

'That was a long time ago, Anna.'

'And yet, you haven't forgotten the Bible.'

'Not all of it,' he said. 'As I recall, the story from Daniel, Chapters two and three, goes something like this: in the second year of King Neb's reign, he was said to have dreamed of a massive statue made of precious metals. The dream inspired him to create a huge golden idol, which he had erected in the Plain of Dura, and commanded that everyone should bow down to it. When the three Hebrew captives Shadrach, Meshach and Abednego refused on the grounds that they worshipped only their one true God, in his kindly way the king ordered them to be thrown into a superheated furnace, supposed to have been seven times hotter than normal fire.'

'Impressive, so far,' Anna said.

'But God sent an angel to protect His faithful, and they

escaped completely unburned from the flames, which impressed King Neb so greatly that he bestowed all kinds of honours on them and decreed that anyone who spoke out against God in future would be torn limb from limb. Probably the all-time fastest conversion to Christianity recorded in the Bible, though Nebuchadnezzar wasn't famous for his consistency.'

'Bravo. You know the story very well.'

'Let's call it what it is,' Ben said. 'A myth. I'm no archaeologist but even I know that no real-life trace of Nebuchadnezzar's golden idol has ever been found. Surely you don't believe any of it is true?'

'That's not the attitude I'd have expected from a theologian.'

'Maybe I'm not famous for my consistency either,' Ben said.

Anna shrugged. 'Legend, myth, call it what you want. Of course, these things are subject to all kinds of possible interpretation, and scholars have picked it all apart for so long that nobody knows what to believe any longer. But interpretation aside, what if there were a core of truth to the story?'

'You mean, what if there really had been a golden idol, just like the golden statue of Zeus that Theo Kambasis spent his life looking for?'

Anna said, 'Well, yes, why shouldn't there have been? Is it so improbable? I mean, if it's possible to accept for a fact that Phidias' Zeus existed, then how justifiable is it simply to dismiss the Babylon idol as pure fiction? They both date from roughly the same time period, give or take a century or so. The technology of the time may have been crude in many respects, but those ancient cultures were nonetheless capable of incredible feats of artistic and engineering ingenuity. Take another of Phidias' lost works, for instance, the colossal gold and ivory statue of the goddess Athena that once stood in the Parthenon in Athens. There's a reproduction of her in Centennial Park, Nashville, Tennessee. At thirteen metres in height, it's the largest indoor sculpture in the Western world. I went there just to stand next to it and get a sense of the size of the thing. It was mind-blowing. Now imagine the sheer mass of a statue which, if the Biblical account of Nebuchadnezzar's idol is accurate, measured—'

'Sixty cubits high by six cubits wide,' Ben finished for her. 'Or so the legend tells.'

'That's *twenty-seven metres* in height, more than double the size of Phidias' colossal Athena, as tall as a nine-storey building.'

'Hard to hide something that big,' Ben said. 'You'd have thought they would have dug it up by now, if it existed at all.'

'It's more than just conjecture,' she said firmly. 'I take my research very seriously, evaluate the evidence as objectively as a scientist and jump to no conclusions without proof.'

'You're telling me you have proof?'

'I'm working on it. There are a lot of challenges involved in trying to shed light on what was really a very hectic and crazy time in Babylon's history. When Nebuchadnezzar died and his rule passed to his son Amel-Marduk in 562 BC, the new king reigned only a short time, giving way to a succession of weak rulers who paved the way for Babylon's fall just twenty-three years later, in 539 BC, to the Persian king Cyrus the Great, leader of the Achaenimid Empire, the biggest empire in the ancient world, which then assimilated Babylon. Somewhere in the middle of all these turbulent changes, the fabled golden idol vanished – as you say, without a trace.'

'There you have it,' Ben said. 'End of story.'

'Not quite,' Anna said.

Chapter 27

'I know you don't believe me,' Anna said. 'That's your privilege. But a good researcher never accepts defeat so easily, and we don't like mysteries getting the better of us. So, as ever, we begin our hunt by going to the records. Thankfully, even though it was so long ago, that period of Babylonian history is very well documented. Since the nineteenth century archaeologists have uncovered thousands of business documents in Babylonia, written on clay tablets in the Akkadian language. Any trading business of any importance would have teams of scribes employed to chisel away all day long at flat sheets of stone, just like secretarial staff typing notes. These ancient records are typically found in large collections relating to the business transactions of a single extended family, often covering several generations' worth of accounts. Loans, mortgages, contracts, receipts, everything, together with dates of when those transactions were made or agreements struck.'

'I get it,' Ben said. 'Nothing changes. People in history were just the same as people today.'

'Which is exactly what my book was originally going to be about,' Anna explained. 'A new angle on those ancient times, exploring the human hearts and minds beneath the dust of history, revealing who these people really were,

171

bringing them to life for today's reader. At least, that was the idea I was working on to begin with. To that end I spent two months of last year in Iraq, in the city of Hillah, south of Baghdad, adjacent to the site of ancient Babylon itself. The area has been something of a war zone in modern times.'

'Just a little bit,' Ben said, with a thin smile.

'But since 2009 the provincial government of Babil has reopened the ancient site to tourism, and archaeologists and cultural organisations were able to resume the restoration efforts that had long been impossible thanks to political and military upheavals. I spent my time working with a team of dig volunteers from all over the world, supervised by a Turkish archaeologist and specialist in ancient languages. It was very physical and exhausting work.'

Now it was Ben's turn to be surprised, at the idea of the refined, elegant and ever-polished Anna Manzini getting stuck into the grinding heat and dust of a Middle East archaeological excavation, shovel in hand, knee-deep in sand and rock, sweating under the blaze of the same Iraqi sun that had scorched him and his SAS comrades so mercilessly, back in the day.

'But so rewarding,' Anna continued. 'Especially when we uncovered a hitherto-unknown store of ancient Babylonian clay tablets that had lain buried for over two thousand years under the sand. It was when we began to catalogue them and the translation work got underway that I first realised the implications of what we had discovered. Until then, so little had been known about the Muranu family.'

'The who?'

'The Muranus were a merchant dynasty who were active from around 600 BC right through until the fall of Babylon to the Persians. Thanks to this discovery, it's been possible to piece together a great deal of detail about their business affairs. They made their start as rural food merchants, going out into the countryside to buy supplies such as grain, dates, onions and so on, then selling the goods in the city. From such humble beginnings they might never have flourished, but this was a golden age for Babylon, when the economy was booming, the city expanding, fortunes were being made and the spirit of the times was highly optimistic. When King Nebuchadnezzar drafted in thousands of workers to man the construction sites for ambitious new projects like the Ishtar Gate and the famous Hanging Gardens, the Muranu family saw an opening and became caterers to the armies of labourers. The profits they made from feeding the workforce they reinvested into farmland and urban real estate, allowing them to diversify still further by going into manufacturing. As they grew wealthier they also became important moneylenders, making loans of silver for interest rates of as much as twenty per cent a year. The daughters of the Muranu clan married other important businessmen and city officials, so that they gradually worked their way into the highest echelons of the state. Thanks to these connections they received tax breaks, as well as access to state-owned ships and river ports on the Euphrates, on whose banks the city of Babylon was built. The Euphrates runs all through Syria and Iraq and joins up with the Tigris near Basra, becoming the great Shatt-al-Arab River before it empties into the Persian Gulf.'

'I know where the Euphrates is,' Ben said.

Anna replied, 'Then you can appreciate how such a trading route allowed the Muranu family to become even richer, by distributing all kinds of goods throughout the region. Now, as I said, we know a lot about the Muranus from the cache of clay tablets that were found. But one tablet is of particular

173

interest. It dates from 539 BC, which of course was a significant year in Babylon's history.'

'Refresh my memory.'

'By then, Babylon was in terrible disarray politically, economically and militarily. It had been just twenty-three years since the death of King Nebuchadnezzar, who for all his faults was an effective ruler, made the kingdom strong and was adored by the mercantile class. Since his son Amel-Marduk took power in 562, the Muranu family had been watching anxiously as the economy began to slowly unravel under a succession of bad rulers, none of whom lasted very long.'

'Sounds like present-day Europe,' Ben said, swallowing the last of his wine.

'You said it,' Anna chuckled. 'What changes?'

At that point, Talia came to collect their dishes. Ben asked if he could have another bottle of wine, which she brought a moment later. Anna declined a refill of her glass. As Ben got to work on the fresh bottle, she went on:

'But things reached a low point with the rise to the throne of King Nabonidus after his predecessor, the child king Labashi-Marduk, was murdered just months after his inauguration. Nabonidus was a lousy king, almost universally disliked, especially as he spent much of his seventeen-year reign absent from the kingdom, in self-imposed exile in the oasis area of Tayma in present-day Saudi Arabia, having little to do with his kingdom and leaving everything in the control of his son and coregent Belshazzar.'

'Belshazzar, as in, Belshazzar's feast and the writing on the wall in blood,' Ben interjected. 'Daniel, Chapter five.'

Anna nodded. 'The same. Nabonidus' neglect of Babylonian affairs was much resented by the general public, the priesthood, and of course the merchant families. They were right to be anxious, because all the while King Cyrus of Persia was growing ever stronger and his shadow hung over Babylon. Invasion and war were coming, and the elite knew it. There was talk of evacuation, as many people were convinced that the Persians would enslave or execute the entire population of the city. Belshazzar, a strong warrior but a worthless politician, began to panic. Babylon's gold reserves were at a critical low and he desperately needed to raise money to fight off the threat of the Persians.'

'War is an expensive business, right enough,' Ben said. 'Always was, always will be. But what's so important about this one clay tablet you mentioned?'

'It's important because it's one of the very last records from ancient Babylon, prior to the Persian invasion of 539,' Anna said. 'Not just one of the last surviving records; one of the *actual* very last due to its date. And also because it's so unusual in itself. It's a legal document, an official contract agreement between Belshazzar and the Muranu family. Unfortunately, it was too damaged to decipher fully, as it was excavated in pieces with several fragments missing that made it impossible to know exactly what the contract specified. We know only that the merchant family were being asked to broker some extremely valuable item from the state treasury, making use of their established civilian transport infrastructure in a way that didn't tie up limited military resources.'

'But we don't know what valuable item,' Ben said.

'It's not spelled out, but other tablets found with it fill in certain gaps. They describe, in detail, the plans for loading an important and very large item of cargo, to be transported away by boat. The record even shows how many extra slaves had to be taken on to complete the loading, as well as the large number of armed guards hired to protect the cargo en

175

route. Belshazzar presumably couldn't afford to offer them a proper military escort as he needed every last soldier available to man the defences of the city.'

'I understand. You're suggesting that this cargo was Nebuchadnezzar's golden statue, being sold to raise defence funds?'

Anna shrugged. 'It wouldn't be the first time that a troubled state had to sell off its treasures in times of crisis. Here we are in modern-day Greece, where not too long ago the government were talking about selling off national monuments such as the Acropolis to shore up the crippled economy.'

'Next thing we'll know, the Chinese will be buying it and carting it off to Beijing, stone by stone,' Ben said. 'But the problem with your idea is that no ship at that time would have been able to carry something as massive as a gold statue close on thirty metres in length. It would have sunk before it made it halfway down the Euphrates.'

'This is why I wanted to speak to Theo Kambasis,' Anna replied. 'Because I, like you, found it hard to believe that you could just pick up such an object and transport it about. The task would be impossible, even with thousands of slave labourers at one's disposal. Aside from the problem of finding a ship big enough to carry it, a pure gold statue of that size would be so heavy that it would tend to collapse on itself the moment it was moved. As a metal, gold is extremely dense but comparatively soft, with low tensile strength. Not to mention the fact that it's very unlikely that enough gold even existed in Babylonia at that time, or even in the world, to fill a mould so large. Only about a hundred and eighty-five thousand tons of gold have been mined in the whole of human history. I pondered all these problems, until I hit on a new theory. One that Kambasis confirmed just a few minutes before he died, that poor man.'

'Which was?'

'That Nebuchadnezzar's idol could have been created the same way as the colossal statues of Phidias were made during the same era, such as his giant Athena. It's been estimated that the quantity of gold in the original Athena would have amounted to forty-four talents' worth. That's about eleven hundred kilograms, a substantial proportion of the gold reserve of the treasury of Athens but still much lighter than if the statue had been cast solid. What enabled Athena to be transported all the way from Phidias' workshop in Olympia to the Parthenon was that the builders used a brilliantly inventive modular technique, attaching separate plates to an internal core sculpted out of wood. The method makes it possible to create much larger monuments, which from the outside *appear* to be solid gold, sometimes combined with ivory and other precious materials. The parts could then be shipped to any destination and assembled there. The modular structure also enabled any section of the statue to be removed and repaired, in case of damage.' Anna's eyes sparkled with excitement. 'Do you see? If the Babylon idol had been created the same way, it could easily have been dismantled for transportation to its new owner.'

'Piece by piece,' Ben said. 'Like the Acropolis going to Beijing. Makes sense. But there are too many ifs and buts. What you're saying is only supposition.'

'Wrong,' Anna said firmly, fixing him with a serious look. 'The circumstantial evidence is strong enough to be taken seriously. Because the same clay tablet shipping records specifically mention not just one item of cargo, but many large pieces, all wrapped up and packaged aboard an entire small fleet of merchant vessels, which set sail from Babylon's river port in early October 539 BC. We even have a kind of passenger manifest, listing the names of all the important Muranu family members who accompanied their precious cargo down the Euphrates as they fled the coming war. We know, for instance, that one of the passengers was a young Muranu boy named Ashar, who according to the family birth records listed on other clay tablets was around eight years of age at the time.'

'All you need now is a buyer's receipt, so you know where the idol ended up.'

'Sadly, that's something we're missing. No further transactions were recorded, for the reason that events unfolded so quickly afterwards. Belshazzar's plan had come too late to rescue Babylon from the mobilising Persian army. Just days after the ships sailed, Cyrus the Great's forces swept in and invaded the city. The Book of Daniel describes how Babylon fell in a single night. Nabonidus fled but was soon caught. His fate is uncertain: it's very possible that Cyrus had him executed by burning, his favourite method of punishment, though some historians have believed Nabonidus was spared and allowed to live in exile, in what is now Kerman Province in modern-day Iran. We do know for certain that Belshazzar was killed in the defence of Babylon, during what little fighting took place against the massively superior Persian army. And with his death and the collapse of the state, the contract between him and the Muranu family was effectively rendered null and void, along with the need to sell the idol to raise money for the war effort.'

'So the question is,' Ben said, 'what happened to the idol?'

Anna nodded pensively. 'I ask myself, if I had been an elder of the Muranu family, fleeing with our children to a new life in exile far away from our beloved Babylon and probably leaving behind much, if not all, of our worldly wealth, what would I have wanted to do with it? Sell it to restore our fortunes? Melt down the vast quantity of gold into ingots or coins, or smaller statues that we could trade? Or would we perhaps have chosen to keep it for ourselves, passing it down from generation to generation in whatever new place we had made our home, preserved in its original state, in honour of a king we believed to have been the last great ruler of their land, and to commemorate the Babylon that once had been? I like to think that's what I would have done, and what they did.'

'Then they'd have had to hide it pretty well,' Ben said. 'You couldn't leave a ninety-foot golden statue sitting in your backyard and not expect it to draw attention.'

Anna heaved a sigh. 'Who knows what became of it? But one thing's for sure. If just one surviving fragment of the idol could be rediscovered and verified, what an incredible find that would be.'

'Another thing's for sure, too,' Ben said. 'Whether this theory of yours is right or wrong, either way we're beginning to understand why Usberti ordered his men to take you alive. Whatever Gianni told him about what you're searching for, it wouldn't take much for Usberti to suss out the rest. He knows the Bible better than most people.'

'That would make sense, given his former profession,' Anna said.

'And he also lusts after gold more than anyone. When I say he's obsessed with it, I'm not joking. He believes that the Nazis were using some kind of alchemy to create gold bars out of base metals, and he tried to do the same. I guess that didn't work out for him, and now he wants to get his hands on as much of the real thing as he can. He also has a long history of kidnapping people he thinks can help him achieve his goals. That would be you, Anna. He wants you to lead him to the Babylon idol.'

'And if he gets it, he'll kill me,' she said with a shiver. 'It's the only thing keeping me alive.'

'Not the only thing,' Ben said. 'I'm here.'

Chapter 28

While they'd been talking, too deep in conversation to notice much of what was happening around them, the restaurant had gradually emptied at the same rate as Ben's second bottle of wine. Now Talia was dropping hints by turning off lights and hovering in the background with her arms folded.

'I think someone's trying to tell us something,' Ben said, rising from his chair and picking up his bag, which had been nestling at his feet all through dinner. It wasn't the first time he'd eaten in a restaurant with a loaded automatic weapon concealed among his personal effects.

Talia led them up a bare wooden staircase and showed them the two upstairs rooms for let, of which they could have their pick. Kris and the family lived on the floor above. 'We'll take both rooms,' Ben said, explaining to the surprised Talia that they liked to spread out. Talia shrugged, as if to say, 'It's your money.'

'All our luggage is in the car,' Anna told her. 'I have nothing to sleep in. Do you think—?'

Talia said she would ask her mother if Anna could borrow something to wear. She disappeared for a few moments, then returned with a pair of well-worn pyjamas several sizes too large for Anna, and a woolly dressing gown. Anna thanked her. Talia smiled and left them alone.

'Good night, Ben,' Anna whispered at her door.

'Good night, Anna. Try and get some rest.'

Ben's room was the smaller of the two, and had an even smaller balcony overlooking the village street. He was dog tired and aching from the day's exertions, but the wine had done little to relax him and he stood out in the cold for a while, smoking and gazing over the rooftops at the starry sky, now that the rain had stopped and the night had cleared. He had to keep fighting the urge to call Sandrine again, even though he knew she'd phone him if there were any changes in Jeff's condition. Maybe he just wanted to hear her voice, he thought. He didn't want to dwell too much on the reason why that might be, and lit another Gauloise to empty his mind.

But it would take more than the effects of a few micrograms of nicotine from a strong, unfiltered cigarette to still his thoughts to some Zen-like state of emptiness. He was thinking about the two Croatian soldiers he'd seen blown up while sweeping for mines in the Bosnian war. One had lost three limbs, the other had been disembowelled; yet the blast hadn't killed them and they'd lain in the dirt for an hour, pleading and screaming for someone to come and put them out of their misery. A memory that had always stayed with him; just the way it had been for Jeff Dekker, after the similar things he'd witnessed in his time with the SBS.

That was why, one night, a long time ago, over a chessboard and a bottle of scotch, Jeff had said to him: 'Mate, if anything like that ever happened to me, I'd rather eat a bullet than spend the rest of my days sucking baby food out of a tube, know what I mean?' By the time they'd reached the end of the bottle, they'd made a pact whereby, worst-case scenario, each could rely on the other *taking care of it* for him.

And that, in turn, was why Ben had already decided that, if Jeff didn't wake up after six months, or a year, then he, Ben, was going to do the right thing by his friend. It would be quick, and quiet, and merciful.

It would be what friends did. They didn't call it 'taking care' for nothing.

Ben was still deep in his thoughts when he heard the creak of his door slowly opening, and turned to peer through the darkness of the room at the figure stepping inside.

'I can't sleep,' Anna said softly, stepping past the single bed and into the light of the window. She was wearing the borrowed pyjamas and the dressing gown, topped off by a patchwork quilt from her bed draped around her shoulders. 'Cold in here,' she whispered.

'I'll close the window.'

They sat side by side on the edge of the bed. Anna moved close to him. For the warmth, he assumed.

'Ben?'

'Hmm?'

'All this talking, and there's one thing I never said to you.'

'What's that?'

'To thank you, Ben. Every time you come into my life, you save it.'

'A man has to make himself useful somehow,' he replied.

'Don't joke. I can't even begin to imagine where I'd be now, if you hadn't done what you did.'

'I'm sorry you had to witness what happened back there,' he said. 'I'm sorry for a lot of things.'

'You've nothing to be sorry about,' she whispered. A pause. Then: 'You know, I always hoped you would show up again one day. Years have gone by, life has gone on the way it has, but I often thought about you. I tried to imagine where you were, what you might be doing.'

'There's not much to tell,' he lied.

'And I've often pictured your face. It hasn't changed. Perhaps a little wiser, a little more rugged.'

'That's a kind way of putting it,' he said.

'And sadder, too,' she said. 'I can see that in your eyes. Has life been unhappy for you, Ben? Do you have love? Are you lonely?'

He said nothing.

She moved closer again, her shoulder pressing against his, and he realised she was about to kiss him on the lips. As gently as he could, he avoided the kiss and pushed her back.

'Why?' he said, because he didn't know what else to say.

'To thank you. And because . . . I . . .' Her words trailed off. She rested her hand on his thigh. Her eyes were shining in the starlight from the window and her breath had quickened. He could feel its warmth on his cheek. The quilt slipped off her shoulders.

He laid his hand on top of hers, and squeezed it affectionately. 'I don't need that kind of thanks, Anna. But I appreciate the sentiment.'

'Isn't it what you want?' she murmured, backing off from him. 'You don't like me?'

'Let's not complicate things,' he replied softly. 'You and I are going to be together for a while until we get this business sorted out.'

She paused. The moment had passed, the tension easing. 'I had assumed you'd be going home.'

He shook his head. 'I can't leave you, Anna. Not while Usberti's still out there. Tomorrow, we head back to Italy, where I'm going to make sure you're safe. But I won't be far away, I promise.'

'I'm not going back to Italy, Ben.'

'What are you talking about?'

'Not yet. Greece was only a stop on my journey. From here I plan on travelling to Turkey. I have to meet a man in Ankara.'

'What man?'

'Ercan Kavur. I told you about him. The archaeologist who supervised the excavation of the clay tablets. He's one of the few people in the world who can read the ancient Akkadian language in all its Assyrian, Babylonian, Mariotic and Tell Beydar dialects. He's been working on piecing together the damaged tablet we found, with a view to deciphering its meaning.'

'He has it? I'm surprised the Iraqi Ministry of Culture let him take something like that home to Turkey with him.'

'Technically, it would be the State Board for Antiquities and Heritage,' Anna said with a crooked smile. 'But the thing is, you see, we didn't exactly tell them everything we found. I mean, once we began to realise how important it could be, how could I live with myself knowing it was languishing in a packing crate in some government storehouse where it might never be seen again? You hear all kinds of stories of precious items going missing, or being sold off to illegal traders. So Ercan took the pieces of the tablet home to work on. Such a long time went by, and I heard nothing from him. Then just a few days ago, when I had already arranged to see Theo Kambasis, he called to say there had been some developments in his research. He told me that he was running into difficulties with the tablet fragments, which were too badly damaged to decipher.'

'So the tablet was no use after all?'

'Apparently not. I was very disappointed to hear it, but I could sense from Ercan's voice that he was tremendously excited about something. That was when he told me he'd made another related discovery, something hugely important, that he needed to tell me urgently.'

'And?'

Anna shrugged. 'And that's all I know. He wouldn't say, except face to face.'

'Why not?'

'Ercan is very cautious. He doesn't like to talk more by phone than is strictly necessary. He's always worried that someone might be listening in.'

One of those, Ben thought. 'Fair enough. What happened to email or Skype?'

'You don't understand. Ercan is . . . well, he's Ercan. He makes a virtue of mistrusting the modern world, and most people for that matter. If you want to see him, you have to go to him in person. He believes that all modern communications are monitored by hidden powers, and will have as little as possible to do with that kind of technology. That's just the way he is. You have to accept it. And so, it seemed the logical thing to do to extend my journey to see both of them – first Theo Kambasis in Olympia, then on to visit Ercan.'

'But all the way to Ankara, just to talk to one man?'

'For Ercan Kavur to speak even just a few words by phone, it must mean he has something genuinely urgent and important to say,' she insisted.

Ben wasn't liking any of this one bit. 'Tell me one thing, Anna. Did Gianni know about this meeting in Ankara, like he knew about your trip to see Kambasis?'

'Yes, of course. Gianni booked all my travel tickets, so he knows my whole itinerary. My plan was to take the train back to Athens and—'

'Do I need to tell you why this makes travelling to Turkey a really bad idea?' he said, interrupting her. 'We can't afford to assume they didn't press that information out of him too.'

'Olympia is a small town,' she protested. 'Anyone could have found poor Mr Kambasis there. But Ercan is a completely different case. A virtual recluse, with few friends, no family, social life or regular employment, living on the margin of society in a city of over four million inhabitants. Unless you knew his exact address, which Gianni doesn't, you could never find him.'

'My interest here is in keeping you safe,' Ben said.

'Please, Ben. I know it's asking a lot. But I really need you to come with me to Turkey. I can't do this alone, with all that's happening. It's so important to me.'

'I can't stop you going. And I told you I wouldn't leave your side until this is over. I meant what I said.'

'Then you'll come? We'll travel to Turkey together?'

He nodded reluctantly. 'But not by the same route you planned. We'll travel by road instead of train, leaving first thing in the morning.'

'Thank you, Ben. You make me feel safe. I've never been so frightened in my life.'

'Usberti won't hurt you,' Ben said. 'That's a promise.'

A promise which, if he'd known what lay in store, he would never have made.

Chapter 29

Not many dead men lived in such comfort as Massimiliano Usberti. What his new home lacked in scale and opulence compared to his Lake Como estate, it more than made up for in seclusion and privacy. The balcony of his top-floor living room commanded a sweeping view like that from the bridge of a ship, from which you could gaze westwards across five miles of the Ionian Sea towards the distant medieval Sicilian coastal town of Taormina, with the shadow of Mount Etna looming behind; while to the north, on a clear day you could just make out the southernmost tip of Calabria, the toe of Italy.

Very little boat traffic came within pistol shot of Usberti's island even in summer, mainly because there was nothing there except a couple of acres of trees, a rocky cove and a single three-storey house perched on its highest point, surrounded by a few stone outbuildings. Now that winter had come, the fishing ports were quiet and the leisure boating season was over, nobody ventured out this way at all and the only living souls Usberti saw were the members of his retinue. Silvano Bellini, his personal assistant, lived in a basic but comfortable converted cottage adjoining the main house that he shared with his colleague Pierangelo Volpicelli. The remainder of the entourage were content to occupy the rougher outbuildings, as befitted their status as soldiers of the down-but-not-out Gladius Domini.

On a day like today, with gusts buffeting the windows, it was too cold to go outside, and Massimiliano Usberti stood instead at the broad balcony window gazing thoughtfully at the grey sea with his hands clasped behind his back. The 'Agnus Dei' from Monteverdi's *Vespers of 1610* played softly in the background, filling the large room with beatific sounds of reverence that elevated his soul.

Usberti was a far more contented man these days. He was looking and feeling better, stronger and sharper. He'd regained some of the weight he'd lost through the dark times, and felt fired up with a renewed and invigorating sense of purpose. In fact, as he liked to joke to himself, he'd never before felt as fit and healthy as he had since his death.

Hearing the door open, he turned to see Silvano Bellini enter the room. The younger priest had nobody to whom to preach God's word these days, but he still wore the long black vestments and the silver crucifix. He was a slim, tall man, dark-haired and intense, with sharp pallid features that made him look like an alabaster hawk. Unfortunately for Bellini, the deity he venerated hadn't blessed him in the genetics department. He wore spectacles as thick as bottle bottoms to correct his terrible astigmatism, and he walked with a permanent lurch in his step as a result of severe scoliosis, which got worse when he was nervous. His had never been a relaxed personality, but at this moment he seemed more agitated than usual as he limped about the room, looking anxiously at his watch.

'What are you worried about, Silvano?' Usberti asked him.

'Scorceletti, Zenatello and Casini should have reported back from Olympia long before now,' Bellini replied anxiously. 'The other two are on their way back here as we speak, and should arrive any minute. But not a word from the rest. Where are they? What's happened to them?'

'Do not fret, Silvano. If we have heard nothing, it is because the idiots have failed in their mission to capture the Manzini woman, and all three are dead. I cannot say I am entirely surprised. In fact, I had foreseen it. They are not coming back.' He smiled. 'All the better for them. Had any of them survived to return to me empty-handed, I would have had them impaled on spikes by way of punishment for their incompetence.'

Bellini stopped limping and stared at him, turning even paler behind his thick glasses. 'Dead? How can you be so sure, Your Excellency?' Despite the fact that his master had been defrocked before they'd even met, Bellini still addressed him by his former ecclesiastical title. Usberti would have preferred 'Your Holiness', but you couldn't have everything.

'I told you, Silvano. You have not had dealings with this Ben Hope, as I have. He is as difficult to eradicate as a spreading tumour, and he has long been in the habit of eliminating even the most proficient men I have sent to deal with him. The truth is that Scorceletti and his associates would have been lucky indeed to get the better of Hope. But finding men suited to the task is not an easy prospect.'

'Then it's a disaster. What are we going to do?' Bellini hesitated, watching his employer. 'Forgive me for saying so, Excellency, but you don't seem unduly perturbed by this development.'

Usberti smiled again. He walked over to the rococo cabinet by the window and opened its ornate doors to reveal a row of crystalware. Taking out a decanter and a glass, he said, 'Would you care for a small cognac, Silvano? It might settle your nerves.'

'No, thank you, Excellency. It's bad for my ulcer.'

'Shame,' Usberti said without much trace of sympathy. He poured himself a drink and relished a sip. On top of the cabinet rested an oblong object wrapped in damask silk. Setting down his glass, he picked up the heavy item, slipped the silk covering away and held up the glinting gold bar to gaze at it in the pale sunlight from the window. He caressed its smooth length, his fingers lingering over the tiny eagle and swastika stamped on its surface. At one time, he'd been the proud owner of a number of genuine Nazi gold bars just like it, but this was the last one remaining in his collection. He often admired it, reminiscing about the period in his life when he'd aspired to master the ancient alchemical secrets learned by Rudolf Hess in Paris in the 1920s and passed to Hitler's inner circle. Usberti believed to this day that he'd come very close to attaining that incredible wisdom for himself, which would have enabled him to produce an infinite quantity of pure gold bars bearing not the Nazi emblem but the cruciform sword symbol of Gladius Domini.

Now, he no longer needed to dream about a mountain of gold. It would soon be within his reach once again, only this time in a different and unexpected form. The fabled golden idol of Babylon would be his.

Not for the first time, Usberti reflected that if that hulking imbecile Ennio Scorceletti had ever done one worthwhile thing in his life it was to have extracted from Manzini's assistant the truth about what the bitch was up to. Usberti had read her books, followed her work, and for all he wanted her dead he had to concede she was a scholar of the first quality. If anyone could trace the whereabouts of such an unbelievable lost treasure, it was her.

Oh, he would possess it, all right. Whatever it took to get it. And now, he had just the man to help him.

Usberti replaced the gold bar in its silk wrapping on the cabinet and turned to Bellini. 'You are right, Silvano. The loss of a few insignificant goons like Scorceletti, Casini and Zenatello does not bother me in the least. Forget such small fry. We are ready to move to the next phase.'

'What do you mean, Excellency?'

'I would like you to meet someone.'

Usberti went over to a desk and pressed the button on a small intercom console that connected him with the office on the lower floor. 'Pierangelo, you may show our new recruit upstairs.'

Bellini raised his eyebrows. 'This is the first I've heard of a new recruit.'

'He arrived this morning, while you were at prayer. If I did not mention him to you before now, it is because of the great difficulty I have had in locating and contacting him. Now I have found him, he will be a decisive new asset to our cause.'

'Who is he?'

Before Usberti could reply, there were footsteps outside the room, followed by a knock. The door opened. Pierangelo Volpicelli, Usberti's chief administrator and gofer, stood there with another man who was dressed all in black.

'Thank you, Pierangelo. You may leave now,' Usberti said. Volpicelli walked off without a word. Usberti ushered the man in black inside the room. There was no greeting.

Silvano Bellini cautiously eyed the newcomer. Had the priest's vocabulary included such vernacular expressions, he might have described the man as a 'badass'. He wasn't tall, and he wasn't obviously muscular, and yet everything about him exuded a quiet menace. His shaven head gleamed from the razor. A black goatee adorned a jaw as thick and heavy as a Rottweiler's. He stood relaxed with his hands loosely curled at his sides, but Bellini sensed that the man could explode into violence in the twitch of a heartbeat.

He didn't like him. More to the point, he was immediately and intensely afraid of him.

Usberti smiled at his assistant's obvious trepidation. 'Silvano, allow me to introduce our new friend. His name is Bozza.'

Bellini frowned at the name. 'But . . . I thought Bozza was dead.'

'He is,' Usberti said. 'And he is not. Franco Bozza, my loyal aide for many years, the man they called "The Inquisitor", is indeed no longer with us. He was brutally executed some years ago in the south of France, while working for me. Murdered, by Benedict Hope. A piece of information that I have now shared with our new friend here.'

He stepped to the man in black and wrapped an arm around his shoulders, beaming. The man in black didn't flinch. His eyes were like dark, empty pools that betrayed nothing. Usberti said, 'Meet Ugo Bozza, Franco's younger brother.

'Ugo grew up revering his elder brother,' Usberti explained. 'But he followed a different path. While Franco was rising up to become one of the most feared professional killers in Europe, Ugo struck out on his own. Aged seventeen, he enlisted in the Foreign Legion, the only elite military regiment in the world that does not care what a man's background is, or his experience. They care only about his toughness and his devotion, two qualities that young Ugo possessed in such impressive measure that he swiftly became one of the most formidable fighting men the Legion has ever produced. He spent ten years there, perfecting the art of death beyond even the level that his elder sibling achieved, which is saying a great deal. His services are much in demand all over the world. He has recently returned from Bangkok, where he spent a year hunting and eliminating drug dealers – an occupation of which I strongly approve.'

As Usberti spoke, Bozza stood utterly still and seemed barely to be breathing. This isn't a man, Bellini thought. It's some kind of machine.

'He shares many things in common with Franco,' Usberti went on. 'His religious zeal, and his commitment to the same goals as Gladius Domini holds dear. He is as motivated to punish the impure of heart, the debased, and all those who scorn God's word, as his brother was. But in some other respects, he differs. While Franco's primary weapon of choice was the blade, Ugo is more versatile. He is expert with fire-arms, explosives and his bare hands, his unarmed combat form of choice being Muay Thai, in which he has reached the highest rank of proficiency. He does not drink, or smoke, or seek personal wealth. He is a master of destruction in its purest form, a younger, leaner, more lethal version of his brother.'

Bellini glanced at Bozza. 'Why doesn't he speak?'

Usberti replied, 'Ugo has taken a personal vow of silence until his brother's death is avenged. Now that I have informed him of the murderer's identity, it means he will not speak until Ben Hope is dead. To kill Hope is the only reward Ugo seeks in return for working with us.'

Bellini was about to reply when a movement from the window distracted him and he turned to squint through his lenses at the motor launch that was mooring up at the jetty down below. 'They're back,' he said.

Moments later, Groppione and Iacono presented them-selves to their master on the top floor. They were the two Gladius Domini agents whose job it had been to locate the

Manzini woman's base in Greece, in case the others missed her at the Olympia site. By working local rental agencies they'd found the property a few kilometres from the ruins, but – as Usberti had anticipated – she hadn't been there.

'We found this,' Iacono said, holding up a bag from which he produced a small Dell laptop. 'She had stuff encrypted on it. Probably thought it was safely protected, the stupid *puttana*.'

'But not from a professional like you, Luca,' Usberti said. 'I assume you had no great difficulty in breaking the passcode?'

Iacono grinned. 'Took me a whole minute. Piece of cake. You're going to love this, boss.'

'Show me,' Usberti said. Groppione placed the laptop on the desk, powered it up and tinkled a few keys, and moments later he had a pair of windows opened up side by side on the screen. One was a digital diary, filled with carefully organised notes. The other was an address book displaying a list of contacts with all the necessary details. He stepped aside to let Usberti look at them.

Usberti studied the screen, scrolled up and down to drink in the information, and his eyes glittered with satisfaction. 'This is excellent, men. Excellent. It confirms, and expands most usefully upon, what we had already learned from her assistant Garrone. Now that we know her exact destination, we need only ensure that we get there ahead of her. The spider will spin its web and wait for the fly to stumble straight into the trap.'

'Thought you'd be pleased, boss.'

'You will be handsomely rewarded for your efforts, men. There is food and wine awaiting you downstairs.'

Once the foot soldiers had filed out of the room looking forward to getting happily drunk, Usberti went over to the framed world map that covered much of one wall. He pointed his right forefinger at their present location in Sicily, then slid his fingertip to the right, squeaking against the glass, until it landed on Turkey. The capital city of Ankara was marked by a red blob. He tapped his finger against it three times and turned with a flourish towards Silvano Bellini and Ugo Bozza.

'Ugo, you are going on a journey. Silvano, instruct Volpicelli to arrange the flight, and to contact our good Catholic allies in Istanbul who will arrange everything Ugo and an additional four-man team require on arrival. No expense is to be spared. We cannot afford to fail this time.'

'Yes, Excellency.'

'And now everything is falling into place,' Usberti said, almost rubbing his hands in glee as he walked to the window and gazed out at the Ionian Sea. 'Before long the idol will be ours, Ben Hope will be dead, and Gladius Domini will be on its way to being restored to its former power, and more. Our time is coming, gentlemen. It is coming sooner than I ever dared to dream.'

Chapter 30

The next morning heralded another day of icy rain as Ben and Anna hurried through a simple and silent breakfast of coffee and toast in the empty restaurant, sitting at the same table they'd had dinner at the night before, with what little luggage they had packed and ready at their feet. Anna was all buttoned up in her coat, but still looked cold and miserable. 'I have to get new clothes. These are ruined. A hobo wouldn't wear trousers this filthy.'

'No army surplus store in town,' he said.

'Maybe a Versace boutique, do you think?'

'You Italians. It's like a disease.'

'Careful.'

At 8.30 a relic of a Lada Niva taxicab rattled and wheezed to a halt in the street outside, and a younger, less ursine version of Kris Christakos jumped out, left the engine running and came bursting enthusiastically inside his brother's joint.

'I am Nick,' he announced brightly, striding up to their table like the ninth cavalry coming to the rescue of these poor, helpless, stranded tourists who so badly needed his services. He threw himself down in the empty seat next to Anna and showed her all his teeth in a wide grin. 'I am mechanic. I take you to your van and fix her up, okay? Is no problem.'

Ben looked at him. 'You say you can fix up the van?'

Nick grinned. 'Sure, sure. Price is two hundred euros.'

'Sounds a little steep,' Ben said.

'Hey. You know how it is. Parts are expensive. You give me the money now, we go fix her up, then you go on your way to Messini. Okay?'

'Change of plan,' Ben said. 'We're not going to Messini any longer. We need to get to Thessaloniki instead. Can you take us there?'

Anna was staring at Ben, bewildered. Nick was staring, too. 'Thessaloniki is the other side of the country.'

'I'm well aware of that,' Ben said. 'We'll pay you for your trouble.'

'What about your van?'

'We'll come back for it,' Ben said. 'Some other time.'

'You are crazy. Three days, it will be gone. These kids now, they steal anything.'

'They're welcome to it. So will you drive us to Thessaloniki or not?'

Nick chewed his lip and looked doubtful. 'Is too far, take too long. I have much mechanic work to do, you know? This time of year, it is most of my business.'

'Tell you what, I'll give you five hundred euros for the ride,' Ben said, reaching into his bag and showing Nick a bundle of banknotes from his stash. 'That's better than two hundred for the repair job.'

Nick boggled at the sight of the money and swallowed hard. 'I would love it, but then, my customers . . .'

'Thessaloniki is what, four hours away?' Ben said. 'You'll be gone eight. I doubt whether your customers will even know you're gone.'

Nick's face was busy for a moment as he churned it over. 'Okay. I do it. Give me the money first.'

'Half now, half when we get there,' Ben said.

Nick pulled a grimace, then nodded. 'Okay, okay.' He grabbed the two-fifty from Ben's hand and stuffed it in his pocket. He glanced at their bags. 'You ready? We go right now. Let me go to toilet. I come right back.'

'See you in a minute,' Ben said, finishing his coffee. He watched as Nick stood up and hurried off in the direction of the toilets. The instant the mechanic was out of sight, Ben snatched up their bags and said to Anna, 'Let's go. Quickly.'

Before she could reply, he was whisking her outside towards the idling taxi. He tossed the bags on the back seat and clambered in behind the wheel. 'Anna, come on.'

'What are we doing?' she asked, getting in.

'Getting out of here as fast as we can,' he said.

'But he's supposed to drive us. You gave him money.'

'No, I bought something from him.'

'What?'

'His life.' Ben slammed the Lada into gear and they took off.

'I don't understand.'

'I'm sure Kris is an honest guy,' Ben said, skidding around the corner. 'Decent and hardworking, like his wife and daughter. But I'm not so sure the brother is as trustworthy. Or, for that matter, very intelligent.'

'How did you figure all this out?'

'He gave himself away in the first three sentences,' Ben said. 'When we talked to his brother last night, we told him our car had broken down. I never said anything to anyone about a van, did you? And yet Nick offered straight off to fix our van. Not our car.'

'Oh,' Anna said, realising.

'That was his first mistake. After that, the next test he

failed was turning down five hundred euros for a few hours' drive.'

'Why would he do that?'

They were heading out of town now, as fast as the old taxi would go. 'Only one possible reason,' Ben said. 'Because he was desperate to lead us into an ambush in the woods.'

'It was a *trap*?'

'It's probably all over the local news by now that the desperadoes who shot up Olympia are running loose about the countryside. My guess is that our friend Nick found the van up there in the forest, saw the bullet holes, put two and two together and figured out a way to get some money out of this. He's probably got an even stupider buddy waiting behind a tree with a shotgun. The minute we rolled up they were aiming to nab us, rob us blind and then turn us in to the police for whatever extra reward they could get. He's calling his mate right this minute, telling him there's been a change of plan so they can rendezvous somewhere else along the road. Except it wouldn't work out the way they expected, because I'd have had to kill them both. And I'd rather lose two hundred and fifty euros than kill anyone, even if they are brainless idiots.'

'But when he realises we took his car, he'll call the police.'

'And he'll tell them we're headed north-east, for Thessaloniki,' Ben said. 'Why else would I have mentioned it?'

'We're not going to Thessaloniki?' Anna asked, confused. She glanced out of the window. Andritsaina was out of sight behind them and they were winding further down the woody mountain road, veering through one hairpin bend after another with all the agility Ben could coax from a worn-out Lada taxi.

'Nowhere near,' Ben said. 'We're going the other way,

south-east to Athens, and from there to see your guy in Ankara.'

'We'll never make it to Athens in this car. The police will be searching for it.'

Ben nodded. 'And when they find it, we'll be long gone. Relax.'

Anna said, 'Relax? We're escaping in a stolen car and we're being hunted by the police and a gang of professional killers who want to kidnap me, and everywhere we go the locals are trying to trap us and rob us at gunpoint, and you say relax?'

'Don't exaggerate.'

'What if the police arrest us at the airport?'

'What occupation does your passport say?'

'Author.'

'If they're looking for anyone specific at all, the only lead they have right now is for some unnamed history professor. As long as none of the cops have read any of your books and twig the connection – and I seriously doubt these guys read much other than comic books – we'll be fine. For now, at any rate.'

'This is how you live all the time, isn't it?' she asked him, arching an eyebrow. 'This is just a normal day for you.'

'You'll get used to it,' Ben replied. 'In the meantime, let's concentrate on getting out of Greece as fast as possible.'

'This isn't exactly what I would call fast,' she said, eyeing the speedometer. The old Lada was struggling to reach a hundred kilometres an hour as they roared along a straight section of the mountain road.

'The moment we spot a nice Ferrari, we'll do a switch. What colour would you like?'

The chance for a switch came unexpectedly as they were winding down through the hills before hitting the motorway.

It wasn't a Ferrari, and there was little choice of colour. Their new vehicle was a mud-brown, rust-speckled Ford Granada that Ben spotted in the backyard of a row of rundown cottages outside a village. Nobody was about, and a barking dog was the only witness to their presence. Moments later, Ben was inside the Granada and hotwiring it, to Anna's consternation.

'I don't know if I'm comfortable with this, Ben. I've never stolen a car before.'

'You're not doing anything.'

'I'm a witness to a criminal act.'

'Then close your eyes. In any case, we're not stealing it, we're buying it.'

The Ford fired up and seemed to run well enough, so true to his word he left a generous roll of cash, more than the thing was worth, on the cottage's kitchen table. Which meant he first had to get inside the house, a quick and easy job.

Anna was shaking her head. 'Let me get this right. You break into someone's home to pay them for the car you just stole?'

'Where else can I leave the money? Someone might steal it.'

Chapter 31

They were soon back on the motorway, speeding along in the second dodgy old car Ben had been forced to buy since landing in Greece only yesterday. He wasn't sorry to be leaving the country. Just over four hours later, they arrived at Athens airport. By late afternoon, they were in the air, heading for Turkey.

But the long, frustrating journey wasn't over yet. The only plane they'd been able to board at such short notice was terminating at Istanbul, making it necessary to jump on a domestic flight to take them the extra five hundred kilometres south-east to Ankara. That ate up a lot more time, and until the last minute it was uncertain whether the internal flight would even depart, with adverse weather conditions and threats of severe snow in the capital.

Finally, late that evening, they touched down in a sub-zero, white-frosted Esenboga International Airport outside Ankara, where crews were working hard to clear ice off the runways. The airport was teeming with a heavy paramilitary police presence in the wake of terror bombings by Kurdish separatists, to add to the failed attempt by rogue elements in the Turkish Army to overthrow the government a few months earlier. Ben and Anna filtered slowly through the scrutiny of customs, who paid close attention to the contents of Ben's battered green canvas haversack.

'Is this a bullet hole?' asked one of the officials, poking his finger through it.

'Cigarette burn,' Ben told him. Which, of course, wasn't the case. The official, a dumpy little guy in what looked like a military uniform, did a lot of frowning before he finally let them through. The bag would have excited him a good deal more if Ben hadn't dumped the MPX machine pistol and ammunition on a quiet mountainous stretch of their drive through Greece.

Esenboga Airport abounded with gift boutiques, cafés and restaurants, and even featured its own dozen mosques for travellers to catch up on their prayers, but to Anna's bitter disappointment she couldn't find anywhere to buy clothes and had to endure the humiliation of wearing the same travel-stained rags as before. Ben was more concerned about getting her some appropriate winter wear. She was shivering with cold as they left the airport and searched for a taxi rank, but it took more than freezing temperatures to diminish her fascination for history.

'Did you know that right here, on this very spot, more than six hundred years ago, a huge battle was fought?' she said. 'It was a bloody conflict between the Mongolian warlord Timur the Lame and the Ottoman Sultan Bayezid the First, and it achieved very little. The Ottomans were defeated but would return to take back Ankara just the following year. It's claimed there were more than a million soldiers on the battle-field, exactly where we're standing now.' She shook her head. 'A million men, full of hate and trying to hack each other to pieces, and all for nothing. I can't even imagine what it must have been like. It's so senseless. What makes people want to wage war and slaughter one another like that?'

Ben ignited a Gauloise and clanged his lighter shut. 'You mean, aside from money, power, territory and the fact that most of them were probably just doing what they were ordered? You're the history expert. What would I know?'

'But you were a soldier. You must surely know.'

'War is what human beings do best,' Ben said. 'Always has been. It's what sets our species apart from all the others and until we wipe ourselves out, that's how it will always be.'

'When you fought in wars, did you believe you were doing a good thing?'

He looked at her. 'Sometimes. Mostly not. That's why I left.'

'Why did you join?'

'You know, I really don't remember.'

'The more I study history, the more I realise what very strange creatures men are.'

'You don't need a doctorate to work that one out,' Ben said.

Soon afterwards, they found a solitary taxi waiting at a rank nearby. The engine was running to keep the heater going, melting the snow into a pool below its steaming exhaust. Anna had Ercan Kavur's address on a slip of paper, and passed it to the driver through the window. The driver nodded. They got in. The inside of the car was stifling. 'Hey, no smoking,' the driver complained as Ben climbed in with his Gauloise. Ben replied in Turkish, 'Who are you kidding? This shitbox smells like an ashtray. Let's go. And you can start the meter. I know all the tricks.'

Cheated out of the opportunity to stiff a couple of tourists by quoting a fixed rate fare, the driver sullenly set off. Ben kept glaring at him in the mirror. Roguish cabbies weren't his favourite people right now.

'I didn't know you could speak Turkish,' Anna said.

'Just phrasebook stuff. Let's hope this guy Kavur is at home tonight.'

'Ercan doesn't get out much,' she replied. 'He used to be married, until he became too eccentric to keep his job at the University, and his wife left him. Nowadays, if he's not on a dig somewhere, which he wouldn't be at this time of the year, he spends nearly all his time in his study, translating ancient languages and deciphering old manuscripts and tablets. He'll be there, I'm sure of it.'

The white-dusted motorway flashed by for half an hour as the taxi's wipers slapped away drifting snowflakes and the spangling expanse of city lights gradually swelled on the horizon. Coming into Ankara, the taxi cut eastwards towards the centre, through streets piled at the edges with dirty brown slush. They passed the Grand National Assembly building, Turkey's parliament, which had been badly hit by F16 strikes during the military coup attempt and was now half-hidden behind scaffolding as it was slowly pieced back together. It hadn't been very long since tanks and troop convoys had been rolling through these same streets as the government and rebel factions struggled for power. 'There's the Kocatepe Mosque,' Anna said, pointing out another of Ankara's landmarks with its lit-up dome and four tall towers piercing the night sky like spikes.

Ercan Kavur lived right across town on the south-eastern edge of Ankara, within an area called Doğukent Caddessi, where crumbly traditional red-roofed houses intermingled with suburban high-rise developments that looked unfinished and neglected. Arriving in a narrow street with houses spaced far apart and back from the road, Anna told the driver to pull up. The night air seemed to have dropped another degree as they stepped out of the car. Their breath fogged in the chill. Snowflakes spiralled gently down to add themselves to the whiteness of the empty street.

'That's his house there,' Anna said, pointing, as the taxi disappeared into the night. 'I think I see the study light on. What did I tell you?'

Ben glanced at the house, a squat single-storey building that looked from a distance like a concrete bunker. A small area of garden in front was lined with bushes that were caked in snow. A winding path led through a gate to the front door. All the windows were dark except one, from which a chink of light was shining through a narrow gap in the drawn curtains.

'I take it you've been here before,' he said.

She nodded. 'After finishing with the excavations in Iraq, Ercan and I brought the pieces of the damaged Muranu tablet back here together. I stayed with him for three days, during which time he showed me some of his work. He's a fascinating man. Dry as a rock and a little strange, but fascinating nonetheless. You'll like him.'

'A little strange how exactly?'

'You'll soon see for yourself. Let's just say that his world view goes a little bit beyond not using telephones and email.'

It was after midnight. Anna led the way towards Ercan's gate. The slab pavement was slick with frozen snow, and Ben held her arm to catch her if she slipped. Italian designer shoes weren't made for this.

'Walk on the crunchy bits,' he said.

'I go down, we both go down,' she replied, flashing a nervous smile at him.

Ben was about to reply when he looked down, his eyes narrowed to slits and he stopped. His grip tightened on her arm.

'You say Ercan lives here all alone? Doesn't get out and has no friends?'

'Pretty much.'

Ben pointed at the path leading to the house. Anna looked down where he was pointing, and her smile dropped. At least four sets of footprints led from the front gate and up the path towards the front door.

'Then his social life must have improved since you last saw him.'

Ben bent down to examine the tracks. The prints were mostly overlapped and the individual sole treads hard to make out, but judging by the clearer imprints he reckoned the tracks had been made by at least four different people, rather than by just one person going back and forth. The crushed snow was powdery, the impressions of the sole treads not yet frozen hard by the cold night. Enough to discern that Ercan's visitors had been wearing boots with chunkier treads than regular shoes. Which wasn't too much of a tell, in itself, on a cold and snowy night. Then again, as Ben knew well, a good solid pair of boots were good for other things than walking. That was why soldiers wore them, and assault teams who might have to kick down doors and get a little rough.

One of the sets of prints was unlike the others. Shoes, not boots. Making sloppy drag marks, like the footsteps of someone too drunk to walk steadily and needing to be supported. The tyre tracks that curved away from the kerb and merged with the fresh ones just made by the taxicab explained where Ercan's visitors had gone.

Anna was reaching the same disturbing conclusion Ben was. 'Someone's been here before us,' she said, looking at him anxiously.

'And not long ago, or they'd be covered by fresh snowfall.'

208

'Ben, you don't think—?'

Ben walked up to the front entrance. The door was reinforced, set into a steel frame that made it as strong as concrete. To the right of the door was a panel with keypad and an intercom speaker behind a grille. A wall-mounted camera stood guard over the doorway, its red power light blinking at them.

'I thought you said he hated technology,' Ben said as Anna caught up with him.

'Only when it's for communication,' she replied. 'Not when it's for security. I told you, he's a very cautious man.'

But not cautious enough to keep his front door shut. It was hanging ajar by half an inch. Ben gave it a shove and it swung a quarter open on its reinforced hinges. It was a beefed-up security door, welded steel like the entrance to a bank vault. It would have needed some kind of serious dedicated door-breaching munitions to take out the lock, but there wasn't a scratch to suggest forced entry. Whoever they were, the four booted visitors who'd called earlier that night hadn't had a hard time getting inside.

No sound, no movement from within. The house felt empty. But there was only one way to find out for sure.

Ben put his finger to his lips, telling Anna, 'Quiet', then held the finger up to signal, 'Wait here.'

Ben eased the heavy door open the rest of the way and stepped inside the dark silence of Ercan Kavur's house.

Chapter 32

In that vulnerable moment when the eyes need time to adapt to the darkness and the other senses step protectively in to provide the missing data, Ben stopped, set down his bag and stood completely still, as alert as a wild animal tuned into the tiniest sound, even a scent, that could alert it to danger. He could hear nothing.

As the darkness began to resolve itself into distinct shapes and shadows, he moved on deeper into the house. The small entrance hall was cold from the open door, but not freezing, telling him that the door hadn't been lying ajar all that long. The hallway extended into a long, narrow corridor that passed through the middle of the building and was sectioned off by first one heavy glass interior door, then a second.

It was an unusual layout, but Ben didn't have time to dwell on that now. Other doors radiated off left and right, leading to rooms that he checked one by one. For a few moments he experienced a strange sense of déjà vu, like a replay of entering Carlo Scanzi's office in Florence, and he half expected to find a dead body slumped across the floor, bled out from a slashed throat like Anna's agent. Or a sudden violent attack from multiple armed intruders. Ben's whole body was jangling into full-on combat mode, ready to explode into action any instant and inflict serious damage on anything that moved.

The inside of the house was warm and smelled closed up, with aromas of stale cigarette smoke and cooking oil and spices that all but smothered an unpleasantly familiar background chemical tang lingering in the air which Ben couldn't quite put his finger on. Daring to risk a little light, he dug his torch from the bag on his shoulder and flashed it around him. It wasn't a big house. In the ninety seconds that it took him to sweep its half-dozen rooms he found no mutilated corpses, and no lurking intruders either.

But he did find the obvious signs of a struggle in the spare bedroom that Kavur had converted into a chaotically cluttered study. The overturned chair and the upset desk lamp, lying on its side in a sea of scattered papers and books, told him that Kavur had been deep in his work when his first set of unexpected visitors that night had turned up.

And now Ben understood what that odd, lingering chemical odour was, because he could smell it loud and clear inside the small study. The same type of alcohol-based sedative that Anna's would-be kidnappers had intended to use on her in Olympia. This time around, the snatch had been successful. That explained the dragging footprints in the snow outside. Kavur had been dragged semi-conscious from the house and bundled into a waiting vehicle.

'Someone was here, all right,' Ben said when he went back to bring Anna inside and retrieve his bag. 'Been and gone. And your friend with them.'

He shut the door and flipped the hallway light switch. Decor-wise, Kavur's home was as drearily and unimaginatively furnished as might be expected of a reclusive single guy with no interests outside of his work. Except now that it was all brightly lit up, Ben could see a few unusual details about the place. The heavy glass doors that divided the corridor into sections were internal security doors with sophisticated electronic locks and full-height mesh-reinforced panes, probably capable of deflecting a rifle round. The doors off the corridor were set into metal frames and likewise fitted with combination keypads. The alarm system master control panel in the front hall near the door could have belonged in a high-security prison.

'Who took him?' Anna asked, eyes darting nervously about as though Kavur might still be hiding in a recess, waiting to jump out and surprise them.

'You want to hazard a guess?'

'But how did they know where to find him?'

'And why did he let them in?' Ben added. 'Doesn't it strike you as strange that a guy who obviously hasn't spared any expense when it comes to security would just open the door to a bunch of kidnappers?'

'Speaking of security –' Anna flipped open a cover on the master control panel by the door. 'July twentieth, 356 BC,' she muttered to herself as she tapped in a code with a polished red fingernail.

'You seem to know your way around,' Ben commented.

'That's an easy one to remember, for a historian. It's the birth date of Alexander the Great.'

'Of course.'

Anna pointed at the alarm system. 'Now we're safe in here. Windows and doors are sealed and the electrified perimeter circuit is armed, but none of the internal security devices, like the pepper blaster, will activate. That was the first thing I made Ercan show me when I was here, in case I set it off by mistake.'

Ben stared at her. 'Electrified perimeter? Pepper blaster?'

'He was left some money by a rich relative. Rather than buy

a house in a better part of town, he spent most of it on turning this place into a fortress. You have to disarm the system every time you open the front or back doors, or you can get an electric shock from the handles. And those –' She pointed upwards at a small nozzle that pointed down at them from a ceiling light fitting. Ben noticed three more of them poking discreetly from elsewhere overhead. 'Those will spray liquid pepper at any intruder who sets off the motion sensor. And you see those vents on the wall? An infrared tripwire triggers a fog device that fills the whole hallway so you can't see.'

'Which you couldn't anyway, if your eyes were full of pepper spray.'

'Those are just some of the modifications Ercan has made. Even the windows can withstand bullets.'

'You told me he was a little strange,' Ben said. 'I wouldn't say that at all.'

'No?'

'He's a raving paranoid headcase.'

'It's not paranoia if they're really after you,' Anna said.

'Hasn't done him much good. They got in and grabbed him as easily as falling off a log.'

'So it seems, and I don't understand it,' Anna said, anxiously chewing her lip. 'What can have happened? Oh my God, I hope he's all right.'

'We'll worry about that later. For the moment, let's make sure that we are. Given that your friend is so obsessive about security, any chance he keeps a firearm around the place? Any kind will do.'

'No, Ercan hates guns. He believes they're responsible for war and violence.'

'That's logical. Did those million Mongolians and Ottomans all fight with guns at the Battle of Ankara six hundred years ago?'

She shrugged. 'I guess he hates swords and spears and arrows too.'

Ben grunted. 'Never mind. I'm sure he has plenty of lethal weapons in his kitchen, like normal people do.'

He returned to the tiny kitchen. Pots and pans and plates were stacked all over the place. He jerked open a drawer, found a carving knife and tucked it diagonally through his belt, pirate-style. 'If you can't have a gun, you can still have an edge,' he said to Anna, who was staring at him. He could see she was on the edge of panic. He touched her arm and felt the rigidity of her muscles through the sleeve of her coat.

'Where could they have taken him?' she groaned. 'What could they want with him?'

'I can't answer the first question,' Ben told her. 'And you already know the answer to the second. Whatever he discovered and was going to tell you that was so important, it's important to Usberti as well. They took him away to work on him.'

He regretted that last part the moment he said it. It was a little more information than Anna could handle. But it was out now, and too late to retract it.

'*Work on him?*'

'Like they did to Gianni. Whatever it takes to get them to open up.'

'Will they torture him?' she blurted, horrified. 'Kill him? Ben? Answer me.'

He said no more, deciding to keep his thoughts to himself. Such as the fact that he sensed something not quite right about the situation. This was a solidly built house, with thick walls, extremely efficiently sound-insulated by so many layers of security doors and well detached from the nearest neighbour. If you wanted to tie a guy up and torture information

214

out of him, you'd have all the privacy you needed right here on the spot, and plenty of time to get your victim to spill whatever information you were after.

So why, in fact, had they taken Kavur away? That was another question Ben couldn't fully answer – and not knowing was triggering his trusted sixth sense for danger and making him feel unsettled.

'Now we're here, let's stay calm and have a look at what we came to see,' he said after a few moments. He led her up the corridor, through the first security door, and to the room on the right which was Kavur's study.

'Look at this place,' Anna breathed when she saw the state it was in.

'This is where they took him,' Ben said. 'Seems he put up quite a struggle before they doped him. Now, we don't want to stay here any longer than we have to, so show me what's what.'

She pointed at a framed picture that was hanging away from the wall on a hinge. 'That's where he was keeping the pieces of the tablet.'

'The old hidden wall safe,' Ben said. 'Not the most original hiding place.' It was the size of a shoebox and inset in a rectangular hole in the plasterwork, with a small combination panel built into its half-inch steel door. The door was open. Ben peered inside. Empty, naturally.

'They took the tablet fragments,' she said.

'They seem to know a lot, don't they?'

As Anna stared helplessly around the wrecked study, Ben went to the window and tugged at the edge of the drawn curtain to take a look at the empty, snowy street outside. The uneasy feeling nagging at him kept intensifying as the minutes ticked by.

'Wait,' Anna said. 'Of course. The document safe. That's

215

where he would have hidden whatever he had to tell me about.'

'I hope it's in a better place than the first one.'

'Under the floorboards, somewhere about there,' she said, pointing down at the large sheepskin rug that covered most of the floor. 'Can you help me? We have to shift the desk to get to it.'

She removed her coat and laid it neatly over the back of an armchair. Ben was too warm inside the house but kept his leather jacket on. He went over to the desk and hooked his fingers under it to test its weight. It would be considerably lighter without the piled stacks of archaeology books and papers that littered its surface. He swept them to the floor with a crash. The place was a mess anyway.

'Careful. Some of those books are rare and valuable.'

'I think Ercan has bigger problems right now than a couple of dented books,' Ben said. He heaved the desk aside, crouched down and pulled away the corner of the rug. The boards under it had been sawn to make a square trapdoor about two feet across. Ben used the carving knife to prise it up, revealing the upward-facing grey steel door of the floor safe.

'Locked,' Anna said with grim satisfaction. 'They wouldn't have thought to look here.'

'Or they drugged him up before he could tell them about it. Either way, unless you have a crowbar in your handbag we're going to need a key to get into this thing.'

'Kitchen,' she said. Ben followed as she hurried from the study, turned right, darted further up the corridor, heaved her way through the second glass door with a small grunt, then entered the room on the left. As he joined her she was bent down by Kavur's fridge and entering a code to unlock it. The kitchen was tiny, with a small table and a single chair shoehorned in between worktops and cupboards. The back door was another high-security affair. As, it seemed, was at least one of Ercan Kavur's appliances.

'Don't tell me,' he muttered. 'The fridge squirts poison gas at anyone who tries to pinch Ercan's beer.'

'Ercan doesn't drink beer, he's a Muslim.' Anna opened the fridge door, slid open one of the plastic compartments at the bottom and took out a large iceberg lettuce. Before Ben was able to make comment, she turned it upside down and he saw that it was actually a convincing resin fake, hollowed to contain a small key safe with another press-button number pad.

'Mail order from the paranoid shop,' Ben said.

'Fourteen fifty-three. Fall of the Roman and Byzantine Empires with the conquest of Constantinople by the Ottomans under Mehmed the Conqueror.' Anna tapped in the number, and the hidden compartment flipped open to let a key drop into her palm.

'You need a damn good memory to live in this place.'

'The code to get inside the document safe is the most important of all,' Anna said. 'Ercan wanted me to know it, in case anything happened to him. He suffers from a lot of medical conditions, most of them probably psychosomatic, and has always believed he could die at any minute.'

'This gets better and better,' Ben said. 'What friends you have.'

'But neither he nor I could have predicted what's happened to him now.'

Ben took the key from her hand. 'Let's go and find out what he had to tell you.'

Chapter 33

Back in the study, Ben crouched by the trapdoor, unlocked the floor safe and hauled open the heavy steel door. It wasn't booby-trapped. Standing anxiously over him, Anna let out a gasp of relief when she saw the stacks of papers inside. '*Grazie a Dio!*'

Ben lifted out the entire contents of the safe and dumped them on the floor. Anna fell on her knees next to him to start sifting through the heap. The papers were a mixture of photocopied images of ancient carvings, stone tablets and other relics, and loose sheets covered in handwritten scribbles made up from an alphabet that didn't look to Ben like any modern language. It wasn't Arabic, nor did it much resemble the ancient Hebrew or Aramaic script that he'd laboured to comprehend as a student at Oxford, way back in another life.

'Old Anatolian Turkish,' she explained. 'Not used since the fifteenth century. Ercan uses it as a kind of code for all his written notes. He works the same way as I do, recording everything he does in a kind of diary form for later reference. Except, of course, my notes are all in Italian.'

'And you can read this?'

'Not as well as he can, but I can get by,' she said. 'I've spent some time studying a variety of these ancient

218

languages.' From her handbag she snatched a leather spectacle case with PRADA emblazoned across it. Putting on a pair of designer glasses that only emphasised the perfection of her eyes and cheekbones, and smoothing her long black hair away from her face, she took a thick handful of the handwritten notes to the desk and began to study them intently under the light of the lamp, flicking from one sheet to another.

Ben had never much relished the chore of poring over ancient languages during his theology days, and he disliked codes and ciphers even more. Watching Anna bent over the desk, totally absorbed in her work, the memory flashed through his mind of the fiendish code he'd had to crack years earlier at the height of his running chase with Usberti's hired killers in the Languedoc region of southern France. It had been the same sultry, summer night that Anna had been attacked in her villa by the near-indestructible Franco Bozza, who would have carved her into pieces if Ben hadn't raced to the scene when he had. Holed up in a hotel suite later that night with Roberta Ryder fast asleep nearby, he'd struggled deep into the early hours to decipher a set of maddeningly cryptic alchemical riddles and number puzzles that had almost driven him over the edge. Ercan Kavur's scribbles didn't seem any less impenetrable to him. He was glad that Anna was here to figure them out.

Letting her get on with the task, he returned to the window for another check of the street outside. More snow clouds were gathering in the sky. Thick flakes were drifting down in spirals that caught the glow of the streetlights like swirling haloes. The footprint tracks on the path were slowly disappearing under a fresh layer of white. A lone car hissed by on the snowy road, taking it slow and easy in the slippery conditions.

'This is strange,' Anna muttered from the desk.

'Make anything of it?' he asked, glancing over.

She shook her head, not looking up from the papers she'd carefully arranged on the desktop. 'I thought Ercan was working on the Muranu tablet, but instead he seems to have been going into a whole other set of historical archives. Nearly all this material is sourced from the PFA.'

'The what?'

'The Persepolis Fortification Archive,' Anna explained, fluttering a sheet of paper at him as though scolding him for not being informed on such elementary stuff.

'That makes everything so clear to me.'

She frowned. 'Persepolis, literally "City of the Persians", was the seat of the Achaemenid Empire in what is now Iran, founded in 518 BC by Darius the First, grandson of Cyrus the Great who overthrew Babylon. The archive was set up in 1933 after a team of archaeologists from the Oriental Institute of the University of Chicago, who were excavating the ruins of palaces of the Persian kings, came across a fantastic cache of clay tablets hidden in two rooms in a bastion of a fortification wall. Hence its name, the Fortification Archive.'

More excavations, more tablets. Ben was scarcely in the mood for another lecture on the history of archaeology. 'I get it. Or maybe I don't. What about it?'

'They found tens of thousands of tablets, which to this day haven't all been deciphered. It's a monumental task that will take many more years to complete. The archive mostly comprises administrative and bureaucratic records dealing with matters of local government, transport, trade, food distribution and so on. It's been a really important source of our knowledge of everyday life during the Achaemenid period.'

'I'm sure that's all spellbindingly fascinating,' Ben said, 'but I fail to see what it has to do with us.'

'So do I, frankly,' Anna replied, frowning back at the sheet of paper in her hand. 'This comes as a complete surprise to me. It's as if Ercan had taken a totally different tack.'

'He did say that the tablet fragments were too badly damaged to work with,' Ben reminded her. 'Maybe he just gave up on them altogether.'

She nodded, looking even more mystified. 'That would fit with what he told me.'

'Or else this is something entirely different he was working on,' Ben said. 'Nothing to do with your Muranus or your Babylon idol at all.'

'Quiet. Let me read this.'

'Fine, but don't take too long.'

She fell back into a concentrated silence as she went on examining the notes. Ben struck up another Gauloise, wondering whether maybe Ercan had smoke detectors built into the place that would drench him with water. Nothing happened, but Ben was more and more on edge. He wanted to get out of this place.

'I think I understand,' Anna suddenly exclaimed. 'This is amazing. This is it. This will lead us to the next step.'

Ben asked, 'What next step?'

But before she had time to explain what she'd found, he heard the sound of engines outside. He snapped back around to peer out once again through the crack in the curtains.

Oncoming headlights made him blink. Four of them, carving beams through the thickening snow. A pair of vehicles approaching fast. Unusually fast, for the slippery road conditions. Heading for the house. The one in front was a big, boxy Volvo SUV. Behind it was a muscular black Audi saloon. Both cars slithered to a halt outside Kavur's front gate. Their lights went dark.

'We have company,' Ben said quietly.

Anna looked up from the desk, startled, plucking off her reading glasses. 'Let's get out of here!'

'Too late for that now,' Ben said, watching. Two men jumped from each vehicle and gathered in a group in the empty street. And one thing was for sure: they weren't stopping by for a friendly social call.

The briefest glimpse of them was all Ben's trained eye needed to take in every detail. They were dressed in black like a tactical raid team, which was exactly what they appeared to be. Their faces covered by goggles and gas respirator masks. The same combat boots on their feet that had made the earlier tracks in the snow, tactical combat gloves on their hands. They knew how to move, fluid and fast, especially the one whose obvious command over the others singled him out as the leader.

He wasn't tall, wasn't muscular, but he exuded power and authority and confident expertise in just the same way as a thousand top-level operatives Ben had seen, known and worked with in the past. This guy was a soldier, or had been.

From their equipment, he and the others could have passed for a Turkish police SWAT team. The leader and one other man were armed with stubby 9mm automatic carbines fitted with tactical lights. The third was armed with a full-size assault rifle bombed up with a grenade launcher attachment that Ben guessed from the masks was loaded with tear gas. The fourth was what military close quarter battle teams designated as the breacher. His weapon was a radically cut-down shotgun with a jagged muzzle attachment designed to be pressed hard against a lock or hinge. Special frangible door-busting ammunition would blow through just about anything that stood in the assault team's path. Ben had gone through plenty of doors that way, back in olden times.

The leader signalled the breacher to lead the way to the house. They hurried in long, purposeful strides towards the door, boots crunching on the fresh snow. Ben slipped the knife out from his belt. Now he understood what his sixth sense had been telling him all this time.

Usberti's men had returned in full force. Except it wasn't strictly a return – because the fact was, they'd never really left. It was the answer to the question why they'd taken Ercan Kavur away: to leave an empty house as bait for their real targets to be lured inside, to feel safe and let their guard down while the assault team waited and watched somewhere nearby, preparing to come back and catch them unawares.

It was a carefully considered move, tactically speaking. The team could have been lurking hidden inside the house to surprise them on arrival, but they knew who Ben was and what he was capable of. They knew, or had been instructed, that a man like him wouldn't walk into an ambush unprepared. They knew, or had been warned, that there would have been a fight. Ben was a dangerous threat to be eliminated, but Anna Manzini was a precious asset to the employer. She could have been hurt, or killed, or escaped. Their orders were not to let any of those things happen, under any circumstances.

And it was a strategy that begged too many questions for Ben's liking. The enemy had known he and Anna were coming here. Usberti was cunning, but he wasn't a mind reader. How could he have predicted their moves so well?

Answers might come later, or they might not. Either way, the trap was sprung.

And Ben and Anna were caught right in it like a couple of rats.

Chapter 34

Trapped inside a strange house, on unfamiliar ground with little sense of the lie of the land, unarmed except for a kitchen knife, with four heavily tooled-up professional thugs about to attack at any moment and a matter of seconds in which to figure out a contingency plan. Ben had been in similar scrapes before now, and survived. But it wasn't something to make a habit of.

Then again, Ercan Kavur's home was not the typical middle-class suburban residence.

Ben jumped over to the desk and turned off the lamp, plunging the study into darkness. Too late. The attackers already knew which room their targets were in. Through the window he saw the lithe figure of the team leader signal to the one with the grenade launcher, who planted himself on the patch of lawn in front of the house, braced himself and fired straight at the study window with a loud report that Kavur's thick security glass muffled to a WHOOMPH.

Ben instinctively dived away from the window, grabbing Anna and yanking her down to the floor. If the grenade was high explosive, they were both dead anyway; but if his guess was right and the assault team were using tear gas, he'd have to try to get to the study door in time to escape the worst of it.

The juddering impact seemed to shake the whole house as the grenade whacked into the glass. A normal window would have shattered into a million fragments that would have covered Ben and Anna's prone bodies like an ice storm, but Ercan Kavur's home improvements paid off. Instead of smashing through the window the missile just bounced off.

Once, while training on a pistol shooting range, Ben had been hit square in the chest by a forty-calibre slug that had bounced straight back at him from a steel plate target and left him shaken and bruised. These things happened, time to time. Up on his feet instantly, still clutching Anna's arm, Ben saw the grenade rebound towards the shooter who had launched it, catch him right in the face and knock him off his feet with his visor cracked. The grenade dropped to the ground next to him, blowing out a pressurised stream of CS gas that billowed and dispersed into the night air. The team leader quickly kicked the grenade away and it rolled harmlessly into the bushes. The fallen guy jumped back up, ripped off his damaged mask and threw it away in disgust.

The assault hadn't started well, but the team now wasted no time to move on with the next phase of the attack, to get inside. That was when the fun would begin.

'Time to leave,' Ben said. He snatched up his bag and slung it over his shoulder, reached down and pulled Anna sharply to her feet.

'The papers—' she began.

'Leave them.' He hauled her towards the study door. There was no time to grab her coat or handbag, either. The electrified perimeter might deter a casual burglar but it wasn't going to be an obstacle to these guys. As Ben wrenched open the door he heard the explosive BLAM of the breaching shotgun taking out the lock on the front entrance.

Then they were in.

At the instant that Ben emerged from the study and bounded into the corridor, knife in one hand and Anna's arm clutched in the other, the front door crashed open. Through the reinforced glass of the security door separating them he saw the four men burst into the hallway. Their boots were rimed with snow. Weapons pointing. The leader was first in, carbine at the hip, finger on trigger, eyes glinting behind his visor, moving with a fluid violence that looked as if he lived for these moments.

Next, three things happened. First, the alarm system activated a whooping, shrilling siren that filled the house. Second, as the invaders charged into the breached hallway, they were met with streams of vapour that shot like smoke from the wall vents either side of them, instantly engulfing them in thick fog. Third, the overhead nozzles built into the light fittings went into action, scooshing jets of red fluid downwards into the impenetrable mist. It looked like blood, or brake fluid, but it was neither.

With gas masks on, the three men still wearing them were protected from the pepper blasters that would have reduced any normal intruders into an incapacitated jelly, and they pushed on blindly through the fog to make it to the first glass door a few paces in front of them. The guy who had torn off his damaged mask didn't fare as well. From the muffled scream that Ben heard through the security glass, it was obvious that Ercan Kavur's pepper spray must be the proper undiluted tactical capsaicin agent that would put the most determined attacker out of action for a good half-hour, and not the attenuated dilution for sale to civilians in those few countries where governments still trusted citizens to defend life and property. The guy wouldn't be much of a threat for a while.

Ben had to smile. Round two to Kavur and his home improvements.

The leader never even glanced back at his fallen man. First to reach the security door, he shouldered and kicked and beat it with his gloved fist, but the alarm system had sent it into lockdown mode. In a fury he motioned to the breacher to take out the lock. The breacher stepped forward, jacked another round into the chamber of his shotgun, jammed the jagged muzzle tight up below the door handle, pulled the trigger, and BOOM, they were through. First came the leader, then the breacher, then the third guy dragging their incapacitated comrade out of the smoke and dumping him on the floor, where he lay writhing and rubbing his eyes as if they were on fire.

By then, Ben and Anna were already through the second glass door, Anna frantically punching in the four-digit code from memory to override the lockdown mode long enough for them to dart through and slam it shut behind them. The electronic lock reactivated on closing with a solid clunk, audible over the screech of the alarm siren.

The leader sprinted towards them and slid to a halt as the second door blocked his way. He ripped off his goggles and respirator.

Ben had been about to hurry on, but he held back. He and the man were just feet apart, almost close enough to reach out and touch if the security glass hadn't separated them.

The man's eyes seemed to bore into Ben's.

Ben stared back.

Chapter 35

Ben was good with faces. Never forgot one, and certainly wouldn't have forgotten this one. He was certain he'd never met, or seen, this guy before in his life. Yet, as he lingered for a moment that seemed suspended in time, he experienced the strangest feeling of semi-recognition. It wasn't the facial features themselves – the shaven head, the solid cheekbones, the square heavy jaw behind the goatee beard.

No, it was the eyes. They were like the eyes of a shark watching him. Dull, lifeless, yet filled with such an intensity of inhuman hatred that Ben had only ever seen once before on a man's face.

That man was dead. Ben had seen him die. And yet—

Then the moment was over. The man's lips curled into a kind of snarl and he raised his weapon and loosed a fully automatic burst of gunfire at his side of the security door. He disappeared from sight as the reinforced glass became an opaque web of cracks.

Ben turned away from the door, took Anna's hand and they ran away down the corridor.

'That man—' Anna gasped as they hurried on. It seemed to Ben that she had more to say, but there was no time for conversation. The attackers would be through the second door in moments.

Ben and Anna sprinted for the kitchen. Her shoes weren't made for running and she stumbled and almost fell. They burst inside the kitchen, past the table and chair, and to the back door.

'I hope you know this combination too,' Ben said, pointing at the panel on the wall. 'Or this is going to be a very short escape.' She nodded and started tapping in a number with a shaking hand. Just as she finished entering the code there was a muffled blast behind them as the breaching shotgun took out the second security door.

'There,' she said.

Ben kicked open the back door and the cold night air rushed in. The temperature outside seemed to have dropped several more degrees. He pushed Anna out of the door, then followed, slamming the door behind him. There were two steps down to a path that wound back around the side of the house towards the front. The flagstones were covered in two inches of fresh snow over a layer of ice. Anna slipped and went down on her side with a cry. Ben scooped her up and got her back on her feet. Her flimsy blouse was wet and clinging to her skin where she'd fallen. No time to stop and ask her if she was hurt. A security light flashed on as they ran, illuminating them like a floodlamp shining on a pair of escaping prison inmates. Their pursuers would be out of the house in seconds.

Now Ben and Anna were racing around the corner to the front of the property, down the driveway, towards the gate, slithering on the ice, their breath fogging in huge clouds. Lights were coming on in neighbouring houses as residents became alarmed at the commotion. Faces were peeking through curtains. Nobody would dare venture outside, but someone would be bound to have called the cops. The police might already be on their way, a complication that Ben pushed to the back of his mind as he ran through the gate and into the empty street.

Slabs of fresh snow had layered the roofs and bonnets and windscreens of the Volvo and the Audi. Ben's eye landed on the big SUV and he thought, *Kavur*. It was the kind of car in which a drugged-up kidnap victim could be bundled in the back. He let go of Anna and wrenched open the tailgate, but the cavernous boot was empty.

Big it might be, and built like a Sherman tank, but the Volvo was the slower car compared to the Audi, and speed was what Ben wanted. He ran to the saloon. The driver's door was open. No key dangling from the ignition. His guts gave a twist of panic, but then he noticed the keyless start button and the fob lying in a moulded recess in the centre console. He shoved a foot inside the footwell, pressed the brake and touched the button and the engine instantly powered into life. He hurled his bag onto the back seats. Flicked on the lights and wipers. The frozen blades juddered, then sprang free and sliced away the brittle layer of snow on the glass.

Anna hovered uncertainly nearby, as if paralysed by the bitter cold. Ben pointed at the passenger side and ordered her to get in, and his sharp command spurred her back into life. As she scurried to the passenger side, she was looking fearfully at him as if to say, *What are you doing?*

Ben leaped back towards the Volvo. The dirty tyre tracks in the snow were already beginning to freeze over into hard ruts. He knelt behind the big boxy rear of the car. Clumps of snow were clinging to its wheels. He planted the tip of the carving knife horizontally against the sidewall of a rear tyre, and used the heel of his left hand on the handle to punch the blade through the rubber. When they did it in the movies, the tyre burst in a spectacular explosion. In real life it just gasped a loud hiss of bad-smelling air and the Volvo sank down at one corner.

Ben was about to do the same with the other rear wheel when he heard Anna's panicked voice from the Audi, screaming his name. He looked up and saw the three armed men charging around the corner, sprinting across the garden for the gate. The leader was in front, his boots pounding the frozen ground as he ran like a madman, his gun raised to the shoulder, eyes darting from side to side, hunting for his escaping targets.

Ben leaped to his feet. Head low, he covered the few steps to the Audi in two leaps. The leader saw him and opened fire. The sharp *rat-a-rat-tat* cut through the silence of the empty street. Bullets chittered off the Audi's bodywork. Ben reached the driver's door, ripped it open and threw himself inside. Anna was saying something, but her words were coming out in a terrified gargle.

The men were racing closer. More gunshots raked across the Audi's windscreen. The left side-door mirror burst apart as a bullet smashed into it. Anna screamed. Ben pressed a hand against her shoulder and forced her roughly down into the passenger footwell. He rammed the stick into drive and stamped down hard on the gas, and the Audi's wheels spun with a tortured scream as it leaped forwards.

Steering with one hand and pressing Anna down with the other he aimed the nose of the car at the oncoming attackers and hammered the wheels up onto the snowy kerb straight at them. The Audi absorbed a dozen more snapping gunshots before the three men scattered out of his path. One slipped on the ice and went down in his haste to avoid being run over. Ben swerved away from the gateway and accelerated along the pavement, scraping past the parked Volvo. Swerved again, bumping down off the kerb and onto the road and booting as much power as he could force from the Audi's screaming engine as the wheels bit down on the slippery surface and he sped fishtailing away from the scene. A glance in his remaining mirror told him the three men were piling into the Volvo. The leader was getting behind the wheel. Its headlights flared into life and it took off in pursuit.

The chase had only just begun.

Chapter 36

Ben had a start on their pursuers, but it was only a tenuous one and he intended to widen the gap as fast as he could. The worsening weather conditions weren't going to make that easy. It was turning into a blizzard out there and the driving snow was splatting the windscreen faster than the wipers could bat it away. What little he could see of the road as he sped down the street was a blanket of virgin white, drifting up against the edges of the kerbs and mounding on the roofs of parked cars.

The street on which Ercan Kavur lived was long and narrow, lined with a clutter of dilapidated houses and apartment buildings. By the time Ben reached the end of the street, he was going over eighty kilometres an hour. Much too fast for the conditions but the glare of the Volvo's headlights filling the cabin of the Audi pushed him on faster. The SUV should have been crippled by its punctured tyre but its driver was coming after them like a madman, wallowing and skidding all over the road in their wake. If Ben slowed down, it would be right on their tail.

Shots cracked out. The Volvo's passengers were hanging out of its open windows, firing at the speeding Audi. Their aim was wild but they could get lucky. The Audi's rear window blew out and a bullet punched through the back of the passenger seat. Now that they had Ercan Kavur, maybe they were no longer as concerned about keeping Anna Manzini alive as Ben had thought.

'Stay down,' he yelled at her over the roar of the engine. She was bundled up in the passenger footwell, getting thrown about with the motion of the car.

Ben had no idea where he was going, but as he reached the bottom of the street and there were suddenly no more buildings he could tell they must be on the extreme eastern edge of the city, on the cusp between the last suburban developments and the start of open countryside. The Audi's wheels hammered over a road surface that was pocked and rough under the snow, hardly more than a track with snow-clumped scrubby grass and tangled bushes marking its edges. The Audi shot by a broken-down house with junked snow-covered cars in its front yard. Then a sharp right bend flashed up without warning, and Ben piled the car into it too fast and felt the wheels losing traction and going into a slide.

A dilapidated fence rushed towards them in the head-lights. With his heart in his mouth he swerved to avoid it, felt the tyres bite again and accelerated harder up the track. Trees and bushes tore past. If it had been a clear night, he might have been able to see the sprawling craggy hills stretching away from the city dotted with scrub vege-tation and snow-laden conifers, the lights of Ankara clustered and twinkling to his left in the distance, maybe a pylon or a mobile phone mast here and there on the high ground, some of the outlying pockets of residential areas where the spreading city had engulfed surrounding villages, and the mountains in the distance. But all he could see was a steady stream of snowflakes rushing at him like twin arcs of tracer fire in his headlights, and

234

behind it the flat greyness of the blizzard blanketing the night.

The Volvo kept on coming. This guy just wouldn't give up. In Florence, Ben had been the hunter. Now he was beginning to feel decidedly like the hunted. The shooters kept up their crackling fire, missing more than they were hitting, but still hitting plenty. Lots of damage. The Audi's perforated bodywork was soaking up pounds of lead. Warning displays were burning like Christmas tree lights all over the instrument panel. Superior German engineering or not, there was only so much punishment the car could take.

The rear window on Ben's side disintegrated in a shower of glass. Another bullet smacked through the headrest of his seat and he felt it part the hair above his ear before it bit a chunk out of the steering wheel an inch from his fingers and buried itself in the dashboard. That was about as close a call as he wanted. But the car's core vitals were seemingly still untouched and it kept going, tearing along the rough road that was now so bumpy and potholed that the suspension was hammering against the stops and the revs were screaming up and down as the wheels constantly struggled for grip on the treacherous surface.

The Volvo was still right there behind them, its lights burning into the windowless back of the Audi, muzzle flash popping from its flanks. Its driver was demented, reckless, suicidal. He was pushing them all to the brink. As if survival instinct meant nothing to him. Only the chase, and the kill at the end of it.

This couldn't go on. Ben knew he had to do something, or any second now this journey would come to a swift and sudden halt. From a bullet or a crash – either way it wouldn't matter once they were both smashed to a pulp.

'Hang on tight,' he yelled. Anna had nothing to hang on to, but she wedged herself tighter into the passenger footwell as he sawed at the wheel and left the road, belting down an even narrower track that veered off to the right through a sudden gap in the bushes.

An instant later he knew it was a bad turning. The track disappeared and he found himself hammering over rough grassland covered in two feet of snow, lurching up and down hillocks, the bottom of the car grinding and scraping over hidden boulders and rocks. Behind them, the Volvo's headlamps were bucking and bouncing like the lights of a ship on a stormy ocean. Ben gritted his teeth and pressed on through it for several hundred yards until the grinding and banging stopped and the Audi cleared a grassy knoll to come bouncing onto an actual road. It had eighteen inches of snow over it, but under the snow was smooth solid tarmac and now Ben could take advantage of the Audi's speed and four intact tyres. He pressed his right foot down all the way. The engine note soared. The Volvo's lights, which had reached the road in his wake, now began to recede in the mirror. The gunfire had stopped.

The road seemed to be leading back towards the edge of the city. Walls and railings and gateways flashed by, too fast to see anything except the speeding tunnel ahead, Ben wrestling the wheel to keep it between the hedges as he ripped a racing line through one twisting bend after another. The Volvo kept falling back, shrinking away in the rear-view mirror. Ben felt a smile spread over his face. *Bye-bye, you bastards.* They wouldn't catch him now.

That was when a new warning light in the instrument cluster began flashing urgently at him to catch his attention, and he tore his eyes away momentarily from the road to glance at it. What he saw there clenched at his guts like an icy fist.

A bullet must have clipped the Audi's fuel line or holed the tank. The gauge was almost at zero. The car was running on fumes and very soon it was going to run out altogether.

Chapter 37

Ben had barely processed the realisation in his mind when the engine coughed and seemed to falter for a moment before it caught again. That was the kind of warning he couldn't ignore. *Not good*, he thought. He slackened his pressure on the gas, afraid to use up what little was left too soon.

By now, the chase had carried them into some kind of sprawling industrial zone on the outer reaches of Ankara. Snowy-roofed factories and warehouses, huts and store buildings and chain-link fences rimed with white zipped by, all in darkness like a ghost town. Ben had no idea how long his remaining fuel would last, but before too long at all he was going to have to abandon this car and either find another or look for a place to hide.

Anna squirmed out of the footwell and into the passenger seat, looking tousled and frightened as the questions poured out of her. 'What's happening? Where are we? Are we getting away?'

'You don't want to know,' he said. Glanced in the mirror and saw the Volvo's lights growing larger again as its driver came on like a demon, rapidly closing the gap.

Definitely not good.

'Buckle up,' he told her. 'This isn't over yet.'

The network of roads and alleyways branching off in all

directions between industrial buildings large and small was like a maze. Ben turned left, right, right, left, picking junctions at random and throwing the car into one after another, not slowing down, kicking up sprays of ice and powder snow as the Audi fishtailed crazily through the bends. Strapped into her seat, too terrified to look, Anna was clutching the door handle and had her eyes clamped shut. Behind them the Volvo skidded, spun on the ice, lost ground, came after them again. The Audi's engine gave another faltering cough. Air in the fuel line. Ben was pretty sure all he had left was whatever remained in his carbs. Any moment now, the engine was going to die. That was if the fuel pump didn't overheat and seize up first from lack of lubrication.

A long straight rushed towards them, with no side roads to duck into, nowhere to hide. The Volvo was coming up fast. Its rear tyre was completely shredded and flapping off its wheel, but the driver was thrashing it on like the coachman from hell. His two guys were hanging out of the side windows, their jackets and masks covered in snow. More shots snapped off. Ben's remaining door mirror blew apart. He didn't need it. Didn't need reminding of what was behind him.

Or, of the fact that they were now heading right into a dead end. The way ahead was barred by a massive chain-link fence that was heavily padlocked. Anna opened her eyes at the wrong moment and let out a cry as she saw the gates coming and realised he was going to crash right through them.

They hit the gates with a shattering clang of metal on metal and went tearing on through, bits of ripped wire and metal fencepost trailing along behind them as they entered a separate section of the industrial park. To their left as they raced up a narrow alley were unbroken, uneven rows of what looked like disused railway sidings and maintenance sheds, with piles of rusty equipment and lengths of dismantled aluminium barrier and sleepers and other assorted junk. To their right was a long, tall ribbon of wire fence that ran on beyond the reach of the car's headlights.

The Audi began to splutter and shake. The Volvo was gaining fast. Bullets punched into their tail. Ben felt the back tyres go and the rear of the car begin to sway like a pendulum. Heard Anna yelling his name, but barely registered it. They were going to die unless he did something *right now*, but he didn't know what.

Not yet.

In such extreme situations, the average human brain easily becomes so flooded with acute stress and terror that it can cease to function properly. Rational faculties and decision-making ability are overwhelmed by panic as the heart rate shoots into the red, hyperventilation causes dizziness and weakness, neurochemical connections fire off too fast for thoughts to be processed and a massive overload of sensory impressions quickly leads to total mental shutdown and physical paralysis.

But Ben Hope's was not the average human brain. The way his mind worked, the closer he came to impending violent death, the more extreme the immediate threat, the more relaxed he became. In this moment, speeding into darkness at over a hundred and twenty kilometres an hour with automatic gunfire hacking and chopping the car to pieces around him and the engine screaming its last before it ran out of gas and Anna shrieking in his ear, he felt as calm as if he was lounging in a hammock on a lazy summer afternoon, lulled half-asleep by the singing of the birds in the trees above, a cool drink in his hand. Everything slowed down. Seconds became minutes. He had all the time in the world to figure out a plan.

And then it came to him.

Crazy. Utterly insane. But he'd had crazier ideas in his life, and he was still here.

To his right, the other side of the mesh fence and running parallel with it, the rough ground sloped upwards into an embankment that a snatched glance out of his shattered window told him was a section of the Ankara high-speed railway line that skirted the city. That explained two things: first, the presence of the rail maintenance sheds and train-related junk on the left. Second, it explained the fact that the sudden dazzling brightness of the light filling the back of the Audi couldn't only be coming from the headlamps of the pursuing Volvo.

A train was approaching. Moving fast. Roaring up on their right rear quarter, set to overtake and come ripping past at any moment, just a stone's throw beyond the fence.

And in his slowed-down ultra-calm near-death state of mind, Ben had also noticed what lay ahead. A dumper truck had tipped a massive load of gravel on the inside of the fence; a whole hill of the stuff, spilled against the wire and bulging it outwards. Presumably some crew of workers, now most likely fast asleep in their beds, were meant to come and spread it or make whatever use of it was intended, but for the moment it had just been left there. As had the lengths of aluminium railway barrier that had been carelessly dumped across the mound at an angle, ramped diagonally upwards towards the fence. It had been there long enough for the snow to drift thickly up against its base and freeze hard, glittering like a small sugar mountain in the headlights of the speeding cars and the glare of the approaching train.

Ben saw his chance. Thought, *fuck it*, and stamped his

foot on the gas and veered the car a few degrees to the right to steer straight for the base of the ramp. Whatever last few dribbles of fuel remained in his carburettor float bowls propelled the Audi towards it like a rocket.

And whatever words were about to burst from Anna's screaming mouth, it all happened too fast for them to come out. The Audi smashed up the ramp in a storm of exploding ice and snow, so hard that it felt as if its wheels had been ripped off. The brutal wrench of the impact almost tore the steering out of Ben's clenched fists. He felt his body pressed back into the seat and his stomach sink as the car left the ground and its nose tilted towards the sky and it hurtled upward at a forty-five-degree angle. The revs soared up an octave, one final tortured howl before the last drop of fuel finally burned away.

The car launched into space. Its momentum carried it straight into the mesh fence and beyond as it ripped a hole right through the wire and sailed high over the snowy embankment and over the tracks in an arcing parabola. An unguided missile, carrying Ben and Anna with it.

Straight into the path of the oncoming train.

Chapter 38

The giant monster was almost on them. An unstoppable force moving so fast that its driver could have done nothing to scrub off the slightest bit of speed as the car came bursting out of nowhere across his path, sailing high over the tracks. The train's blinding white glare filled the inside of the airborne Audi like the flash of a nuclear explosion. The thunderous roar was the loudest sound Ben had ever heard. Louder than an artillery battle at close range. It completely drowned Anna's scream, filled every space and vibrated every cell inside his body.

And then they were dead. Or they should have been, the car squashed flat on impact and then smashed down onto the tracks and pulverised by the train's wheels, their bodies reduced to mincemeat in a fraction of a second.

But the impact never came. The car passed in front of the train's nose by a matter of inches and began to drop towards the ground. Its front wheels hit first, slamming into the downwards slope of the embankment on the far side of the tracks. Ben and Anna were hurled against their seat belts with the force of the landing. Behind them the train hammered past, the moving pocket of air at its nose slapping them like a shockwave as it came hurtling by. The car bounced and seemed about to flip and cartwheel; but then all four wheels were back on solid ground and they were moving again, rolling away from the roaring clatter that made the air tremble and blasted a blizzard of swirling snowflakes in its slipstream. The train kept coming and coming. The ground trembled as if an earthquake had struck.

'*Sei completamente pazzo!*' Anna yelled in Ben's ear over the deafening noise.

Ben heard that one. He couldn't agree more: he probably was completely mad, but at least they were still alive, just about. As Anna kept up a rapid-fire torrent of abuse about how utterly insane he was and how he'd almost killed them both, he grabbed the steering wheel and yanked the Audi's gearstick into neutral. The engine had given all it had to give. The dead car began to roll faster down the slope of the embankment. The train was still clattering past, seemingly infinite in length – but all too soon it would be gone into the night and their pursuers stranded on the other side of the tracks would be able to find a way to come after them. Ben knew he had limited time to make his escape.

The rolling car picked up speed down the slope. It was steeper and longer than Ben had anticipated, which was both a good thing and a bad thing. Bad, because the snow had drifted up thick against the side of the embankment making the terrain so treacherous that one touch on the brakes would send them into a sideways slide that would turn into a roll, and then a lethal tumble all the way down to the bottom of the hill.

Worse, the landing had destroyed the car's headlights. They were free-falling blind, crashing through mounds of snow that splashed up all over the windscreen and obliterated what little forward vision they had. Moments earlier the Audi had been an unguided airborne missile – now it was an uncontrollable bobsleigh plummeting through the darkness, ripping through unseen shrubs and bushes as it went. Ben gritted his teeth and tried to steady the slithering, gyrating, bucking car, but it was out of his hands. If a tree or a rock were in their path, they wouldn't even see the obstacle coming before the car came to a sudden, crunching halt, and maybe their lives with it.

When the crash came, it wasn't a solid tree trunk or a boulder they hit, but an abandoned wooden storage hut at the bottom of the hill. It was a hidden rut beneath the snow that saved them from a head-on collision, bouncing them sideways at the last instant so that the car's flank took the worst of the impact. Ben was flung against the driver's door, and Anna against him. Ripped bits of planking flew all around as the car ploughed through the flimsy wall of the hut and spun through several full turns, demolishing the building totally before it finally came to rest on the snowy hillside.

Then there was eerie stillness, just the ticking of hot metal and the rasp of their breathing as they sat still for a moment in the darkness of the wrecked car, gathering their wits and slowly realising that they were still alive.

'You okay?' Ben said at last.

'I think so,' Anna replied shakily, not sounding too sure.

The driver's door was too badly twisted to open, so the two of them had to scramble out of the passenger side. The snow was almost up to their knees, and fresh billows were still tumbling from the sky. The night air felt deeply refrigerated. Ben could already feel his cheeks beginning to tingle before they started going numb. He and Anna were still warm from adrenalin, but the cold would start getting to them quickly, especially her. He peeled off his leather jacket and, despite her protests, made her put it on and zip it up to her neck. He was worried about her feet, pressed deep into the snow. His own would stay warm and dry for hours in his heavy waterproof boots, even if the rest of him froze. Hers were almost totally unprotected in those flimsy little shoes.

Ben retrieved his bag from the back seat and shone the flashlight up and down the length of the car. Its rear bodywork panels were bullet-shredded and perforated beyond recognition. The front suspension had collapsed. A trickle of smoke was rising from its rumpled bonnet. Or maybe steam. Ben was far from being an expert mechanic, but he knew enough to recognise a vehicle that wouldn't be going anywhere from here. He pointed the light beam up the hill, could see no lights, nobody coming after them. Not yet, but they soon would be.

He made Anna lean against the side of the car and shone his torch over her to check for anything broken. He could find no damage. Lucky.

'Still think this Babylon idol of yours is worth going after?' he asked her.

She glared at him, her temper flaring up. 'Do you think I would be so weak that I would give up, just because I'm a woman?'

'Not in the least. I've known some pretty crazy women.' He thought of Brooke, fighting her way out of the armed South American compound in which she'd been held captive and hiking alone through miles of Amazonian jungle. Roberta Ryder, picking up his Browning pistol in the middle of a firefight with multiple attackers after he'd been shot, and getting them both to safety. That made him think of Father Pascal, who'd looked after him during his recovery. That in turn made his thoughts cycle back to Jeff, picturing him lying there with the tubes and the needles, maybe never to regain consciousness. He sighed.

'I won't give up,' Anna snapped, shooting daggers with her eyes. 'I'm perfectly capable of seeing this through to the end. Besides, nobody could possibly be half as crazy as you, Ben Hope. What kind of *deficiente* would have done what you did back there?'

First he was called a lunatic, now he was a moron too. But he wasn't in a mood to get offended. 'Now you know why the car hire companies won't touch me with a bargepole any more.'

'It's not funny,' she fumed at him, in no way mollified. 'And if you would mind not pushing and pulling me around and speaking to me as though I were one of your soldiers, that would also be very much appreciated.'

He spread his hands. 'My apologies,' he said graciously. 'Now if you don't mind, at the risk of telling you what to do, it's my opinion that we should be getting out of here before our friends come looking for us. Can you manage to walk?'

'I can manage fine.'

Ben wasn't so sure that she could, but he said nothing.

Chapter 39

They abandoned the car and started making their way down the hillside, picking out a wandering path between the snow-laden conifers and thorny bushes that dotted the steep incline. If the hut hadn't arrested their descent when it had, they might have come down the hill much more quickly, with a one hundred per cent chance of getting killed in the process.

Ben had no idea where they were going, just that they needed to keep moving in the hope of finding either some kind of shelter, or some kind of vehicle. But keeping moving in near-blizzard conditions wasn't an easy thing to do. Without his jacket, he could feel the killer cold gradually seeping into his body.

The ground levelled out into a wooded valley where the snow wasn't quite as deep. Every so often a fallen tree blocked their way, making them skirt around or scramble over it. An hour passed. The going was slow and they hadn't come far in real terms, but as the wilderness closed in around them Ankara could have been a thousand miles away. On the far side of the wooded valley the terrain became rougher and rockier, full of hidden boulders lurking beneath the snow that could easily trip an unwary foot. Ben walked behind Anna so that he could keep an eye on her. His relief at giving their pursuers the slip was overshadowed by his concern for how she was doing. Her temper had long ago subsided and she was very quiet as she struggled gamely on, kilometre after painful kilometre, stumbling more often and slowing her pace until she eventually halted and slumped on a big rock that jutted out of the snow.

'My feet. I can't feel them any more.'

Ben knelt in the snow in front of her, clamped his flashlight in his teeth to see by, unshouldered his bag and undid the straps. From inside he took out both pairs of spare thick socks. 'Put your feet here,' he said, pointing at his thighs, and she did. He pulled off each of her shoes in turn and tossed them away. They disappeared in the snow.

'Those are Prada.'

'I'm sure some fashionable Turkish lady will find them in the springtime and cherish them forever. You don't need them any more.' He rolled up the hems of her flimsy trousers, then peeled off her thin socks and threw them away too. They were soaking wet. Her toenails were carmine red, while the skin of her feet, ankles and calves was almost blue with cold.

'Am I going to get frostbite?' she asked anxiously.

'Can you wiggle your toes?'

She wiggled them. 'Just about.'

'Then we won't have to chop them off anytime soon.' He rubbed everything dry with a spare T-shirt, then pulled the socks onto her feet, two pairs apiece. He used a length of duct tape to attach them to each trouser leg, so they couldn't slip off. 'Good enough for the Norwegian Army,' he said. 'And those blokes know a thing or two about keeping your feet toasty in cold weather.' He closed up his bag, stood up. Anna peered at her feet, holding them clear of the snow to keep them dry.

'They feel warmer already, but now I can't walk.'

'You don't have to,' he said. He reached down to pick her up. 'Put your arm around my neck.'

'You're not going to carry me?'

'That's exactly what I'm going to do.' He lifted her off the rock, one arm around her torso and the other under the crook of her knees.

'But we're in the middle of nowhere. You can't carry me all that way.'

He gave her a reassuring smile. 'You ever been to Wales? There's a mountain there called Pen Y Fan. In winter it makes this place look like Miami Beach. For SAS training we were expected to march right the way over it in full pack, plus rifle and ammunition. My bergen alone was heavier than you.'

But that pack had been on his back, held tight to his body by wide webbing straps, the science of weight distribution and ergonomic efficiency all carefully worked out by military minds. Even that kind of load, carried for too long, occasionally proved enough of an endurance test to claim the lives of strong, fit young warriors twenty years or more his junior. Ben knew all that even as he set off with her in his arms, but outwardly he just smiled and acted as though it was nothing.

After a mile, though, his arm muscles were screaming, his spine was arched backwards to counter the forward drag and his neck felt ready to snap off. He was afraid of stumbling in the snow and dropping her. The big fat flakes were falling even more thickly from the sky, drifting down like feathery moths that clung to his hair and eyelashes, making him blink. The temperature was still dropping. The cold was seeping deeper towards his core. His face was numb. His denim shirt was soaked through to the skin. He was

250

trembling and his teeth were chattering. Which was a good sign. It was when they stopped chattering that you needed to start worrying.

Just one of the tell-tale signs of hypothermia. Others included headaches, loss of coordination, blurred vision, slurred speech and increasing stupor that eventually led to unconsciousness. After another mile, he was still doing reasonably okay himself but he was worried that Anna was becoming drowsy and unresponsive. 'Hey,' he said close to her ear. 'What was the birth date of Alexander the Great again? Remind me.'

She mumbled back, 'Three fifty-six BC.'

'What month?'

'August,' she answered after a pause.

'Wrong. It was June. What day?'

'I don't know,' came the slurred reply. 'Why are you asking me all these questions?'

He marched on, trying to keep her talking, but before long she stopped answering and her arm drooped loosely from his neck, putting even more dead weight on his straining biceps. If he didn't find shelter for them both before the night was out, her core temperature was going to drop to critical point, her organs would begin to shut down, and she was going to freeze and die.

Then, sometime afterwards, exactly the same thing was going to happen to him. Nobody would find them until the snow melted, sometime next year. Perhaps never at all.

He marched on, half-blinded, snow in his eyes. Snow in his hair, snow down his neck. The chill gnawing right through him. His feet were two blocks of wood and he could no longer feel his arms. His blood was chugging to a stand-still in his veins. He had thought he'd been cold crawling from the Arno River in Florence. He couldn't take much

251

more of this, but he made himself do it anyway. Step after step. *Always a little further.* Like the words of the James Elroy Flecker poem that adorned the wall of the SAS chapel at the regimental HQ in Hereford.

> *We are the pilgrims, Master; we shall go always a little*
>   *further:*
> *It may be beyond that last blue mountain barr'd with snow,*
> *Across that angry or that glimmering sea.*

The poem had always inspired him, kept him fighting and struggling and driven him to survive even when the odds appeared insurmountable. And that was what it did now.

And then, through the swirling blizzard, he saw the dark shapes of the buildings up ahead.

Chapter 40

The farmhouse was in a whole different order from Ben's solid stone-built home in France. As he got closer and played his torch beam over it through the falling snow he saw it was little more than a log cabin, long and low, the green paint old and peeling. Its corrugated roof extended outwards all around to make a veranda whose wooden steps had rotted away and were buried under a mound of white. An iron stovepipe chimney jutted from one end of the roof and icicles as long and thick as unicorn horns hung from the rusted guttering. Some of the windows were boarded, others broken.

Next to the house was a lean-to barn that was in no better state, snow drifted deep against its chained and padlocked doors. Old animal pens stood empty and forlorn nearby. The patch of land around the homestead, maybe a couple of acres, was planted with the corpses of dead trees, gnarled ghosts of what had once been a small apple orchard. Whatever smallholder family had tried to make a go of it here had probably packed up and left not long after the trees had died, and their livelihood with them. It was a sad and gloomy place, but for Ben, it was a miracle haven whose discovery was almost enough for him to start believing in God again.

Almost.

Struggling up the broken-down steps onto the porch with Anna in his arms, he kicked open the front door. The smell of dank and decay wafted out of the dark interior. There was no need to call out, 'Anyone at home?' Nobody had been at home for years. Inside, he booted the door shut with his heel and lowered Anna gently down to the bare plank floor. She stirred, muttered something incoherent. He shone the torch around him. Life here had been as rustic as it could get. The smallholders obviously hadn't thought their few sticks of simple furniture worth taking with them when they left. In a corner was a chopping block made from a section of apple tree, with a small pile of kindling and logs and a rusty hatchet next to a spartan old wood burner.

Shivering violently, he knelt by the wood burner and laid his torch on the floor to give him some light. His hands were so numb that he could hardly get his fingers to work enough to scrape away the damp ashes clogging up the grate. With luck, the stovepipe chimney wouldn't be packed solid with generations of bird nests.

Luck was on his side. In a few minutes he had a fire going, a small smoky flame that he carefully built into a crackling blaze. The cast-iron stove soaked up the heat, clicking and ticking as the metal warmed and threw out a glow that began to chase the cold air from the room. He moved Anna close to the spreading warmth.

'What is this place?' she asked groggily.

'We'll be safe here for a while,' he said. 'Let's get you out of these wet clothes.'

Anna was too cold to have many inhibitions. They both stripped to their underwear, huddling and shivering as close to the fire as they could without burning themselves. The smallholders had fixed up a rack for drying clothes from a pulley above the stove. Ben hung their things from it, and soon there were clouds of steam billowing from the soaked material. He joined her on the floor and the two of them sat pressed up close together, feeling the wonderful heat sinking into them and the blood beginning to circulate once more through their half-naked bodies. He wrapped an arm around her bare shoulder and rubbed her back and arms to get the circulation going.

It was several minutes before Anna's shivering died away and she was able to talk normally. Ben uncapped his flask and shared a little whisky with her. She spluttered at the taste of it, but gratefully took a few more sips. The firelight glowed amber on her skin and danced in her eyes. 'Thank you for looking after me, Ben. I'm sorry I snapped at you before.'

'Sticks and stones,' he said. 'Better than bullets and grenades.'

'They won't find us here, will they?'

'Not unless they're psychic, and riding on polar bears.'

'Perhaps they are psychic. I can't understand how else they got to Ercan's house before us.'

'I've been asking myself the same question,' Ben said. 'They seemed to know exactly where we were headed, and that's a little too much of a coincidence. You said that nobody could locate Ercan unless they had his address. Unless I'm missing something, there's only one place they could have got that. From you.'

'From me?'

'Specifically, from your laptop,' he said. 'You left it behind in Greece.'

'Because you told me I couldn't go back for it.'

'What exactly was on that laptop, Anna?'

She shrugged. 'Everything.'

'Such as?'

'When I'm researching a project I keep a diary of all my thoughts and ideas as it takes shape. My travel plans, everything.'

'Including the names and contact details of the people you were intending to visit?'

'It's all in my address book.'

'Which is on the laptop too?'

'That's where people keep them nowadays.'

'Do they? I have a leather book that sits by the phone.'

She said nothing.

'And the laptop was where?' he asked.

'It was in my travel bag, along with my clothes and other things. I didn't try to hide it. Why would I? In any case, Ben, as I told you, the material in the computer is encrypted.'

'There's encrypted and "encrypted". How hard would it be to access?'

She looked flustered from his questioning. 'I'm not all that expert with computers, and in any case I wasn't expecting anyone to pry into it. You just have to enter a code to get in. The thing asked for a password of twelve digits or more, so I used "Nebuchadnezzar". I suppose, if Usberti had hold of it, he might have—'

'Yes,' Ben said. 'I suppose that too. In which case, he'd have known exactly where in Ankara you were headed.'

'I suppose,' she said.

He thought for a minute. 'Among these personal details, did you write down Ercan's various security passwords and combinations?'

'On the last day I stayed with him, he ran out of provisions and went out shopping. I was terrified I would set off the alarms while he was gone, so I got him to list them all down for me and I copied them down. But only the numbers, not what they were for. I had my own system for remembering what was what. Nobody else could have used them.'

'What matters is that they knew they were dealing with a paranoid nut,' Ben said. 'Which is also why they were able to get inside his house so easily. Usberti's no fool. He would have known the place would be on lockdown and Ercan would never open the door to a bunch of strangers. I'll bet he used a decoy.'

'What kind of decoy?'

'It wouldn't be hard to find a nice-looking woman of about the right height and build, dress her up to look stylish, put a long black wig on her, stick some money in her pocket and tell her what to do. A hooker, maybe, happy to earn easy cash for a change. All it took was for her to ring his doorbell and say into the speaker "Ercan, it's me, Anna, I've come to see you," and his whole security system was worthless. The instant he deactivated the alarm to open the door, the heavies jumped out of the bushes, pushed their way inside and that was it. Then they took him away and waited nearby for us to walk into the trap.'

Anna looked crestfallen. 'I can't believe this is happening. It's like Theo Kambasis all over again. How could I have known Ercan would be in danger?'

'You couldn't,' Ben said. 'So don't beat yourself up over it.' Which was some advice, coming from the man who had spent much of his life plagued by guilt over things he couldn't control.

They were silent for a few minutes, listening to the crackle of the fire. Ben tossed on another log.

'There's something else,' she said. 'This may sound crazy to you.'

'Try me.'

'That man back there. The leader. It seems insane, but somehow I felt that I recognised him.'

'Me too,' Ben admitted, 'and it's been bugging me the whole time. I'm certain I've never come across him in my life, and yet . . . it's as if I'd seen the bastard before.'

'It's the eyes,' Anna said shakily, gazing into the flames with a troubled expression, as if she saw something there that haunted her. 'I can't ever forget those eyes. They are the same eyes that looked at me that night in France, years ago, when I thought I was going to die.'

Ben turned to face her. She wasn't joking. 'What are you saying?'

'Bozza,' she replied, tight-lipped. There was total conviction in her voice.

'That's impossible,' Ben said. 'Franco Bozza's been dead for years. And in any case, he was bigger, taller.'

'Then this man is related to him. His son?'

'Too old for that.'

'Then his brother, perhaps. Is it possible?'

Ben shook his head grimly. He didn't want to believe it, but his instinct told him Anna might be right. 'I don't like it, but it's not impossible. It would mean—'

'Ben? What would it mean?'

'First, if you're right, it would mean this guy has more motivation than whatever cash sum Usberti's paying him to do a job. He wants revenge for his brother's death.'

'And he knows you killed him.'

'Or thinks I did. As it happens, the blind woman shot him. Two rounds from an old broom-handle Mauser pistol. The first got him in the throat, the second blew the top of his head off.'

'That sounds like very precise shooting from a blind woman.'

258

'That's because she was only pretending to be blind. Had us both fooled.'

'Oh.'

'And secondly,' Ben said, 'if you're right, it means we're up against someone a lot worse than your regular rent-a-thug. The first Bozza was bad enough, and he was just a plain-vanilla hired assassin, sadist and torturer. Little brother, if that's who he is, is a tougher prospect. He's done some army time. Maybe quite a bit of it.'

'You can tell?'

'Like day from night.'

'He was a soldier like you?'

Ben shook his head. 'If he'd been a soldier like me, or like any of my guys back in the day, he wouldn't have confined his assault to the front door. He'd have split his men up and hit the front and back both at once. Then we'd have had a real problem getting out of that house. What that means is that he was never in Special Forces, in anyone's army. That's the good news. The bad news is, you take a man with the screwed-up psychopathic genes of a Bozza brother and put him through any kind of serious military training, teach him how to fight with weapons or bare hands, how to endure physical punishment and ignore pain, you're bound to create some kind of monster. But then, we've already had a taster of what he's like.'

'He won't stop coming after us, will he?'

Ben shook his head again. 'Nope. Not until it's over. We'll be seeing him again, for sure.'

'This won't end well, will it?'

'For someone, it won't.'

'This is my problem, not yours. If I have to face it alone, I will. You don't have to stay with me.'

Ben looked at her, saw the earnestness in her face, and

his heart went out to her for her courage. 'You're not getting rid of me that easily,' he said. 'We're getting through this together, or not at all. You and me.'

'You, me and Ercan. We have to save him, too. Before those animals harm him.'

'I wouldn't bet on Ercan's chances, if I were you. His only value to the enemy is the information inside his head. How long he lives depends on how long it takes for Usberti's guys to get it out of him. My guess is, not long.'

'Then we have to get to him first,' Anna said firmly. 'The sooner we find Usberti, the sooner we find Ercan, alive. It all boils down to our search for the idol. We're all in the same race, hunting the same clues. And now I know where the next clue is leading us.'

Chapter 41

By now, the glow of the fire had spread through the whole cabin. Ben and Anna's bodies were warm, the whisky flask was empty and they felt as safe and cosy as two people in their predicament ever could. Ben took their dried-out clothes from the rack over the stove and handed Anna's down to where she sat on the floor. He kept his eyes discreetly averted as she stood up to dress.

'Such a gentleman,' she said. 'You can look now. Oh, it feels so good to be warm again.'

'You were saying you knew where we have to go next. I'd be interested in knowing that myself.'

She nodded. 'Thanks to Ercan. At first, when I read the papers from his document safe, I didn't understand. But then I realised. He figured it out. I told you he was a genius.'

'He must be, considering it now turns out the fragments of the Muranu tablet are of no use after all.'

'The tablet was . . . what's the expression? A red sardine.'

'A red herring,' Ben said.

'That's exactly what it was. Ercan realised that the pieces were too badly damaged to be decipherable, leaving him with no choice but to abandon them. But he's as tenacious a scholar as any detective. When you find one avenue of investigation becomes a dead end, you retrace your steps, go back to the starting point and look for another. This time he took a completely different approach, in order to try to trace the movements of the Muranu family after their escape from Babylon. The problem was, no such records existed. Instead, he found the solution buried in the administrative records of the PFA.'

'The Persepolis Fortification Archive,' Ben said, remembering.

Anna nodded.

'And?'

'Let me set up the context for you, or none of it will make sense. As we know, the Muranu family and their mysterious cargo left Babylon in October, 539 BC, literally days before the Persian army of Cyrus the Great swept in, conquered the city and took over the whole Babylonian Empire as part of their own, which it would remain for many years. Cyrus eventually died and his son Cambyses became king for eight years, until he died also and his son Darius took over in turn. In some ways, Darius was to the Persian Empire what King Nebuchadnezzar had been to Babylon, a highly capable empire builder. He expanded and consolidated Persia's conquests in territories including India. Like his father and grandfather before him, initially Darius used the city of Babylon as his capital; then in the year 518 BC he founded Persepolis—'

'City of the Persians,' Ben cut in. 'His new capital, in what's now Iran. You already told me this part.'

'But as the empire grew, so did the number of rebellions he had to deal with. Darius was very adept at putting down rebels. We can see that from the famous inscription carved into the rock of a cliff at Mount Behistun in Iran's Kermanshah Province, studied in depth by a British Army officer called Sir Henry Rawlinson who was the first to scale the mountain in 1835. The carving depicts Darius as a mighty warrior crushing a rebel underfoot.'

'What's the point of this?'

'Stop interrupting,' she said testily. 'All this background is important. Now, we also know from various records that minor insurrections began to break out all over Darius' empire in those years. Most of these rebellions Darius could entrust his local governors to quell. Law enforcement records, including records of executions of insurgents, would be gathered together in a central database, if you like, in the rapidly growing capital Persepolis. Do you follow me?'

'Every step. I just don't know where we're going.'

'You must have been a terrible student. Did your tutors never tell you that patience is a virtue?'

'It's also a luxury.'

'Well, now here's where we get to the really interesting part. When Ercan gave up on the tablet fragments and turned instead to the records of the Persepolis Fortification Archive, he found there a translated account of one particular uprising against the Persian authorities. It was led by a man known as The Babylonian, whose force of rebel bandits occupied the ruins of an old fortress in the hills near the city of Harran, within the Persian Imperial Province of Athura.'

'And?'

'And, as Ercan confirmed when he cross-checked the story against other historical records, it seems that The Babylonian and his rebels were a real stone in the side for the Persians.'

'A thorn in their side,' Ben corrected her. 'Or a stone in their shoe.'

'But you get the idea. They were a skilled guerrilla militia who scored a lot of success in attacking army convoys and supply routes, disrupting them very considerably. This went on for some time, until in 516 BC, the Persian-appointed governor finally sent a mass of soldiers who stormed the fortress and caught many of the rebels. The surviving prisoners were brought to the local garrison, where they were horribly put to death. All of which was entered in government records and later became part of the PFA archive. But while the authorities had managed to eliminate most of the outlaws, the leader himself managed to evade capture, and was never caught. Now, by cross-checking all the sources he could find, Ercan discovered that this enigmatic character was also known by another name: Ashar the Babylonian.

'Ashar the Babylonian,' Anna repeated, looking at Ben with a sparkle in her eyes. 'Do you see?'

Ben thought. The name sounded familiar, but where had he heard it? Then he remembered. 'You told me about him. The boy on the ship.'

'That's right. The eight-year-old Muranu child listed on the passenger manifest when they fled the incoming Persian invasion in 539, never to see their beloved home again. So it's thanks to the very precise records of old Babylon, and then the detailed law enforcement database of the Persian authorities, that for the first time we can pinpoint where the Muranus went after leaving Babylon.'

Ben did the arithmetic. Twenty-three years later, Ashar Muranu would have been thirty-one. A grown man, and a dedicated rebel against the imperial invaders who forced his family into exile. Ben thought about that, then revisualised the map of the ancient Middle East that he'd spent all those hours studying in his youth. 'Harran, in Mesopotamia. In the Book of Genesis, it's where Abraham and his wife settled en route to the promised land of Canaan. To get there, the Muranus must have sailed a long way up the Euphrates, and then continued eastwards overland. Quite a journey, in those days. Even so, they can't have reached beyond Persian territory.'

'Something like eight hundred kilometres from Babylon,' Anna said. 'And you're right, Harran was still within the borders of the Achaemenid Empire. After the conquest of Babylonia, it was now the biggest empire in all of classical antiquity, covering such a gigantic territory that it was simply too huge for normal travellers to escape from.'

'Then again, the Muranus weren't exactly normal travellers. Why not keep moving?'

Anna shrugged. 'Perhaps they were content to compromise, by settling in a corner of the empire as remote and far-flung as possible, in order to try to get on with their lives. There may have been a Babylonian connection, albeit a tenuous one, as some scholars believe that Addagoppe, the mother of King Nabonidus and grandmother of Belshazzar, may have been from Harran. In any case, in those days Harran was a reasonably busy trading outpost, where they might have thought they could resume their merchant business. But it seems they never returned to their former greatness. Meanwhile Ashar, who clearly had never forgiven the Persians for what they did, seems to have gone his own way. I don't suppose we'll ever know all the facts. But that's history for you.'

'What about the idol?' Ben asked. 'Did they have it, or didn't they?'

'We've already speculated that they could have sold it, or melted down the gold plates into enough coinage to make them fabulously rich.'

'In which case, why hang around in some backwater outpost of the same empire that had ravaged their home? With that kind of money they could have travelled as far and wide as they wanted, settled anywhere they pleased, and lived like kings and queens.'

'It was a bigger world then. Distances seemed much greater than they do to us now, and foreign lands were mysterious and frightening. Especially with wars raging everywhere. Perhaps they still retained enough affinity with the region to make them want to stay.'

'Or perhaps it's more than that,' Ben said. 'Ashar's political involvement suggests that at least some of the Muranus must have been sympathetic to the rebel cause. Maybe they hoped that the kingdom of Babylon would one day be restored and they could go back. That could have been why they stayed.'

She shook her head. 'I doubt anyone could have thought that way. The Persians were too powerful. It would have seemed like a lost cause.'

'And history's full of lost causes that people never gave up fighting for.'

'That's just speculation,' Anna said doubtfully. 'You can't know these things for sure.'

'Not for sure,' Ben said. 'But close enough. And it changes everything.'

Chapter 42

Ben said, 'Put yourself in his shoes. Think like him. By the age of thirty-one, Ashar would have risen up to be a fairly senior member of the Muranu clan. From what we've learned about him, he must have been a pretty strong personality, probably with a lot of influence within the family. Yet he broke with family tradition in a big way. He could have chosen the easy path and become a merchant trader like the whole dynasty before him, but instead he chose a life of hardship, war and risk. To make that kind of sacrifice, he must have been highly driven. And nothing drives a guy like that more than ideological ambition. Then there's the value of symbols. Ancient people placed far more importance on them than we do.'

Anna looked puzzled, studying Ben's face intently in the firelight. 'I'm not sure what you're telling me here,' she said.

'Say the idol was still in the family's possession, still intact after all those years. A vast, magnificent monument to the fallen king they'd once revered, under whose reign Babylon had flourished. To a dedicated freedom fighter locked in a death struggle against the hated Persian oppressor, it would have been more than just a heap of gold. It would have represented more than just wealth. It would have been a massively powerful political icon, symbolising a future return to the glory days of Babylon under the rule of a mighty king like Nebuchadnezzar. Darius wasn't a popular sovereign, or else there wouldn't have been revolts sprouting up like mushrooms all over his empire. What if Ashar's dream was to overthrow it altogether, rallying together all the discontented and disenfranchised peoples of the empire under the symbolic totem of the golden idol?'

'Then he would have kept it carefully concealed until the time came when he could use it. If my theory is right about its modular structure, he could even have scattered its parts in various secret hiding places.'

'That's what I would have done,' Ben said. 'And I would have been extremely cautious about who I trusted with the knowledge of those hiding places. Maybe just a handful of my closest and most faithful followers. I certainly wouldn't have allowed my family to know. For their own protection as much as anything else.'

'That makes sense. Go on, I'm listening.'

'He had a lot to lose. And a lot to gain. When the day finally came when the idol could be reassembled in its proper home, the guy who could pull off a coup like that would be sure to become the new king of Babylon. Except it never happened. Ashar's dream fell apart when his rebels were decimated and he became just another renegade fugitive. What if he was the only one left who knew where the pieces of the idol were hidden? Or, what if he was killed too, in some skirmish with imperial forces that never made it to the official record?'

Anna had her head bowed in thought, beginning to nod to herself as she gradually came round to Ben's idea. 'Or that did, but the official record is still lying in a storeroom of the Persepolis Fortification Archive with a thousand others, waiting to be translated? I told you, there are still years of work left to be carried out.'

'In which case', Ben said, 'he'd have taken the secret to his grave. And if he'd chosen his hiding places half as carefully as I would have done—'

'It could still be there,' Anna finished for him.

'Not just the single piece you were hoping for. But the whole thing. You'd just have to know where to dig.'

Her eyes sparkled from the flames. 'You're right. This changes everything.'

'It's just a theory,' Ben said.

'But an excellent one. All the more reason why we need to go to Harran.'

Ben thought back to his mental map, picturing what the vast territory of the Persian Empire looked like in ancient times. Then he set it side by side in his mind with a modern map of what the region looked like in the present day. 'My ancient geography's a little rusty after all these years.'

'Like your Bible knowledge.'

'But if I'm getting it right, our destination is right here in Turkey.'

Anna nodded. 'I already worked out the location. Harran is about forty kilometres from Sanliurfa, which is just six hundred kilometres to the south and west of Ankara, with a motorway connecting them. Except we don't have a car. How are we even going to get out of here?'

Ben kept the wood burner going all night. When he ran out of logs he smashed a chair for firewood, taking it outside first so as not to wake Anna who was sleeping peacefully in the glow of the fire with his jacket over her as a makeshift blanket. After the last spar of the chair was burned up, he carried out the wooden table and broke that up too, then tiptoed back inside carrying an armful of splintered pieces. Being on fire duty kept him from thinking too much about all the things that would have crowded his mind and kept him from sleeping anyway.

As the red tendrils of dawn came creeping in over the eastern forest skyline, he quietly left the cabin and went exploring about the smallholding. He took the hatchet with him, partly for wanting some kind of weapon just in case, and partly for its usefulness in helping him to get inside the chained-up barn, which was what interested him most. Specifically, what he might find inside. The snow had stopped; the rising sun shone its ruby glitter across the hard-frozen white ground. It was going to turn out a gloriously crisp, perfect winter's morning. You could almost forget you had a bunch of crazed murderers after you, and a best friend back home who was deep in a coma.

The rural property was too far out in the middle of nowhere to have been of interest to vandals and thieves. Judging from the thick rust that had seized the padlock, the barn hadn't been opened since the day the smallholders had departed. Ben used the shaft of the hatchet like a crowbar to prise the rusty screws holding the hasp to the rotted wood of the door. The chain fell away, he creaked the door open and sunlight shone inside for the first time in years. The floor of the barn was covered in musty straw. Shovels and rakes and a pickaxe leaned against one wall. A small tractor stood partially dismantled, never to run again. Next to it, tucked away behind piles of old boxes and crates and covered by a dusty tarpaulin, was a large object whose shape there was no mistaking.

The old sedan was a Peugeot 404, the car whose design the East Germans had pinched for their papier-mâché Trabant. It was about the same age Ben was, though it had been enjoying a far more restful existence for quite some time, doing little except provide a home for generations of mice. The key was in the ignition but the battery was totally dead, its terminals badly corroded, which Ben guessed might have been the reason why the smallholders had abandoned it.

Ben had never been much of a car person but he did happen to know something its former owners might not have been aware of: that this model was one of the last saloon cars to incorporate a manual starting crank. Hence, it didn't need a battery or a starter motor to turn the engine over. Knowledge like that was the kind of thing Special Forces soldiers found useful on occasion, such as when commandeering improvised transport in tricky situations in Third World countries where such ancient vehicles tended to proliferate. He'd once seen a pickup version of the 404 in Yemen, carrying two live camels in the back. These old crates could survive just about anything.

He smiled when he found the crank handle buried under a heap of junk in the boot, still in its original plastic pack. The smallholders might have dismissed it as some kind of oddly shaped wheel brace or other tool whose purpose they couldn't figure out, or they might never have spotted it at all. Along with the crank handle Ben found a tatty, mouldy old road atlas of Turkey and a battered but serviceable pair of wellington boots. Where they weren't caked in old chicken shit they were pink, with flowers all over them. Fashionable footwear for a farmer's wife or teenage daughter.

Ben walked around to the front, found the hole below the rusty front grille where the handle could connect to the crankshaft, gave it a turn, and the engine coughed into life amid a massive cloud of blue smoke. Now he was smiling even more. He tossed the crank handle and the map on the back seat, along with a shovel and the pink rubber boots. Brushed the mouse droppings from the driver's seat, climbed in and engaged the steering-wheel gearstick, and the car rattled out into the morning sunshine, tyres crunching on the snow.

He parped the horn twice. Moments later, Anna appeared in the doorway of the cabin, wide-eyed in amazement.

He stepped out of the car and leaned on the door. 'Did you say something about a motorway trip to Sanliurfa?'

'In that?'

'It's a classic.' He slapped the bodywork. 'No recycled Coke tins in there.'

'It looks like something we could have excavated from the ground in Iraq.'

'Suits me fine,' he said. 'These modern cars, a couple of little knocks and they just fall to pieces.'

'How are we going to drive in deep snow?'

'We'll dig our way out, if we have to. That's what you have me for.'

She ventured out onto the veranda, stopped short and looked down at her feet. I've got no shoes.'

Ben grabbed the rubber boots from the back. 'Sorted,' he said, tossing them to her. They landed on the veranda. She bent to pick them up, tentatively sniffed them, pulled a face and held them at arm's length as though they were two dead fish.

'I'm supposed to *put my feet* into these?'

'Might not cut the mustard on the Florence catwalk, but at least now you'll be waterproof. Now let's grab our kit and get out of here. Next stop, Harran.'

Chapter 43

Some hours earlier

Massimiliano Usberti stood by his window overlooking the dark sea, hands clasped behind his back, deep in thought and ignoring the presence of his assistant Silvano Bellini. At this late hour, the house would normally have been all in silence, except only for the continual hiss and boom of the waves breaking in the rocky cove below.

Tonight, instead, the room was filled with the sound of agonised screams.

The screaming was coming from the fifty-eight-inch LCD television screen that had been set up especially for the occasion by Pierangelo Volpicelli who, unlike his employer, was handy with technology. Usberti had never used Skype before. The idea seemed like science fiction to him, not to mention faintly vulgar for its populist appeal. Yet he was willing to admit its usefulness in certain applications, and he was enjoying the show playing out on the big screen. Bellini, though, judging by the contorted frown on his face, was not.

The image showed a bare, starkly lit and lugubrious room with mould-streaked walls and peeling plaster. Usberti knew exactly where it was, in an abandoned rat-infested hovel in a shanty-town district of Ankara, although nothing on the screen would have given away the location.

The scene was framed from the point of view of a webcam positioned not far above floor level, on a stool or a box. In the middle of the screen stood a cheap, narrow wooden table. Perched on top of the table was a cheap wooden chair. Lying arched on his back across the seat of the chair, elevated so that his legs dangled in empty space down one side and his head, arms and upper torso dangled down the other, was the source of the inhuman cries of pain that were filling Usberti's living room.

Ercan Kavur was naked, which wasn't a particularly pretty sight. He was lashed securely to the seat of the chair by a rope around his middle. A second length of rope was attached to his ankles, and a third to his wrists, which were outstretched beneath his head. The ropes were tautly connected at a downward angle to makeshift iron rings on the floor, each of which consisted of several thick nails hammered halfway into the boards and bent over to make an inverted U for a rope to pass through, with a strong man keeping up the strain on each end: Groppione and Iacono, both hidden off-camera at opposite sides of the screen. Ugo Bozza, overseeing the proceedings with a completely blank and deadpan expression on his face, could be seen to the left of the frame. The only crew member with little to do was Maurizio Starace. The bulging eyes that were caused by a thyroid disorder were even more manically bugged out than usual as he enjoyed watching the spectacle from the wings while puffing on a cigarette.

The torture was called 'the German chair', though as far as Usberti knew it had no particular association with Germany, and its use was popular in various parts of the world by virtue of its sheer simplicity. Why mess about with elaborate equipment when some of the most effective torture methods required only the minimum of basic essentials? The tension on his arms and legs was stretching Kavur backwards over the seat of the chair, arching his spine to breaking point. If the brutal screams were anything to go by, it was causing him appalling pain. Usberti's understanding of anatomy and physiology was somewhat limited, but even he could see that if the strain on the victim's arms or legs increased by another inch, it would cause irreversible damage. Or worse. Kavur already wasn't the world's most prime specimen of the male sex. God had not blessed him with a fine physique to begin with, and decades of bad diet and deskbound study had atrophied his muscles until he looked as scraggy as a diseased old cat. Any more of this punishment would break him, literally – and Usberti didn't want Kavur dead. Not just yet.

'Enough,' he commanded. Far away in the shanty hovel in Ankara, Ugo Bozza's stonefish eyes flickered across and down to the laptop on the crate, from which his employer's face looked up at him. Bozza nodded to Groppione and Iacono, and the tension on both ends of the rope slackened. Kavur gasped, still in tremendous pain, but his back no longer about to snap like a stick of celery.

Usberti stepped closer to the big screen. 'Look at me, Ercan.'

Slowly, painfully, Ercan Kavur craned his neck to peer at the smaller screen on the Ankara side of the Skype connection. Sweat dripped from his body despite the freezing cold that had his torturers all wrapped up in coats and gloves.

'You do not want to die, do you, Ercan?' Usberti said.

A slow, agonised shake of the head. No, Ercan didn't want to die.

'Of course you do not. Nor would I wish to inflict such

a cruel and untimely end upon a scholar of your calibre. On the contrary, my dear Ercan, I want you alive, fit and healthy, so that we can go on a journey together. A journey of discovery. One that may bring untold rewards. That's right, Ercan. For you too. You know what journey I am speaking of. You know where the Babylon idol is.'

'No!' Kavur managed to gasp through his pain. 'Nobody knows if—' a fit of coughing seized and racked him pitifully for a few moments before he could finish. 'If it even exists.'

Usberti's face darkened. 'You are lying to me, Ercan. I warn you, you must never, ever, lie to me. It exists. And you know where it is. You are going to lead us to it. Because if you do not . . . well, let me show you what. Ugo?'

Bozza needed no further prompting. He stepped around the side of the table. Kavur let out a strangled cry of terror and tried to wriggle away from him, but he couldn't move. Groppione and Iacono tensioned the ropes just a little more, to prevent the victim from struggling. Kavur hung arched backwards over the raised chair, eye to eye with Bozza. 'Please,' he quavered. 'Whatever it is you're going to do to me – please!'

From the look in Kavur's wild eyes, it was easy to imagine what kind of anticipatory terrors were running through his mind. Knives, needles, blowtorches, pincers, all the usual horrors associated with physical mutilation.

But what was coming was worse than any of that.

Bozza's face remained completely expressionless as he removed first one glove, then the other. He flexed his fingers, rubbed his hands together, then reached out and lightly, almost delicately, ran his fingertips over the clammy flesh of Kavur's right shoulder. Kavur flinched violently at his touch, but the strain on his arms held him tight.

Bozza slowly moved his fingertips up and across Kavur's

scrawny upside-down upper torso, like a caress, and stopped just at the point where the top of the ribcage met the base of his stringy, wasted right pectoral muscle near the armpit. His fingers seemed to hover there like a concert pianist about to hit the opening notes of a concerto.

'Ugo's late, lamented brother was a master at inflicting pain,' Usberti said. 'I should know, as Franco was my trusted and loyal servant for many years and I personally witnessed him at work on countless occasions. His methods with the knife and the razor were brutal and highly effective, and earned him a well-deserved reputation in certain quarters as well as the equally deserved moniker "The Inquisitor". In fact, I doubt whether the torturers of the Spanish Inquisition could have plied their craft as skilfully. But in retrospect, now that poor Franco is no longer with us, I would say that his techniques were somewhat crude, frequently requiring a great deal of cleaning up afterwards. The room would often have to be completely screened with thick plastic sheets. I am sure you can imagine, sparing me from having to enter into graphic descriptions.'

Usberti paused. Bozza hadn't moved or shown any flicker of expression. He stood there poised for his next command.

Usberti went on: 'By contrast, what I have learned of Ugo's skills has persuaded me that his mastery of the art of pain has transcended even that of his elder brother. Even without the use of such crude implements as steel blades, he is capable of elevating the human pain response beyond all imagining, and in this respect has reached a level of virtuosity to which few expert practitioners could aspire. Ugo, perhaps you could offer a small demonstration of your considerable skills to our friend?'

The nerve centre that Bozza had singled out was known to acupressure practitioners as Gall Bladder Point 23 or, to give it its traditional Chinese name, 'Zhe jin', meaning 'flank sinews'. Like all such points, the right application of pressure could be used to heal, or it could be used to inflict pain and damage. A sharp strike or excessive pressure on GB23 could cause liver damage or even death. However, just the right touch could, without inflicting permanent harm, trigger a jolt of the most excruciating agony possible.

And that was exactly what Ugo Bozza now did to Ercan Kavur. He dug his index finger and thumb into the pectoral muscle and mashed the nerve centre in an iron pincer grip. The inhuman scream that burst from Kavur's lips almost made Groppione and Iacono drop the ends of the rope and clamp their hands over their ears, and this was far from being their first torture.

The scream went on and on, ululating, piercing, bellowing. Bozza held the pressure for a few seconds and then released it. Kavur fell silent and hung there quivering, his breathing coming in great shuddering gasps. Sweat pattered the table and the floor like rain. His eyes had rolled up in their sockets so only the whites showed.

'On a scale of one to ten,' Usberti said, 'one being roughly equivalent to the pain from a handful of finely ground sea salt being vigorously rubbed into a raw and open wound, and ten being the most unimaginably hideous torment of Dante's purgatory at the hands of demons, I would estimate that what you have just experienced was approximately level four. Each successive point of the scale represents a significant increase of agony. The real measure of Ugo's skill is the effortlessness with which he is able to extract such a response from his victim. He is perfectly able to continue for hours. And we have all night. Shall we now explore what a five would feel like, or would you prefer to talk instead? The choice is entirely yours.'

And it was a choice Kavur wasted no time in making. The information flowed out of him so freely that once he'd started talking, he wouldn't stop. He told them every last detail of what he'd encrypted into his research notes. And every last detail of his fresh discoveries since making those notes, yet to be written down.

As Kavur talked on the big screen, Massimiliano Usberti listened, and smiled, and paced back and forth with his hands clasped behind his back. Silvano Bellini stood near the window, looking edgy and thoughtful. At last, when the terrified man had given all he had to give, Usberti stopped pacing.

'So let me make sure I understand this correctly,' he said. 'We already know, from having seen them scattered all over the floor of your study, that the Manzini woman was able to locate your research notes. We can equally take it that she must have acquainted herself with their content, being admirably educated herself and quite capable of translating the old Anatolian Turkish that you used as your code. Unfortunately, she is not here to confirm this fact in person, but it is a reasonable assumption to make. Moreover—' He held up a finger. 'We also know for a fact, assumptions aside, that her knowledge must necessarily be limited to what she has seen and read. It is impossible that she could have become aware of these further discoveries of which you speak, as they are so fresh that you had not yet committed them to note form. Interesting. Very interesting. In short, what this means is that she believes the idol to be located in Turkey. Which we now know, and she cannot know, is not the case. Or, to put it another way, we have a significant advantage thanks to superior intelligence. Am I correct?'

Too exhausted to utter another word, Kavur just nodded.

Usberti pursed his lips. His eyes gleamed. 'Very well, here

is what we will do. Ugo: you, Luca, Aldo, and Maurizio, all remain where you are. The time has come for me to leave this island. I will travel incognito from Sicily and rendezvous with you in Ankara as soon as possible. Pending my arrival there, you will make the necessary preparations for our journey south to Harran.'

Bellini frowned. 'But, Excellency, as you just said yourself, the idol is not in Harran.'

'No, Silvano, it is not,' Usberti replied with a chuckle. 'But Hope and Manzini are currently lacking that information. Nor does Hope appreciate how well I know him; how clearly I can anticipate his moves. When they reach Harran they will make their way to the ancient ruins there. Like the soldier he is, Hope's strategy will be to establish a temporary base as nearby as possible, from which he can determine the whereabouts of the rebel fortress of Ashar the Babylonian. He is by nature independent of spirit and his first instinct will be to locate the fort himself. Whereas Manzini, being both a pragmatist and a woman, will be more inclined to seek local assistance in the matter. In his foolish gentlemanly way, Hope will relent rather than force his own inclinations on a female. Thus, after some discussion, they will doubtless opt for her way of thinking and make inquiries to find a guide in the town of Harran who can convey them to the site.'

'You confuse me, Excellency. You speak as though you knew exactly where this fortress can be found.'

'My dear young friend, as ever you are one step behind me. Be assured, I have precious little interest in either the fort itself or its location. My sole concern lies in ensuring that Hope and Manzini are brought somewhere conveniently remote, and very private. The perfect location for us to strike.'

On that note, Usberti cracked a broad, toothy smile and turned to the big screen, where Bozza, Iacono, Groppione, and Starace had gathered in a group, all peering down at the webcam and waiting for their instructions. Starace looked like a mad Pekingese.

Usberti said, 'Gentlemen, get ready for the final phase of our plan.'

'What about him?' Iacono asked, pointing at Kavur.

And Usberti told them what to do.

Chapter 44

'It's me.'

'I know it's you. There's something nowadays called caller ID, you know? Anyway, you don't have to keep phoning me all the time. I told you I'd be in touch if there was a change.'

'Which there hasn't been?'

'He's stable. But there's no improvement in his condition. I wish I could tell you more, but that's it.'

'I'm sorry if I disturbed you. I won't call again.'

'No problem.' A hesitant pause in her voice, then: 'I like it when you call.'

He said nothing.

'When are you coming back?' she asked.

'I can't say.'

'Where are you now?'

'Stopped for fuel at a motorway services in the Urus Mountains, about three hundred kilometres south-east of Ankara, Turkey.'

'What are you doing there? What's happening?'

'It's a long story.'

'That's what I was afraid you'd say. Don't do anything—'

'Stupid? You already said that.'

'Or whatever.'

'You want to come and hold my hand?'

'I would, but I'm too busy holding Jeff's.'

'Keep doing that. Talk to him. He'll hear you.'

'It's your voice he needs to hear. Come back soon, okay? I'm worried about you.'

'Why?' he asked her.

'I don't know why. I hardly know you.' Another pause, longer this time, as if she was searching for more words but didn't want to commit to saying them. 'Just come back soon, okay?' she repeated. 'And promise me you'll look after yourself, Ben.'

He put the phone away and got back in the car. 'Here, I got us some sandwiches,' he said to Anna, holding up two plastic packs. 'Lamb or cheese?' She picked the cheese. They sat in silence for a moment, ripping open the plastic twinpacks, both just now realising how hungry they were. Anna wolfed down half of her first sandwich with little care for ladylike manners, then paused for breath and asked, 'Who were you talking to just then?'

'Sandrine Lacombe, the doctor looking after Jeff.'

'That's who I thought it was. I take it there's been no change in your friend's state?'

'Not yet.'

'I'm sorry.'

'Me too.'

'I wish there was more I could say.'

'I know.'

'He'll pull through it, I'm sure.'

'Maybe,' Ben said. 'Thanks for the thought.'

'You're welcome,' Anna said, and then a small smile curled the corners of her lips. 'She likes you, doesn't she? And you like her, too.'

'Don't be ridiculous,' Ben said through a mouthful of lamb sandwich.

'I can tell. From your face when you talk to her.'

'What about my face?' he said, hardening it into a scowl.

'It certainly doesn't look the way it does now. The opposite. And I could tell from the warmth of your voice when you were talking to her. And from the way you didn't want to end the call.' Anna smiled. 'Is she nice? Tell me about her. What colour eyes does she have? What colour hair?'

'This is a daft conversation,' he said, tossed away the empty sandwich pack and twisted the ignition. The battery was fully recharged from all the driving, and the engine fired instantly.

A hundred kilometres further down the road he broke his silence and said, 'Blue eyes. Blond hair. Don't ask me any more questions about her.' Anna made no reply. The little smile on her face remained there for a long time.

The old car was sedate, but it was comfortable and reliable, and the heater worked fine. Anna dozed off now and then, while Ben smoked the last of his cigarettes with the driver's window wound open a crack and the icy wind whistling at his ear. As the journey rolled further southwards they left the snow and the mountains behind for the more temperate climate of south-eastern Turkey. It was still cold, but the roads were clear and the sky was blue.

Six hours after setting off from the hills of Ankara, they were arriving in Sanliurfa. A city of half a million inhabitants, built on a plain eighty kilometres east of the Euphrates. Anna knew it as the birthplace of some twelfth-century Armenian historian she mentioned. Ben knew it as the site of massacres during the First World War. Then again, just about everywhere had been the site of massacres during the First World War, like the second, and most likely the third too.

By the time they were driving into the city, Anna's mood

had changed and she was looking sombre. 'What were we thinking? Now we're here, I have no idea what to do next.'

'One thing at a time,' Ben told her. 'First let's see about getting you kitted out with some decent shoes and clothes. Then we'll think about establishing a base somewhere nearby, preferably as close to Harran as possible. *Then*, we'll worry about what we're going to do next.'

They might have had different ideas about what constituted decent shoes and clothes, but thanks to the limited options available in the stores they checked out, it was Ben's that mostly prevailed. She stalked out of the store wearing leather winter boots, heavy denim jeans and a good, warm, if utilitarian, thigh-length jacket that padded out her figure with thick quilting. She was grateful for being able to junk the pink wellingtons, but the new coat wasn't such a hit. 'It's like something you'd put on a horse,' she said, looking disapprovingly at her shapeless reflection in a shop window. 'Is this meant to be part of my re-education? Learning to live the Ben Hope way?'

'You look fine,' he had to say at least six times before they reached the car.

Now that that task was taken care of, it was time to make their way to their destination, Harran. The road from Sanliurfa seemed at first to be taking them due south, straight towards Syria; then just a few kilometres before reaching the border town of Akçakale it veered eastwards. The ancient site that had been the stopping point for Abraham in the Old Testament was a sprawl of ruins scattered over an arid plain of semi-desert scrubland, encircled at a distance by the modern town of Harran. Like a couple of sightseers, Ben and Anna trekked on foot across the barren scrubland of the plain and spent a while wandering about the ruined sandstone walls and archways and towers that were all that remained of the place. It was like Olympia, but with none of the serenity and little of the mystique. The only intact buildings on the plain were the clusters of beehive houses that had been built a lot more recently, centuries rather than millennia ago, from the stones of the ruins. Incongruously surrounded by pylons and wires that hummed in the cold desert wind, some of the beehive houses appeared still inhabited – until it turned out that they were strictly used as a tourist trap by locals ever-ready to exploit the unwary for all they could get. The children were less subtle about it, crowding around Ben and Anna every-where they went like a cloud of mosquitoes, clamouring for money. Ben noticed that some of the kids were speaking Arabic. Refugees from over the Syrian border, just twenty-five kilometres away. He felt pity for them, until one of the little urchins pulled out an imitation 9mm Beretta realistic enough to have caused most tourists to soil their pants, pointed it at Ben and yelled 'Bang, bang, you're dead!' Ben replied to him in Arabic. The kid lowered the gun, stared at Anna in horror and then beat it along with his crowd of friends.

'What did you say to him?' Anna asked.

'I told him you were a Seventh Dan Karate master, and you were going to break both his little arms and shove his gun where the sun doesn't shine.'

'This is a dismal place. There's nothing for us here anyway. We should be looking for Ashar's fortress.'

Ben shook his head. 'It's getting late, and we wouldn't know where to start. I suggest we get a place to rest up for the night, a shower and a meal.'

The modern town of Harran wasn't much less dismal than the ancient one, but had a motel handily situated right on the edge of the plain. Anna wasn't impressed with their adjoining rooms, and even less so with the shared bathroom. 'There are cockroaches.'

286

'It's winter.'

'They're hibernating. But they're here. Don't tell me you've seen worse, because such a thing isn't possible.'

'Except maybe in summer,' he said. 'When the cockroaches all come back out to play.'

The narrow street leading up from the motel was crowded with tawdry gift shops, coffee bars and a handful of restaurants that looked more or less in the same league as the motel, but within a five-minute walk they found a café that was a little better than the others. Over dishes of Urfa kebab and chicken and rice, they talked about the possibility of hiring a local guide to help them locate the fort, or at any rate the site where it had once stood. 'There must be dozens of them in this town, with little work during the low season,' Anna pointed out. 'And in a place like this, where everyone knows everyone, it's just a matter of asking.'

'What are the chances that some local guy just happens to know where this fort is?' Ben said.

'I've used guides before, on research trips. It's surprising how knowledgeable some of them can be.'

'Maybe you're right,' Ben said. 'But assuming we even find anything out there, it could be a long trek. And the terrain will be rough as hell. I could go alone. I've spent a lot of time in places like that.'

'You think I'd let you find the golden idol of King Nebuchadnezzar without me?' she fired back. 'I've survived this far. I'm ready for anything.'

Chapter 45

Anna survived the night, as well, with no cockroach sightings to report when morning came. Breakfast was a cup of Turkish coffee so strong you had to chew it, taken in the empty dining room. 'I think we're the only guests here,' Ben commented.

'What a surprise.'

Ben left her to finish her coffee while he went over to the reception desk to enquire about hiring someone local to show them around the surrounding area. As it turned out, Anna had been right about everyone knowing everyone in Harran, but wrong about the abundance of suitable tour guides.

'There's only one man I know of who might be able to help you,' the manager said. 'Wait a minute.' And kept Ben waiting for several of them while he took his time looking up the number in a grubby old diary. 'Here he is. Diya Sharifi.' The manager scribbled the name and number down on the back of a scrap of paper and showed Ben the way to a payphone.

An hour later, Diya Sharifi was sitting with Ben and Anna in the empty motel dining room, over more of the chewy coffee. He was an ethnic Arab, about thirty years of age, who said he'd lived in the area all his life and knew every inch of terrain from Gaziantep to Batman. His manner was relaxed but his eyes were sharp and his English fluent, even though it had been learned from American TV. He confirmed that he could make space in his frantically busy schedule to help them out, and listened as Anna outlined to him what they were looking for.

'The place we're trying to find would be very, very old. It was already a ruin in ancient times, possibly the remains of an Assyrian fortress dating back four thousand years. There might be virtually nothing left now, except a few scattered pieces of rubble. Yet it's vitally important that we find the right place. Do you think you can help us?'

Sharifi considered the request. 'Most tourists, they want something they can take a picture of, you know? You're asking me to take you someplace that doesn't even exist any more?'

'It would be on high ground,' Ben said. 'Somewhere right up in the hills, a good vantage point where you could see an enemy approaching miles away. The kind of place a lightly equipped guerrilla force would have had no problem slipping in and out of, but regular infantry would've found difficult to access, even harder to attack.'

'Do I look like a military tactician to you?' Sharifi said, then broke into a grin. 'Relax, man. Happens I do know a place that kind of sounds like what the lady was talking about. You could say it was a fort, or was once, what's left of it. Might be the same one you're looking for, maybe.'

'You can take us there?' Anna asked, leaning forward in her chair.

'It's a long way up in the hills. Kinda hard to reach, but I have a good truck. Sure, I can take you there. Gonna cost you a little extra, though. It's real close to the border. Lots of trouble still going on in some of those places. You hear stories of ISIS fighters slipping across and killing folks.'

Ben and Anna exchanged glances. His, dubious. Hers,

flashing with excitement. 'It's as good a place as any to start,' she said.

'I still think it's best if I go alone,' Ben replied.

'Over my dead body.'

'That's what I'm trying to avoid.'

Anna dismissed the idea with a wave of her hand. 'You have the job, Mr Sharifi,' she said.

'The price will be five hundred lira,' Sharifi said. 'And please, call me Diya.'

'That's fine, Diya. We're anxious to reach the fort as soon as possible. How quickly can you be ready to leave?'

'Let me go fuel up the truck,' Diya said, knocking back the dregs of his coffee and getting to his feet. 'I'll meet you outside in one hour, ready to rock. You should bring some food and water. Gonna be a long day.'

Ben watched him go, then turned to look at Anna, saying nothing.

'What?'

'Are you sure you want to play it this way?' he asked her.

'You heard him. It sounds as if he might be able to take us to the right place. And for a good price, too.'

'I don't care about the money,' Ben said.

'It's just that you don't trust anyone.'

'I trust myself.'

'But you don't know where the fort is. You said so, remember?'

An hour later, Diya Sharifi screeched up outside the motel in a Dodge Power Wagon pickup truck that looked as though it had spent the last thirty years hauling rocks over the desert, complete with enough ancillary lighting to fry a camel crossing the road and knobbly tyres so oversized that Anna could barely clamber up inside the crew cab.

'You can dump your bag in the back, boss,' Diya said. The rear bed was filled with a clutter of various junk. One big steel jerrycan for fuel, a plastic one for water. A crammed metal tool box with all the paint knocked off it. A spare wheel, wearing the same pattern of knobbly tyre, tethered to the side of the flatbed with rope. Some shovels and other well-worn wooden-handled utensils carelessly rolled up in a frayed bit of canvas tarp tied in the middle with a length of twine. Ben always found it interesting what people carried with them for travelling in the wilderness.

'You coming, boss?'

'I'll be right there,' Ben said. He shoved a few things aside to make space for his bag, made sure it was secure and then walked slowly back towards the front passenger side. He paused at Anna's window. 'Last chance to change your mind.'

'I told you, I'm coming. I wish you wouldn't keep asking.'

'Fair enough,' Ben said. He pulled open the front passenger door and hauled himself in. The dashboard was covered by a colourful patterned cloth to protect it from melting in the summer sun. An Islamic ornamental pendant dangled behind the windscreen from the mirror stem. Less traditional was the sat nav device suckered to the inside of the glass.

Diya grinned at his passengers. 'Hang on tight, folks. I drive real fast and we're taking the road where there *is* no road. Let's go.'

Chapter 46

They set off, quickly leaving Harran behind as their guide sped out into open country, talking and joking animatedly as he drove. From March through October, it would have been the kind of unbearably hot, dusty trek that Ben had endured a thousand times before. In winter, it was just unbearably uncomfortable as Diya charged up into the barren hills, never slowing down for a rock or boulder smaller than a watermelon or bothering to avoid a rut unless it threatened to engulf the entire truck. Ben wedged his feet against the door and transmission tunnel to prevent himself getting too badly thrown about. Behind him, Anna was being bucked out of her seat at every bump, but she was too excited to complain.

The landscape was an arid panorama yellowed by sand and sun, dotted here and there with sparse vegetation. They passed through the outskirts of a village where feral children came out to throw stones. Deeper into the wilderness they had to slow for a sheep herder leading his flock across their path. Further on again, they passed the bleached-white skeleton of a camel; then the carcass of a wrecked and overturned car, blackened by fire and peppered with large-calibre bullet holes, a silent witness of the warfare that now and then strayed over the border into south-eastern Turkey.

'In your line of work I'd carry a weapon for self-defence, Diya,' Ben said in Arabic over the roar of the engine. 'What with all the trouble in these parts.'

Diya glanced at him in surprise that he could speak the language, then shrugged and replied, 'Forget it. That's a sure way to get yourself killed, around here.'

'I'd take the risk, personally,' Ben said.

'Rather you than me, chief.'

'So you don't have a gun?'

Diya shook his head, all the way left, then all the way right, in an exaggerated motion for emphasis. 'Never wanted one, never needed one, never will.'

'Sorry I asked,' Ben said. 'Just wondered, that's all. So, are you really the only guide in Harran?'

'Only one worth his salt.'

'Nice little monopoly you have there. No competition. You make much money?'

Diya shrugged and grinned wider. 'A man has to earn his crust. You know how it is.'

'Yeah, I think I do know how it is,' Ben said. 'I'll bet your phone never stops ringing, does it? I'll bet it was ringing even last night, sometime after she and I got into town.' He pointed a thumb back at Anna, who was gazing out of the window and oblivious of the conversation.

Diya looked at him uncertainly, the grin wavering. 'You ask a lot of questions, chief.'

'Bad habit of mine,' Ben said.

Soon afterwards the terrain began to climb. Diya took a winding hill path up and up through all sorts of spectacular ravines and canyons and escarpments. Anna was watching it all roll by, gazing out of the window in fascination. Ben was watching Diya. For the last few kilometres the guide had stopped smiling and talking. He kept glancing at his watch, biting his lip. Peering this way and that as though checking for landmarks, then consulting the GPS reading on the sat nav.

Ben asked him, 'What's the matter, Diya? Lost your way?'

'No chance,' Diya replied. 'I been coming out this way all my life, chief. Nobody knows it better than me.'

'Maybe you're in a hurry because you have a plane to catch later, or a hot date.'

Diya threw him another uncertain look. 'No worries, man. Almost there. Just a couple more minutes.'

'This'll do,' Ben said. 'You can drop us off here.'

Diya stared at him. 'You crazy? This is no taxi ride.'

'You heard me. This is far enough.' Ben reached out and yanked the handbrake. The truck skidded to a halt at an angle across the track. Anna was thrown forwards against the front seats.

'Ben, what are you doing?'

The engine had stalled. Diya clutched the wheel and kept staring at Ben. He was sweating. Ben said nothing, either. Before Diya could speak or attempt to restart the engine, Ben threw open his door and jumped out. They had stopped in a shallow canyon that a million years ago could have been the bed of a fast-flowing river. Its banks sloped upwards on both sides in a wide V. Here and there, landslides had brought part of the canyon walls down to form piles of boulders around which scrubby bushes had sprung. Ben hit the stony ground with both boots and started striding fast towards the rear of the truck. Stepped up on the tow-hitch, reached into the pickup bed among the wooden-handled utensils carelessly wrapped inside the piece of frayed canvas tarp, grabbed something solid and heavy and slid it out of the roll with a sharp tug.

Ben always found it interesting what people carried

with them for travelling in the wilderness. Especially when one of the items in their tool roll wasn't a shovel or a pick, but rather a clumsily concealed bolt-action Mauser main battle rifle of the sort that had flooded Turkey by the million during and since World War Two. And even more especially when the same rifle's owner insisted he carried no weapon. By anyone's standards, the 8mm Mauser was a *hell* of a weapon, as lethally effective now as when it had rolled off the assembly point at the Steyr-Daimler-Puch factory in Austria, 1943, and into the eager hands of the Waffen SS.

Diya was clambering out of the truck. Anna peered open-mouthed from the dusty window. 'Let me guess,' Ben said, clutching the rifle. 'This old thing has been bumping around so long in the back of your truck, you forgot it was there. Is that right, Diya?'

Diya made no reply. Ben cracked open the bolt and saw the big, long, bottlenecked rounds stacked on top of each other in the receiver. He pulled the bolt all the way back, then pushed it all the way forward, feeling that famous slick Mauser action, and locked it down tight. Now there was a round in the chamber.

'You really shouldn't leave firearms lying around like that,' he said. 'Too many nasty, dishonest people around. The kind of people who might point a loaded rifle at you when they pretended they were unarmed.'

'Ben, what's happening?' Anna called from the truck cab.

Diya took a step towards him. In one fast motion Ben swivelled the butt of the rifle to his shoulder and fixed the battle sight right on Diya's centre of mass. The 8mm Mauser cartridge was good for over a thousand yards and could penetrate light armour at half that distance. At this range it would blow a man in two.

Diya presumably knew that, it being his rifle. He took a step back and raised his hands.

Ben said to him, 'Let's have a little bit of truth, Diya. You can start by emptying out your pockets. Nice and easy. If I thought you had a pistol in there, I might get really nervous. And nervous folks have twitchy fingers.'

Diya moved slowly, partly because he didn't want to get shot with his own rifle, and partly because he was understandably reluctant for Ben to see what was in his jacket pocket. More precisely, what was in his wallet, which he left until last to pull out. The worn leather was stuffed as thick as a double burger.

'Open it up so I can see inside,' Ben said.

Diya's eyes bulged. He held open the wallet. A fat wad of banknotes fell out, scattered and caught the wind and swirled about his feet like autumn leaves, but he made no move to pick them up.

'Business really has been good for you, hasn't it?' Ben said. 'Looks like another couple of thousand Turkish lira, on top of the five hundred you stood to get from us. Why don't you go crawling after it, before it all blows away? Wouldn't want you to have sold us out for nothing.'

Anna's door opened and she peered out. 'Ben, please tell me what's going on here.'

'What's going on is that there *is* no ancient Assyrian fort anywhere nearby,' Ben told her, still keeping the rifle pointed at Diya. 'And if there were, our deceitful friend here wouldn't care one way or the other. Because he didn't drive us out into the middle of nowhere for an archaeological excursion, but for a prearranged rendezvous with a certain someone. Isn't that correct, Diya?'

Diya boggled at him. 'They said to bring you here. That's all I know. Said it was for a surprise.'

'You're an idiot, Diya. The biggest surprise would've been

when they put a bullet in you and took the money back. And if you thought packing a rifle as insurance was going to save your worthless skin, you have no idea who you're dealing with. When did they call you? Yesterday?'

'Last night,' Diya admitted.

'And they didn't wire you that cash through the bank. They paid it to you in person. Which means they're here, in Harran. Who did you meet?'

'I don't know his name. I don't know anything, I swear.'

'The last bloke who swore to me he knew nothing died pretty soon afterwards.'

'Okay, chief, okay. One was in charge. Older than the rest, with white hair, maybe in his sixties. A big man, spoke with a foreign accent. Italian, sounded like. He had three others with him. Heavy-looking guys. Two who spoke, one who didn't. Just kinda looked at me.'

'Bozza,' Anna breathed.

Ben asked Diya, 'They came to your place?'

Diya nodded reluctantly. 'Told me to expect your call in the morning. Gave me the money. Half now, half when the job was done.'

'The job being to cart us out into the middle of nowhere like two lambs to the slaughter,' Ben said. 'And you knew just the spot to bring us. So far, the only thing you haven't lied to us about is that you know this area like the back of your hand. You probably even gave them the GPS coordinates, which is why you kept checking your sat nav as we got closer. And my guess is that you called them just before we set off, which is why you kept checking your watch, too. Because they're up ahead, waiting for us.'

Diya nodded. He pointed mutely deeper into the rocky canyon, about five hundred yards further on. 'Where I was taking you.'

'That's all I need to know,' Ben said. 'You're a very lucky man, Diya. A less nice person than me would have blown your brains out and left you where you dropped, for the jackals and lynxes and whatever other hungry things live out here. I'm just going to make you walk home. You'll have to pray you make it back alive.'

But Diya wasn't going to make it back alive, and Ben might as well have shot him anyway.

Because in the next instant, his brains burst all over the side of the truck.

Chapter 47

The bullet that spattered Diya's brains was travelling about three thousand feet per second, more than double the speed of sound. So the crack of the shot reached Ben's ears almost exactly half a second after it hit. Diya was stone dead but still standing, his knees crumpling under him, beginning to drop. Anna's cry was still forming in her mouth.

But by then Ben already knew exactly where the hidden sniper was positioned among the rocks some five hundred yards away. And he was already spurred into action, leaping behind the truck and yelling at Anna to get down, *Down!* Through the rear cab window, all grimed with dirt and dust, he saw her duck between the seats. Out of sight, not out of danger.

The truck lurched on its suspension and went down at the front left corner. Quarter of a second later, another boom sounded from the distant rocks and echoed up and down the canyon.

The sniper fired again. Same result, second front tyre. He was immobilising the truck. Once he'd contented himself with that, he might very well start shooting at them. Using the big Dodge as cover wasn't an option. A high-velocity rifle would zip through vehicle metal like paper.

Ben had no intention of hanging around for whatever

might come next. Jumping up onto the cluttered pickup bed he yelled to Anna to turn her face away. Military Mauser bolt-action rifles were made with a thick steel butt plate, ideal for smacking down onto the concrete of the parade ground, or for staving in an enemy's teeth, or for smashing windows. He jabbed it hard against the dirty glass, felt the splintering crunch, whacked it again and kept hammering at it until the entire rear window was in pieces over the back seat. He reached an arm inside. She clasped his hand and he half helped, half hauled her out through the glassless frame. At the same moment she scrambled onto the pickup bed, the truck's windscreen dissolved into a mass of fissures with a round hole punched cleanly through its middle. Ben ran for the tailgate, leaping over the junk and tools, dragging her behind him. They jumped. Hit the stony ground at the rear of the truck. Anna was wild with terror. Ben pushed her down into a crouch behind the tow-hitch.

It was time to give the sniper back a dose of his own medicine. Ben brought up the Mauser and used the side of the pickup bed as a rest to steady his aim. The hidden shooter was almost certainly using a modern rifle with a telescopic sight, surgically accurate enough to pick off flies at long range. Ben had only crude iron battle sights, through which even a relatively close target looked tiny. He couldn't expect to pick flies off at this distance.

But a man is a much bigger target than a fly.

Then he saw what he was looking for: the briefest flash of reflected sunlight glinting off steel and glass, just long enough to give away the sniper's position. He was hunkered in tight to the rocky slope of the canyon, about thirty feet up and about ten degrees left. Ben estimated the range at around 485 yards. He sighted on the spot where he'd seen the flash. Took up the first pressure on the trigger, drew in a breath, let half of it out, felt his body go still and pressed the trigger the rest of the way. The Mauser was loud. Its recoil jolted the steel butt plate against his shoulder. The bullet was in flight; a fraction of a second later he thought he saw the puff of dust as it struck the rocks. Close enough to the sniper's position to get him worried.

Ben worked the bolt, ejected the smoking spent cartridge case, slammed another in the chamber. He wondered how many Wehrmacht soldiers back in the day had shared the same worry he was having now, which was the limited magazine capacity of their standard infantry rifle. One gone, only four to go.

Then he would just have to make them count.

He scanned the rocks through the sights. A tiny movement caught his eye. He fired again. The same loud crash, the same hard-kicking punch to his right shoulder, the same split-second interval as the bullet flew. There was no puff of dust this time. He thought he saw a dark shape flit past a gap in the rocks. Had he hit his mark?

The return shot that cracked off the side of the truck an instant later told him he hadn't. Now the sniper had *his* position. Not good. And sheltering behind the flimsy-skinned truck was no kind of shelter at all. Ben glanced at a pile of landslide debris ten yards to their left, where a large boulder had broken loose of the canyon wall at some time in its history and come tumbling down to the foot of the slope to provide perfect cover for a moment like this. The sniper could blast away all day and never put a crack in it.

'I'm going to count three,' Ben said to Anna. 'Watch my fingers. Take my other hand and don't let go. On three, we're going to run for that rock there, quick as we can. Ready? One – two – *go.*'

They burst out from behind the truck and raced over the

stony ground, threw themselves behind the safety of the big boulder and crouched there. Ben re-cocked the Mauser. The empty case flipped out and rolled in the dirt. Two rounds gone, three to go. Less than ideal, considering the sniper probably had a ten-shot magazine and a whole box of ammo resting at his elbow.

Anna was gaping at him. 'Ben, how are we going to get out of this?'

'Same way we always do,' he replied. 'I'll do something crazy, you'll tell me I'm a lunatic, and we'll live to find more trouble another day.'

'I don't care what you do, as long as you do something.'

'I'll quote you on that.'

'Is it Usberti?'

'Not in person,' Ben said. 'The archbishop never was a trigger puller and I doubt whether he'd risk himself in a gunfight. Like a good general, he'll be leading his troops from the rear.'

'Bozza?'

Ben smiled grimly, nodded. 'I don't know if he's the one sniping at us, but he's here, all right. I can smell him.'

'What can we do?'

Ben said nothing. Because the fact was, with only one gun and just three rounds, they weren't exactly option-rich right now.

A third bullet cracked off the rocks nearby, ricocheting with a cloud of dust and stone chips and a howl that blended with the boom of the shot.

'He can't see us,' Anna said. 'As long as we stay here, we're safe.'

She was right, as far as it went. The problem was that it didn't go far, because Anna was new to the tactics of war. Ben wasn't. He was all too aware that they were being deliberately pinned down. That was one of the key functions of a sniper, to keep the enemy distracted and unable to shift position while the rest of the unit split up and work their way around in a flanking manoeuvre. That was exactly what he'd have been doing, in Bozza's shoes.

In which case, the rest of them could appear at any moment.

Another shot cracked and boomed. The truck's rear right tyre exploded and the vehicle sagged down at the corner. Another key function of a sniper, in anti-materiel mode to neutralise the enemy's transport. This was getting better and better.

'Ben? What do we do now?'

Chapter 48

'The only thing we can do,' Ben told her. 'Get out of here, and fast.'

'How?'

He nodded in the direction of the truck. 'In that, while there's anything left of it.'

'But the tyres—'

'I'll drive it on its rims if I have to. Won't be the first time.'

'I can believe that.'

He gripped her shoulder. 'Now listen to me. Stay tight, keep your eyes peeled and don't move. If I'm not back in two minutes, run like hell. Okay?'

She nodded, eyes huge and moist. 'I'm frightened.'

'Being frightened is good. Helps you run faster.'

'Come back quick.'

'Quicker than you can say "*precipitevolissimevolmente*".'

'I'll say it slowly.'

Ben winked, then snatched up his rifle and broke cover. The sniper had been waiting, poised to shoot, and his reflexes were sharp. Ben was halfway to the truck when a bullet zipped much too close for comfort behind him. Still running, he sacrificed another bullet with a snap shot intended more to cover himself than hit anything. He reached the truck and ducked behind it. He glanced back at the rock. Anna was out of sight.

Ben inched his way up the left side of the truck. The angle at which it sat meant that if he kept pressed against its flank, he was shielded from view. Diya Sharifi's body lay sprawled with one arm outflung under the rocker panel. His blood had soaked into the dirt to make a dark, almost purple patch on the ground. Ben stepped over him. He worked the rifle bolt one more time. *Shlick-shlack.* Chambered the fourth round. Just two cartridges left. He was almost at the open driver's door. He could see the bunch of keys dangling from the ignition. If he could scramble inside the cab without getting shot, fire up the engine and slam the truck into reverse and hit the gas as hard and fast as he could while locking the steering all the way right, he had a fair chance of getting the vehicle backed up close to where Anna was hiding behind the big boulder. A lot of things could go wrong. But it was a plan.

Then the plan fell apart even before it began. Ben was so focused on getting to the door that he almost didn't notice the movement sixty yards the other side of the truck, halfway up the right-side bank of the canyon. A man in a dark jacket, carrying a submachine gun.

It was just as Ben had feared. They were closing in around their flanks.

He and the man both saw each other at the same instant. And now the slow, exploratory exchange of fire erupted into a full-on gun battle. The guy swivelled his weapon and fired, but he was in too much of a hurry and his footing was bad on the rough slope. Bullets thunked into the truck and blew out the passenger window. Ben swung the Mauser up, caught his target in his sights, and let loose his precious fourth and penultimate shot.

The bullet took the guy right in the head. The pink mist caught the wind. He crumpled at the knees, then dropped straight down like a sack of washing. His weapon went clattering down the slope.

Ben worked the rifle bolt. *Shlick-shlack.* One guy down. And one round left. Like a pauper's last penny in the world, with a stack of debts and bills to pay and bailiffs beating on the door.

Which meant the last thing Ben wanted at this moment was to be forced to use it. But in war, just as in life, what you want is seldom what you get. A second later, another figure of a man appeared – on the left this time, high on the canyon bank, clutching a black rifle with a compact ACOG scope. He was directly above Anna and tracing a zigzag path down towards her. From the way he was peering down the slope, Ben realised that he had a line of sight to her. He was raising his gun to his shoulder. Watching her through his scope. All he had to do was squeeze the trigger, unless Ben did it first.

Ben did. The perfectly timed and balanced reflexive aim-fire. The ultimate synthesis of man and machine, as though the battle rifle had been an extension of his mind and body.

But then it went horribly wrong. At the exact moment that Ben pressed the trigger, the sniper fired again, punching a hole through the open door of the truck next to him. It missed Ben, but it also caused him to jerk his shot. The last bullet from the Mauser vanished somewhere beyond the empty horizon. The figure on the slope quickly scurried for a cluster of rocks and ducked under cover. He needn't have worried. Ben was now clutching a steel and wood club.

But the sniper was still happily in business – and let off another shot to prove it. The truck shuddered from the impact. The tell-tale *ping* of a pointed copper-jacketed bullet penetrating deep into metal, carving a channel of destruction through the vehicle's vital innards. The sniper followed that one up with another that blasted out the driver's side window and showered Ben with broken glass.

And then it got worse.

The cry that rent the air was full of pain and fear. Anna's voice. Ben felt the blood freeze in his heart and wheeled around.

Bozza had her.

Chapter 49

He'd found his way down the slope unseen, and had come up behind her. He had jerked her upright, dragged her out from the shelter of the boulder behind which she'd been hiding and was clutching her tightly in front of him, one hand clamped over her mouth, the other holding a pistol against her head. Her eyes were rolling and she was struggling in his grip, but he was too strong for her. It was a replay of Olympia, except this time Ben was unarmed and helpless to do anything about it.

Anything except a strategy that had worked well for him in the past, and saved his life a couple of times. Pure brazen bluff.

Ben wasn't thinking about the sniper as he walked towards Bozza and Anna. *Let the bastard shoot*, he thought. If he allowed this woman to be killed on his watch, it was what he deserved anyway. He pointed the rifle at Bozza and worked the bolt one last time, ejecting the fifth and last spent case and making a big show of slamming a non-existent sixth into the empty chamber.

'Put it down, Bozza,' he said as calmly as he could make his voice work. He saw the tiniest narrowing of the man's eyes at the mention of the name.

'It is Bozza, isn't it? Franco was what, your elder brother?'

The man gave a slow nod. His expression didn't change. The eyes stayed narrowed, piercing into Ben's with a blaze of hatred.

Ben took another step closer. 'Tell me, are you trying to uphold some kind of family tradition?' he said. 'Dying in the line of duty, to serve a nutcase like Usberti? Or did you just take this job to get back at me?'

The man said nothing. He screwed the gun muzzle harder against Anna's head. A muffled whimper of pain squeaked through his black-gloved fingers. She tried to bite him, but he just gripped her more tightly.

Ben took another step closer, holding the rifle steady. He said, 'I'll bet you always wondered how Franco died. I was there, so I'll tell you. He was shot with a small-calibre pistol. Not much more than an antique one, at that. Once in the throat and once in the head. The second shot damn near took the whole top of his skull off. You should have seen it. But that was nothing next to what this rifle will do. At this range it'll peel you like a banana. The question I'd be asking myself in your position is: is she worth it? And then I'd let her go, right sharpish. I'd advise you to do the same.'

Bozza still didn't speak. The cold burning light in his eyes flickered downwards for a few moments and he looked at the rifle in Ben's hands. Running up and down its length, taking in the detail of form and dimension as if he was digitally scanning it with his brain. Then his eyes flicked back up to lock Ben's once more, and a ghost of a knowing smile twitched one corner of his lips. He took his left hand away from Anna's mouth. Ignoring the torrent of furious Italian that poured out of it, he kept his eyes on Ben. He held up his left thumb, then his forefinger, then the other three. Counting, *one, two, three, four, five*. Then he pointed at the rifle and the smile spread into a twisted kind of smirk that said, 'I can count, my friend. You fired five, that's a 98k you're holding there, and you're clean out of ammo.'

'Shoot him, Ben!' Anna yelled.

But Ben knew what Bozza knew: that if he was going to use the rifle, he'd have to cover the remaining distance between them faster than the pull of a trigger, and beat his enemy's brains out with it. That steel butt plate was good for all kinds of uses. If it had been just him and Bozza, he might have chanced it, even if it risked taking a bullet. But the added element in this equation was Anna. One move, and Bozza would kill her before Ben was even halfway there. Ben could read that clearly in his eyes.

Ben looked at Anna. He shook his head and saw the despair flood through her face. Then he looked back at Bozza. 'Some other time, then,' he said. He let the rifle drop from his hand. It clattered to the ground at his feet.

He might have expected his victorious enemy to offer some kind of comment at a time like this. But Bozza said not a word. His eyes darted up the canyon. Waiting for his buddies to arrive, the ones Ben hadn't killed. Ben gave Anna a reassuring wink. Like saying, 'This is just a temporary setback, we'll be fine.' He wished he could be so sure of that himself.

One by one, the others showed themselves. First came the one Ben had missed with his last shot. He slithered and scrambled down the rocky slope to join Bozza, keeping his submachine gun carefully pointed at Ben the whole time. He was a heavy-set guy with greying hair and bulging eyes like an exophthalmic fish. If he'd been one of the assault team back in Ankara, Ben didn't recognise him without his gas mask.

'You're the luckiest man alive,' Ben said. 'Better enjoy it while it lasts.'

Popeye held his gun one-handed while he fetched a small walkie-talkie handset out from his jacket, turned it on with a squawk of static and said into it, 'Mission accomplished, boss. We're one man down. Iacono didn't make it, thanks to this piece of scum. Be with you shortly.'

'Same old Usberti,' Ben said. 'Leading from the rear. Letting the expendable grunts do the dying for him.'

'*Stai zitto, bastardo inglese.*'

'That would be "*bastardo metà irlandese*",' Ben said. 'Let's get this right.'

'One more word,' Popeye warned him, 'and I'll shoot you in the balls.' He put the radio away and then used his free hand to take a set of steel handcuffs from another pocket. Stepped behind Ben, pressed the muzzle of the gun against the back of his neck. Grabbed one arm and jerked it behind Ben's back, then the other. Ben could have broken his spine in two effortless moves, three at most. But Bozza's pistol was still trained on Anna. Ben felt the bite of cold steel bracelets on his wrists and knew that his window of opportunity had just closed. For the moment.

The third guy to appear was the sniper. He emerged from a fissure between two big rocks on the canyon slope and ambled towards them with his scoped precision rifle slung casually over one shoulder, a bandolier of ammunition draped around the other, as though he'd come prepared to fight off a battalion. Like Bozza and Popeye, he was wearing a black quilted cold-weather jacket, black high-leg combat boots, black gloves and a black beanie hat. As he reached the assembled group he flashed a lurid grin at Anna. 'Aldo Groppione, *al tuo servizio.*' He ran his tongue over his lips.

'*Vai a morire ammazzatto,*' she fired back at him. Italian for: 'Go and die murdered.'

'*Maledetta puttana,*' Groppione sneered in disgust, then

turned a cocky grin on Ben. He pointed at the Mauser lying on the ground. 'Not bad shooting, from an antique musket.'

'Not so bad yourself,' Ben said. 'I'll bet you could hit an unarmed man in the chest from a kilometre away in high wind and snow. Taken any trips to Normandy recently?'

Groppione chuckled. 'That was me, all right. Most fun I ever had with my trousers on.'

'Shame you got the wrong guy,' Ben said.

'Yeah, well, you Brit pricks all look alike. Stupid shit never knew what hit him.'

'I meant shame for you,' Ben said. 'There are consequences for that kind of mistake.'

'Such as?'

'Such as, first chance I get, I'm going to stretch your neck like a chicken.'

Groppione stared at him. 'Like a chicken?'

'That's what I said,' Ben told him. 'You'd better believe it.'

Groppione laughed loudly. 'You got some *coglioni* on you, man. I'll give you that. It's almost gonna be a shame to have to plug you.' Turning to Popeye he said, 'I say we do him here. What do you reckon, Starace?'

Fish-eyed Starace shook his head. 'You know the boss said to bring both of them in alive if we could.'

'Yeah, well, what if we didn't? Accidents happen, right?'

'You want to piss him off? Nor me. Let's go.'

Groppione pointed at Anna. 'You going to cuff her too?'

'What's the matter, Groppione? You afraid of a woman?'

'I like a bitch tied up, know what I mean?'

Prisoners now, Ben and Anna were marched at gunpoint up the canyon, then up a winding path through the rocks that took them past the nook where Groppione had set himself up. It was a well-chosen spot, Ben had to admit.

The ground was littered with empty cases and screwed-up Power bar wrappers. A busy assassin's working lunch.

A little way further on, the slope peaked and then dropped away into a barren plateau where the cold wind whipped up little dust devils and rustled the few hardy shrubs that could find a place to grow. Snaking across the plateau's outer edge was a rough, unmade single-track road, the kind that needed passing places every few hundred yards so that on the rare occasions two vehicles met, they could squeeze by one another.

The nearest passing place was a short walk up the road. Filling its entire length was a stationary vehicle that was an incongruous sight out here in this empty wilderness. It wasn't a van, or even a lorry. It was an American-made six-wheeled RV the size of a touring coach. Its acres of colourful paintwork were streaked with whorls of dust and dirt from a lot of road miles. It looked as though it must have been parked there for some time, long enough for whoever was inside to make themselves comfortable. Hydraulic slide-out sections were extended on both sides. A haze of warm air was streaming from a heating exhaust vent at the rear. Pull-down blinds screened the inside of every window.

'Cosy,' Ben said. 'A mobile command centre fit for a king. Or maybe just a dead former archbishop. You boys have a hot tub in there as well?'

'Shut your mouth,' Popeye said, and prodded him in the back with his submachine gun barrel.

Bozza led the way up to a side door and stepped up an extending metal gangway. The door opened with a whoosh of hydraulics. Ben and Anna were prodded and shoved after him. 'Welcome aboard, girls,' Groppione said with a leer.

Warm air and the soft strains of a Bach choral cantata

wafted from the RV's interior as Ben climbed the steps, Anna behind. The inside of the huge motor coach seemed even more cavernous than it looked from the outside. It smelled of leather and new carpeting. Walnut cabinets and faux marble tops reflected the light from clusters of LED ceiling spotlamps. At the very front, the driving cab looked like the bridge of a starship. Between it and the side entrance, a massive swivel armchair upholstered in tan cowhide was turned with its back to Ben and Anna. The chair slowly rotated around to face them.

'Major Benedict Hope,' said the familiar voice of the chair's occupant. 'Professoressa Manzini. How happy it makes me to welcome you both to my humble domain.'

Chapter 50

Massimiliano Usberti drew himself up and stepped towards them, arms spread as though greeting long-lost friends. He was dressed in an immaculate double-breasted suit tailored from white silk over a black shirt. His hair was carefully slicked back and the gleam of his shoes was as dazzling as the Panerai watch on his thick wrist.

Usberti's men spread out around him. Groppione stalked over to the driving cab and lounged in an armchair not much smaller than his boss's throne. The bug-eyed Starace stayed near Ben and Anna, covering them cautiously with his weapon. Bozza was as motionless as a hunter-killer cyborg in standby mode, recharging itself before the next electronic data command sent it back into combat. Hovering nervously in the background stood a tall, stooped, gaunt, bespectacled younger man Ben had never seen before. The way he was standing hinted at some kind of severe spinal curvature. He certainly didn't have the look of one of Usberti's typical foot soldiers, either, wearing a shortened version of priestly black vestments and a large silver crucifix on a neck chain.

'I really hate being called that,' Ben said.

Usberti affected a look of surprise. 'It bothers you to be addressed by your former rank of major? Please accept my sincerest apologies. I must have forgotten what a modest fellow you are.' Smiling, he turned towards Anna. 'Likewise, I must confess it had previously slipped my notice just what a truly attractive creature the professor is. No photographer's lens could accurately capture such radiant beauty. I am honoured and delighted to make your acquaintance in person at last.'

Anna said, rapid-fire, '*Usberti, ficcati una barca in culo con i remi aparti.*' Or, 'Stick a boat up your ass with the oars out.'

Ben was impressed. Jeff Dekker himself couldn't have come up with a more colourful turn of phrase, or said it half as well.

'Unfortunately, her magnificence is betrayed by the ugliness that spouts from those pretty lips,' Usberti said, his smile unbroken.

'You're looking rather well yourself, old boy,' Ben told him. 'I have to say, death becomes you. Should try it for real sometime. I could give you a hand with that. In fact, I intend to, and soon.'

Usberti gave a gracious nod. 'I admire your bravado, Benedict. Am I permitted to call you Benedict? We are old friends, after all. On this occasion, however, your defiant spirit is much misplaced. You know as well as I do that you are outmatched, outgunned and outwitted, with no possibility of escape.'

'Maybe I just wanted to see if it was really you,' Ben said.

'In the flesh, as you see. Rumours of my demise have been, as the saying goes, greatly exaggerated.'

'And the poor sod they fished out of Lake Como with half his face chewed off was who, another of your old Gladius Domini cult followers? You always did look after your own.'

If Usberti objected to the word 'cult' he didn't show it. 'I believe the acronymic term used in the British Army is a "Ponti",' he said. 'A person of no tactical importance. One who had the misfortune to bear a striking physical resemblance to me.'

'Of all the bad luck, eh?' Ben replied. He flexed his wrists behind his back. The cuffs were tight. They hurt. He cast a glance at the tall, stooped priest. 'I see you found yourself a replacement for Fabrizio Severini.'

'This is Silvano Bellini, my new assistant,' Usberti said.

'Let's hope for his sake that he does better than his predecessor,' Ben said. 'Otherwise known these days as Prisoner Five-Six-One-Three-Nine.'

Usberti's eyes narrowed. 'Interesting that you should know that.'

'That's me, full of useful information.'

'May I ask how you came by it?'

'Being your partner in crime is a bad deal all round,' Ben said. 'They don't last long, do they? Those that do, end up hating your guts. Severini hated yours so much that he wrote me a letter from his prison cell, warning me that you might be up to your old tricks again. Imagine my surprise that you hadn't learned the error of your ways and become a reformed character.'

'A letter,' Usberti said, pursing his lips. 'I wonder what could have motivated him to do such a thing?'

'He said God told him to. Seems that even the Almighty has it in for you these days. Which puts the rest of us into pretty good company.'

Usberti's tall, gaunt assistant hadn't uttered a word since Ben and Anna had arrived. He was shifting nervously from foot to foot, looking ever more bent over and staring down at the floor with his brow corrugated by a deep frown. Ben thought that maybe he didn't like the Lord's name brought into this. Or maybe the idea of ending up in jail as a consequence of running around with crooks like these had never occurred to him before now.

Anna hadn't taken her eyes off Usberti since they'd walked in, glaring at him as though she wanted to slit his throat. 'Where's Ercan? What have you done with him?'

Usberti looked at her a moment before replying. 'Oh, he is nearby. And I must say we owe him a debt of gratitude for his contribution to our knowledge regarding the possible whereabouts of the idol. Having seen the fruits of his research, you do not need me to tell you what a truly diligent scholar he is. So diligent, in fact, that he was able to share with us a number of his most recent discoveries that you would not find in his notes. Discoveries of which you are as yet unaware, but which have cast a very important new light on our little quest.'

Usberti paused, smiling at Anna as if inviting her to say something. When all she did was stare at him in hatred, he went on: 'You did not know, for instance, that within the last few days your associate, dissatisfied with the progress of his research, delved yet deeper into the Persepolis Fortification Archives to unearth fresh information. He additionally made further inquiries from a contact of his, one Dr Serge Munoz of the Joint International Syrian Expedition, currently surveying the ancient city and Roman legionnaire garrison at Al-Rafina. We now learn that the Babylonian renegade Ashar Muranu did not remain long in Harran, though what became of the rest of the family is unknown. Hitherto-unresearched PFA records show that he fled from here to the ancient city of Karkemish, where he established a new base, attracted new followers, and attempted further acts of insurrection against the authorities. It was in

Karkemish that, in 515 BC, he was finally caught and executed. There his story ends, while ours is only about to begin.'

'Ercan told you all that?' Anna said in disbelief.

'Oh, and much more besides. Consequently, it appears that our search must now take us towards Karkemish. A place so steeped in heritage, filled with such ancient wonders. But I would not presume to lecture a learned historian on the subject – perhaps you would like to share your considerable wealth of knowledge with a mere amateur such as myself?'

'The only thing I share with you, you murdering pig, is the air inside this stinking camper van, so –' She finished in Italian. '– *vaffanculo a chi t'è morto!*'

Which, roughly translated, was telling Usberti to go and screw the souls of his dead family members. It was hard to tell which offended him more, that or calling the huge luxury RV a camper van. His face purpled for a moment, but he quickly recovered his urbane demeanour.

'Then you leave it to me to sum up what little I know of Karkemish and its ancient past. Formerly a monumental capital city in north-western Mesopotamia, no more than seventy-five or eighty kilometres from where we stand, to the west and a little to the south. Frequently mentioned both in scripture and in extra-Biblical texts. Once upon a time, an important seat of power for Hittite and Neo-Assyrian dynasties, as well as the site of the defeat of the Egyptian Pharaoh Nacho the Second at the hands of the forces of King Nebuchadnezzar himself, six hundred and five years before our beloved Lord Christ walked this earth. Surely it cannot be a coincidence that Ashar the Babylonian would have chosen such a symbolic location for his last stand against the Persian Empire? And what a fitting resting place for the golden idol crafted in honour of Babylon's greatest ruler.'

Ben was barely listening to Usberti speak. He was too busy picturing that mental map again. And what he was seeing there wasn't good news.

Usberti continued: 'All that remains today, of course, are scattered rubble fields where once stood proud palaces, temples and mighty ramparts. Excavation attempts there have been somewhat sporadic, beginning in 1878 for only three years, then recommenced in 1911 by notable archaeologists including Britain's own T.E "Lawrence of Arabia". Sadly, the advent of World War One interrupted these activities with no further resumption until as recently as 2011, when a joint team of Turkish and Italian scholars led by Professor Nicolò Marchetti of Bologna University resurrected the excavation project and campaigned for the ruins of Karkemish to be designated a UNESCO heritage site. However, once again, such worthy efforts were to be hampered by the same endless litany of human conflict and destruction.'

It was the conflict and destruction that Ben had been thinking about, with a sinking heart as he began to realise where Usberti was intending to take them.

Because in modern times the ancient site of Karkemish was overshadowed in every sense by its near neighbour. Just a mortar shot away, straddling the Turkish–Syrian border in one of the most fiercely contested territories of the ongoing Syrian civil war, was Jarabulus.

Ben had had a bellyful of military goings-on during his Army career, and followed little of what was in the news – but he knew enough to know that Jarabulus had been occupied since 2013 by forces of the Islamic State of Iraq and the Levant, better known as ISIL, who had used it as a

320

base from which to lob rockets and shells over the border into Turkey. It was only months since Turkish land forces and troops of the Free Syrian Army had responded in a military push called Operation Euphrates Shield, dropping heavy bombardment on Jarabulus and supported by air strikes from US Air Force jets, in an attempt to oust the militants. The last he'd heard, FSA troops had pressed their advance far enough to storm Jarabulus, only to find the city emptied of insurgents and ISIL forces largely pulled out of the area ahead of their invasion. But all kinds of battles were still being fought over the region as the two sides went back and forth in a desperate effort to take and retake the same old ground.

Not just two sides: it was an increasingly confused nightmare welter of warring factions. New Syrian Army, Free Syrian Army, Democratic Syrian Forces, Syrian Islamic Liberation Front; then there were the Russians, supporting the Assad regime, and the Americans, trying to destabilise it, having themselves a fine little replay of the Cold War. The Abu Amara Brigade, the Jaysh al-Islam, the Jabhat al-Shamiya, the Mujahideen, the Kurdish YPG Militia, and probably a thousand more, all slip-sliding around in an ocean of blood and ever-shifting internal allegiances. It hadn't surprised Ben to hear reports that British Special Forces units were unofficially roving about in the middle of the big ugly tinderbox that was just waiting to kick off into a third world war, if and when the politicians proved insanely stupid enough to let that happen.

In short, it was the last place he wanted either Anna or himself to be.

'You talk too much, Usberti,' Anna said. 'I asked about Ercan. You said he was nearby, so let me see him. Right this minute, you hear me?'

'How can I refuse a direct request from a delightful lady?' Usberti said. 'By all means.' He turned to Bozza. 'Ugo, would you oblige the professor by reuniting her with her learned associate?'

Bozza wordlessly walked down the length of the RV and went to what Ben guessed must be the door to a bathroom or bedroom, at the tail end of the vehicle. Bozza opened the door, stepped through it and closed it behind him.

What Ben expected to happen next was for Bozza to re-emerge clutching Ercan Kavur, drag him up the aisle and dump him at Anna's feet. Probably doped up to the eyeballs and semi-conscious, which would explain the silence from behind the door. Most likely battered and bruised, too. It seemed unlikely that he'd have fed so much information to his captors without being under some duress. It wouldn't be a pretty sight, and an upsetting one for Anna.

But Ben was dead wrong.

The door reopened. Bozza came out alone, carrying something in his hand. It was a blue plastic cool box with a folding handle, the kind of insulated container people took with them to keep their beer cold on a camping trip. Bozza walked back up the length of the RV. Minute tremors of its suspension rocked the floor under his weight. He carried the box in front of him at arm's length. Set it down on a table. Then he folded down the handle, unsnapped a catch at each side, lifted off the lid, and tilted the box towards them to display its contents.

It wasn't a chilled six-pack of beer.

And that was when Ben saw how mistaken he'd been. They hadn't beaten Ercan Kavur up at all. Or, if they had, they hadn't touched his face, which looked perfectly unbruised as it stared at them from the blue plastic box.

They'd cut off his head.

Chapter 51

This wasn't the first time Ben had found himself in the presence of one part or another of a decapitated body. But Anna had led a more sheltered life than he had. Her cry of anguish and horror filled the RV. Her knees folded under her and she covered her mouth with her hands.

'Take her outside, Ugo,' Usberti said, grimacing. 'I would rather not have the carpeting covered in vomit.'

Bozza replaced the lid on the cool box, stepped over to Anna and hauled her upright by the arm. He marched her to the door, activated a switch that made it whoosh open, then shoved and dragged her down the metal gangway and let her go so she could bend double at the side of the road and throw up.

'They don't call you Mr Charm for nothing, do they?' Ben said to Usberti. 'What did you do with the rest of the guy, feed him to your lapdog?'

Usberti shrugged. 'There is a limit to every man's usefulness. Regrettably, we reached a stage where Signor Kavur no longer served any purpose to us. Moreover, I see no need to employ the services of two expert historians, when one will do me just as well. Now that she is up to date with her colleague's latest discoveries, Professor Manzini will be quite able to help us achieve our objective. As for what to do with you, my dear Benedict, I have another purpose in mind. One for which your particular skills qualify you better than any of my men; or should I say, my *remaining* men. Once again, you have demonstrated your perplexing habit of diminishing my human resources.'

'They'll be diminished a lot more by the time we're done,' Ben said. He couldn't point, so he jerked his chin in the direction of Aldo Groppione. 'Starting with him there. But he already knows that.'

'Fuck you,' Groppione said. 'Boss, I'm telling you, it's a mistake to keep this fucker alive. He's tricksy. You can't trust him.'

'You can trust me,' Ben said. 'You can set your watch by me. Start counting the minutes you have left. I'll save you till last, Usberti. Just so I can see the look on your face when you're all alone and it's time to say bye-bye.'

'I would expect nothing less from such a worthy opponent,' Usberti said. He motioned towards Groppione and Starace without looking at them. 'And I have no doubt that, left to your own fearsome devices, you would have little trouble disposing of these men. But Ugo Bozza is another matter. His lethal expertise is second to none, and he has waited a long time to avenge his elder brother.'

'Or to join him in hell.'

'We shall see. As they say, may the best man win.'

Bozza came back inside, shoving Anna in front of him. All the defiance had gone out of her and she looked waxen and utterly defeated. Bozza slung her into one of the long leather sofas that lined the sides of the motor coach's opulent interior.

'I believe we have some trash to dispose of,' Usberti said. 'Then let us get underway. There is no time to lose.'

'How about taking off these cuffs for me?' Ben said.

'Seems a shame to be travelling in this thing and not be comfortable.'

Starace just snorted in reply. He slung his weapon over his shoulder, grabbed the cool box, carried it outside and drop-kicked it into the scrub bushes that edged the road. He came back inside wiping his hands, then walked over to a digital display panel with a cluster of buttons and pressed one. The door sucked shut behind him. He pressed another, and there was the whirring of an electric motor as some hidden mechanism folded the extending gangway steps into a recess beneath the door. The third button activated a hydraulic system that retracted the extending slide-outs on both flanks of the vehicle. The walls and floor sections closed in, suddenly transforming the RV's interior back from a penthouse apartment to something resembling a luxury narrowboat.

'Take a seat, asshole,' Starace said to Ben, unslinging his weapon and using it to motion at the sofa where Anna was sitting. He leaned back in one opposite, now much closer across the narrowed centre aisle, with the gun resting on his thigh and pointing lazily at Ben.

Meanwhile, Groppione was getting behind the wheel of the starship. The diesel engine started up with a muted snort, rippling the length of the huge vehicle with faint tremors of vibration. Groppione pushed the oversized chrome gear selector into drive and the motor coach shuddered against its brakes. Usberti returned to his throne. His assistant, Bellini, perched on a fold-down seat nearby. Bozza hovered towards the stern end of the coach, his eyes never leaving Ben. Ben ignored him and sat close to Anna, but she was in a world of her own.

There was a hiss as Groppione released the airbrakes. Then they began to roll.

The winding track meandered downhill for several kilometres. The coach had been built to cruise the glass-smooth, arrow-straight interstates of North America, not for hacking through the camel trails of south-eastern Turkey. Groppione was taking it very easy, but still the suspension was rocking and bouncing, and the rear end was swaying like a pendulum through the twists and turns. Ben couldn't lean back on the soft leather sofa with his hands cuffed behind him, so he sat leaning forward and watched the road.

Nobody spoke. Bellini looked deep in his own worries. Starace's eyes were closed, but he still had his finger on the trigger of his weapon. Bozza's were wide open and fixed on Ben like a chameleon watching a fly.

They eventually joined a windswept highway and Groppione was able to put on some speed. The road carved through the flat, wintry semi-desert landscape for an hour without meeting any traffic. Usberti seemed to be enjoying the ride, a contented smile on his face as though the golden idol was already in his hands. Or a treasure map with a big red X that marked the spot where all they had to do was start digging. Either he was delusional, Ben thought, or he knew something they didn't. Was it possible that Ercan Kavur had figured it all out? Found the key to a secret that had eluded the best of the world's historians for two and a half thousand years?

'You seem to have a very good idea of exactly where we're headed,' Ben said to him. 'As you've press-ganged Professor Manzini into serving as your archaeology consultant, it might be appropriate at this point to fill her in on the details.'

Professor Manzini didn't seem to give a damn one way or the other. But Ben needed to form a strategy. In tactical planning, if you weren't thinking ahead, you were going backwards.

Usberti wasn't about to be drawn, however.

'All in good time, Benedict. All in good time,' he said.

Which confirmed what Ben had been thinking, but didn't detract from his suspicion that Usberti was at least partly delusional. Because no matter how confident he might be that he knew where the idol was, he was seriously underestimating the trouble they were going to have getting there.

And the closer they got to the Syrian border, the more Ben could see the signs of trouble growing. Slowly at first, then with dramatic speed, the highway around them began to crowd with traffic rumbling in both directions. Most of it was military. Dusty olive-green convoys of troop transports, armoured personnel carriers and heavily loaded supply trucks, giant articulated trailer lorries carrying tanks and artillery, formations of four-wheel-drive pickups crammed with men and ordnance. The majority of the army traffic was Turkish, while the rest belonged to Syrian forces allied to President Erdogan's regime. So far, nobody seemed to be bothering with the RV, but it was only a matter of time before they were pulled over by one lot of soldiers or another.

'Great plan, Usberti,' Ben said. 'This carnival float sticks out like a hot-dog stand at a Jewish wedding. You think you're just going to go waltzing into the middle of a war zone?'

Usberti said nothing.

Ben knew the border control was up ahead long before Groppione was forced to slow down for it. Both lanes of the highway and a whole stretch of dusty, sandy terrain either side of it were teeming with troops and vehicles. The checkpoint itself was hardly visible through the confusion, but it was clear that what little civilian traffic was attempting to pass through was being stopped and searched. Several vehicles ahead, a dirty, battered Toyota farm truck loaded with goats was rolling at walking pace towards the checkpoint when a group of soldiers clustered around it with rifles pointed and a burly Turkish officer in wrinkled combat DPMs and a blue beret blocked its path with a raised hand. One of the soldiers banged on the driver's window and made an exaggerated motion telling him to step out of the vehicle. The guy was dressed in Arab garb, wiry and grey-bearded. The soldiers yanked him out of the Toyota. They weren't being particularly gentle about it. They pushed and poked him around as the officer yelled something in Turkish. The old Arab guy started nervously reaching around inside his garb for his papers, surrounded by threatening guns.

Groppione turned round behind the wheel of the RV and threw a look at his boss that said, 'What do we do now?'

Usberti still said nothing.

As the soldiers waited impatiently for the old goat farmer to produce his papers, Ben saw the Turkish officer glance over at the RV. As if the huge gaudy bus could be missed, even in all the chaos and half-camouflaged with road dust. The officer issued a brusque nod to some more of his men who were standing on the sidelines. Four snapped to attention and came running over towards the RV, clutching their weapons. MPT-76 battle rifles, standard issue to Turkish infantry. Ben had used one in the past. It was a good tool. Not one that anyone wanted to have pointed at them.

Ben said, 'Let's see you talk your way out of this one, Usberti.'

The soldiers came closer. They spread out around the front of the motor coach. Three of them planted themselves right in front of it, aiming their rifles at the windscreen in a triangular formation. The fourth marched up to Groppione's driver window, which was so high off the ground that he had to stand back to be seen. He used his weapon to rap on the glass and started gesticulating angrily.

'Boss?' Groppione said, throwing up his hands. 'Tell me what to do here? The guy wants to see papers. We don't have any.'

'We are going through regardless,' Usberti replied calmly. He turned and looked at Bozza, who had quietly stepped past Anna and Ben and was standing close to the big leather throne, looking expectantly back at Usberti.

The soldier was still rapping on the window.

The officer who had given the order was stepping away from the goat truck and walking towards them to see what the problem was.

'We are going through,' Usberti repeated. 'Nothing can stand in my way. If God wills it, we will fight our way into Syria. Ugo, shoot the soldiers.'

Bozza responded without hesitation, without the smallest flicker of doubt on his face. He grabbed the submachine gun from Starace. Checked it, flipped off the safety, and walked to the front of the RV.

'Call him off, Usberti,' Ben said. 'He's about to get us all killed.'

Bozza took aim through the window at the nearest soldier.

Chapter 52

All Ben could do was brace himself for the gunshot. About one second after Bozza squeezed the trigger, every soldier at the checkpoint would respond with a concentration of gunfire that no one inside the RV would survive.

When it came, the blast was stunning, like a massive clap of thunder. Beyond any gunshot Ben had ever heard before. The whole coach rocked violently on its suspension, as though a powerful percussion wave had slapped into it from outside. Windows shattered and cracks appeared all over the windscreen as Groppione ducked behind the steering wheel and covered his head with his arms. Bellini tumbled out of his seat and hit the floor. Ben felt Anna tighten up with sudden terror next to him.

After an instant's confusion, he realised what had happened. Bozza hadn't fired the shot. The blast had come from outside. The scene he could see through the RV's now-cracked windscreen was one of total carnage. The Turkish officer and a dozen of his soldiers had been laid flat by the explosion. Several of them were torn apart. Blood was everywhere. Body parts were still falling from the sky. Separated limbs were strewn across a circle fifty feet in radius. Not just human ones. Pieces of goat lay twitching with the fur singed and smoking. Then the screaming began as dozens more injured men at the edges of the blast circle realised the horror of the damage done to them.

At the centre of it all, what was left of the Toyota farm truck was a black, torn shell engulfed in roiling fire. Surrounding vehicles had been blown over onto their sides by the massive shockwave, flames belching from their scorched insides. Nothing at all remained of the wiry little Arab guy who had been reaching inside his garb for his papers – and pulled out a remote detonator switch instead, triggering what the military called a VBIED, or vehicle-borne improvised explosive device – what everyone else called a car bomb. Twenty or thirty pounds of Semtex cleverly stashed where few soldiers would think or care to search, under a pile of stinking goat bedding in the back of the truck, had done their work.

The result was a slaughterhouse. Ben had been close to car bombs before, but never close enough to see the immediate aftermath from a ringside seat. The checkpoint instantly fell into wild chaos. Some soldiers tried to drag the mutilated survivors away from the flames. Others simply ran, fearing secondary blasts if the fuel tanks of burning vehicles exploded. Some began firing off their weapons in confusion at some unseen enemy hidden in the black smoke that was billowing up and blocking out the sunlight.

Usberti surveyed the scene with an air of unflappable calm, then said, 'Groppione, drive on.'

Groppione was too stunned to speak. He slammed the selector back into drive, put his foot down, and the coach went lurching through the mayhem. It had taken some shrapnel from the blast, but they were still in the game. A soldier ran in front of them, yelling and waving his gun. Groppione just accelerated towards him and he dived out of the RV's path.

'Keep moving!' Usberti commanded. 'We do not stop for anything!' The diesel engine grunted and rasped. Groppione drove blindly through the smoke and flames, rolling over wreckage and crushing dead bodies and severed limbs. Then the smoke cleared to reveal the path ahead, which the explosion had carved out of the busy checkpoint. Groppione accelerated harder, and they were through and away, picking up speed. Through the back window, Ben saw soldiers chasing them on foot, shouting, raising their rifles. A crackle of shots sounded over the roar of the diesel. Bullets smacked into the tail of the RV. But the soldiers had more to worry about, and quickly gave up the chase to return to their shattered checkpoint.

Massimiliano Usberti looked as proud as if God Almighty himself had come down and parted the Red Sea to let him through. 'Faith, men. Faith. The Lord is with us.'

Groppione said, 'Amen to that.' Starace closed his eyes and sank his chin to his chest in a moment of reverent prayer. Bozza said nothing, and neither did Ben, though for other reasons. If there was a God up there, Ben was thinking, and if He had any influence at all on what happened down here below, then He truly did move in mysterious ways. Or, if Usberti was just lucky, then given what plans his good fortune might allow him to carry out, that in itself could be taken as pretty good proof that there was no God up there after all.

Or, maybe God wasn't such a good guy.

Ben and Anna sat close together on the leather sofa. The cuffs were constantly chafing and biting his wrists, and there was no way he could sit that didn't hurt, but he was concerned only for her. 'Are you okay?' he mouthed silently. She tried to smile. She nodded. 'I'm okay,' she mouthed back.

Soon, all that could be seen of the border checkpoint was a tower of black smoke far behind them as they rolled onwards into Syria, due south. The sun was beginning to set in the west, casting its pale rays through the Perspex window behind Ben and Anna. Sand and dust were blown in ever-shifting waves across the RV's path by the wintry wind. Warm air whispered through the heating vents. The road went on, and on, through the arid landscape. If the soldiers had radioed ahead to alert other units to the presence of a large, suspicious vehicle in the vicinity, there was no sign of it. They drove past a burned-out tank that sat lopsidedly at the roadside, its armoured flanks perforated and charred black, alone in the desert like a silent monument to the men who had died there. And the thousands more who would before this senseless war passed into history to join all the other senseless wars that men had fought since the dawn of time.

'So are you going to tell us where we're going, Usberti?' Ben said at last.

Usberti was sitting on his throne with its leathery back to them, so that all they could see of him were his feet and elbows. He swivelled round to face them. 'To a place where your talents will be put to good use, Benedict,' he replied. 'I told you I had a purpose for you. That is the only reason I have chosen to keep you alive, for the moment.'

'That's very gracious of you,' Ben said, staring at him. 'Whatever it is, I hope I don't disappoint.'

'I know you will not.' Usberti smiled, then turned his gaze on Anna. 'And neither shall you, my dear Professor. Your own skills will soon be brought to bear, now that our quest nears its end.' He rose from his chair and walked down the length of the RV towards where they sat side by side, steadying himself against the lurch and sway of the vehicle.

'I suppose the time has come for me to reveal to you what your late associate was kind enough, shortly before his demise, to reveal to me.'

'You could even have let him tell us himself,' Ben said. 'It would have saved you the trouble. And saved him some grief.'

'No trouble,' Usberti said nonchalantly. He waved Starace away, then lowered himself onto the sofa opposite them. 'In the bitter winter of 1923 an expeditionary team of Austrian archaeologists led by one Hans Von Grüber came across a mysterious discovery, high on a rocky plateau. It was just a few hours' horse ride across the Syrian Desert from what was then the largely abandoned excavation project at Karkemish. Their find was a set of inscriptions carved into the face of a sheer sandstone cliff, near to what they believed to be the remains of an ancient fortress. The location was extremely hazardous to access, so much so that two of their team fell to their deaths in their attempts to investigate the inscription. Von Grüber and another of his colleagues survived, however, and despite the difficult conditions they were able to record detailed transcripts of their discovery. Von Grüber later compared it to the inscriptions at Mount Behistun in Iran, discovered ninety years earlier. But while the Behistun carvings were of Persian origin, celebrating the glories of the Emperor Darius, these by contrast were writings in an obscure cuneiform language. Moreover, while the Behistun carving is a magnificent work of art crafted by skilled sculptors using the best quality mason's chisels, the Karkemish inscriptions were relatively crude and appeared to have been made by someone in a hurry, with an implement such as a dagger or sword point.'

Anna was listening intently. This time, she didn't interrupt Usberti to tell him he talked too much. The look of hostility on her face hadn't softened, but her curiosity was getting the better of her.

'Von Grüber returned to his home city of Graz in early 1924, severely afflicted by pneumonia contracted during his expedition, whereupon the transcript of the carvings was placed on display at a private historical and art collection in Berlin. Sadly, the building that housed the collection was flattened, along with so many others, in 1945 when the British and Americans bombarded that city with over seventy thousand tons of bombs. The only existing physical record of Hans Von Grüber's discovery was among the many artefacts lost forever. Von Grüber himself had died twenty years earlier; having never recovered from his sickness he succumbed within months of his return from Syria. But in a letter written shortly before his death to a colleague, one Professor Claude Desmoines of the Sorbonne, he described the clifftop inscriptions near Karkemish and expressed his fervent and unshakeable belief that they constituted some form of map. More correctly, a set of directions which, accurately translated, could direct the seeker to unearth a great treasure. Von Grüber wrote, "Beneath every footstep in Syria may dwell the legacy of ancient civilisations, undiscovered wonders and, for the seeker who will risk all to find them, riches beyond imagining." Like so many ancient mysteries yet to be solved, neither the nature nor the precise location of that treasure have ever been determined.'

'It's incredible,' Anna said in a low voice. 'It could really be true.'

To Ben, the idea of carving a treasure map on a cliff face seemed a little baffling. But then, he wasn't an archaeologist. Carving stuff on rocks and stones seemed to have been the thing in those days. Plus, he supposed that if you were a desperate bandito hiding out in the hills with enemy soldiers closing in all around you, and you found yourself bereft of a convenient piece of papyrus to use as notepaper on which to scratch out your last message to your gang, you might not have any other choice.

'There is more, my dear Professor Manzini. I told you that Kavur had recently been in contact with a fellow archaeologist. Dr Serge Munoz of the Joint International Syrian Expedition is a highly respected authority; he is also, like your late colleague and, I believe, you yourself, an expert on ancient cuneiform languages. He claims to have seen not only a copy of Von Grüber's 1924 letter but a rare pre-war photograph of the Berlin exhibits themselves, which he was able to partially decipher. Following his discussion with this Dr Munoz, Kavur became convinced that the clifftop inscriptions near Karkemish almost certainly point to the exact whereabouts of a fabulous buried secret.'

Usberti's eyes gleamed. He went on:

'Thanks to you and Signor Kavur, who alone among historians have traced the path of the exiled Muranu dynasty from Babylon, there can be little doubt that we stand on the brink of finding the great lost treasure of Nebuchadnezzar.'

Chapter 53

Ben could see the internal forces splitting Anna in two. She was face to face with the man who had personally sanctioned the murder of Theo Kambasis and Ercan Kavur, ordered the attack on Gianni Garrone at her villa, and who had been trying to kidnap her since Olympia. Yet she'd come this far and been through so much to find the Babylon idol – and if what Usberti was saying was right, the nearness of its discovery was driving her wild. She was thinking so fast that her eyes were darting.

'Now I understand what Ercan wanted to tell me, and why he had to share the secret with me in person,' she said. 'Ashar the Babylonian, the fort at Harran, was only the beginning of the story. It all makes such sense. Ashar was constantly at war with the Persians. If anything had happened to him, if he was killed or captured, he knew the idol must be preserved at all cost. Perhaps he left the inscription as a message to his followers when he realised he was about to be caught. That would explain why the work was crude and done in a hurry, carved with whatever weapon he carried with him. And also why it was so high on the cliff, to keep it hidden from enemy eyes. And it must also mean—'

She hesitated, glanced at Usberti. Ben read her expression

of self-annoyance for letting her passion for her subject make her say more than she should have.

'What must it mean, Professor?' Usberti asked with a gloating kind of smile that Ben wanted to slice off him with a knife.

She paused. 'I was going to say . . . it must mean that the idol is nowhere near Karkemish. I mean, the Persian soldiers were all over the region.'

Usberti went on smiling. 'You try to deceive me, Professor. On the contrary, and as I know perfectly well you were going to say before you checked yourself, the idol's guardian would have wanted to ensure that it was safe. To that end, he would have visited its location frequently, in secret, and in person. Which would imply that it was concealed within convenient travelling distance from his base, as too much time spent journeying back and forth would have constituted a risk of capture. Say, half a day's ride, there and back, and possibly much closer. In any case, the map will soon provide all the information we need.'

'That's if you can find it,' Ben said. 'You might not be so lucky this time.'

Usberti waved a hand. 'Luck will not be necessary. The account in Von Grüber's letter was detailed enough for Serge Munoz to pinpoint the precise navigational position of the cliff.' He took a small GPS device from his pocket and held it up. 'Once again, Signor Kavur's assistance proved most useful in providing us with the coordinates.'

'Isn't that handy,' Ben said.

'Indeed it is most fortunate,' Usberti replied, smiling even more broadly now. 'One might say, serendipitous. An act of fate, even, that the wheels of discovery should have been set in motion at exactly the right moment for us – or should I say, for me. It was only a matter of time before some other intrepid scholar picked up the trail and followed it to its fabulous end. The idol of King Nebuchadnezzar, a magnificent statue of pure gold, sixty cubits tall, buried beneath the sand. But I will get there first and stake my claim. If my calculations are correct, and I am confident they are, such a quantity of gold will make me one of the richest men in the world.'

'Now we get to it,' Ben said. 'And there was I thinking this was all about the pursuit of theological truth.'

'Even if you found it,' Anna said to Usberti, 'you can't know what to expect. Nothing in archaeology is ever certain.'

'But God's word is,' Usberti said. His smile fell away and irritation twisted his face. 'It is the most certain thing there is. And the Bible is God's word. If the Bible says the king of Babylon created a golden statue sixty cubits tall, then that is what I shall find there. To doubt that is to doubt the Holy Creator Himself. To question God is to be a heretic, and heretics shall be punished with death. Is that not so, Ugo?'

Bozza made a single up-down motion of his head.

'Then we mustn't doubt the Creator,' Ben said. 'You'll be the wealthiest man in the loony bin and the world will be a happier place for it.'

'Major Hope thinks he can provoke me with his taunts,' Usberti said to Anna. 'His ploy is that, if he can anger me sufficiently, it may trigger some reaction on my part which he can exploit to his advantage. For your own sake, Professor, and for his – as it has not escaped my notice that you have some inexplicable degree of feeling for him – please impress upon him that such an attempt would not only be quite futile but also counterproductive, in that it would produce only a worsening of the means by which he is to die, when that time arrives, as it will soon enough.'

Anna looked at him. 'I was right, Usberti. You do talk too much.'

The sun was sinking lower over the desert as they slowly ground towards their destination. Usberti and Groppione had worked out a route using GPS to get them there without skirting too closely by the town of Jarabulus itself. So far, the plan had worked and they'd seen no sign of trouble. No sign of anything at all, or any living person. Just sand and rock and the increasingly difficult terrain that was becoming more challenging with every passing kilometre. For most of the journey the landscape had been flat and endlessly wide and almost featureless except for undulating hills and clumps of scrubby, stunted vegetation eking out an existence in the sheltered dips and hollows. A hard place to survive: seared by brutal heat for two-thirds of the year, while the winter months brought blasting winds and temperatures that could sink far below zero.

Which was exactly what was happening out there right now. Strong gusts of icy wind rocked the RV and the darkening sky seemed to threaten snow. Ben couldn't tell exactly where they were, but judging by the lie of the land, Jarabulus was somewhere to the east of their position. To the west the horizon grew wilder, overshadowed with rocky escarpments that were turning to purples and blues in the fading light. And it was into the high country that the GPS was directing them, tracking the same approximate route that had led Hans Von Grüber's expedition to the site of their discovery – for two, their deaths.

The RV had long since left behind anything resembling a road. It was lurching and pitching and rocking crazily as it crawled over the impossible terrain. Groppione was no kind of an expert off-road driver, but even if he had been, the size and weight and low ground clearance of the vehicle was a major handicap. Three times in succession, he ploughed them into rocky hollows that had the suspension jarring against its stops, the wheels spinning for grip, and Ben almost certain that they wouldn't get out. But Usberti's luck was holding.

Now they curved due west, away from the falling sun and the flat desert panorama that dropped away behind them as they climbed into the rocky escarpment. It was like navigating a ship through a frozen ocean, with lanes of open water ever-tightening into narrow fissures and icebergs looming on all sides. The long, low chassis scraped and clanged and dragged painfully over ruts and boulders. The way ahead became steeper, and steeper, until they were down to first gear and the engine was straining badly and sounded as though it was overheating. Ben could smell diesel fumes and hot oil, and hear the whirr and whine of the cooling fan struggling to pull enough air through the radiator.

Undeterred, Massimiliano Usberti stood behind the driver's seat, clutching his GPS device, pointing ahead and urging Groppione onwards with terse commands and threats of what would happen to anyone cowardly enough to refuse to keep going. Groppione was hunched over the wheel, looking as if he hardly dared to breathe. They squeezed through a pass that was almost too narrow for the RV's bulk, sheared off one of its mirrors and crumpled their flanks and left deep gouges in the Perspex windows.

Up, and up. And up some more. To their left, the escarpment formed a sheer cliff face almost touching the side of the coach. To their right, across the aisle from where Ben and Anna were sitting, was a vertical drop to the desert below. To the front, what little track there was to follow was narrowing into a rubble-strewn mountain path where even a Syrian Awassi sheep herdsman would have hesitated to take his flock. It seemed to Ben that if it narrowed any more, the coach would topple off its precarious edge and go hurtling down to its destruction. And *he* was supposed to be the crazy one. Starace looked about ready to collapse from terror, darting pug-eyed glances out of the window every few seconds and pouring with sweat. Bellini was sitting near the front, head bowed in grim silence, his fingertips white where they clutched the arms of his seat.

Usberti scrutinised his GPS one last time, held up a hand and said, 'That is far enough.'

Groppione braked to a halt and fell back in the driver's seat, as limp and pale and spent as a man running a high fever. Starace let out a wheeze of a sigh and rubbed his eyes. Bellini let go of the arms of his seat and looked at his employer in bewilderment. Even Ugo Bozza seemed relieved.

They couldn't have travelled any further in any case, even if the track had gone on and on. The way ahead was completely blocked by the rubble of a rock fall. Just before that, there was a large craggy opening in the cliff face to their left, easily the height of the RV, deep enough for two nose-to-tail and wide enough for three, side by side. Groppione's driving duties weren't over yet.

'Turn us around,' Usberti ordered him, circling a finger in the air. Groppione suppressed a groan, engaged reverse, backed up a few yards with a careful eye on the remaining mirror, then gently eased the RV inside the cave. The rasp of its engine was suddenly amplified and echoey. Groppione had to spend the next few minutes pulling a complicated multi-point turn to get the RV reversed out of the cave mouth without backing right over the edge and killing them all, then turned around and straightened up to point the opposite way down the track. By the time he was done, the cave reeked with sickly-sweet diesel exhaust fumes.

'Thank you, Aldo,' Usberti said. 'You may kill the engine now. Everyone, please disembark.'

Bozza activated the hydraulics to open the side door, which was now on the RV's inside flank, between it and the cliff face. The gap was a tight squeeze as, one by one – Ben first, then Anna, and Usberti last – they all stepped down the gangway. After so long inside the warm vehicle, the freezing, whipping wind cut like a razor. Anna immediately began to shiver despite her heavy jacket. Usberti seemed unaffected by the chill. His men gathered round him. Ben watched. And listened. He could hear something over the fluting note of the wind. A distant sound that his ears were attuned to by virtue of oft-repeated experience.

Somewhere beyond the horizon, there was a fight happening.

Usberti frowned up at the sky. Particles of moisture too slow and heavy to be rain were drifting diagonally on the wind. The temperature was dropping perceptibly now that the sun had sunk all the way behind the broad western horizon. 'There is not much time,' he commented.

'Not much time for what?' Ben asked. Though he was afraid he already knew the answer to his question.

Usberti turned, gazed at Ben, and a look of cruelty and triumph split his face into a crooked grin. He pointed a finger straight up into the air.

'Time for you to show your mettle, Benedict. You are going to climb the cliff for me.'

Chapter 54

Ben craned his neck to peer upwards in the direction of the pointing finger. The cliff loomed over them. Maybe a hundred feet, maybe three times that. Hard to tell. The angle of the rock face was past vertical, so he couldn't see the top.

He normally enjoyed climbing. Now and then, on a Sunday morning when the schedule at Le Val allowed, he would take the old Land Rover to a Normandy beach near a place called Étretat, with a sea kayak strapped to the roof, paddle out to the base of the famous chalk cliffs of the so-called Alabaster Coast and relish pitting himself against the challenge.

This was a whole other proposition. Ben didn't like to use the word 'impossible'. But if there were an enemy position up there on top, and orders dictated that it were imperative to capture that position, the SAS would have looked for another way.

'Now you see my purpose in keeping you alive,' Usberti said. 'Why should I risk the lives of my own men, when I have you? Aldo, you may uncuff him. No tricks, Major, I beseech you.'

'You can't make him do this,' Anna said.

'Of course not. He will make the climb by his own will.

344

Because he can all too well imagine the harm that may come to you, my dear, if he refuses.'

'You need me just as much as you need him,' she said. 'More, even. Unless you suddenly became an expert translator of ancient cuneiform languages.'

'The human body is remarkably adaptive to even the most atrocious mutilation,' Usberti said. 'I have seen double, even triple amputees capable of some amazing feats of dexterity. Consider for a moment, Professor, the minimum physiological requirements necessary for translating a piece of writing from one language to another. All that is really needed is a brain to think with, one eye to read with, one hand to write with, a heart and a pair of lungs to keep the abbreviated organism functioning. A marvel of economy, thanks to the genius of God's design. But what a pity it would be to reduce so beautiful a feminine form to such a pitiful state. And how upsetting for Major Hope, knowing such an outcome could have been avoided.'

'I'll make the climb,' Ben said. 'But I can't do it with my bare hands. Though I'm sure you already thought of that.'

'Naturally.' Usberti turned to Starace. 'Maurizio, fetch the equipment from the vehicle.' Starace walked to the rear of the RV and opened up a compartment big enough to accommodate a Smart Car. A light came on inside. The compartment was empty except for a black holdall. Starace knelt down to unzip it, and pulled out a large coil of thin rope, climbing gloves, body harness, pick, hammer, pitons, a lightweight flashlight, and a belt pouch with the legend NIKON. A small digital camera, Ben guessed, for taking pictures of the inscriptions.

'These items were obtained at the last minute before we departed from Ankara,' Usberti said. 'I trust they meet your requirements?'

Ben inspected the pile of equipment. The rope was the kind of super-strong cord that could lift a tank but would stretch to soften the jerk on a falling climber. The karabiner clips, pitons and belay device were all decent stuff, light and robust. Then he looked up again at the cliff. It was little wonder that two of the Von Grüber expedition hadn't survived it, back in 1923 when rock climbing gear was a lot more primitive.

'No climbing shoes?' he said.

Usberti spread his hands. 'Forgive me. I did not know your size.'

'Goggles?'

'I am sure you can manage without them. Whenever you are ready, Major Hope. I suggest you do not tarry too long, the light is failing rapidly. The rest of us will shelter in the cave and await your safe return.'

'You don't have to do this,' Anna said.

'You know I do,' Ben told her.

'Please be careful.'

'This is a walk in the park,' he said. 'I'll be back before you know it.'

Usberti was right about one thing. He didn't have a lot of time before nightfall made climbing ten times harder, and weather conditions were worsening every minute. The freezing rain was turning to snow, driving down harder on a stiffening wind that was making his hands and face numb. He quickly put on the harness, strapping up the Velcro and buckles good and tight. Made sure the various loops and connectors were properly fitted, clipped the camera pouch to his waist, slipped the hammer and pitons into their respective pouches, pulled on the gloves and fastened their wrist straps, and he was as ready as he'd ever be.

All he had to do now was scale the damn rock and get back down again alive.

He spent a few moments with his neck craned upwards to scan the sheer cliff face for handholds and footholds, and cracks into which to hammer his pitons. Once he had a rough route figured out, he reached up and hammered in his first piton, then hooked up his rope. Took a deep breath, and began his ascent.

It started out bad, and it got quickly worse. Without proper climbing shoes his toes were slipping all over the smooth, damp cliff face. And having to keep his face constantly tilted upwards with no goggles on left his eyes unprotected from the steadily thickening snow. It was the frozen wastes of Ankara all over again, except then he hadn't been clinging to a past-vertical incline with a lethal drop and a bunch of gangsters holding Anna hostage below him. Sometimes, you just don't realise how lucky you are.

He climbed. One hand over the other, feet scrabbling for grip, fingers numb and raw even inside his gloves, unable to feel his toes inside his boots. Pausing to grope for cracks above him, reach for his hammer, tap in another piton. Clipping and unclipping ropes as he went, so that there was always a safety line to anchor him to the wall and another to haul himself up another few feet before the process had to be repeated over. Ten minutes of solid, constant, muscle-ripping effort. Then twenty minutes. Night was falling fast. His mind emptied of all the anger he felt against Usberti, Bozza and the rest. Gravity was the enemy now, the deadly presence that wanted to reach up and grab him by the ankles and yank him to his death. He was shivering and sweating both at once. His eyes were burning and watering from the bite of the cold wind.

And all through it, he could hear the sound of war growing louder. It was coming from the north, the unmistakable crash and sonic boom of heavy artillery carried on the wind like rolling thunder, interspersed with ragged volleys of crackling small arms fire. Pausing to catch a breath, he let the rope hold his weight and dangled freely, used his feet to rotate himself around to look to the north and saw the strobe-flashes and arcs of light on the dark horizon.

It was heading their way. A running battle: tanks and mobile rockets and light armour, moving fast. Another twenty minutes, half an hour, and they would be much closer, perhaps too close for comfort. A full-scale military engagement was no thing to be a spectator to. He was worried about Anna's safety down there. For a few seconds he thought about abandoning his climb – but returning back down the cliff empty-handed wasn't going to do either of them much good.

In which case, there wasn't a moment to lose. He kept on climbing, but now it was getting too dark to see, so he took the lightweight torch from his harness pouch, switched it on and clamped it between his teeth so that it pointed wherever he looked. There was a ledge right above him. With a huge effort he managed to drag himself over its lip. He hauled his rope up and recoiled it, then knelt on the craggy rock and shone the flashlight around him. The ledge was maybe twenty feet deep, and part of it had been cut away in edges and angles much too straight and regular to be the work of nature. He swept the torch beam left, right, up and down over the cliff wall, hoping to find what he'd come here for.

No inscriptions anywhere to be seen. Nothing but craggy rock and broken sections of weathered, time-smoothed block wall that he quickly realised were the remains of a millennia-old fortification of some kind.

The last holdout of Ashar the Babylonian. It had probably been ancient even when the band of outlaws had taken up residence there, originally built by an even older civilisation back when this ledge had been part of a much bigger overhang on the cliff face. Sometime in the last couple of thousand years both it and, presumably, the narrow cliff path that allowed the renegades access to their base must have been carried away in a major rock slide, perhaps as a result of an earthquake.

But as interesting as that might be to an archaeologist, all it meant to Ben was that he was unlikely to find the inscriptions here. A bandit leader wily enough to elude the might of the Persian army for as long as Ashar had wouldn't have been foolish enough to carve the vital clues as to the whereabouts of his treasure right where his enemies could find them.

Which meant Ben had to keep searching, and keep climbing.

Leaning back as far as he could over the edge of the lip, he pointed his torch beam vertically through the swirling snowflakes and saw a second, smaller overhang another fifty feet or so higher up. A long, long way above the ground. Whichever one of the Von Grüber party had first spotted the inscriptions from down below must have been packing a hell of a pair of binoculars. Assuming the inscriptions were even there, and not eroded away to nothing or destroyed in another rock slide.

Only one way to find out.

A Gauloise would have been nice about now. Better still, a slug of scotch. Ben hugged his sides, then clapped and rubbed his hands and kicked his feet to try to get some sensation back into his extremities. He checked his harness pouch and saw he was running short on pitons: just enough left, or so he hoped, to make the final leg of the climb. The wind was blowing harder. The snow was gusting strongly, clinging to his hair and eyelashes, and creeping icily down his neck. His body was racked with shivering. He looked towards the north. The flashes on the horizon had advanced a considerable distance. Usberti and the others might not be able to see the faraway explosions as well as he could from so high up, but they'd be deaf if they couldn't hear the battle inching ever closer.

Time was running short.

Ben climbed on. He was getting very tired, and very cold. He was beginning to make mistakes as the creeping chill got to him. A couple of times, he failed to hammer a piton deeply enough into its crevice, only to see to his horror that it was working its way out when he had the full strain of his weight on the rope. Only luck and speed saved him. When he misjudged a foothold and his numb toes slipped and he felt himself going, it was the strong, stretchy rope that kept him from falling to his death.

Maybe there was a God, after all. Ben thanked him, just in case.

And at last, the second ledge was right above him. He was down to his last piton as he dragged himself up onto the narrow crawl-space. His hands no longer seemed to belong to him, but he managed to anchor himself with a loop of rope around a spike of rock, then take out the torch.

And that was when he saw the inscriptions carved on the cliff wall right in front of him.

Chapter 55

There was no mistaking what he'd found. The carving was made inside a crude rectangle hacked and chipped out of the pitted surface, roughly six feet wide by three feet high. Just about large enough for an observant spotter on the ground to pick out with modern optics, but much too small to be visible to the naked eye. The latter being, Ben guessed, exactly Ashar's idea when he'd carved it.

Inside the rectangle was a mass of script. The stone was so weathered and eroded by endless cycles of wind, rain and sun that parts of it were smoothed away almost to nothing. The parts that Ben could make out were written in a language like no alphabet still used in modern times, made up of scratchy little wedge-shaped markings and crooked crosses and irregular arrows and squiggles that meant absolutely nothing to him, or to the vast majority of people alive on the planet. He had only fleeting memories of seeing writing like it before, long ago in his student days. Maybe if he'd paid more attention in class, he would have known whether it read from left to right, or right to left like Hebrew, or top to bottom like Chinese.

But he wasn't here to work out what it meant, only to record what it looked like. He wiped away the dusting of snow that the wind had blown against the rock, then unzipped the small camera from its pouch on his climbing belt. It was all set up for him with flash and autofocus, so all he had to do was point and shoot. He zoomed out to take shots of the whole panel of inscriptions, then zoomed in again to take close-ups of the parts that were still faintly legible. He snapped about fifty images, working quickly but careful to miss nothing out. For the moment at least, Anna's life depended on what he brought back to Usberti.

Once he was satisfied, Ben zipped the camera carefully back in its pouch. Job done. Now it was time to get back down there, and fast. The crashes and booms of the battle were growing constantly louder to the north. He could see the moving shapes of tanks and smaller vehicles clearly now, silhouetted against the flash of explosions and fireballs. It looked as if a whole tank company, probably Turkish Army Leopards or Sabra M60s although it was hard to tell, was pursuing a smaller enemy force across the desert. Ben guessed those would be Syrian insurgents, belonging to any one of a hundred factions. They were using armoured pickup trucks equipped with rockets and heavy machine guns. As Ben watched, one of the trucks took a direct hit from a tank missile and went up with a bright white-and-yellow flash that lit up the desert. The running battle was headed straight towards the escarpment. It was several kilo-metres closer than it had been just ten minutes ago. Not a healthy development.

Ben's one consolation was that his descent would be a hell of a lot speedier than the climb. Fast-roping from heli-copters and abseiling down buildings and mountains was trained into him like tying shoelaces was for normal folks. As a young SAS trooper, he'd been so agile at bounding down vertical drops that his instructors could barely keep up. Now he'd have to be even faster. He stuck the torch back between his teeth and untied the short length of rope anchoring him to the ledge. *Here we go.*

Two deep breaths, and he dropped like a stone over the side of the ledge. He swung dizzily in empty space for a few instants, blinded by the driving snow, then felt the rope go taut and the soles of his boots touch the cliff face twenty feet down. He kicked hard, swung out, swung back in, met the impact with bent knees, then kicked again, losing more altitude at every downward leap. With gravity working in his favour, what had taken him the best part of an hour to achieve going up, was less than three minutes' work in reverse.

Anna rushed out of the cave to meet him as he landed on the ground. Bozza was just a step behind her, with a gun at her back. 'Ben!' Her cry was half drowned by another explosion. The battle was now just a couple of kilometres away, and still closing.

'Told you I'd be back soon,' Ben said. He clasped her hands and kissed her gently on the forehead. She pressed her face into his shoulder.

'You feel so cold,' she said.

'So do you.'

'I don't think I can ever be warm again.'

'Don't be too sure,' he said. 'I get the feeling things are about to start hotting up around here.'

Usberti emerged from the shadows, followed by Starace and Groppione, both pointing their weapons at Ben. 'Pardon me for interrupting this tender scene. Congratulations on a successful mission, Major Hope. I trust you have something for me?'

Ben unhooked the pouch and tossed it on the ground at Usberti's feet. 'Here you go, Your Grace. Now I'd suggest getting out of here, unless you want to find yourself in the middle of a tank battle.'

Starace picked up the pouch and passed it to his master. 'It is their war, not ours,' Usberti said, clutching the camera as though it was a gold ingot. The momentary flash of a rocket blast lit up his face, and Ben saw the crazed glint in the man's eyes. He wanted to snap his neck. But now wasn't the time, not with Bozza's gun an inch from Anna's back.

'Cuff him,' Usberti said. Groppione kept his weapon in Ben's face as Starace stripped away the climbing harness, dumped it on the ground and grabbed Ben's wrists behind his back. *Snick-snack,* and the hardened steel bracelets were back on, tighter than before.

'Now let us depart,' Usberti said. Bozza already had the RV's side door open for him. Usberti hurried aboard first, closely followed by the silent Bellini, and headed straight for his throne. Ben and Anna were hustled unceremoniously in after them and shoved into their seats while Groppione dived behind the wheel and restarted the engine. Starace took up his sentry position on the leather sofa across the aisle. Ugo Bozza was the last one aboard, not taking his eyes or his gunsights off Ben. Ben ignored him and watched through the window as the flashes of artillery fire kept creeping closer. The ground was beginning to shake under the wheels of the RV with every percussive blast. 'You'd better start praying this was all worth it, Usberti,' he said.

'Shut your fucking mouth, English,' Starace growled, but his words were lost in another tremendous explosion that made the whole vehicle shudder. Groppione slammed the RV into gear and they began to pick their bumping, lurching way back down the track.

'Faster,' Usberti urged him.

'Boss, if I go any faster in the darkness I'm gonna rip off

a wheel or ground us on these rocks,' Groppione protested in a strained voice.

It took nearly fifteen minutes for the RV to bounce and grind its way off the escarpment road and get back to level ground.

Too long, by at least five minutes. Because now the whole place was a raging war zone.

Chapter 56

Just as Ben had feared, the battle had arrived virtually on top of them. A broad stretch of desert was lit up like daylight by scores of madly bouncing headlights and the strobe effect of muzzle flashes from rocket launchers and machine guns, punctuated every few seconds by the blinding glare of high-explosive blasts as heavy missiles blew craters in the ground. Ben thought he could count nine tanks rolling through the chaos. He could hear the harsh squeal and patter of their treads cutting through the gunfire as they scuttled like living dinosaurs over sand and rock.

And now he realised he'd been wrong about them being Turkish Leopards or Sabras. They were Russian T-90 main battle tanks, one of the most formidable and feared war machines ever made. Russian tank companies were made up of three platoons, consisting of three tanks each plus the command tank, for a total of ten. The tenth tank was the stationary blazing wreck several hundred yards back from the advancing column, hit by a lucky rocket strike from one of the fleeing rebel armoured trucks. But a force of even just nine T-90s were a terrifying enough opponent to send just about any militia army into total flight mode: that was what they were witnessing, and it was all happening less than a football field's length away as

Groppione pressed his foot to the floor in desperation to get them out of here.

A tank shell hummed overhead and exploded among the rocks just fifty yards to their right. The RV surged unscathed through the bursting shrapnel but the violence of the shock-wave sent them into a wild skid that had Groppione yelling and wrestling the steering in a frenzy to stop them from overturning. He somehow managed to right the coach and accelerated harder across the undulating sands, crunching over boulders, no longer giving a damn about tearing off half the chassis.

For Usberti, it was as if they were out for a Sunday drive in the countryside. He was sitting calmly on his throne. Or as calmly as it was possible to sit, as he too was being thrown about by the bouncing suspension. He had the small Nikon camera in his lap and was wearing half-moon reading glasses, intently scrutinising the images on the camera's glowing screen.

'Professor Manzini, your expertise is required. Would you please come and look at this?'

'Are you crazy?' Anna screamed back at him. 'Don't you know what's happening? You think God can save you from tanks?'

'Ugo, assist her.'

Bozza was only too glad to oblige. He grasped Anna roughly by the upper arm and hauled her up the aisle. Usberti pointed to a nearby seat, opposite where Bellini had taken up his usual position, hands clasped in his lap, eyes darting nervously behind his thick lenses. Bozza dumped Anna into the seat. At the same instant, another rocket blast shook the RV from stem to stern and Groppione let out a yell of 'Jesus!' that drew a very disapproving look from his employer.

'Now, Professor,' Usberti said, handing her the camera,

'our present circumstances dictate that you conduct your work with as much alacrity as possible. So please, get to it, and do not compel me to bring Ugo into this. Aldo, a little more haste from you would also benefit us greatly.'

'It won't go any faster, boss. Not on this surface.'

The RV was going so fast, it felt as though it could shake apart at any moment. If a random tank shell didn't reduce them to splinters first. Watching from the window, Ben sensed there was a roughly fifty per cent chance of that happening. The RV was widening their distance from the battle, but only slowly. It was mayhem back there. The Russian gunners were very, very good. Another rebel truck blew apart in a fireball that turned the snowy sky golden-red. Then another, in a solid hit by the turret machine cannon of one of the T-90s that set off its target's fuel tank and blasted it into a tumbling wreck.

But the insurgents were fighting back hard, even as they beat their retreat. Stabs of rocket fire erupted from the rearward-facing guns of the fleeing trucks. The leading tank burst into flame, rolled to a halt and sat there burning as its eight remaining platoon comrades rumbled and squealed past it, keeping up their steady fire. The Russians were getting more than they'd bargained for from the rebels, that was for sure.

Not for long. The sudden screeching howl from above came out of nowhere and made everyone inside the RV except Ben, Bozza, and Groppione clap their hands over their ears at the sheer massive deafening noise. The Russian tank commander had called in air support. The jets had come streaking in so fast out of the night that not even Ben had time to recognise them as MiG 29 fighters – they must have deployed from a carrier off the Syrian coast.

The air strike was over in seconds. The jets were already

gone when a vast curtain of fire erupted into the sky in their wake. Like summoning the forces of death from the bowels of the earth to rise up and smite the enemy at a single stroke. Ben felt the heat on his face through the window as he watched dozens of armoured vehicles instantly vaporised in the awesome fiery blast. A hundred men blown limb from limb or reduced to a fine ash that was swept away by the desert wind. Maybe two hundred. Few people would ever know, fewer still would care, and a palatable version of their brutal destruction would be served up in the media sound-bites, to be forgotten moments later.

The RV bucked and bounced away from the carnage. Ben turned to see what was happening up front: Anna was being made to study the images on the camera; Bozza was standing menacingly over her, hanging on to a rail for support; Usberti had produced paper and pens for her to write her translation of the cuneiform inscriptions Ben had photographed, as if anyone could write or even read in a shaking, rattling bus hammering over unpaved wilderness at breakneck speed. A patient man, that Usberti.

Then Groppione glanced in his remaining mirror, turned the colour of parchment and announced in a quavering voice, 'Oh, no. Oh, shit. Boss, we g-got company.'

Chapter 57

Ben twisted back around to peer out of the rear window, and saw what Groppione had just seen. Vehicle lights in their wake: two sets of headlights supplemented with grille and roof spotlamps, all bobbing and gyrating crazily like Chinese lanterns in a storm. A pair of rebel trucks that had managed to escape the devastation of the MiG air strike had broken off from what was left of their fleeing column and were in pursuit.

'What the hell do they want with us?' Starace yelled.

'Why don't we stop and ask them?' Ben said. 'Maybe they're lost and need directions. Or maybe they think we're a bunch of coalition "spies" they can capture and do to us what you guys did to Ercan Kavur.'

'Outrun them,' Usberti ordered Groppione.

'Are you kidding me?' Groppione yelled back, near panic.

'Remain calm, Aldo. We are in no immediate d—'

But now Usberti's luck seemed to be running out at last. The flash of a grenade launcher from one of the pursuing trucks was followed almost instantly by a violent explosion right at the RV's rear. Everyone went sprawling. Groppione was thrown hard against the steering wheel. The RV went into a weave that degenerated into another bad skid, and almost overturned before Groppione, gibbering like a lunatic and sawing at the wheel, somehow got it back under control and stamped his foot down even harder. The RV surged ahead, crashing and bounding insanely over terrain it was never meant to handle even at a snail's pace.

Ben struggled upright and looked to the rear. On the bright side, it looked as though the rebels had run out of rockets. On the pessimistic side, the RV's massive bodyshell was made of flimsy stuff that even an air rifle could punch through. The grenade blast had torn a gaping hole in their tail end. The rear window was gone, along with a large section of bodywork. Ben could see exposed chassis members and ripped wiring and twisted brackets where light fittings used to be. Small fires were crackling everywhere and the smell of burning filled the vehicle. The electrics began to flicker. Bellini had been thrown out of his seat and was scrabbling around for his glasses. Usberti had managed to scramble back into his throne and was shouting at Anna, on her hands and knees in a sea of scattered paper.

'You! Hurry up with that translation!'

'Go to hell!' she screamed back at him.

The pair of rebel trucks were gaining fast, one taking the lead, the other right behind it. Their lights were glaring into the windowless back of the RV. Bozza staggered up the aisle to the rear, planted himself with his feet braced against the wild swinging of the vehicle, aimed his submachine gun through the ragged hole and rattled off its whole magazine at the lead truck. He couldn't have hit much, because a second later the rebels returned fire.

And they were packing somewhat heavier hardware. The snorting blast from the large-calibre machine gun ripped into the body of the RV, punching through it like an over-sized cardboard box, shredding everything to pieces. Woodwork splintered. Bits of carpet and leather upholstery flew. Bozza flattened himself to the floor. Anna screamed. Starace screamed louder. Too slow to hit the deck, he caught a bullet in the throat and his blood splashed over the bullet-riddled sofa he'd been sitting on.

Now the trucks were splitting up and overtaking the RV on both sides. Ben caught a clear glimpse of the rebel gunner on his side as the guy swivelled his machine gun around on its mount behind the cab. His face was covered with a cloth mask, just wild eyes and clenched teeth showing through the holes. Ben saw no more, because a millisecond later he was diving for cover as the machine guns poured fire into the sides of the RV, virtually ripping it in half horizontally.

Groppione had lost control, both of himself and of the vehicle. In his panic, he let go of the controls and threw himself down under the dashboard as both side windows shattered simultaneously to his left and right, showering him with glass. He got himself wedged deep in the footwell and cowered there, one hip pressing the accelerator pedal hard against its stop, neither hand on the steering wheel. Ben glanced forwards. He saw Anna curled up in a foetal position on the floor. No blood. That was good. Then he saw the rocky outcrop racing towards them in the glare of the driverless RV's headlights. That wasn't good.

It was the rebels who saved them from the head-on collision against the rocks. Maybe they were used to firing on armoured vehicles that would offer a little more resistance to their bullets. Or maybe they were just incredibly stupid. Either way, as their two trucks sped in parallel up the flanks of the RV, pumping high-velocity machine-gun shells at point-blank range and in opposite directions at once through its flimsy skin, they hadn't reckoned on where those bullets would go next. The occupants of the truck on the right soon found out. Bad timing. A tactical lesson in the risks of friendly fire. One of the most inappropriately named phenomena in the combat manual, because there was nothing remotely amicable or heart-warming about being shredded to bloody chunks by the firepower of your own inept comrades. Nor was it much of a practical lesson, if you died learning it.

The badly judged storm of bullets from the left-hand truck passed straight through both sides of the RV and hit the right-hand truck, killing every rebel on board instantly. The truck skidded, hit a rut, flipped a somersault in the air and cannoned against the right flank of the coach with enough force to send it veering off course to the left. It missed the rocky outcrop by a matter of inches. It was the truck that hit it instead, with a crunch as the two dead soldiers up front went through the windscreen and the gunner in the back went sailing over the roof and his body broke on the rocks.

But the impact that saved the RV from a terminal head-on smash also caused it to go into a furious skid. It was a very large, very heavy vehicle with comparatively undersized wheels and lot of momentum. An experienced driver might have stood a small chance of correcting the skid and regaining control. With nobody at the wheel at all, there was less than zero chance. All six wheels lost traction in the soft sand and it began to spin on itself. In what felt to Ben like a slow-motion dream, the length of the shattered RV rotated anti-clockwise until it was skidding sideways like a ship about to broach. There was a tortured groaning and creaking from the twisting chassis, and then the world seemed to flip over as the thing crashed onto its side, rolled and rolled again in a tumult of self-destruction.

If the driver of the remaining rebel truck had reacted in

time, he might have avoided the path of the crashing RV. He didn't. The truck's wheels locked up and its front end ploughed at high speed into the wreckage.

Then everything went still.

Chapter 58

Ben opened his eyes to a glare of white light. He looked down at the floor and realised his back was stuck to the ceiling. Then he blinked, and realised that he was actually lying on his back looking up at the floor, because the floor was above him. It took a moment for his brain to orient itself and remember why that was, and why his hands were pinned together under him.

He squirmed and elbowed himself up onto his knees and looked around him at the wreckage. The source of the bright light was the remaining headlamp of the rebel truck whose crumpled front end and still-turning front wheels were buried in the overturned wreck of what used to be the luxury motor coach. Most of the RV's bodywork was an unrecognisable rumpled mass of plywood and aluminium. Smoke and dust drifted through the smashed interior. He could smell diesel oil fumes and toilet chemicals and battery acid, all mixed together in a sour olfactory cocktail with the stink of death. Starace's body was hanging, gently swinging, from the upside-down floor, arms outflung as though he'd been crucified, bug eyes staring blind, a leg trapped in the broken frame of the sofa on which he'd died, its leather upholstery smeared with his blood. More was dripping down to the inverted ceiling.

'Anna,' Ben said.

She was curled up among the wreckage nearby. Her face and hair were grey with dust. At first he thought she was dead, too; then at the sound of his voice, she pushed herself up onto one elbow, looked at him with dazed eyes, and broke into a fit of coughing.

'Lord be praised, we are alive,' Usberti said, getting to his feet. He had the camera in his hand. A cut above one eye was dribbling blood down his cheekbone. He wiped it with his fingers and flicked them clean. 'Ugo, Silvano, Aldo, Maurizio . . . Maurizio? Ah, there he is.' He gazed up for a brief moment at the hanging corpse as though Starace were some dead crow stuck in a tree. 'No matter. He was of little use in any case. Silvano, are you badly hurt?'

'I don't think so, Excellency,' Bellini replied, dusting himself off. His glasses were bent out of shape, perched unevenly on his nose.

'Help the others to salvage what weapons and supplies we can. We must continue on our way.'

'You could do with an extra pair of hands to get us out of this,' Ben said to him. 'How about letting me loose from these cuffs?'

Usberti shook his head. 'You do not think me that stupid, surely. Now would be the perfect time for you to try one of your tricks.'

'I'm just as invested in getting out of this situation as you are,' Ben said. 'Especially as we won't be alone here for long. See there.' He couldn't point, so he nodded his head towards the smashed front end of the RV, which now faced in the opposite direction. There was just a big ragged misshapen hole where the windscreen had been. Through the hole, still a long way off in the distance but approaching at some speed, more vehicle lights were visible. 'Looks like more of our friends are about to join us.'

'Then there is not a moment to lose,' Usberti said. 'Ugo, see how serviceable that truck is.'

Bozza seemed as unfazed by the incident as he was unhurt. He waded through the wreckage to get to the half-buried Syrian rebel truck and pulled away the remains of Usberti's leather throne that was lying upended across its cracked windscreen. Both the driver and the gunner were dead, but the front passenger was still alive, blood all down his front from his broken nose and smashed teeth. Bozza wrenched open the door, grabbed him by the collar, hauled him out of the cab, dumped him in a heap and drew out a pistol. The guy groaned and tried to move.

'Don't kill him,' Anna pleaded, but it was to no avail. She looked away, screwed her eyes shut and covered her ears as Bozza put the gun to the Syrian's head and pulled the trigger twice. It was cold and brutal, but Ben reckoned it was probably a more humane end than came to most of Bozza's victims. Bozza walked around to the driver's side, hauled out the dead man behind the wheel and clambered inside the truck. He used his pistol to knock away the remains of the windscreen glass, then twisted the key to restart the stalled engine. The front of the truck was buckled and twisted, but its heavy-duty grille bars had taken most of the brunt of the impact. The engine coughed into life. Bozza put it in reverse and, with some effort, managed to disentangle and back it out of the wreckage.

Usberti turned to Bellini and tossed him a torch. 'Silvano, go and check the other vehicle back there. Six are too many to travel in one truck.'

'How about we kill this fucker?' Groppione said, pointing his gun at Ben. 'Then there's only five of us to worry about.'

'He may yet be of use to me,' Usberti said. 'This is not over yet.'

Bellini reluctantly obeyed the order. He limped his way out of the wreck and picked a hobbling path off through the darkness towards the rocky outcrop where the other truck had crashed. Ben watched his torch beam dart around the vehicle. Bellini didn't look as though he had the physical force to haul out the driver the way Bozza had, but as the guy had already exited via the windscreen, he didn't have to try. Moments later, the truck fired up in a cloud of blue smoke. The rattle coming from under the crumpled bonnet didn't sound too terminal. Both its headlights were smashed, but the two roof-mounted spotlamps that hadn't been knocked askew by the gunner's flying body still worked fine. Their light shone brightly over the slick of blood that three dead men had left all over the rumpled bonnet and the rock in front of it. Bellini engaged reverse and gingerly pulled away from the mess.

Usberti smiled. 'Two working vehicles. Professor Manzini, you will accompany me in the first. Aldo, you will drive us. Ugo, you drive the second with Silvano and the major. Stay close behind us. We will find a place to shelter for the night, where the professor can finish her translation. Come morning, we will complete our quest.'

The approaching lights were getting gradually closer. The way they were moving suggested that they belonged to a larger, slower transport, maybe a troop carrier full of Syrian rebels fleeing from the Russian tanks. Ben was no more anxious to hang around and find out than the others. The pickup truck's bench seat was just about wide enough for three. Usberti hurried Anna to the passenger side of the first truck and pressed his bulk in after her, making her squash up in the middle as Groppione loaded bags from the wrecked RV into the pickup bed and took the wheel from Bozza. Bozza pointed his pistol at Ben and walked him to the second truck where Bellini was waiting. Bellini climbed out of the driver's side. Bozza gave him the pistol, then got in behind the wheel.

'After you,' Bellini said, training the gun on Ben's head.

'Are you sure you know how to work that thing?' Ben said.

'Well enough. Get in, please. I don't want to have to shoot you.'

'All the better for you,' Ben replied. He squeezed in, hands painfully trapped against the seat in the small of his back, one foot either side of the transmission tunnel, his left shoulder pressed against Bozza's right. It felt like granite. Bellini stiffly clambered into the passenger seat to Ben's right. The door mechanism had been damaged in the crash and wouldn't close, forcing Bellini into an awkward position with his arms crossed over his lap, holding the door handle shut with his left hand so he could keep the pistol pointed at Ben in his right.

The lead truck took off into the darkness, its single working headlight bobbing and bouncing as Groppione hustled across the desert as fast as he could. Bozza followed, silent and grim as ever.

'Talkative, isn't he?' Ben said. 'Once you get him started, you can't shut him up.'

'Ugo doesn't speak,' Bellini said. 'Not to me, not even to Usberti. Least of all to you. He's taken a vow of silence. And I would advise you to follow his example. Don't make this worse for yourself.'

They kept moving fast over the desert. It was a rough ride, but Ben had had rougher. A blast of freezing wind, snow and dirt kicked up by the wheels of the lead truck whistled through the broken windscreen and all around the inside of the cab. The bobbing tail-lights ahead were barely visible. Meanwhile the headlights behind them gradually receded to pinpoints in their wake and finally vanished altogether, leaving their little convoy alone in the vastness of the night.

Ben was picturing Anna sitting there in the lead truck next to Usberti, wondering what the bastard was saying to her, wishing he could have done something to prevent the situation getting so bad. And he was thinking about all the possible ways he could disarm Bellini and kill both him and Bozza without using his hands.

The first part wouldn't have been too hard. Speed and surprise would be half the battle. Ben's upper body was already canted slightly forwards out of his seat because of his cuffed wrists in the small of his back, which potentially gave him an advantage. A violent curved lunge to the right, one good solid head-butt straight to Bellini's forehead, and he could smash the guy's glasses off, break his nose, then use his elbow to knock the weapon out of his hand before he pulled the trigger, and then flip himself around to kick hard with both boots and send Bellini flying right out of the damaged door. One down, maybe three seconds.

But taking on Bozza no-handed was a different matter. It would be the most efficient form of suicide imaginable. Ben closed his eyes, willed his mind and body to relax, and resolved to wait for a better opportunity.

After a few more minutes he sensed that they were slowing down. He opened his eyes again, expecting to see the lead truck doing the same. It wasn't. The gap between them was widening, Usberti leading further and further ahead. For a moment Ben thought something was wrong with the engine, even though the rattle from under the bonnet hadn't got noticeably worse. It wasn't fuel, either. The gauge was reading a third full. Then he realised that Bozza was deliberately slackening his pressure on the gas. The speedometer needle dropped to forty kilometres an hour. Then thirty-five. The dirt spray from the lead truck would obscure most of what Groppione would be able to see in his mirrors. They wouldn't know what was happening behind them.

And something *was* happening, for sure. Ben could sense it almost telepathically, just like he could feel the strange energy emanating from the silent killer sitting next to him.

'Ugo, why are we slowing down?' Bellini said. He was shivering so much from the cold that his voice was full of tremors. 'What are you doing? I don't understand.'

But Ben understood.

He wasn't the only one planning his moves, waiting for the right moment.

Bozza let the truck roll to a halt.

Then he turned off the engine.

Chapter 59

They were in the middle of nowhere, nothing to be seen except the twin strips of illuminated ground in the beams of the spotlamps, snow drifting gently through them to coat the desert in a sprinkling of whiteness. The sound of the lead truck was so distant as to be barely audible.

Bellini repeated, 'Ugo, what are you doing? Keep moving. Usberti said we were to follow close behind.'

Bozza said nothing. Instead, he reached for his door and opened it and stepped out of the truck. He walked around its front, casting a monstrous shadow across the landscape ahead. Before Bellini could say anything more, Bozza pulled the passenger door open and punched him hard in the face. Bellini brought the gun around defensively to point his way, but Bozza was much faster. He snatched it from Bellini's fingers, seized his collar and dragged him from the truck and punched him twice more, breaking his nose and smashing his glasses. Bellini went limp on the ground.

Bozza spoke for the first time. 'Fuck Usberti. And fuck you, *priest.*'

By then, Ben was already out of the truck. Nowhere to run.

He wouldn't have run, anyway. Not from this man. He would fight, even with his hands tied behind his back and no possible chance of winning. Sometimes, it was the fight that mattered, more than the outcome.

Bozza left Bellini lying semi-conscious in the dirty snow and walked slowly back around the front of the truck towards Ben. He was smiling. He pointed the pistol.

'Get on your knees.' His voice was raspy and pitched an octave lower than a normal man's.

'You know I won't do that,' Ben said.

Bozza shrugged, like saying, 'Fair enough.' And shot Ben in the left leg.

Agony lanced like a blade through Ben's thigh. His left knee gave way under him and he fell hard on his side. He rolled and looked up at the man's silhouette standing tall above him against the lights of the truck.

'You going to shoot me in the head? Go for it, if you've got the guts.'

Bozza laughed. 'You want me to make this easy for you, Ben Hope. But I am in no hurry. I have waited for this.' He held the gun up in the air and tossed it over his shoulder. It hit the ground a couple of feet behind him. He took a step closer to Ben, and kicked him in the stomach.

Shot in the leg with the wind knocked out of him, Ben would have loved to jump up and get in the fight. Bozza laughed again, a strange raucous cackling that wasn't quite human. He peeled off one glove, then the other. Folded them carefully away into his jacket pocket. He spat on his hands and rubbed them together. Just as he'd promised, he intended to take his time.

Ben expected the knife to come out next. No matter what training a person has received, no matter how skilled in combat, no matter how brave in the face of impossible odds, no sane human being yet born did not experience visceral fear at the thought of cold steel plunging into their defenceless flesh. Ben knew he was about to get cut: badly, deeply, slowly, expertly, probably fatally. But he also knew he would not sell his life cheaply to Ugo Bozza.

He was wrong about the knife. And he couldn't have fully imagined what was about to happen next.

Bozza hovered over him and then, as fast as a falcon swooping on a mouse, reached down with fingers splayed like talons. Still gasping from the gut-kick, Ben wasn't quick enough to ward him off. Bozza's fingers gripped Ben's shoulder muscle, near the base of his neck. They squeezed like no grip Ben had ever felt before. The pain that exploded through him was as if red-hot wires had been inserted into every cell of his body and simultaneously hooked up to a million-volt electrical pulse generator. There was no physical way to control his response to it. Nothing he could do to resist what Bozza was doing to him. But he wouldn't scream. He wouldn't utter a sound, not if he had to bite his own tongue off.

'I am going to make you suffer like this for hours, Ben Hope. Scream. You know you want to. You will die screaming.'

Bozza released the nerve centre. His hand drew back and his eyes darted up and down Ben's body as though he was deciding where to hurt him next. Then the hand darted back in like a snake. Ben felt the agony course and quake through him. He was on fire, tearing apart, exploding into a thousand pieces. The pain of his wounded leg felt like nothing by comparison.

A voice from very far away shouted, 'STOP!'

Bozza released his torturous grip. He turned. Bellini was standing by the truck. There was blood pouring from his nose. The broken glasses were gone.

Bellini repeated, 'Stop. You're going to kill him.'

Bozza nodded impassively. 'Yes. And you, if you stand in my way.'

'Usberti will punish you if you don't let him go, right now.'

'Usberti can die too,' Bozza said. 'You think he matters to me?'

The two of them seemed to lock eyes for the longest moment. Then Bellini's gaze flicked down at the gun on the ground. It lay a couple of paces closer to his feet than it did to Bozza's. Bozza could see what he was thinking, and smiled at the idea that this limping cripple, this half-blind gawky preacher, thought he could beat him – *him*, Ugo Bozza – to the drop.

Then Bellini went for the gun.

Except there was something Bozza couldn't have predicted. Bellini was no longer the limping cripple, and he could see just fine without his glasses. He got to the gun first and scooped it up and wheeled away just in time to duck out of the path of Bozza's fists. Backing off three fast steps with the pistol thrust out in both hands, he yelled, 'On the ground! You're under arrest!'

Bozza sneered at him. Then attacked like a charging tiger.

The gunshot rang out. Bozza recoiled, blood spurting from a hole in his shoulder, eyes wide more with incredulous surprise than the shock of being shot. He clutched his shoulder and stood there for an instant as Bellini kept the weapon pointed at him.

'I said, on the ground, NOW!' Bellini yelled. His whole manner and behaviour were suddenly completely changed.

Bozza hesitated one more second, then bolted into the darkness.

Bellini watched the man sprint away. He lowered the gun and hurried over to where Ben lay clutching his injured leg. 'You're bleeding badly.'

Ben had already assessed the damage. A gunshot to the

thigh can kill a man within minutes, but that wasn't going to happen to him. Bozza had deliberately aimed off and only clipped the outside of the quadriceps muscle, in order to bring him down without injuring him too badly. He didn't want his victim to bleed out from a ruptured femoral artery. That would have been much too quick and merciful an end.

Ben looked up at Bellini. 'Who are you?'

Bellini said, 'We'll get to that. First I'll see if there's a med kit in the truck.' He hurried over to the vehicle, dug under the seats and returned a moment later with a tatty olive-green plastic box that he set on the ground next to Ben and opened up. 'Okay, we have pressure bandages, rolls of gauze, surgical tape, antiseptic, some penicillin that's about three years out of date and a bunch of morphine syrettes that look like military surplus left over from the Vietnam War.'

'How many syrettes?'

'Enough to kill a platoon. Or turn them into hopeless addicts.'

'That'll do. First you need to help me get these damn cuffs off.'

'I have no key.'

'Then shoot them off me.'

'Gun's jammed.'

'Then unjam it.'

Ben had never seen a priest who could field-strip a pistol the way Bellini could. He ejected the magazine, worked the slide back and forth to clear the jam and then released a catch to allow the slide to pull free of its rails. Next he took out the barrel and spring, wiped down and blew into the mechanism and then put everything together again just as fast. 'All right. Now hold steady. I'm going to blow the chain in half. That's the best I can do. If I try for the bracelets it's going to take your hands off.'

Ben gritted his teeth from the pain in his thigh as he rolled onto his side and kept his wrists braced as far apart as he could. He felt Bellini lever the muzzle of the pistol between them, pressing against the chain. 'The blast's going to hurt like a bastard,' Bellini warned him.

'Do it,' Ben said. Bellini fired. The explosion of hot gases that burst from the muzzle in the bullet's wake seared his flesh. His hands jerked free. He flexed his arms. The steel bracelets were still clamped too tightly around his wrists, each dangling a few links of broken chain. The flesh was blackened and bloody where the hot nitrocellulose propellant gases had broken the skin, but he had worse pain elsewhere.

'Give me one of those syrettes,' he muttered, feeling faint from the agony of his leg. Bellini pulled one from the med kit. Ben tore open the wrapping and jabbed the needle into his thigh, a few inches from the gunshot wound. The pain relief would be rapid, in exchange for some temporary wooziness, and maybe a hallucination or two. He could live with that, especially if the drug took away the lingering, burning torment of what Bozza had done to the nerves of his neck and shoulder.

'You'd better wrap that leg,' Bellini said. 'Not to mention start looking for a hospital.'

'What hospital? Anyway, it's just a scratch.'

'Looks like more than a scratch to me.'

'Why did you let Bozza run?'

'I didn't. I was going to shoot him again, but like I told you, the gun jammed. Sand and grit in the slide rails. Fucking Glock piece of shit. Anyway, he's wounded and he can't survive long out here. I hope the fucker gets beheaded by ISIL or skinned alive in a dust storm.'

'You certainly don't talk like a priest.'

'That's because I'm not. But my father was. I've spent the last six months trying to be him, basically.'

'Then who the hell are you?' Ben asked.

'First, my name's not Bellini. It's Janssens. The rest is a long story.'

'I want to hear it,' Ben said. 'But not here.'

'Where?'

'In the truck. We have some bad guys to catch up with.'

Chapter 60

After Ben had cleaned up his leg, disinfected the wound area and taped it up with a pressure bandage to stem the bleeding, Janssens helped him back to the truck. 'I'd better drive,' Janssens said. 'Apart from not being able to work the clutch, that morphine's going to knock you for six.'

'Can you follow tyre tracks over this terrain?'

'Not when they're covered up with fresh snowfall,' Janssens admitted.

'Then I'd better stay awake, hadn't I?'

They took off, chasing the faint tracks of Usberti's truck. The snow was gradually easing off, but the wind was blowing harder and Ben guessed from the way Janssens started shivering again that the temperature had dropped still further. He couldn't feel it, with the effects of the morphine elevating his body heat. The drug was kicking in full blast now. He had to keep blinking to stop himself from falling asleep. The nicotine rush from a few good, strong cigarettes would have been ideal, but Janssens didn't smoke.

'Talk to me,' Ben said.

'You want my life story? My name's Marc Janssens. Son of a Belgian priest and an Italian schoolteacher. Hence, the fact I could pass myself off as Italian, as well as a man of the church.'

'You told Bozza you were arresting him. You're a cop?'

'I prefer "undercover law enforcement agent",' Janssens replied.

'What agency?'

'A leading one.'

'INTERPOL?'

Janssens took one hand off the wheel to make a vague gesture. 'Whatever. You know, we're all the same soup. Let's just say I was sent into deep cover to infiltrate Usberti's operation.'

'To investigate what? He was cleared of all charges, years ago.'

'Precisely,' Janssens said. 'Elements within the agency were unhappy with the way he got off the first time. There were suggestions that he used his power, money and contacts to leverage his way out of trouble, letting others take the fall for him.'

'Like Fabrizio Severini.'

Janssens nodded. 'But now we've got more than enough evidence to blow the case back wide open and put that piece of shit away for the rest of his life.'

'If he lives that long,' Ben said.

Janssens smiled. 'So, have you puzzled it out yet?'

Ben looked at him, confused.

'The letter,' Janssens said.

'It was you?'

'No, the letter was for real. But it wasn't God who gave Severini the word that Usberti was back in business. It was me. Personally, I thought the whole divine inspiration bit was too kooky. I was afraid it would put you off. But I couldn't think of any other reason why a crazy old coot in jail might have the inside track on what Usberti was doing.'

'Why contact me at all?' Ben asked.

'Three reasons,' Janssens said. 'First reason, you were the guy who did more than anyone else to nail him the first time round. If only he hadn't managed to slip through the net in the end, it would have been all down to you.'

'Not just me. Luc Simon did his bit, too.'

'You can play it cool if you want. Second reason, as a result of the first, we knew you were Usberti's top target and about to become involved anyway. Sadly, he made his moves against you and the others sooner than we anticipated.'

'Meaning that you could have saved them,' Ben said. 'If you people had come to me sooner, all this could have been prevented. Father Pascal and Luc Simon would be alive now. Jeff wouldn't have been shot.'

'I know. I'm sorry. If you let me explain the third reason, you'll understand why that couldn't be helped.'

'It had better be a good one.'

Janssens said, 'When I said I worked for a big law enforcement agency, I was telling the truth. Thing is, I work for Europol. Now do you understand?'

Ben narrowed his eyes. 'Europol are just an organising body with limited powers. In effect, you're a paper tiger. You don't have the authority to arrest criminals, or even to conduct criminal investigations inside Europe.'

'You're right. Technically, we're strictly an intelligence agency, and obliged to delegate those powers to INTERPOL, a whole other and totally differently-structured organisation. Unless, that is, we decide to do things off our own bat.'

'Which is what happened in this case?'

'That would be one way of putting it,' Janssens said.

'Meaning that this isn't any kind of official investigation,' Ben said. 'You're off the radar and in direct contravention of your own rules, just by being here.'

'Yeah, right. Just like the CIA are technically prohibited from performing internal security functions within North America, but they say screw that and do it anyway. Wake up. The rule books were tossed a long time ago. When it suits them, at any rate.'

'Go on.'

'And so, a group of Europol agents, pissed off about the way Usberti got off the hook, took it upon ourselves to reopen the case privately.'

'How big a group?'

'Me, and four other guys. I was elected to be the under-cover person, first because I can speak Italian fluently, second because I'm supposedly on medical leave, so I was free not to go into the office every day like the others.'

'The back thing? I thought you were faking it. Like the glasses.'

'Exaggerating it, as part of my cover. I damaged my spine in a motorcycle crash last year. But it's a lot better now than it was. Thank you for asking.'

'If you're looking for sympathy, you can look somewhere else,' Ben said.

'Says the guy whose ass I just saved.'

'Keep talking, Janssens.'

'It took a long time to work my way inside his organisa-tion and gain his trust, but I played my role well and it worked. Slowly, I began to understand what the devious scumbag was up to. He was planning to fake his own death, using a body double, a man called Gennaro Tucci who he found by chance in some small village in Umbria. They grabbed Tucci one night from his home, brought him back, imprisoned him and then slaughtered him.'

'The body in the lake.'

'These people are monsters. And now I really thought we

had them. An open-and-shut murder case that my guys and I could simply hand over to the correct authorities.' Janssens shook his head bitterly. 'How wrong I was. That was when it all started falling apart. It seems Usberti still has one or two sympathisers in high places. The moment we filed our report, certain agency chiefs – we believe in collusion with certain EU ministers, although we can't prove anything – came down on it like a ton of *merde*, buried the whole investigation and my team with it.'

'Fired?'

'Suspended indefinitely without pay pending an internal inquiry, which amounts to the same career death, whichever way you look at it. At least they could go home and be with their families, go fishing, find something else to do, or whatever. Not me. I was suddenly left hanging. I couldn't depend on my colleagues' backup any longer, and I couldn't trust the department. It was like being stranded on a desert island, except this particular island was full of predators who'd torture me to death and put my head on a spike for the seagulls to peck if they suspected the slightest thing. I was desperate.'

'So you decided to call in outside help,' Ben said.

Janssens shrugged. 'I didn't know what else to do. I looked you up, found your training centre's website and your address in France. Except how could I contact you directly? What if you didn't believe me? It could have backfired on me, and I'd be dead. I had to find another way.'

'By working Severini.'

'It was all I could think of. When Usberti sent me on an errand to Brescia I managed to slip away long enough to drive to Milan and pay a visit to Bollati prison. Severini hadn't had a visitor in years. He was glad to talk to someone. Even gladder when I told him we were *this* close to nailing his former employer once and for all. Nobody, and I mean nobody, hates Usberti as much as he does.'

'I doubt that very much,' Ben said.

'He agreed to help me in whatever way he could. We composed the letter together, and it went into the prison's outgoing mailbag the same day.'

Now it was clear why Janssens had looked so uneasy back in Turkey, when Ben had mentioned to Usberti that Severini had contacted him.

'I was out of the country when the letter turned up at Le Val,' Ben said. 'If I'd received it a few days sooner—'

'I assumed it was either that, or you'd just torn it up. Either way, it looked as though my plan had failed. My only consolation was that there was no possibility of it coming back on me.'

'And my friends paid the price instead.'

Janssens was silent for a moment, gripping the steering wheel tightly and staring at the desert. Then he nodded and turned to look at Ben.

'It's true,' Janssens said. 'How can I tell you enough times that I'm sorry for all that's happened? And what good are words, anyway? There's only one thing to do now. We have to set things right. For them.'

Chapter 61

Groppione had driven quite some way through the dark desert by the time Usberti happened to glance back and realise that the second truck was no longer there.

'Maybe they broke down,' Groppione suggested.

'You should have been paying attention.'

'I'm sorry, boss. What do you want to do? You want me to double back and go look for 'm?'

Usberti thought about it, then shook his head. 'No, we must keep moving. Ugo is equipped with a satellite tracker device linked to mine; he knows my exact location at all times. He will find us. The mission must come first.'

Anna was shaking inside, but she wouldn't let them see it. Swallowing her fear, she laughed. 'Now I know what you've been doing with yourself all these years. Watching bad movies full of lines like "the mission must come first" and dreaming of yourself as the big hero.'

'I would not be so brazen, if I were you, Professor. Your very survival depends on my continued goodwill.'

'You know what's happening, don't you, Usberti?' she said. 'You made a big mistake, turning your back on Ben Hope. Now your little flunkies are both dead and he's coming after you and this other *idiota* here.'

'Shut your filthy mouth, slut,' Groppione growled at her.

'You know it's true. And there's not a damn thing you can do to stop him. He took you down the last time, and this time he's going to take you down for good.'

'We shall see about that,' Usberti said. The anxiety in his voice made Anna smile to herself, despite her own terror of what might soon happen to her. In the darkness he reached inside his jacket and took out a small pill bottle. She watched as he unscrewed it, shook two pills into the palm of his hand and swallowed them. Was that a slight tremor she noticed in his hands? If it was, she was glad.

Soon afterwards, they came to the edge of a plateau where clusters of strange rock formations and clumps of vegetation offered a break from the freezing wind. Usberti ordered Groppione to halt the truck.

'Unpack the equipment, Aldo,' Usberti said as they stopped. 'This place will serve as a rest point while our guest makes herself useful.'

Groppione got out and dragged the bags from the back of the truck. Inside one of them was a portable paraffin stove that he set up in the lee of an overhanging rock and busied himself lighting. As it hissed and ticked and popped fiercely, he went back to the bag and took out an Italian stovetop coffee percolator that he set on top. The aroma of good espresso soon began to steam out of it. 'All the comforts of home,' Anna said acidly. She kept glancing at the horizon. Expecting, praying, for Ben to appear at any moment, but the seconds kept passing and there was no sign of him. Where was he?

By the light of two rechargeable lanterns, Usberti directed Anna to a sheltered spot close to the warmth of the fire, told her to sit and tossed the camera in her lap. 'I am going to enjoy a cup of hot coffee. By the time I have finished, I expect results from you. And I hope for your sake that they are all I could wish for.'

'Are you crazy?' she retorted. 'This isn't something you can work out in five minutes. Cuneiform script is more than just some simple code, it's a whole system of different languages from all kinds of different cultures across thousands of years. These inscriptions could take a team of experts weeks, even months, to decipher.'

'I am not an idiot, Professor. This is the very same variety of Akkadian as was used in ancient Babylon, as I know perfectly well. I also happen to have it on good authority, that is to say the late Signor Kavur, that you have studied it in some depth during the course of your considerable research. That said, I do not expect an eloquent translation. Only the essence of what is there. Aldo, how is that coffee coming along?'

Groppione poured the bubbling espresso into a pair of tin mugs, for himself and his boss. Usberti paced and sipped, then paced some more as Anna studied the various images Ben had taken of the clifftop carvings. The camera allowed her to enlarge the pictures to examine detail more closely. Groppione perched on the edge of a nearby rock and watched her with a glinting leer as she worked. He was nursing a big black Walther pistol in his lap in case she tried to run. And just in case a pistol wasn't enough hardware to shoot down an unarmed woman, a submachine gun stood propped within easy reach against the rock.

'Your time is up,' Usberti said when he'd drained the last of his coffee.

She glared at him. 'I have no idea what any of this says. None. It's totally illegible to me.'

'Then it appears I have employed the wrong translator. Aldo, you have my permission to dispatch the professor in whatever manner pleases you.'

It was just the order Groppione had been waiting for. He

eagerly jumped down from his rock and stepped towards her, grinning. Anna backed away.

'Unless', Usberti said, holding up a hand, 'she has changed her mind. Have you changed your mind, my dear?'

'All right, all right,' she said, relenting. 'I can't be totally sure, but I think this first line translates something like "Where Nimrod sleeps".'

'Curious, the way a little pressure can suddenly bring focus and clarity,' Usberti chuckled. 'Now perhaps we are getting somewhere. Nimrod, son of Cush, himself son of Ham, who in turn was the youngest child of the prophet Noah. The Book of Genesis tells us that Nimrod was the founder of a mighty kingdom in the land called Shinar, whose capital many scholars believe was the city of Babel. Babel being, of course, the name given in the Hebrew Bible to none other than Babylon itself.'

'Then this line "Where Nimrod sleeps" obviously points back to Babylon,' Anna said. 'What does that mean? The idol never left the city?'

Usberti pondered the question for a moment, then shook his head. 'I believe there is another interpretation. As their revered founder and first great ruler, Nimrod was later deified by the Babylonians as a personification of the sun god. The phrase "where Nimrod sleeps" may be thus taken to signify the position of the setting sun. In other words, a simple instruction pointing us towards due west. Please carry on, Professor. What does the next line say?'

She swallowed, controlled her pounding heart and scrutinised the camera's screen. 'It's mostly worn away. I can only read a few of the markings.'

'After such a promising start. Aldo?'

'Okay, okay,' Anna said quickly. 'The part that I can make out says something about, "one and one half *beru*".'

'What the fuck is a *beru*?' Groppione muttered, annoyed that he'd been cheated of yet another bit of fun.

Usberti silenced him with a hard look, then turned his gaze back on Anna. 'The professor can explain that, I am sure.'

Anna nodded. It wasn't a request. She had no choice but to cooperate. 'In ancient Mesopotamian texts, the *beru* was a commonly used measure of time,' she explained, keeping her voice steady. 'The so-called double hour. So, logically, one and a half *beru* would make three Babylonian hours. But how long would that be in our time measurement? I have no idea.'

'I believe you know better than that, my dear. I would be most disappointed to think you were trying to trick me. The *beru* was also a measure of distance, equating to the amount of ground that a marching army could cover in that time. Correct?'

She looked at him, beginning to realise he was a step ahead of her. 'All right,' she conceded. 'But how far is that? We would just be guessing.'

Usberti clicked his tongue. 'Wrong once again, and that was your last warning not to try to deceive me. You are playing a dangerous game, Professor. Now, let us backtrack for a moment. Having foreseen that deciphering any sort of treasure map would entail understanding the units of distance involved, I have taken the trouble to research the Babylonian system of weights and measures myself. The smallest unit of distance used by their culture was one *she*, the size of a barleycorn, approximately one-third of a modern centimetre. Six *she* was what?'

'A *shu-si*,' Anna said reluctantly.

'I tried some of that raw fishy shit once,' Groppione said. 'I was sick for a week.'

Anna ignored him. 'It's about one point eight centimetres in modern measurement.'

'Wonderful, how your memory returns,' Usberti said with a smile. 'If mine serves me right, the length of thirty *shu-si* was known as a *kush*.'

'About half a modern metre,' Anna admitted.

'And twelve *kush* was one *mindan*, or approximately six metres. Next comes an *ush*, equating to sixty *mindan*. Are you with me?'

Anna sighed. 'One *ush* would measure about three hundred and sixty metres.'

'Which brings us full circle to the *beru*,' Usberti said. 'The largest of the ancient Babylonian units of distance. Which you and I both know to be the equivalent of thirty *ush*, therefore measuring . . .'

'A little less than eleven kilometres.'

'Around ten point eight kilometres, to be more exact. A figure that we can verify with some degree of accuracy, based on a text of the earlier Babylonian ruler Nebuchadnezzar the First, which records the distance from the Sumerian city-state of Der to the Sha'ur River as being some twenty-four *beru*. Now, having checked this myself, I can confirm the distance to be exactly two hundred and fifty-seven kilometres. Divide that figure by twenty-four, and what do we have?'

Anna quickly crunched the numbers in her head. 'Ten point seven kilometres.'

'Your skill at mental arithmetic does you credit, Professor. Close enough confirmation, do you not agree? And now I believe we come to the final part of the inscription. Please translate.'

Anna knew she couldn't bluff him any more. 'The last line says, "There you will find the glory of the king".'

'"The glory of the king",' Usberti repeated, clasping his hands. 'No interpretation is needed to understand such an obvious reference to the legacy of Ashar the Babylonian's revered former monarch, King Nebuchadnezzar the Second. Not only his legacy, but his actual, physical treasure. And at last, we can now put it all together. In summary, the inscription is directing the seeker of this treasure to travel a distance of one and a half *heru*, or just over sixteen kilometres, due west from Ashar's base.' He pulled the GPS device from his pocket. 'We can easily calculate the precise coordinates using this wonder of modern technology. As we approach our target, I would expect to find there some form of landmark in the shape of a rock or other object, perhaps put there by Ashar himself to denote the exact spot.'

'You're a very clever man,' Anna said. 'I'll give you that.'

'Oh yes, indeed. Furthermore, I possess an unerring sense of when I am being lied to, Professor Manzini. You would not by any chance have attempted to accidentally misread these markings, would you?'

'You asked me to translate; that's what I did. If there's a mistake, it's not my fault.'

'Are you perfectly sure of that?'

'I'm sure.'

'Let us find out how sure you really are. Aldo, be a good fellow and remove the little finger of the professor's left hand.'

Chapter 62

Even after all these years, Anna still had horrible nightmares about Franco Bozza's attack on her. The memory had never left her: that sense of dread when she'd realised an intruder was in her villa; the maniac suddenly appearing from the shadows and chasing her up the stairs; the violent blow that had stunned her; the blade of his knife slicing her. She'd never forgotten the terror and the pain.

This was worse. Much worse.

With her back to the rocks, there was no escape as Groppione advanced on her. She struggled frantically to fight him off, but it wasn't enough. He beat her to the ground, pinned her body down with his weight. She smelled his foul breath in her face, heard him laugh, felt his iron grip take a hold of her left hand and prise the little finger free from her clenched fist. Then screamed as she felt the sharp steel bite hard and deep into her flesh, sawing through the cartilage of her finger joint. Then the awful, sickening sensation as the finger came away. He climbed off her, still laughing. She clutched her damaged hand to her chest, unable to look at it but feeling the hot blood jetting out of it and soaking into her jacket. The pain was so stunning that she could barely breathe. Tears flooded down her face. She rolled and writhed, wanted to hit her head on the ground and knock herself out to ease the terrible agony.

'I don't think she likes me, boss,' Groppione said, grinning. 'Gave me the finger. See?' He waggled the severed digit in the air, then tossed it away. He wiped the bloodied blade of his clasp knife against his trousers, folded it up and slipped it back in his pocket.

Usberti said, 'Professor, I am still waiting for your assurance that you have been honest with me. You have nine more fingers and thumbs before we start removing pieces elsewhere. And we have all night. So, I repeat: are you sure?'

Anna mustered up every molecule of air in her body and screamed, 'I'M SURE!'

'I believe it,' Usberti said. 'She is telling the truth. Which means I now have all the information I need. Consequently, like her associate Kavur before her, Professor Manzini has now reached the end of her usefulness to me and it is time to terminate our association. Over to you, Aldo.'

Groppione lit up like a gluttonous child presented with a giant chocolate Easter egg. 'Can I do her before I kill her?'

'The terms of your employment', Usberti replied calmly, 'are that you do exactly as I command at all times, in return for which you receive financial recompense plus additional bonuses of a more recreational nature. She is yours with which to amuse yourself as you desire. But do it out of my sight. I have no desire to observe the repulsive things you are capable of.'

That was no problem at all for Groppione, who at that moment was bursting with gratitude towards such a generous and benevolent employer. While Usberti walked off to make himself another pot of coffee, Groppione snatched up one of the lanterns, grabbed Anna by the collar of her jacket and started dragging her over the rough ground towards a recess among the rocks where he could privately exercise all the urges that had been eating him up ever since they'd captured her.

The recess led to a triangular stone cleft, almost a shallow cave, out of the cold wind and just about high enough to stand up in. *Perfect*, Groppione thought. He hauled her inside, dumped her on the hard ground, set down the lantern to shine on her, and stood at the mouth of the cleft to admire her for a moment before the party began. He took a grimy handkerchief from his pocket and flung it at her. 'Bandage your hand up with this, bitch. I don't want you pissing your dirty blood all over me.'

Blinking away the tears of pain, Anna spat at him like a cornered wildcat. 'Murdering pig. You're going to die.'

'See, no, you're getting that all back to front, babe. *You're* the one going to die. But not just yet. First I'm gonna show you what a real man is. Then I'm gonna strangle you with your own panties. How's that sound?' He thought it sounded incredibly funny. As he started unbuckling his belt he threw back his head and roared with laughter.

So absolutely hilarious, in fact, that he was still cackling and chortling to himself when something thin and black dropped lightly from somewhere overhead and brushed his ear. He swatted at it as though it were a fly, too preoccupied with his imminent carnal prospects to fully register it. Less than a second later, when the slender rope noose jerked tight around his neck, it was already too late for Aldo Groppione to save himself. He boggled upwards in horror, and then his feet left the ground.

From where Anna lay sprawled on the floor of the rock crevice, it looked as though her would-be rapist was suddenly levitating in mid-air. His hands went to his throat, desperately clawing, legs kicking. His feet jerked another six inches higher, scrabbling like crazy and finding no purchase on the smooth rock. His tongue protruded from his gaping mouth. He tried to cry out, but produced only a dry, rattling croak.

On the ledge above him, Ben tied off the rope, then jumped down. The morphine was still working nicely and he barely felt the jolt in his injured leg. But his stomach twisted and he turned cold when he peered deeper into the rock crevice and saw Anna lying there in the pool of light from the lantern, her face streaked with pain, nursing her mutilated hand.

'Ben!' she cried out. He shouldered past Groppione, swinging the dying man like a carcass on a slaughterman's hook, and fell to his knees next to her. 'What did they do to you?'

Anna was trying to reply when she saw Janssens appear at the mouth of the cave and her eyes widened in horror. 'It's okay, he's with us,' Ben said.

Janssens stepped past the hanging, struggling, gasping Groppione, took out Bozza's Glock and offered it to Ben. 'I'd happily shoot this rapist scum myself, but I think you'd rather do the honours. One in the balls, then one in the head.'

'I'm not shooting him,' Ben said. 'I'm keeping my promise to him.'

'What promise?'

'That I'd stretch his neck like a chicken. Maybe he's taking it seriously now.'

'He's got a strong neck on him. Might take a while.'

'Fine by me,' Ben said. 'In the meantime, run back to the jeep and get me the med kit. Hurry.'

While Janssens was gone, Ben heard the wheeze and rasp of a starter motor and the sound of an engine revving wildly as a truck sped off into the night. Anna heard it too, through the mist of her pain. 'Usberti—'

'Let him run. He's on his own now.'

'You're hurt,' she gasped as she saw his leg.

'Don't you worry about me. Let's get you patched up, okay? Look at me. Breathe. You're going to be fine. That's another promise.'

Janssens came running back. 'The other truck just took off.'

'I know. We'll catch up with him after,' Ben said.

Janssens held up a submachine gun. 'I found this.'

'Keep it handy.' Ben tore open the med kit and pulled out a syrette. He jabbed it into Anna's arm. 'This will dull the pain for a while. It's pretty good stuff, let me tell you.' Next he pulled out all the surgical dressing left over from binding his leg wound, and got to work. He taped the pressure bandage into place over the bleeding stump of her finger and then looped a thick wrap of gauze round and round her hand. Lastly, he helped her sit up so that he could place a makeshift sling around her neck to keep the arm supported at an upwards angle across her chest. 'Everything will be all right now,' he assured her.

Her eyelids began to flutter. 'I feel strange,' she murmured.

'That's just the morphine kicking in,' he said. 'Go with it. Close your eyes and sleep. I'll take care of you. You haven't a worry in the world.'

Anna was getting faint. Before she passed out, she whispered, 'Ben . . . I . . . I love you, Ben.'

Which Ben attributed to the effect of the drug on her brain. He gazed sadly at her as she fell unconscious. 'We need to get her to a hospital,' he said.

'What hospital?' Janssens said.

Ben stood and turned to check on Groppione.

'Still hanging in there,' Janssens said. The thin rope was cutting deeper into Groppione's neck and his eyes looked about to pop out. His tongue was stretched grotesquely out from his mouth. His movements were becoming less and less as his brain was starved of blood and oxygen.

'That'll more or less do it,' Ben said. He patted Groppione's pockets, found the clasp knife in one of them, and a soft-pack of Italian Nazionali cigarettes and a brass Zippo lighter in the other. 'Well, well, look what we have here.' He put the cigarettes and lighter in his own pocket and snapped the knife open. It was still sticky with Anna's blood. He reached up and sliced the rope, and Groppione flopped to the ground like a sack of dirty laundry.

'That'll more or less do what?' Janssens said, looking down at the crumpled heap.

Ben took out the pack of Nazionalis, drew one from the wrapper, screwed it between his lips, clanged the Zippo and took in a deep pull of sweet smoke. He felt better already.

'Cerebral hypoxia,' he said. 'He'll lie here in a coma until his body starves to death, or something eats him. Maybe someday I'll get to tell Jeff all about it.'

'Your friend? The guy he shot, right?'

'What goes around comes around,' Ben said. 'And he had this coming from the moment he pulled the trigger.'

'What about Usberti?'

Ben took another long, silent drag on the cigarette.

Then replied, 'Let's go get him.'

Chapter 63

The first crimson-hued streaks of dawn were breaking over the horizon behind him as Usberti sped due west with the GPS device on the seat beside him, guiding him on. The snow had resumed, whirling down in gusts from the grey sky and making the flat desert appear even more featureless.

It had been so long since he'd driven any kind of motor vehicle, let alone a primitive militarised four-wheel-drive truck, that he'd barely remembered how to operate one. Similarly – even if he'd been able to grab one as he made his hasty escape earlier – he'd never used any sort of firearm in his life and would have had no idea about its functioning. Leadership and power had rendered him aloof from the realities of the world and utterly dependent on the men who had followed him, out of loyalty or out of fear.

Now, for the first time in his life, more so even than when he'd lost everything in his fall from grace years before, he felt utterly alone, defenceless and frightened.

Lord, keep me safe and protected.

He had another cause to feel afraid, and it wasn't just the prospect of running into more Syrian troops, or even Ben Hope. It was the private terror he'd harboured for months and confessed to nobody, whose existence he'd tried hard to deny even to himself. The tremors were back, and they were growing worse. So was the nausea that plagued him day and night, and the dull ache he could feel burning sometimes in his shoulder, spreading down his arm. Feeling it now, he reached for his pills as he drove, shook one out and swallowed it dry.

How, how, *how* had that pestilential man Hope been able to thwart him yet again? Why had Silvano been there with him? Usberti had scarcely been able to believe it when, secretly spying on Groppione in the hopes of catching an eyeful of what he was getting up to with the Manzini woman, he'd spotted Hope and Bellini suddenly appearing from nowhere, looking for all the world as though they belonged on the same team.

Had Silvano betrayed him? Had the insidious Hope somehow persuaded him to go over to his side? Or paid him to do so? Which would mean that Hope must be working for Them. Perhaps he had been all along: an enemy agent, sent to do Their evil work. Usberti knew all about Them. They were the Darkness, the powers of Satan, gaining control of the world step by step. Dark times indeed, if God's chosen few failed to stand and fight.

Where, also, was Ugo? If the unthinkable had happened and Hope had managed to defeat and kill him, that was all the proof needed that he must surely be backed by devilish powers.

And if his loyal, devoted Ugo was gone, now he, Massimiliano, was completely alone. It was all up to him now.

'So be it!' he yelled out loud into the snow-dusted emptiness of the desert. 'I will show them, Lord. I will not let you down!'

The GPS on the seat by his side was his last remaining ally, and proving extremely useful. Using the coordinates of Ashar the Babylonian's cliff as his starting point, Usberti had calculated fresh coordinates of his new destination lying sixteen kilometres west of that location. The tank battle and chase with the rebels had driven his quest a long way off course, but he would soon make up the distance.

However, when he got there not long afterwards, Usberti could see nothing but bare terrain in all directions. Not a marker, scarcely a bush, in sight. Something was terribly wrong; and yet the technology was insisting they were exactly sixteen kilometres west of Ashar's cliff.

Usberti was gripped by sudden doubts. Had that bitch Manzini lied to him after all? Given him a false translation, so that she and Hope could make their way to the right place and steal the treasure that was rightfully his?

The thought made his heart thump. He wiped the cold sweat from his brow. *Calm, Massimiliano, calm.* Steadying his mind, he remembered that the measurement of one and a half *beru* equated to a little *over* sixteen kilometres: a margin of error allowing for the inexact distance calibrations of the day, which could add as much as two, three hundred or more metres to the figure. That would take him over the crest of the rise he could see ahead, a long north–south ridge glowing crimson from the rising sun at his back.

Bolstered with renewed optimism, he gunned the truck towards the rise, reached its apex –

And there it was. Standing like a monolith in the middle of the emptiness, bathed red by the dawn, the tall solitary rock could be nothing if not some kind of manmade marker. *X marks the spot.* He'd found it at last!

Usberti went skidding down the slope towards it. He halted the truck and scrambled out, virtually babbling with excitement. The rock was more than twice his height, solidly planted in the ground. He hardly dared to touch it, in case it was some strange vision dreamed up by his fevered imagination – but, no, it was real. He ran his hands over its craggy face. As he wiped away the snow and dirt, he realised with a shock of pure joy that it was carved with markings that – once he'd examined them more closely through his half-moon spectacles – looked just like more of the same kind of cuneiform patterns as the cliff inscription. They were illegible to him, but he could imagine their meaning: '*Here lies the fabled treasure of dear old King Nebuchadnezzar; congratulations, friend, you've hit the jackpot*'.

'Thank you, Lord!' he shouted up to the sky. Almost weeping with happiness now, he ran back to the jeep and dragged out the bag he'd managed to salvage in his escape. He tore open the zip and pulled out the folding shovel.

Massimiliano Usberti had never performed any kind of manual labour in life, and so it took him a while to understand how to unfold the shovel. Finally, he picked a spot at the foot of the standing rock, stabbed the pointed end of the blade into the ground, and began to dig frantically. He soon scraped through the thin layer of snow to expose the sand underneath. It was harder work than he might have imagined, made even more frustrating by the way the sand and stones kept sliding back into the hole. But he would not be deterred from this glorious moment. He stabbed and dug as fast as he could, grunting like a wild man, sweating profusely despite the freezing wind.

The hole grew deeper and longer, until he'd excavated a trench large enough to bury the truck in. He paused, gasping for air, then went back at it even more ferociously. He had little sense of time, but it must have been another hour of frantic digging before the shovel blade hit something solid under the sand. A larger rock? No, it couldn't be. It mustn't be.

Lord, don't let it be a rock.

Usberti hurled away the shovel and threw himself flat on his belly at the edge of the trench, using both hands to dig like a dog. As his fingers came into contact with the buried object he scraped more furiously still, expecting at any moment to see the magnificent glint of gold sparkling up at him in the dawn's red glow. Gold! *His* gold!

This was it.

This was the moment where everything would change for him.

He'd won.

It was a while after sunrise when they found him. Ben was the first to spot the empty truck parked at the foot of the rise. As they came closer they could see the trail of footprints in the thin snow, leading from the vehicle towards the tall standing rock. At the foot of the rock was a large trench some thirty yards long by four wide. Judging by the hills of freshly dug sand, dirt and stones that stood heaped all around its edges, it looked as though someone had been busy.

Janssens pulled up, killed the engine and yanked on the brake. He and Ben looked at each other and climbed out without a word. Ben had Bozza's Glock, Janssens had Groppione's Walther, and each man was ready to open fire as they advanced cautiously.

Ben's leg wound was aching badly now that the painkiller was starting to wear off. Anna remained curled up in the truck with her eyes closed. Her system was still comfortably pumped with the effects of the morphine, along with the past-date antibiotics Ben had dosed her with out of the Syrian rebels' med kit. She'd spent the drive drifting in and out of consciousness, making it hard to get coherent directions out of her. That, combined with the fresh snow gradually obscuring the tracks of Usberti's truck, had slowed their pursuit.

But here they were. And so was Usberti.

He was lying still at the edge of the enormous trench, as though asleep. He didn't stir at their approach. Janssens shot Ben a puzzled look as if to say, 'What the hell—?'

As they stepped closer, Ben noticed the military-style metal folding shovel lying in the dug-up sand nearby. It looked new and relatively unworn, except for the blade which was all scuffs and paint chips. There were no other tracks on the ground. Usberti had clearly done all this digging himself.

And he'd evidently found something down there as a result.

Ben peered into the trench and became the second living person to bear witness to the ancient, historic object that had, until now, lain buried in this remote spot through most of recorded history.

Janssens looked down into the trench and whistled. 'Wow. I think maybe Anna would want to see this.'

'Yes, I think she would,' Ben said.

Anna must have read their thoughts, because she'd already clambered gingerly out of the truck and was making her unsteady way towards them, pale and fragile and clutching her bandaged hand, but her eyes filled with wonder. She said, 'Is it—? I mean, did he—?'

'It is, and he did,' Ben said. He put an arm round her shoulders to steady her, and led her to the edge of the trench.

'There you have it,' he said, pointing. 'You were right, Anna. It did exist, all along. The lost golden idol of King Nebuchadnezzar, lost for thousands of years and now rediscovered in all its glory.'

Chapter 64

All three of them gazed down at the huge, ancient object that Usberti had excavated from the sand: a wizened, blackened stump of desiccated wood, like the remains of a prehistoric oak tree that had become hardened like iron with extreme age and preserved by the dryness of the desert climate.

Nobody spoke for a long time. 'Well, so much for that,' Janssens said at last.

Anna shook her head. 'And so, my theory was correct. The idol was created on a modular system, out of gold plates that could be dismantled and packed away for transport. That's how the Muranus were able to smuggle it away from Babylon.'

'There's not much left, is there?' Ben said.

'Only the wooden core of the structure,' she replied sadly. 'We'll never know what became of the gold plates. Pillaged by robbers, or taken by the surviving members of Ashar's rebel group after his death, either for their personal gain or to help fight a lost cause that nobody would ever remember. Maybe the plates were discovered by Persian soldiers and taken away as spoils of war. Or, perhaps the family treasure was reclaimed by the Muranu descendants and minted back into coins to support themselves in their exile from their homeland.' She sighed, clutching her hand to her chest. 'Who knows? Whatever happened to it, the gold is long gone. All that remains is worthless, except to an archaeologist. If they could prove what it was.'

'What it is, is a big lump of firewood,' Ben said.

'Not a bad idea. We should chop it up and burn it,' Janssens said, rubbing his hands together. 'Get some warmth happening around here.' Then he glanced over at Usberti. 'What about him?'

'He looks dead,' Anna said.

Ben left her side and limped over to where Usberti lay. After a moment he called back, 'He's not dead.'

Usberti wasn't unconscious, either. But something was wrong with him. His open eyes were glazed and strangely unfocused. His lips were moving as he muttered inaudibly to himself. In one curled hand he was clutching a small pill bottle, from whose unscrewed top what remained of its contents had spilled on the ground.

It was only when Ben reached down to take the pill bottle from his limp fingers that the old man seemed to register his presence. The glazed eyes rolled dolefully up at him, but nothing else moved. Ben read the medical brand name printed on the label to see what the yellow pills on the ground were, and then tossed it away. The patient wouldn't be needing them any more anyhow.

'What's happened to him?' Anna said.

'He's had a heart attack,' Ben told her. 'Or a massive stroke. Either way, it's all over for him.'

'I've seen him popping more and more of those pills lately,' Janssens said. 'He didn't think anyone noticed. Seen him clutching his heart once or twice, too. All this digging must've brought on the attack. He's got to have shifted three tons of sand here, at least.'

'Or maybe it was the shock of finding what was under it,' Ben said. 'I'm sorry. It's a shame.'

Janssens looked surprised to hear Ben say such a thing. 'A shame that there was no gold after all, or a shame that this poor, dear, once-great leader of men is now reduced to a drooling vegetable? I can't believe either would bother you that much.'

'Neither does,' Ben said. 'I mean, I'm sorry that I didn't get to see the look on his face when all his sick little dreams fell apart. The moment he realised that hurting my friends, murder and torture, all of it, was for nothing, and that he was never going to live to find his precious gold, and that he was going to die alone and miserable.' He bent closer to Usberti, saw the eyes roll up at him again. 'Isn't that right, Archbishop? You can hear everything I'm saying, can't you?'

Usberti's lips moved and he whispered something. Ben leaned closer still, so he could hear.

'*Shoot me . . . Don't . . . don't leave me like this . . . Please.*'

'I'd shoot a dog,' Ben said, 'if I thought it was suffering. I'd put any innocent creature out of its misery. But I'd make an exception for you. You don't merit it.'

'*I . . . beg . . . you . . . Finish it.*'

'You should shoot him,' Anna said.

'He's already in hell,' Ben said. 'Why waste the bullet?'

'Because it's the humane thing to do.'

'Does he deserve humanity?'

'Doesn't everyone?' she said. 'Give me the gun. I'll do it, if you won't.'

'Will it make you feel better?' Ben asked her.

'No. It won't. It will make me feel sick for the rest of my life. I'll never be able to close my eyes again without remembering what it felt like to take a life. Even one like his.'

'Then I'll do it,' Ben said. 'I'm not like you, Anna. When

I go to bed every night, this bastard's brains all over the ground will be the last thing I picture before I drop off to sleep with a big cheesy smile on my face.'

He put the Glock to Usberti's head.

'This is for Father Pascal,' he said. 'For Luc Simon, for Jeff Dekker. For every life you ever reached out and destroyed. And for all the rest of the people in the world who'll be that little bit safer once you're gone, even if they'll never know it. Say hello to the Devil for me, Usberti, because you'll be with him in about one second from now.'

The shot rang out across the desert. Its echo rolled and boomed for miles. Ben stood up. A jolt of pain ran through him. He felt dizzy and weak, and infinitely sad. Not for what he'd just done. But for the fact that he hadn't done it years sooner.

'And that's that,' Janssens said. 'May the best man win, just like he said.'

Ben was about to reply when a triple stitch of red holes blew out of Janssens' chest and he went straight down on his back, dead before he even started toppling.

Ben seized Anna's good arm and sent her spinning over the edge of the trench, then dived in after her as Ugo Bozza loosed off another burst from the submachine gun that Janssens had left in the truck. For a man with a bullet in him, he'd sneaked up on them with incredible stealth.

Ben poked the Glock over the edge of the trench and snapped back two double-taps in quick succession. He saw the snow skip at Bozza's feet, heard the clank of a copper-jacketed 9mm bullet perforating the truck. Bozza jumped over its side and disappeared behind it. From Ben's low angle he could see the man's feet under the truck's wheelbase. He took aim and fired again, and this time he heard a sharp yell as his bullet punched into the heel of Bozza's boot.

Bozza went down on one knee, but before Ben could fire again he rattled off another stream from under the truck that made the fresh sand at the edge of the trench dance and sent Ben slithering down for cover. Anna had managed to crawl over to the wooden statue and was cowering behind it. 'Stay there and don't move!' he yelled at her.

'I won't,' she yelled in reply.

Ben fired. Bozza fired back. Ben fired back again. The gunshots boomed and rattled and echoed over the desert. They could go on like this all day, except for one crucial issue. Trench warfare, with both belligerents hunkered down under cover either side of no-man's land, was a war of attrition whose outcome basically came down to whichever side's ammunition supply could outlast the other's. Ben had started with a near-full Glock, and a Glock was a high-capacity weapon with a thrifty one-at-a-time appetite for bullets. You could load it on a Sunday and shoot all week long. Whereas Bozza's submachine gun was to ammo what a supercharged V12 Chevrolet engine was to fuel, and with no spare magazine the odds were long against him.

Bozza knew that.

And so, he shortened them.

When Ben heard the truck engine starting up, he thought for a second that Bozza was beating an escape. When he saw it racing straight towards him, he knew he couldn't have been more wrong.

The truck came roaring over the edge in a storm of dirt and snow. Its nose tipped forwards and its spinning front wheels slammed into the loose sand and it bounced and careered down the sloping bank of the trench to slam hard into the wooden hulk at the bottom, making Anna crawl frantically out of the way to avoid being crushed to death.

Bozza came piling out of the driver's side, teeth clenched in a look of manic hatred.

Ben was there to meet him.

The close-quarter battle was virtually toe to toe. Ben shot Bozza in the chest. Bozza flinched. Ben shot him again. Bozza twisted. The submachine gun snorted out a three-round burst. Two of them missed Ben.

The third one did not miss.

Ben felt its impact rock him on his feet, but he didn't take his eyes off the pistol's sights or the target behind them. He fired again. A third eye opened up at the exact centre of Bozza's forehead. He seemed to hang in mid-air for a split second, and then dropped soundlessly into the sand and was dead.

Ben stood there looking over Bozza's corpse. Then he sensed the ground falling out from under him, and suddenly he was looking up at the pale sky with Anna's anguished cry echoing in his ears from somewhere far away.

Chapter 65

Anna came scrabbling over to him, crying out his name, shaking him. Ben blinked. His vision swirled, then drifted into focus. He rolled his head to one side and saw Bozza lying nearby, staring lifelessly into his eyes with a thin red trickle oozing from the hole in his brow. Then Ben turned his head back upwards and saw Anna kneeling over him, her long black hair dishevelled and hanging down past her tear-streaked face.

'That guy Bozza takes a lot of killing, doesn't he?' he said.

'So do you, Ben Hope. You hear me? More than anyone!'

'I don't know about that,' he replied. He smiled at his feeble joke, but Anna didn't seem to find it amusing. He lifted his head and peered down the length of his body, seeing it as though it belonged to someone else. Then saw the blood pouring from the gunshot wound in his side, and understood why she wasn't laughing.

'Oh, God,' she sobbed. 'You're so badly hurt. It's all because of me.'

'Don't be daft,' he said. 'I do this kind of thing all the time.'

'We have to get out of here.'

'Can't you just let me lie here a while? I'm feeling a little tired.'

411

She wiped away her tears. 'No! Put your arm around my neck. Let me help you. We have to go.'

Anna helped him get to his feet, but he couldn't stand properly without her support. Blood seemed to be everywhere. 'Fine. But I'm driving,' he said, and collapsed again.

When he woke up, he was in the truck. They were tearing across the desert, bucking and bouncing crazily, Anna driving with one hand. He couldn't see straight. The seat under him felt wet. He was so cold.

'Don't move,' she yelled over the engine noise.

'Where are we going?'

'To a doctor.'

'There are no doctors,' he said. 'Give me some more of that morphine, and I'll be right as rain.' The idea was an appealing one. He could kill himself with an opiate overdose or just sit here and bleed to death. An easy choice.

'We'll find help,' she said, staring intently ahead as she hammered the truck over the rough terrain. 'If it's the last thing I do.' Then she looked down at the dash instruments and her mouth fell open. 'No! No!'

'What is it?' he asked drowsily. He soon understood. The truck began to judder, then to slow, then stalled and coasted to a complete halt.

'We can't be out of fuel!' Anna yelled. She thumped the wheel with her good hand. 'We *can't be*!' She kicked open her door and clambered out. Ben heard her cry of frustration from outside.

'Let me guess,' he said as she ran around the truck and opened his door. 'Some idiot shot a hole in the fuel tank. It happens all the time.'

She nodded, ashen and distraught. 'I don't know what to do.'

'Not your fault,' he said. He managed to haul himself out

of his seat and lean against the side of the truck. His legs wouldn't hold him up. He slowly sank down to the cold, hard ground. The desert was huge and empty and still and quiet all around.

'There must be something,' she said. 'I have to think of a way to help us.'

'You can help yourself,' he said. 'Take the pistol and start walking.'

'I don't have the pistol,' she said.

'Then start walking without it. Someone will find you. You'll be fine. Go home to Italy. Get that hand seen to. Finish the bloody book. Tell the world all about the great golden Babylon idol.'

'And you?'

'Who gives a damn? Not me.'

She shook her head. 'It doesn't work that way. Do you remember what you told me?'

'Whatever it was, it was probably wrong.'

'You told me that you wouldn't leave my side until this was over. And now I'm telling you, Ben Hope, that I won't leave yours.'

'That's a hell of a responsibility to lay on me,' he said.

'That's the way it is,' she replied.

'Then we either stay here together, or we walk out of here together,' he said. 'Yes?'

'Yes. What are you doing?'

'What does it look like? I'm getting up. See? I'm fine.'

But he wasn't fine. Not remotely. He wobbled on his feet for a second, then his knees buckled and he was down again. 'Fuck it,' he muttered. He battled upright again. He wouldn't give up. If he died, he'd die standing. He put an arm around her shoulders.

'Let's go,' he said.

The two of them struggled away from the dead truck. Apart from the desert wind that whistled and crackled and peppered them with flurries of snow, they were the only things moving on the whole massive, barren landscape. Two tiny insects crawling over a vast plateau of white nothingness.

'That rise ahead,' Anna said. 'If we can get to the top of it, we might be able to see a village or a town where we can get help.'

Ben would have told her there were no villages or towns for miles and miles, but he had little energy left for speaking. Or for much else. The dark was clawing at him, beckoning to him, whispering in his ears.

Come down to us, it said in a silky voice.

Come on down.

'I'm not dead yet,' he mumbled.

They were halfway up the rise when the loud rumble of an engine came out of nowhere and a vehicle suddenly came roaring over the top. It came lurching and bouncing their way, and pulled up. Under the film of grime and slush that caked its bodywork, the jeep was painted up in desert camouflage. It had spare tyres and fuel cans and weaponry slung from everywhere. There were four guys inside.

Soldiers. Swathed in desert winter clothes. Their eyes hidden by wraparound dark glasses that reflected the pale sunlight, faces shielded from the cold wind by bandanas. All four stepped out. Automatic rifles in their gloved hands.

Ben blinked. His vision was hazy from blood loss, and he couldn't make them out too well. Turkish soldiers, maybe, he thought. Or Syrian ones. Or rebel fighters. Or just about anybody else. Whoever they were, they didn't look friendly.

Ben said, 'Come on, you bastards. If you're going to shoot us, get it over with.'

One of the soldiers stepped forward. He lowered his

weapon. Peeled off his dark glasses and stripped the bandana away from his face, and peered at Ben with piercing, steely grey eyes.

'Jesus Christ. Don't I fucking know you?' said the soldier. 'Bloody hell, it's a small world.'

Ben focused on the man's grizzled, bristly, weather-beaten face. Muttered, '*Tinker?*' Then went whirling into a black void that tunnelled through the centre of the Earth and carried him to the stars.

Chapter 66

SAS, SBS, US Navy SEALs, French GIGN, Israeli Sayeret Maktal and a dozen others: the sphere of Special Forces meant a lot of different things to a lot of different people across the globe.

For some, whether they chose to pit themselves against the challenge and seriously aspire to be all they could be, or whether they just dreamed about it and stuck posters on their bedroom wall, it was the epitome of warrior cool. For others of a different political bent, the shadowy military elites represented the ultimate embodiment of the dark, sinister forces that ruled the world.

But of all the many things that Special Forces might have been or seemed, to those chosen few within the circle it was, above all else, a family. Once you were in, you were in for life. Loyalty was all, the bonds of brotherhood sacred. Guys would do anything, break any rule, take any risk, to protect their own. It didn't matter if you were still in, or if you'd been out for decades. All that mattered was to have paid your dues as part of that tight-knit community – to have lived with them, trained with them, broken bread with them, fought and bled with them, shared in the sorrow of fallen comrades or the elation of victory. Together, as one.

And Ben Hope had been an integral part of that family

for many years. Almost the same span of time had passed since he'd eventually quit and walked away; but in that period of his life he'd done things that, whether he liked it or not, had earned him the reputation of a legend in the eyes of young warriors like Tuesday Fletcher and a hundred others. His name was mentioned with awe and reverence by a generation of Special Air Service soldiers who'd never met him. And it was remembered with fierce pride by those who'd had the experience of serving alongside him.

Soldiers like veteran trooper Rab 'Tinker' Taylor, currently engaged on his fourth tour of duty as a platoon commander in the savage, blood-drenched nightmare that the apparently never-ending civil war had made of the beautiful land of Syria.

Small world, indeed.

The four-man SAS unit had tended to the two injured travellers while waiting for an emergency CASEVAC chopper to whisk them to safety. Ben's identity had been formally confirmed via the Ministry of Defence while he was unconscious on the operating table at the US Army Unit Base Camp's military hospital in Damascus, before being flown to the UK for further treatment. The close-knit SF network had quickly cranked into action, doing what it did best. Strings had been pulled, corners cut, the usual authorities neatly left out of the loop, the usual complications associated with two Western travellers found wandering and mysteriously injured with neither passports nor ID in the middle of a foreign war zone studiously avoided.

As for the matter of the bodies of various known members of the Italian crime fraternity, together with a now twice-dead former Vatican archbishop and an off-the-radar Europol agent, scattered in their wake, the report Ben would later submit to the SAS chiefs in Hereford would be filed away in the deepest recess of classified military records, never to be seen again.

That was that – and this time, it really was.

Twelve days after leaving Syria, and two days after Ben was released from hospital, Anna Manzini was flown home to Italy. Ben last saw her as she boarded the military transport plane at RAF Lakenheath.

'Now I'll always have something to remind me of our time together,' she said, holding up her bandaged left hand.

'How is it?' he asked.

'It doesn't hurt so much any more. It feels a little strange, a little lighter. Perhaps not the ideal way to lose weight. But I'll get used to it. What about you?'

'Hardly much pain,' he lied. 'Just stiffness, really. I'll soon be able to ditch the walking stick.'

'We were lucky,' she said. 'If you can call it that. I've learned my lesson. No more adventures for me.'

'I'm glad to hear you say it.'

'Writing books is safer. And I can still do that with nine fingers, from the comfort of my villa. It's a good thing I didn't make my career as a concert violinist.' She paused, looking at him, knowing she wouldn't see him again for a long time, if ever. 'Are you going home too?' she asked.

He nodded. 'Yes, I'm going home.'

'No more adventures for you either. You have to promise.'

'That's one promise you know I can't make,' he said.

'I didn't think you could.' She kissed him, and held him tightly for a long moment. 'Stay safe, *caro mio*. Whatever the future holds. And remember—'

'Remember what?'

'If you ever find yourself in Florence, you must give me a call.'

He said nothing more. Just smiled, then stood back and

gave her a last wave as the RAF guys closed up the hatch. The plane taxied into position. Minutes later, Ben watched it take off into the wintry English sky.

'And home we go,' he murmured to himself when it was gone.

To find what awaiting him, he didn't yet know. In between trying to call Roberta Ryder to give her the all-clear, he'd left three messages on the voicemail of Dr Sandrine Lacombe, asking after Jeff's condition and telling her he'd be back in France tomorrow evening. He was still waiting for Sandrine to reply. And that worried him. It worried him a great deal.

Epilogue

It was worrying him even more as he trudged up the front steps of the farmhouse at Le Val the following evening.

It was his intention to stop off at home for a few hours, get cleaned up a little, change his clothes and inspect his dressings, before calling another taxi to drive him up to Cherbourg. He'd given up trying to call Sandrine. Either she'd switched jobs, or she'd taken an unexpected holiday and left her phone at home, or she had something to tell him that could only be said face to face. That could only be one thing, and it filled him with dread that made his wounds ache so badly he craved more of that Syrian rebel army morphine.

The farmhouse was totally dark, not a lit window in the place. He found the door locked, so he took out his key and let himself in quietly. The house felt dead and sombre, to match his mood. He hung his jacket on the hook in the front hall, as well as the walking stick that he'd need to use for a few weeks, until his leg healed up completely. He limped slowly into the dark kitchen. Without turning on any lights, he opened a cupboard and took out the bottle of Laphroaig and a glass.

The best part about not being able to drive a car for a while was that you could drink as much as you needed to.

Which, in Ben's case, was going to amount to a lot of drinking. That was his intention, too.

He was finishing his glass and about to pour another when the kitchen door opened and Tuesday walked in. 'I saw the taxi come and go.'

'Then you know I'm back,' Ben said.

'How come you're sitting in the dark?'

'Because it feels like a good place to be right now,' Ben said. 'How come all the lights are out?'

'I was in the back,' Tuesday said, as though that explained anything.

'You want a drink?'

Tuesday shook his head. 'Nah. I'm okay, thanks. So . . . what've you been up to?'

'I had a few things to sort out.'

'Sorted them?'

Ben nodded. 'Pretty much.'

'We good?'

'We're good,' Ben said.

Tuesday nodded and made no reply. Ben looked at him. Tuesday could be inscrutable at times. 'Anything you want to tell me?' Ben asked him.

Tuesday gave a noncommittal shrug. 'One bit of news. Looks like we're off the hook with the cops. They've reinstated our licence. The armoury stuff all came back yesterday.'

'Fancy that,' Ben said. 'Anything else?'

'There was one other thing,' Tuesday said morosely.

'And what's that?'

'You'd better come with me.'

'What for?'

''Cause I need to show you something,' Tuesday said.

'Show me what?'

Tuesday said nothing.

'Can't you just tell me?'

'It's best you see it. I can't describe it.'

Tuesday led Ben from the dark kitchen, down the dark hallway, towards the living-room door. He turned the handle and pushed the door open. The living room was dark, too.

Ben limped inside the room. 'What the hell's this about?' he was about to snap irritably at Tuesday, when the lights all came on at once.

'SURPRISE!'

Ben nearly fell over. Partly out of shock, and partly because Sandrine flew at him and hugged him so hard that he almost lost his balance.

Everyone was there. Boonzie McCulloch, accompanied by his wife Mirella and clasping a bottle of whisky that he'd already drunk too much of to be able to speak coherently. Fry, Blackwood, McGuire and the other two ex-SAS guys Boonzie had drafted in to look after things in Ben's absence, all loud and hearty. Marie-Claire, busily topping up empty glasses. Chantal, smiling radiantly but still eclipsed by the terawatt grin that was suddenly splitting Tuesday's face in two. Lynne Dekker and her guy Kip, the crocodile farmer, both pink-faced with mirth and booze. Storm and the rest of the dogs, happily wagging their tails and lolling their tongues.

And Jeff.

He was sitting in a wheelchair in the middle of the crowded room. He'd lost weight and a couple of shades of colour. But he was alive, and awake, and laughing out loud at the expression on Ben's face. 'Look what the cat dragged in,' he hooted.

Ben didn't know what to say. He managed, 'Welcome back to the land of the living, Dekker. Hope you had a good sleep while the rest of us were out working.'

Sandrine clasped Ben's hand. 'You look awful,' she said. He couldn't have said the same thing about her. Her hair was loose, all the way down past her waist.

'I tried to call you,' he said.

'I got your message that you were coming back tonight. And I thought you'd like a surprise.'

'When did he wake up?'

'Six days ago.'

'Six days of hell, mate,' Jeff laughed. 'These women won't leave me alone. This doctor lady, she's a slave driver, I'm telling you. You never met an RSM half as tough.'

'I like the chair,' Ben said to him. 'It's a good look.'

'Just for show,' Jeff replied. 'You want to see me dance the tango?'

'Some other time,' Ben said. A twinge made him step to the nearest sofa and lower himself stiffly into it.

'Fuck, mate, you look even more banged up than I am. What happened?'

'You want to hear a story?' Ben asked him.

'Just what I need.'

'I have a story for you,' Ben said. 'It's about a guy who got his neck stretched like a chicken.'

'Sounds great.'

'I don't think we need to hear that story now, *chéri*,' Chantal said, stepping behind Jeff's chair and putting her hands on his shoulders.

'Later,' Jeff said with a wink to Ben.

It was too much. Tears melted into Ben's eyes as he sat there, surrounded by laughter and light and warmth. Sandrine looked tenderly at him and squeezed his hand. 'Are you okay?'

'I am now,' Ben said. 'I am now.'

Read on for an *exclusive* extract of the new Ben Hope
adventure by Scott Mariani

The Bach Manuscript

Coming November 2017

Prologue

Nazi-occupied France,
July 16th, 1942

All four family members were at home when they came.

Monsieur and Madame Silbermann, or Abel and Vidette, were in the salon, relaxing in a pair matching Louis XV armchairs after a modest but excellent lunch prepared by Eliane, the family house-keeper. Vidette was immersed in one of the romantic novels into which she liked to escape, while Abel was frowning at an article in the collaborationist newspaper *Le Temps*, reading of much more serious matters. Things in France were growing worse. Each day seemed to bring a fresh round of new horrors.

Seated at the piano, framed by the bright, warm afternoon light that flooded in through the French windows, their seven-teen-year-old daughter Miriam was working through the most difficult arpeggiated right-hand passage of the musical manuscript in front of her, pausing now and then to peer at the handwritten notes, some of which were hard to read on the faded paper.

Though she played the piano with a fine touch, Miriam's particular talent lay with the violin, at which she excelled. The real pianist of the family was her little brother. At age twelve, Gabriel Silbermann's ability on the keys was already outstripping that of his teachers, even that of his father. Abel had been a respected professor of music at the Paris Conservatoire for over twenty years, until the venerable institution's director, Henri Rabaud, had helped the Nazi regime to 'cleanse' it of all Jewish employees under the premier *Statut des Juifs* law, which had come into effect in 1941.

For the last two years Abel Silbermann had managed to get by teaching privately. Things were not what they had been, but he had always convinced himself that the family money, dwindling as it was, would get them through these difficult times. Abel was also the proud owner of a fine collection of historically important musical instruments, some of which he'd inherited from his father, others he had picked up over the years at specialist auctions in France, Switzerland, and Germany – all before the war, of course. It had nearly broken Abel's heart when, six months earlier, he'd been forced to sell the 1698 Stradivarius cello from his collection, to help make ends meet. He often worried that he might have to sell others.

But Abel Silbermann had far worse things to fear. He didn't know it yet, but they were literally just around the corner.

'*Merde, c'est dur,*' Miriam muttered to herself. Complaining how tough the music was to get her fingers around. Gabriel could rattle through the piece with ease. But then, Gabriel was Gabriel.

'Miriam, language!' her mother said sharply, jolted from her reading. Miriam's father permitted himself a smile behind his newspaper.

Miriam asked, 'Father, may I get a pencil and add some fingering notes? I promise I'd do it very lightly, so they could easily be rubbed out afterwards.'

Abel's smile fell away. 'Are you mad, girl? That's an original manuscript, signed by the composer himself. Have you any idea what it would be worth?'

Miriam reddened, realising the foolishness of her idea. 'Sorry, father. I wasn't thinking.'

'It shouldn't even be out of its box, let alone being defaced with pencil marks. Please tell your brother to put it back where he found it, in future. These things are precious. This one most of all.'

'I'm sure Gabriel knows that, father. He calls it our family treasure.'

'Indeed it is,' Abel said, softening. 'Where is Gabriel, anyway?'

'In his cubbyhole, I think.'

Things had been hard for Gabriel at school since the Nazis invaded. He hated having to wear the yellow star when he was out of the house. Some of the non-Jewish kids pushed him around and called him names. As a result, he had become a rather solitary child who, when he wasn't practising his pieces and scales, liked to spend time alone doing his own things. His cubbyhole was the labyrinth of nooks and crawl-spaces that existed behind the panelled walls of the large house, connecting its many rooms in ways that only Gabriel knew. You could sometimes catch him spying from behind a partition through one of his various peepholes, and you'd call out, 'Oh, Gabriel, stop that nonsense!' and he'd appear moments later, as if by magic, and disarm everyone with his laughter. Other times he could stay hidden for hours and you'd have no idea where he was. Like a tunnel rat, his father used to say jokingly. Then they'd started hearing the terrible stories coming from Ukraine and Poland, from everywhere, of Jews hiding under floorboards and in sewers while their people were transported away for forced labour, or worse. Abel had stopped talking about tunnel rats.

'I do wish he'd come out of there,' Vidette Silbermann said. 'He spends too much time hiding away like that.'

'If he's happy,' Miriam said with a shrug. 'What harm can it do? We all need a little bit of happiness in this terrible, cruel world.'

Vidette lowered her book and started going into one of her 'In my day, children would never have been allowed to do this or that' diatribes, which they'd heard a thousand times before. Miriam's standard response was to humour her mother by ignoring her. She moved away from the piano and picked her violin up from its stand nearby. Her bow flowed like water over the strings and the notes of the Bach piece sang out melodiously.

That was when they heard the growl of approaching vehicles coming up to the house. Brakes grinding, tyres crunching to a halt on the gravel outside, doors slamming. Voices and the trudge of heavy boots.

Miriam stopped playing and looked with wide eyes at her father, who threw down *Le Temps* and got to his feet just as the loud thumping knocks on the front door resonated all through the house. Vidette sat as though paralysed in her chair. Miriam was the first to voice what they all knew already. '*Les Boches.* They're here.'

In that moment, whatever shreds of optimism Abel Silbermann had tried to hang onto, his prayers that this day would never come, that everything would be all right, were shattered.

From the window, the dusty column of vehicles seemed to fill the whole courtyard in front of the house. The open-top black Mercedes staff car was flanked by motorcycle outriders, behind them three more heavily-armed Wehrmacht sidecar outfits, a pair of Kübelwagens and a transporter truck. Infantry soldiers were pouring from the sides of the truck, clutching rifles, as Abel hurried to the front door. He took a deep breath, then opened it.

You can still talk your way out of this.

The officer in charge stepped from the Mercedes. He was tall and thin, with a chiselled, severe face like a hawk's. He wore an Iron Cross at his throat, another on his breast. The dreaded double lightning flash insignia was on his right lapel, the sinister *Totenkopf* death's head skull badge above the peak of his cap. Just the sight of those was enough to instil terror.

'Herr Silbermann? I am SS Obersturmbannführer Horst Krebs. You know why I'm here, don't you?'

Abel tried to speak, but all that came out was a dry croak. When Krebs produced a document from his pocket, a high-pitched ringing began in Abel's ears. The paper was a long list of many names. It was the nightmare come true. Some Jewish families had fled ahead of the rumoured purges. Abel, choosing to disbelieve that anything like this could happen in his dear France, had made what he was now realising with a chill was the worst mistake of his life by staying put.

'You reside here with your wife Vidette Silbermann and your children Gabriel and Miriam Silbermann, correct? I have here an order for your immediate deportation to the Drancy camp. Any resistance, my men will shoot. Understood?'

Drancy was the transit camp six miles north of Paris that the Germans used as a temporary detention centre for Jews awaiting transportation to Auschwitz. Abel had heard those rumours, too, and refused to believe. Now it was too late. What good would escape have done them, anyway? All fugitives would be picked up long before they reached the Swiss border.

'Take me. I care little for my own life. But please spare my family.'

'Please. Do you think I haven't heard that before?' Krebs pushed past Abel and strode into the house. His soldiers clustered around the entrance. Abel found himself looking down the muzzles of several rifles. The hallway of his genteel family home was suddenly filling with troops, their boots crashing on the parquet, the smell of their coarse tunics mixed with leather polish and gun oil, a harsh and alien presence. The Obersturmbannführer turned to his second-in-command and said sharply, 'Captain Jundt, seize everyone whose name appears on the list and have them assembled here in the hall. Make it quick.'

The captain snapped his heels. '*Jawohl, mein Obersturmbannführer!*'

Jundt relayed the command and soldiers surged into the salon to seize both Miriam and her mother, who was mute with horror and virtually fainting as they half carried, half dragged her into the hallway. While his men carried out his orders, Horst Krebs strolled around the downstairs of the house and gazed around him with appreciation for the Silbermanns' good taste. Krebs did not consider himself a barbarian, like some of his peers. He came from Prussian aristocratic stock, spoke several languages and, before the war, had published three volumes of poetry. By chance, he had studied music at the same Halle Conservatory founded by the father of Reinhard Heydrich, the SS chief whom the Czech resistance had murdered only the previous month. Reprisals there had been harsh and were ongoing. Krebs intended to pursue his own duties here in France with equal zest.

Noticing the piano at the far end of the salon by the French windows, Krebs strolled over to inspect it. It was a very fine instrument indeed, a Pleyel. His keen musician's eye passed over it, taking in the beauty of such a magnificent object. Maybe he would take it home to Germany as a trophy of war.

Then Krebs' eye settled on the music score that lay open on the music rest. He raised an eyebrow. Unusual. And very old. He picked it up with a black-gloved hand, and peered at it.

Behind him, the hallway echoed with the cries of Madame Silbermann and her husband's pleas as the soldiers forced them to line up at gunpoint. Captain Jundt was yelling, '*Wo is das Gör? Où est le gamin?*' Demanding to know the whereabouts of young Gabriel, whose name was on the list. Jackboots thumped on the stairs and shook the floorboards above as more troops were dispatched to search the rest of the house.

Krebs heard none of it. His attention was completely on the manuscript in his hands as he studied it with rapt fascination. The age-yellowed paper. The signature on the front. Could it be the genuine thing? It was amazing.

Handling it as delicately as though it were some ancient scroll that could crumble at the slightest touch, Krebs replaced the precious manuscript on the music rest, then swept back his long coat and took a seat at the piano. The six flats in the manuscript's key signature showed that the piece was in the difficult key of G flat major. He removed his gloves, laid his fingers on the keys and sight-read the first couple of bars.

Amazing. If this was the genuine item, he wanted it for himself.

In fact, on consideration, he could think of an even better use for it. He and the now-deceased Heydrich were not the only high-ranking Nazis with a passion for classical music. What an opportunity for Krebs to ingratiate himself at the very highest level.

'*Entschuldigung, mein Obersturmbannführer—*' Jundt's voice at his ear, breaking in on his thoughts.

'What is it, Jundt?'

'We cannot find the boy. Every room has been searched but he is missing.'

'What do you mean, you can't find him? How is that possible?' Krebs was more irritated by the interruption than the news of a missing brat. 'He must be hiding somewhere.'

'The parents and sister refuse to say where, *mein Obersturmbann-führer*.'

'They do, do they? We will see about that.' Krebs rose from the piano stool and marched towards the hallway. Moments like these called for a little greater authority than the likes of Jundt could sum up. Krebs drew his Walther service automatic from its flap holster.

As Krebs reached the crowded hallway, he heard a sudden sound behind him and turned in surprise to see the young boy who seemed to have appeared from nowhere and was now racing across the salon, heading for the piano.

Jundt shouted, 'There he is!' As though his commanding officer were blind.

Miriam Silbermann screamed, 'Gabriel!'

Krebs realised that the boy must have been hiding behind the wood panels, watching him as he sat at the piano. Running to the instrument, the twelve-year-old snatched the manuscript off its rest, and clutched it tightly. He yelled, 'Filthy Boches, you won't take our family treasure!'

His elder sister screamed, 'Run, Gabriel!' One of the soldiers silenced her with a harsh blow from his rifle butt.

And Gabriel ran, still grasping the precious manuscript to his chest as though nothing could persuade him to let it go. He made for the French window and slipped through, dashing towards the lawned garden and the fence at the bottom.

Krebs watched him go. Then calmly, unhurriedly, he walked towards the French window. Stepped through it, feeling the sun's warmth on his face.

The boy was running fast. If Krebs let him run very much further, he would reach the fence and disappear into the trees, and it might take an entire Waffen-SS unit all day to scour the surrounding countryside in search of the brat.

Krebs raised his Walther and took careful aim at the running child's back. It was a long shot, but Krebs was an accomplished pistol marksman.

The gun's short, sharp report cracked out across the garden. Inside the house, Vidette Silbermann howled in anguish.

The boy stumbled, ran on two more staggering paces, then fell on his face and lay still.

More screams from the house, once again cut short by the soldiers. The Obersturmbannführer walked over to where Gabriel Silbermann lay dead, hooked the toe of his shiny jackboot under his body and rolled him over. A trickle of blood dribbled from the child's lips. He was still clutching the music manuscript as if he wouldn't give it up, even in death.

Krebs bent down and removed it from the boy's fingers. It sickened him to see that there was blood on it, but not because it was the blood of an innocent child he had just killed. Rather, it was like seeing a rip in an old master painting. The manuscript had survived all these years, just to be indelibly stained by the blood of a filthy Jew. Disgusting. Krebs carefully slipped the precious object inside his coat before more harm could come to it. Then walked back towards the house to resume his duties. A pretty much routine day had turned out to be a lucky one for him.

Soon, the rest of the Silbermann family would be taken to their temporary new home at the Drancy internment facility, along with more than thirteen thousand other Jews rounded up by Nazi troops and French police in what was known as 'Opération Vent Printanier', or 'Operation Spring Breeze'. From Drancy, not long afterwards, Abel, Vidette and Miriam would find themselves on the train to the death camp of Auschwitz.

Only one of them would ever return.

Chapter 1

Oxfordshire
Many years later

The country estate covered a spread of some seventy-five acres: a fraction of the grounds it had commanded in former, grander days, but still large enough to keep it nicely secluded from neighbouring properties and the nearest village that had, over the last two or three centuries, sprawled outwards into a small town. The estate was entirely surrounded by a ten-foot-high stone wall, built long ago by an army of local labourers, nowadays impossibly expensive to put up. Its main entrance gates were tall and imposing, all gothic wrought-iron and gilt spikes, set into massive ivied pillars crowned with carved stone heraldic beasts of Olde England that had guarded the gateway since 1759 and bore just the right amount of weathering and moss to convey an impression of grandiosity without looking scabby and decayed.

Neatly hidden among the ivy of the pillars were the electronic black box and mechanism for opening and shutting the gates, as well as the small intercom on which visitors had to announce themselves in order to be let in; the rest of the time, the gates were kept firmly shut. Nor could you see it from the ground, but the walls themselves were topped all the way around with broken glass cemented into the stonework, to deter unwanted callers. Technically illegal without a warning sign, but the property's owner was little concerned with their duty of care to protect the safety and well-being of potential burglars, vandals or other intruders.

Entering the gates and following the long, winding driveway that led through a corridor of fine old oak trees and eventually opened up to reveal the clipped lawns and formal gardens, and then the house itself, few people could have failed to be impressed by the scale and majesty of one of the nobler country piles in the region. The manor stood on five floors, comprising over thirty bedrooms and many more reception rooms than were ever in use at any given time. Its multiple gabled roofs sloped this way and that. The red and green ivy that clung thickly about its frontage was kept neatly trimmed away from its dozens upon dozens of leaded windows. Clusters of chimney stacks poked like missiles into the blue Oxfordshire sky, providing a lofty perch for the crows that circled and cawed in the tranquil silence. Down below, parked on the ocean of ornamental gravel surrounding the big house, were rows of Aston Martins and Bentleys and classic Porsches, nothing as vulgar as a Ferrari.

The place might have been the personal residence of someone extremely wealthy, a marquis or a viscount, or the ancestor of some Victorian merchant dynasty still reaping the fruits of the family empire. Old money. Or new money, like a dot-com multi-millionaire or whizzkid software developer who had struck lucky with some new gadget that had set the world on fire. Whatever the case, they would have required a live-in service staff to keep it on an even keel. At least one butler, maybe two, plus the requisite contingent of housekeepers and kitchen staff and gardeners. Or else it might have been open to the public, as a gallery or a museum or a National Trust heritage venue ushering crowds of visitors through its many grandiose rooms during the months of the tourist season.

It was none of those things. Instead, it was a place of business. A going concern, providing a variety of services to its clients. A polished brass plaque above the doorway read, in bold gothic font, THE ATREUS CLUB. Named after a king of ancient Greece, the father of Agamemnon and Menelaus, not that the name bore any connection to the nature and purpose of the establishment. A nature and purpose to which, in turn, few people were ever privy.

The Atreus Club was strictly private, hence the locked gates, and hence the broken glass on the walls. Members only. Expensive to join, and only certain individuals need apply to enjoy the secluded and discreet haven it provided for its exclusive, distinguished membership.

And for good reason, considering some of the activities those pillars of society enjoyed there.

Behind a tall balcony window, up on the fourth floor, one of those activities was currently taking place. The room was large but quite sparsely decorated. It had been a bedroom, and sometimes still was, depending on need. Today, though, it was something else. At its centre stood an antiquated wooden school desk, the kind with the flip-up top and a recess for an inkwell. In front of it was a larger teacher's desk, behind which stood an equally old-fashioned classroom blackboard, complete with chalk and duster. Scrawled in slanting chalk script across the board were the words, '*I must not be a naughty boy; I must not be a naughty boy*'. Over and over.

At the far side of the room, in the light from the tall window, stood a metal frame, seven feet high with a steel bar supported between sturdy mounts either side. Attached to the overhead bar, arms raised above his head by the rubber manacles and rubber chains that bound him firmly in place, stood one of the room's two occupants.

He was naked apart from his socks. A man in his early sixties, grey-haired, tall, slightly stooped, and not in the best of shape physically. His bare buttocks were pinched and somewhat shrivelled and very white, except for where they were striped red from the whipmarks that the room's other occupant had spent the last few minutes inflicting on him.

She was blonde, and at least forty years younger than her client. But not naked, not yet, as specified by the instructions that had to be followed to the exact letter. All part of the expensive services

437

provided by the Atreus Club. And this particular client had specified, as he always specified on his many visits here, that the girl be wearing a mortarboard and one of the abbreviated black academic gowns that Oxford University tradition dubbed a commoners' gown. Both items duly obtained from the official university outfitters, Shepherd and Woodward's of the High. No expense spared. Aside from the academic garb and the matching black fish-net stockings, garters and suspender belt, she was wearing nothing else. Again, as per instructions. The instrument of torture was a whippy rattan cane, the type that schoolmasters had once used to inflict corporal punishment on disobedient pupils, back in the day. The client had never been caned at school, however. He had always been a model pupil, set for academic glory.

'Have you had enough, you bad, *bad* professor, you?' the blonde asked with a wicked smile on her red lips. She spoke with an Eastern European accent that drove him even more crazy.

'No! Hit me again! Ah!'

The client's cry of pain and pleasure was drowned out by the whoosh and sharp crack of the cane as she whipped it through the air and added another fresh, livid stripe to his pale rear end. The velvety tassel on her mortarboard swung with the movement.

'Again! More!'

Whoosh. *Crack.*

This could go on for quite some time. As the blonde knew very well, because it usually did and she was his regular pick. She had the technique down better than any of the other girls. Something in the wrist action. For some reason, she was a natural at it. He knew her as Angelique, which, needless to say, wasn't her real name. The instructions were to call him 'professor' and that was the sum total of her knowledge about him. He could be a judge, for all she cared. Or a cop. A couple of senior Thames Valley Police officers were regulars.

What 'Angelique' didn't know – what neither of them could have known – was that their supposedly private session was, in fact, anything but.

The fine mature oak tree on the front lawn was about as close to the house as it was possible to get without being spotted from the windows, and you could reach it easily enough by darting from hedge to bush. Plenty close enough for the man who was perched high up in its branches. The only challenging part of his job had been getting over the wall unscathed. The rest was easy. Almost fun. He had an excellent view through the window in question, and at this range the telephoto lens on his camera was capable of producing crystal-clear close-ups of both the client and the girl whipping him.

The watcher wasn't so interested in the girl. The client was another matter. Just a few more snaps, and the watcher would descend unseen from his perch and make his way back out of the grounds and over the wall to his vehicle.

The watcher permitted himself a smile as he watched the blonde step back to give herself space, then swing the cane and whack the old perv again. He could almost hear the snap of the thin rattan against soft, loose, white flesh. Framed in the viewfinder the client's eyes were rolled upwards and his mouth was open with a sigh of ecstasy.

The shutter clicked one more time.

A perfect shot.

Someone was going to be happy.

The Bach Manuscript
coming November 2017

TO POSSESS IT, HE WILL PAY IN BLOOD . . .

Has Ben Hope finally met his match?
Read the explosive two-book series

Out Now